Submitted to Work as a Spy

Imaginary &
Tragic Novellas of
Prudence Han Tranduc

First Edition

PAGE PUBLISHING, INC.
New York, NY

First originally published by Page Publishing, Inc. 2014

ISBN 978-1-62838-531-1 (pbk)
ISBN 978-1-62838-532-8 (digital)

Printed in the United States of America

Contents

Author's Note

These novellas are works of fiction. Names of countries and characters, as well as settings and incidents, are the products of the author's imagination. Any resemblances to any real stories of actual persons, living or dead, are entirely coincidental.

Please, forward this Literary Work of Prudence Han Tranduc to your Friends, Relatives, and Acquaintances.

Many readers have commented:

1). The title <u>Submitted to Work As a Spy</u> is not explicit the Theme of the Novellas.

2). My Novellas are more dramatic and exciting than *The Tale of Vuong Thuy Kieu* of Nguyen Du (1765 – 1820)?

Therefore, in the next edition, the title will be:

<u>Women Victims</u>

(Submitted to Work As a Spy)

Eight stories in the book are independent of one another. Dear readers, after reading the "Preface" you can continue your reading on any story you like.

<u>Outlets</u>: Amazone, Barnes & Noble...google

\- - - - -

Do not miss the next Novel of Prudence Han Tranduc

<u>The Clan Divided</u>

Epic & Gripping. Fabricated story but reflects some societies.

Preface

Many beautiful women have been treated as sex objects since the ancient time. Working as harlots and being raped were the two immemorial types. The problem of sex objects has become more and more sophisticated. Even though the Women's Rights Movements and its supporters have attained many huge successes, there still have been women who have become victims as sex objects.

Even today, in every country, the problems of women victims still more or less exist. The total of victims in the world can be from thousands to hundreds of thousands. They are abducted or lured by swindlers, then they are forced to work as whores in their countries, sold to brothels in other countries, or coerced to be sex objects of strangers. Only a few swindlers are punished in countries where laws are respected. Worse, swindlers are unpunished in countries where authorities are inefficient or tolerate their actions. The worst miseries happen to women victims in countries where officials are secret bosses of swindler groups.

The Epic of Gilgamesh is a precious antiquity. In its introduction, author N. K. Sandars states the cases of women's sexual submissions occurred before the beginning of the second millennium BC. The protagonist of the legend was the strong and powerful King Gilgamesh of Mesopotamia (between Euphrates and Tigris Rivers), Middle East. In the setting,

Sandars states one characteristic of Gilgamesh is lust.

He deflowered all young women, even daughters of his warriors or wives of nobles.

Classical Mythology is a very useful literary work. Two authors Mark Morford and Robert Lenardon expound the two poetic sagas *Iliad* and *Odyssey of Homer*. The book states some consequences that happened after the fall of a Trojan citadel. Many Trojan leaders were killed, their wives included. Hecuba and Andromache were arrested and forced to be slaves of Greek leaders. What meaning connotes in the words the women were forced to be slaves? The answer should be sex objects. Surely, daughters of the defeated had the same ill fates. Probably, Greek soldiers of lower ranks also took women of lower rank defeated for their sex objects.

Understanding Human Sexuality is a worthy study. Sociologists Janet Hyde and John DeLamater note legal rapes in Europe in the early Middle Ages. There was a law allowing landlords to deflower peasant brides in their wedding nights before giving them to their husbands!

Different Voices: Women in United States History is an admired document. Historian Emily Teipe points out several rapes in the late seventeenth century AD, such as native women were raped and forced to be mistresses by Spanish men, a native virgin was gifted to Captain Romeo to deflower, and so forth.

The examples in the books prove that many men have been more interested in virgins than other women for their sexual intercourses. Therefore, in some old cultures, brides had to show their virginities in the first night, and bloodstains on towels under buttocks of brides were the proofs. Today, many men still consider virginity is precious; to deflower virgins will bring them good luck.

Other type of sex objects occurred in lots of countries in the Middle Ages. Hundreds of beautiful women were forced to be concubines of sultans, emperors, and kings. Those women were detained in harems or forbidden citadels. Only eunuchs were allowed to contact the women detainees. Similar endurances happened in palaces and mansions where sufferers were mistresses of powerful or wealthy men.

For example, poet Xuan Huong Ho Phi Mai (1772–1822), a concubine of a middle-aged wealthy man, expressed her unhappy and disappointed emotion.

On Sharing a Husband

The woman there is warm in blanket, others are embittered in dispirit;
Damn the unfair fate of sharing one husband I face with.
Occasionally he comes, afterward disappointment harasses me;
One encounter happens each month, but it means nothing.
Enduring for steamed sticky rice, rice is deprived;
Toiling like a servant, servant is not paid anything.

Men who had concubines were lustful. They behaved as if their women were sexual toys. They did not intend to make their women to get satisfaction, or they had no ability to do it.

Third type of sex objects related to brothels that have appeared since the ancient times. Today, this issue becomes very diverse and sophisticated with wicked actions of swindlers and pimps.

In the precious antiquity *The Epic of Gilgamesh*[1], N. K. Sandars implicits this type. Gilgamesh owned a brothel since

1 References: Sandars, N.K. *The Epic of Gilgamesh*, Penguin Books. London. 1972. P. 7
Morford, Mark and Robert Lenardon. Classical Methology. 2nd Edition. David McKay Co. Inc. New York. 1977. P. 325-27.
Hyde, Janet and John Delamater. Human Sexuality. 9th Edition. McGraw Hill. New York. 2006. P. 75
Teipe, Emily. Different Voices. Women in the United States. Cat Publishing. California. 2006. P. 11

jungle man Enkidu asked him for one harlot from the temple; she trained Enkidu how to practice sex and taught him how to live as a noble.

The Tale of Vuong Thuy Kieu

The literary work *The Tale of Vuong Thuy Kieu* (1802) of poet Nguyen Du (1765–1820) describes the miseries of protagonist Thuy Kieu, a very pretty and talented lady who was sold two times to two different brothels.

> Thuy Kieu was the eldest child of Mr. and Mrs. Vuong. Her youngest sister was Thuy Van, and her younger brother was Vuong Quan. The family was a middle class one in the sixteenth century. They lived in Que Huong City.

The tale began when Thuy Kieu was seventeen years old. One morning in March, in the Spring Festival, the three siblings met a *junzi*, a gentleman of the country. He was the son of a noble family in a faraway province, Lieu Duong. He was young, nice, and friendly. His name was Kim Trong.

> *He was handsome and gallant,*
> *Intelligent and gifted (148)*
> *His aspect was gentle and upright,*
> *Chivalrous and refined.*

Vuong Quan and Kim Trong had already known each other from the library of the city. Kim Trong was a diligent student who rented a small apartment near the library and temporary lived there. Vuong Quan introduced Kim Trong to his sisters and his sisters to the *junzi*.

Kim Trong and Thuy Kieu assumed to love each other at the first sight since they conversed harmoniously and did not want to say good-bye.

Intelligent and gifted gentleman met
Beautiful and talented lady. (164)
Their hearts stirred the loveliness,
But they did not dare to say.

Nevertheless, they had to say good-bye at noon. At their different dwellings, they both were in lovesickness. Thus, after several days, Kim Trong rented a small house next to the villa of the parents of Thuy Kieu and looked for opportunity to meet her. After about a week, they met each other at the front gate of the villa. He expressed his love and asked her to marry him. She answered that they had to ask for permission from her parents.

However, in the evening, she snuck in his house. They said that they loved each other and kissed each other. They took vows to love each other for all their lives. They exchanged souvenirs to trust their love. He asked for sexual intercourse, but she refused and said that it would be saved for their wedding night:

"Don't treat our future marriage as a game; (501)
Let me explain, if you respect me until our wedding,
The precious flower has both beauty and fragrance.
The peach garden won't ban the green-bird.
The virtue of a bride, (505)
Chastity is her treasure for her husband.
So soon you wish to pluck the flower; (521)
I'll live long, you'll be completely fulfilled.
If you don't protect my chastity,
I'll be shameful to you later."

He respected her virginity. They shared their talents of

composing poems, playing musical instruments, and drawing. She came back home before nightfall.

Unexpectedly and unfortunately, on the next day, two male servants of Kim Trong's parents came from his native province. They gave him bad news; his father had just passed away.

He was stunned since the filial duty of the traditions required him to return home to mourn his deceased father, and he was not allowed to marry in a period of three years. Thus, he sneaked to the villa, met Thuy Kieu, and said a sorrowful good-bye.

> *"We've so few opportunities to express our hearts;*
> *We don't have enough time to organize our wedding.*
> *Our vows we always hold fast; (541)*
> *Although we live far away, our hearts are near.*
> *Thousands of miles away in three winters,*
> *It's our deep grief, but it'll pass over. (544)*
> *Take care of yourself, my darling gold and jade;*
> *It'll make my mind peaceful in the far-away place."*

Also, Thuy Kieu was very sad; she was confused. She promised that she would keep the vows of fidelity. Then they said good-bye in deep melancholy.

Catastrophically, a human-made disaster came to family Vuong just a week later. Then waves of miseries began to pour down on the life of Thuy Kieu. Corruptive and cruel authorities were the makers of the disaster. Worse, all organizations of the authorities cooperated with one another in the corruptions and despotism. The local authority devised a slanderous blame of a fraudulently clandestine trade and laid the crime on Mr. Vuong and his son. It sent its group of constables to the villa, and they acted like bandits. They took valuable things, smashed many others. Then they tortured Mr. Vuong and his son before Mrs. Vuong and the two daughters.

The whole household was frightened and panic-stricken,
Cries and sobs for innocence echoed from the earth to the firmament. (590)
Though they groveled, and begged all the day,
Deaf ears did not hear pleas, cruel hands did not halt tortures.
Ropes bound their heels, to girders, the victims were drawn
upside down,
Even rock would be painful, they were mere human beings.
Agonies and scariness tormented their hearts and minds.
To far Heavens, they could not appeal this injustice. (596)
All day long, the constables coarsened and tortured.
The havoc was created because of money and gold.

Then the constables dragged Mr. Vuong and his son to the local jail. On the next day, a local organization sent word to Mrs. Vuong and her daughters that if they handed three hundred taels of gold, the victims would be released.

In such a situation, Thuy Kieu decided to save her father and her brother; she persuaded her mother and her sister to let her fulfill her filial duty. She would sell herself to have gold to bribe the authorities. Her mother sobbed bitterly.

The mother had pity on her innocent daughter,
The yoke suddenly bound her life. (616)
She would live in a strange land,
Sacrifice her future and life for the whole family.

However, the mother was in a stalemate; she compared the agonies of her husband and son with the fate of her daughter. She reluctantly agreed with the daughter. Then Thuy Kieu sent word of her volunteering to become a wife or concubine of any rich man who would pay a high price.

Three days later, Ma Giam Sinh, a man older than forty from province Lam Chuy came and viewed her. His aspect, complexion, and trope were rude and impolite, quite opposite to the ones of Kim Trong, her lover.

He rushed to the highest chair and sat insolently,
Urged the mother to show Thuy Kieu to him. (632)
Reluctantly, Thuy Kieu walked out from her bedroom;
Sadly and shyly, her tears dropped down at every step.
The more Ma-Giam-Sinh was impudent,
The more Thuy Kieu was shameful. (636)
He stared at her;
She felt ashamed.

After several hours of haggling, he bought Thuy Kieu for the price of three hundred taels of gold. Then he said that he would come back in the next two days and left the villa.

When the local authority received three hundred taels of gold, it released Mr. Vuong and the son immediately. Thereafter, Mr. Vuong knew that her daughter had sold herself to have the gold to bribe for the releases. He attempted to commit suicide, but his wife and children, especially Thuy Kieu, implored, begged, and soothed him.

> *"Even though you're in old age, (673)*
> *One secular tree supports many branches."*

In that night, Thuy Kieu groaned sadly in her bedroom. She felt very sorrowful because she could not keep her vows of fidelity with Kim Trong. She sobbed because she could not fulfill her duty and responsibility in this life as she had vowed. She promised that after her death, in her reincarnation, she would volunteer to be a horse to serve him in his next life.

> *"Until my death, I cannot pay this debt (710)*
> *The souvenir-of-love is here, how can I resolve?"*

In the next bedroom, her sister, Thuy Van, woke up and heard the groans; she got up and went to the other bedroom. Seeing her sister in tears, Thuy Van asked her sister this:

"Unexpected calamities have come to our family;
You alone must bear the burdens. (715)
You've groaned so long in the night;
Probably, you're preoccupied with love."

Thuy Kieu confessed that she had vowed to marry Kim Trong. Since she could not keep the vows, she asked Thuy Van to replace her to be spouse of Kim Trong, her lover. She handed the souvenir of love to Thuy Van.

"I'm very shy in talking to you;
If I don't ask you, I'll be infidel. (722)
Please, help me to keep the vows;
Sit on this chair, I kneel to prostrate you.
I can't fulfill my duty of being his wife;
Please, replace me to do the duty. (726)
Though my flesh will be crushed and bones broken;
In the Elysium I'll smile. (734)
Here is the souvenir-of-love, take it.
You'll be his wife and live in happiness; (737)
Remember your ill-fated sister, who dies in a strange land;
I'm lost, but my utensils are still here;
Whenever you use them; (740)
Whenever you play my music instruments;
Whenever you ignite incenses in my bronze urn;
You look out at leaves and grass;
If they stir in light wind, you know I return.
My soul still bears the vows; (746)
Though I die, I still feel I don't fulfill my duty.
O my lover, I'm disloyal to you!"

At the moment, Thuy Kieu fell down in faintness. In panic, Thuy Van called their parents and brother. They came and rubbed balm on the body of Thuy Kieu; after half an hour, she regained consciousness.

Ma Giam Sinh came on the next day. The whole family falsely thought that he bought Thuy Kieu to be his concubine. However, he was a professional swindler who sought and bought young women, especially virgins, to deflower them, then he acted as a pimp in exploiting them as courtesans in a short period to get back his gold or money he had paid. Thereafter he resold them to a whorehouse for profit. Tu Ba, a madam who owned a whorehouse, Ngung Bich, in his native province, Lam Chuy, was his client. Thuy Kieu was one of his victims.

It has pity on the young, pretty, and talented
virgin; (819)
Precious flower was sold to a promiscuous
rake pimp.

In that evening, after dinner, Ma Giam Sinh lay on the bed of Thuy Kieu and prepared to deflower her since she already belonged to him. He stared at her charm and prettiness again and again to sketch out his wicked scheme. He would sleep with her in some weeks, then he forced her to be a courtesan for his profit.

In joy he thought, "I've procured the
precious treasure;
The more I stare at the qualities, the more I
realize the values.
It's really the goddess of beauty, the
firmament of scent; Her one smile is worth

one thousand gold. (826)
At first, like plucking a beautiful bud, I deflower;
Then princes and nobles will be bewitched.
Soon I get back three hundred taels of gold;
Thereafter, huge profits will come for sure.
The substantial wealth is within my grasp; (831)
I pay nothing to procure the treasure from the sky.
The peach from fairyland comes into my hands;
It is life, I fulfill my desire firstly. (834)
On this earth, many men think that they pluck buds;
But they cannot feel how the buds are."

The last part of his scheme would be how to counterfeit her virginity to resell her to Madam Tu Ba with a high price.

"A mixture of pomegranate-husk juice and cockscomb blood
Makes deflowered buds show their colors like originals.
Vagueness can often trick fools; (839)
A high price I will ask and get for sure."

He was a lustful, prurient man; he did not wait long. In the very evening, he deflowered Thuy Kieu and fulfilled his sexual desire two more times on her bed.

Alas! the precious bud had to let, (845)
The coarse bee opened all its ways of forth and back.
The waves of gusts hit and swept violently,
No pity on the noble jade, nor sorrow for fragrant scent.
In spring night, she was exhausted in half-dream,
Humiliated on bed beneath the torch light.

After the night of enduring thrice the humiliation, at dawn, she decided to commit suicide with the sharp knife that she had stashed inside her nightgown in the twilight of the day before.

In rain of tears, she felt deeply sorrowful,
Resent at the coarse guest, sad for her dirty body,
"What a fishily stinky creature he appears! (853)
My elegant body is smeared and smudged.
No hope left for me to look forward; (855)
Termination of a life like mine ends all miseries."
Groaned at her ill-fate, cursed on shifty society,
Pulled out the knife, she attempted to stab and cut herself.

At that very moment, she realized that if she died, the rest of her family would be in trouble, so she resigned herself to let her ill fate run its course.

During the next six days, Ma Giam Sinh lived in the villa. Thuy Kieu experienced the rude way he treated her and observed the rough way he behaved to the others. She suspected he was a professional swindler.

At dawn of the last day, in saying good-bye to her father, mother, sister, and brother, she murmured to her father:

"In looking at him during the days, (881)
My life is probably caught in hands of this caddish trickster.
The insolent ways he behaved, spoke, and ate, (885)
Impertinently to superiors, domineeringly to inferiors,
Quite different from a noble or courteous man. (887)
In watching him, we can conclude that he's a pimp."

Though Mr. Vuong also knew that his daughter was the victim of the pimp, he could not help her because all branches of the authorities had shared three hundred taels of goal. He also resigned himself to let the dark future of his daughter run its course.

"Poor daughter, I'm sad but can I do anything? (889)
Painfully you'll live, die, and burry in strange land."

When Thuy Kieu said farewell, the whole household sobbed sorrowfully. In her case. To see one of them again in that century was an impossibility. Sadly, Thuy Kieu had to go with Ma Giam Sinh to Lam Chuy province.

At the house of Ma Giam Sinh, Thuy Kieu had to continue to sleep with him. She was forced to be a courtesan, greeting wealthy customers for the pimp in a period of two months as he sketched his scheme. Then the pimp resold her to Madam Tu Ba, the owner of Ngung Bich whorehouse. She felt upset when she glanced at the madam.

Glimpsed at the crone, whose complexion
was so pale;
What had she eaten? Her body was so tall
and fat. (942)
In front of the cart, the impudent way she
greeted;
But Thuy Kieu had to obey and enter the
house.

At the first sight, Thuy Kieu was shocked. She realized the place was a whorehouse. There were several prostitutes with customers and a pedestal with a statue of the bogeyman of brothels:

Some women with showy faces embraced
pair of
boor men in one corner;
Other girls in gaudy clothes cuddled some
crass
customers at other side;
Heat of fire and incense emanated from the
middle
of the room; (929)
A pale-and-dense eye eyelash statue of a
man was
hung above the pedestal; (930)

Whorehouses usually put statues of him for their talisman;
These businesses decorated this evil as their ancestor.
Incenses and flowers they adored around for days and nights;
Any prostitutes who were unlucky had few clients, (934)
Or any others were rudely ill-treated by customers,
Before the talisman, they added incenses and prayed,
Offered new flowers, old flowers they put under their bed sheets. (937)
Bees would come in plenty, all corners would be busy.

While Thuy Kieu was still in panic, the madam pressed on her shoulders to lower her down before the talisman and prayed.

"Give her plenteous luck with plenitude of clients,
Around for days and nights she gets joyful successes.
Thousands of men crave to love her; (943)
This house enjoys more and more customers.
The presence of this beautiful girl is spread near and far;
She says good-bye a client at the front door, immediately
greets another at the back door (946)"

Frightened and dizzy, Thuy Kieu floundered, but Tu Ba rushed to the armchair nearby, sat with crossed legs, and commanded her.

> *"I'm your mother now; kneel to prostrate me; (951)*
> *Then go to the other house to prostrate your uncle."*

Nevertheless, Thuy Kieu did not obey. She spoke the things that made the madam very angry.

> *"My father and brother were in calamity;*
> *So I resigned to be his concubine. (954)*
> *The marriage was certified by wedding celebration;*
> *Additionally, I slept with him as husband and wife.*
> *I didn't know he led me to this place;*
> *If I knew, I didn't consent. (958)*
> *Sincerely, I submit you my case;*
> *This dirty work, I cannot do."*

Tu Ba threw a tantrum when she heard the words of Thuy Kieu. The madam cursed Ma Giam Sinh, who deceived her. She heaped penalties on Thuy Kieu.

> *"The evidences expose so obviously;*
> *He's not your husband but a blackguard robber.*
> *He ensured me your virginity; (965)*
> *So I bought with the high price;*
> *But he's only an inhuman creature,*

Not only deflowered but also repeat many
times.
Damn! The origin is lost; (969)
High profit cannot be attained as expected.
Hey, headstrong girl, I've bought; (971)
You must do what I say."

Then the madam called the uncle, the pimp, to flog Thuy Kieu before the other prostitutes to show discipline in her whorehouse.

"Uncle, uncle, come here, whip her;
She obeys only under our strong action.
Let us teach her the duty of tameness.
She's so young but lost virginity. (976)
Let she know my power;
Patch three whips together and beat her."

After the whipping, the pimp left the room, but the madam still stood there and did not cease her reviling.

In agony, Thuy Kieu decided to end her life. She pulled out the sharp knife that she had stashed in the sleeve of her gown and stabbed it into her chest.

The victim fell down in trauma; (989)
The madam dismayed and trembled with
fear.

Tu Ba quivered uncontrollably because she had bought Thuy Kieu with a big amount of gold; thus, she ordered some other prostitutes to hold Thuy Kieu onto the bed in the next room, assigned turns for them to take care of the victim, and invited a physician to cure the injury.

On the next day, Thuy Kieu regained consciousness.

Tu Ba used an opposite tactic; she coaxed Thuy Kieu to give up the intention of committing suicide.

"Everybody has only one life; (1005)
You're so young; your springtime will last long.
We're sorry about mistakes we've behaved you;
Persistently you keep your chastity; no more we force you to greet any customer.
However, you're already here; (1009)
Lock yourself in this room to wait opportunity to
marry a good man.
Still living, still having good chances, (1011)
You still have a good lucks to get a noble husband."

Even though Thuy Kieu was soothed by the soft words, she still suspected Tu Ba cheating her.

"If it happens like you say, I'm grateful; (1023)
But I still afraid something wrong will appear.
Customers here are like bees that can make tangles;
To die in cleanness is better than to live in dirtiness."

Tu Ba continued her deceiving words to calm Thuy Kieu. Additionally, the madam swore to a mystical power that she would keep the promises.

"Let be relax;
I don't lie. (1028)
If I don't keep my promises,
The Sun over my head will punish me."

The swearing in of Tu Ba made Thuy Kieu calm down. However, her days in the house caused her to feel very lonely and sad; she missed her parents, sister, brother, and lover. She desperately thought that she could meet them only in dreams.

After about a week, one morning, she heard from the next room two different voices, a man and a woman who composed valuable twin poems. After an hour, she opened the door of her room and stood there. At that moment, the man also stepped out from the other room. The eyes of the pretty girl and the handsome man met. He was well dressed; his gait and gesture made him appear like a nobleman.

After a couple of minutes of conversation, he introduced himself as So Khanh and expressed his emotional sympathy and heartrending pity for her situation.

"Alas! Beauty of a mermaid, fragrance of the sky,
What a pity, you're forced to live here. (1066)
Phoenix is unfortunately doomed in a cage.
Flower of high rank is banished in indignity.
Angry at the old king of firmament,
How can I express my helpfulness? (1070)
The fair lady knows the heroic man,
Who can easily break the kennel to open the cage."

They said good-bye. So Khanh came back to the other room. After some hours of pondering on her unknown period of incarceration, Thuy Kieu wrote her plea for help on a piece of paper.

A bold step she decided to flee, (1079)
Asked him to rescue her from this vale of tears.
In the paper she told him her whole case,
Filial duty and banishment to the utter
miseries.

At dawn of the next day, with the help of a bird, Thuy Kieu secretly sent the paper to So Khanh. At the dusk of the very day, with the help of the same bird, he sent her a small piece of paper with the words "At 9:00 p.m. on the twenty-first."

At the tryst, So Khanh sneaked into the room of Thuy Kieu. Despite of her shameful feeling, she greeted him and knelt before him.

"Like a water-hyacinth, I drift into this house,
Like a stray-bird, I fall in this net. (1097)
Like a nearly drown, I owe your rescue,
This favor, I inscribe in my heart."

So Khanh nodded and ensured her that he would easily rescue Thuy Kieu. Then he bragged about his ability, elegance, and ownership.

You worry because you haven't known me;
Abyss, I will fill it up. (1104)
I've strong horses which can fly through

winds, (1107)
Loyal body guards who will defeat any interferers.
This best opportunity you should hold firmly;
Thirty-six ways, the best is to flee. (1110)
Even in cases of storms or deluges,
You will be safe because of my protection."

After hearing his boasts, Thuy Kieu suspected him, but she was in a stalemate; she decided to risk her life. He guided her to sneak to the front yard. Some men on horses were waiting for them. One horse was reserved for Thuy Kieu. In hurry, they all ran into the forest. Nonetheless, it seemed that her horse was the weakest.

During the night, the horses of So Khanh and his men were running faster than the horse of Thuy Kieu. At dawn, she was alone in the maze of the forest.

Suddenly, a crew of guys marched nearer and nearer. Madam Tu Ba was the leader. Others were male and female servants of her whorehouse. Immediately, Tu Ba grabbed Thuy Kieu and beat her heartlessly.

In great pain, Thuy Kieu asked for mercy and promised to do what Tu Ba would teach, but the madam said that she did not trust her. Among the crew, a woman with the name Ha Kieu asked for mercy for Thuy Kieu. However, Tu Ba required both Thuy Kieu and Ha Kieu to write their guarantee in words on a paper and sign on it.

Back in the whorehouse in that afternoon, Ha Kieu came to the room of Thuy Kieu, who told how So Khanh had cheated her, but Ha Kieu explained this to her:

"Oh, you've been deceived because (1157)
You've just came here, you haven't known him,
A well-known caddish trickster in this province.
He had already destroyed many pretty girls. (1160)
What have just happened to you, their scheme.
Similar swindles had happened in the past." (1162)

Nearly all prostitutes in the house swapped stories of the wicked works of So Khanh to one another. Thus, in the next morning, he walked around the house and reviled loudly:

"I've heard of one girl here, (1172)
Has circulated a false rumor that I've cheated,
Come here to confront with me."

In splenetic mood, Thuy Kieu brought the small piece of paper on which So Khanh had written the words "At 9:00 p.m. on the twenty-first" to face him. When he intended to beat her, many other women had already surrounded them, and several women said that all women in the house had already known his inhuman characteristic. Shamefully, he quickly left the house.

Nonetheless, Thuy Kieu was already shackled in the whorehouse in this strange region without relatives, without acquaintances, and with no way for her to escape.

After a week, in a full-moon evening, Tu Ba came to the room of Thuy Kieu to instruct and train her how to greet and sleep with customers.

"Professions of harlots are very elaborate;
A harlot has to know all their artful
details." (1201)

Thuy Kieu replied that in her situation, she had to venture anything she was instructed and trained. The madam continued:

"All men have same desires; (1205)
They come back here again and again, they
pay;
In the art of sex, there are lots of attractive
facets,
Equivocal by nights, various by days.
(1208)
Practice cleverly and conversantly;
Seven letters in openness, eight skills in
privacy."

Tu Ba gave seven instructions to the whores of her house. They were seven insincere or cheating acts: (1) to make pitiful sobs of pretending love, (2) to cut their locks and present them to customers as love proofs, (3) to make each customer interested by writing his name on the body of the girl, (4) to burn incenses to swear love, (5) to make a tryst to marry, (6) to pretend to ask a customer to escape together, and (7) to pretend to be faint because of love to make each customer deeply attached.

There were eight private skills that the madam trained the whores also. They were acts to be performed during sexual intercourse with customers. The madam continued her lesson.

"A harlot has to make flowers shy, willows surprised,
And her customers madly satisfied; (1212)
Ogle amiable glances, express charming smiles,
Attractiveness of tropes, allure of gaits." (1214)

Thuy Kieu had to conceal her shyness, sorrow, misery, resentment, and self-pity to greet customers.

So many bees knew the way of the pretty flower,
Intoxicated by days, infatuated by nights. (1230)

Rarely, she had time to think on herself, and rarely she had time to think about her parents, sister, brother, and lover; but whenever she thought, she felt self-piteous and missed them.

Days and nights passed. Thuy Kieu dragged on her miserable existence. However, one day, a young man of Clan Thuc, named Thuc Sinh, who often followed his father from province Vo Tich to province Lam Chuy to manage their business, visited the house since he heard of the beauty of Thuy Kieu. After some months, he was captivated by her prettiness, talent, and nicety:

Gradually he deeply attached to her; (1289)
He came not only for lust but also for love.

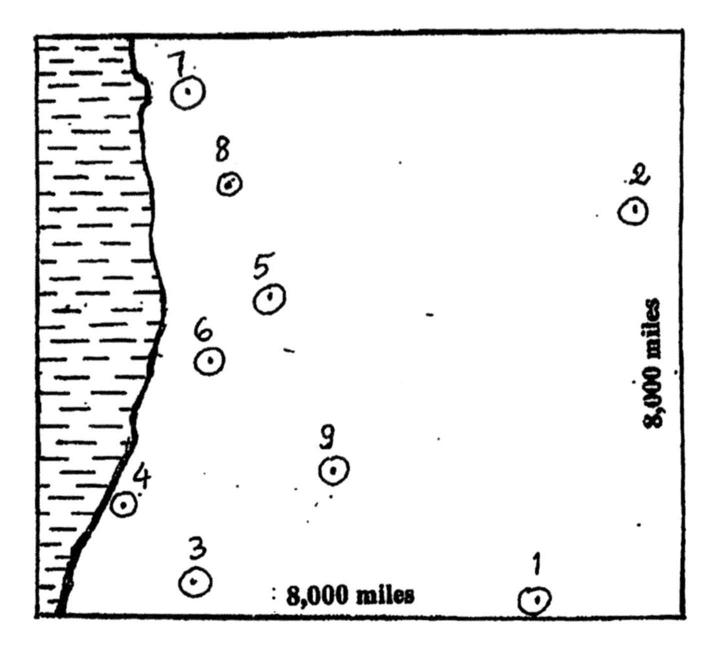

1. Que Huong City: Home of Thuy Kieu, her parents, and siblings
2. Lieu Duong: Native province of Kim Trong, the lover of Thuy Kieu
3. Lam Chuy Province: House of Ma Giam Sinh, the pimp
4. Ngung Bich Brothel
5. Vo Tich Province: Castle of Hoan Thu and Thuc Sinh
6. Rented house of Thuc Sinh and Thuy Kieu
7. Palace of Mandarin Hoan and wife, parents of Hoan Thu
8. Chau Thai Brothel
9. Viet Dong: native province of Tu Hai

Then Thuc Sinh asked Thuy Kieu whether she was the daughter of madam Tu Ba or not. He explained his decision to marry her as concubine, so he wanted to know her origin. She told him not only her origin but also the cause that had made her leave her family and what had happened to her thereafter as well as her worrying on her future.

"Your marriage has been in harmony;
(1341)
My presence in your family may harm it.
To be a secondary rank,
It's usually slighted. (1344)
One hundred intricately difficult conducts,
Am I relatively free?
Do you have smart dealing
To protect me in some respects?
If the first is vicious,
I'm ill-treated by the lion. (1350)
If the first is jealous in love,
I'm miserable thrice."

Thuy Kieu was worried how she would be treated not only by his wife but also by his father.

"Additionally, your father on high,
Does he have any pity on me?
When he does not accept, (1355)
A come-back to brothel will make more
humiliated."

She said that he had to ponder before deciding to marry her as his concubine. However, he calmed her down.

Thuc-Sinh said, "You're so provident;
Why don't you trust my sincerity?" (1362)

Then they took vows of love. He stayed in her room that night. In the early morning of the next day, they asked the madam for permission to stroll into the woods surrounding the house.

Nevertheless, as he had planned, he led her to escape. He hid her in the mansion of an influential man named Hoa Duong. Then Thuc Sinh did two acts in parallel: asking Mr. Hoa Duong to intimidate Tu Ba that he would sue her because she forced a lady from a good family to be a whore and sending an intermediary to the madam to talk about a price he would pay if she agreed to let Thuy Kieu marry him.

The madam agreed on a price. After the payment, Thuc Sinh married Thuy Kieu. However, he did not bring her to his castle in Vo Tich to live together with his wife Hoan Thu. He rented a small house near the provisional dwelling of his father, not far from the mansion of Mr. Hoa Duong. The couple lived there.

Half a year elapsed gently; spring and summer passed.

Suddenly, storms fell down on their heads in autumn. Father Thuc did not accept Thuy Kieu being a concubine of his son when he revealed that she was from a whorehouse. Father Thuc ordered his son to end the marriage and expel her back to the whorehouse. However, Thuc Sinh pleaded:

"I've known my guilty deeds; (1395)
I'll endure any punishments;
But we've lived in one house as husband and wife;
Love doesn't differentiate between foolishness and wisdom;
Though living in harmony just one day, (1399)

Who has a heart to cut the lovely relationship?
If the authority on the high doesn't grant us grace,
We'll die together to fulfill the meaning of love."

Father Thuc knew he could not change the mind of his son, so he complained to the local mandarin that Thuy Kieu, a whore, enticed his son, making his clan undignified. The mandarin sent constables to bring the couple to his office. They knelt before him and pleaded for mercy, but he reprimanded Thuc Sinh as a gullible fool and Thuy Kieu as a deceiving whore.

He delivered the stringent verdict: Thuy Kieu would be sent back to the brothel or flogged to death. Thuy Kieu accepted the death sentence. The mandarin ordered constables to flog her.

Thuy Kieu was hurt. Thuc Sinh felt wretchedly and told everyone there that it was his fault, not hers.

The mandarin stopped the flogging and heard him speak.

He told everyone her noble origin, his asking her for marriage, his guarantee to protect her, and her talents including the ability of composing poems. To check her talent of composing poems, the mandarin gave the title Cange and let her sit on a chair at the small desk on which there were a sheet of paper, an inkpot, and a brush-pen.

Immediately, she raised the brush-pen and wrote the poem of eight lines on the sheet. Everyone was surprised at her talent. Thus, the mandarin praised her, saying that her beauty and talents were worth all the gold on this earth. Then he advised Father Thuc to accept Thuy Kieu to be the daughter-in-law of Clan Thuc. The father accepted.

Thuc Sinh and Thuy Kieu came back to their rented house. Autumn and winter passed very quickly. She felt that they could not conceal their marriage from his wife, Hoan Thu, anymore.

"Since the day you've supported my frail life,
A year passed with the witnesses of swallows and canneries.
No news has come from your own home. (1479)
Warm affection with the second, frigid attitude with the first,
In thinking about common senses, it seems odd;
Rumors and gossips exempt nobody. (1482)
I've heard your first is disciplined,
Living in rules, speaking in etiquettes,
Special guys have usually been frightening;
It can measure depth of river or seas but cannot fathom
human hearts. (1486)
Living together here one whole year;
We cannot conceal your wife anymore.
No news from her in one year, (1889)
I'm afraid something will happen soon.
Let come back to your castle;
Firstly make her satisfied, and then beg her."

Thuc Sinh consented. Thuy Kieu prepared baggage for him. The good-bye moment was melancholic.

Thuc Sinh came back to his castle, but he did not dare to say anything about the marriage with Thuy Kieu to his wife, Hoan Thu. He was a henpecked husband since she was a special woman from important origins, the daughter of the mandarin of the civil office board. She was severe in her sly characteristics.

Her ways of living and behaving were good;
But judging and catching faults were hard. (1534)

In truth, Hoan Thu had sent her loyal servants to spy the works of her husband and she knew all his secrets. Although she was angry, she spoke and acted as if she knew nothing about his secrets. However, his concealments made her angrier.

"Since the garden has been added the beautiful flower;
All guys in the castle murmured but he concealed." (1536)
Fire in her heart made her testier and testier,
She tacitly reproached the disloyal and flirtatious knave:
"If he confesses to me the truth, (1539)
I might give favor to the inferior, I'm the deserved superior.
I'm not fool, I don't want to lose my nobleness,
Not to be labeled as jealous shrew. (1542)
However, he performs concealments,
What a childish, silly, and farcical trick.
Lived in the distance, he has turned infidel. (1545)
He conceals, so I cooperate with him;
The play he has arranged, I don't need to invent.
Crawling around the brim of the cup, the ant can't flee.
I'll make them not to dare to recognize each other;
I'll oppress and humiliate her, she cannot raise her head.
The play will be performed in front of everyone;
They'll see my iron hands." (1552)
The anger, Hoan-Thu passed inside her heart,
Ignored the rumors and gossips she heard.

Nonetheless, one day, two servants directly told her the secrets with hopes to receive some reward; she refused, reviled, and punished them.

> *Lady Hoan-Thu was in tantrum: (1557)*
> *"My husband is the man of ethics,*
> *The immoral acts are fantasized by some whispers,*
> *You dare to swap them to smear him." (1560)*
> *She commanded stringent punishments to the two servants;*
> *Their mouths were slapped, their teeth were pulled out.*
> *Thereafter, nobody dared to say anything about the forbidden.*

Simultaneously, servants in the castle witnessed Hoan Thu behaving sweetly toward her husband. There were nice words, heartfelt smiles, delicious food, high quality liquor, and so forth.

On the other hand, during several meals, when Thuc Sinh intended to confess the marriage, Lady Hoan Thu refuted his intention and changed their conversation into other issues. After these missed opportunities, he thought of this:

> *"The mouth of the bottle is covered tightly,*
> *She doesn't ask, why should I confess?" (1578)*

Therefore, both Thuc Sinh and Hoan Thu lived in differently dishonest situations. Another autumn came. One day, she asked him to let her come to her native province to visit her parents.

At the palace of her parents, in grief, she lamented the infidelity of her husband to her mother:

She confided all the details, (1607)
His disloyalty, her unluckiness.

Then the daughter told her old mother her wicked scheme and asked for some help. She would come back to her castle in Vo Tich. A week later, her old mother would send pairs of hoodlums to the rented house in Lam Chuy where Thuy Kieu was living. They would secretly abduct Thuy Kieu and bring the victim to the palace; the old mother would ill-treat Thuy Kieu in the palace. After a month, Hoan Thu would come to the palace and bring Thuy Kieu to her castle, and Hoan Thu herself would continue her wicked scheme.

"To Lam-Chuy, it lasts one month on roads,
To use boats on sea will be much shorter.
Select fierce servants, (1615)
They chain her ankle.
They make her pain in shame;
They make her unconscious in coma,
To sooth my mind and heart, (1619)
To give everybody ridiculous fun."

The old mother praised the scheme and promised to give her wholehearted help. Then Hoan Thu came back to her castle. Some days later, the old mother began to implement the scheme; she sent four of the most fierce servants to the rented house in Lam Chuy.

That night, after some hours in drowsiness, Thuy Kieu went out to the front yard to pray under her breath. Suddenly, the fierce servants appeared and executed a series of man-made miseries.

In the autumn night, winds blew through the bushes;
Under the crescent moon and three bright stars, (1638)
She lighted some joss-sticks and prayed in her breath.
However, her prayer was half-way through entreaty;
Suddenly, she saw the evil hoodlums in the bushes;
Like loud devils, cruel ghosts, they appeared (1642)
Being frightened and scared, she floundered;
Anesthetic was sprayed quickly and thickly into her face.

The fierce servants, the hoodlums of Old Mother Hoan, put unconscious Thuy Kieu into a jute bag. They laid an unknown corpse that they had picked up by the sea onto her bed and set fire to the whole house.

Dwelling in the house nearby, Father Thuc, his servants, and some neighbors saw the fire. They ran to the burning house, but it was too late. They could not save anything. Then they dug up the heap of ashes; they found a half-burned skeleton, which all of them concluded was the rest of the corpse of Thuy Kieu.

The servants of Father Thuc collected the bones. While Father Thuc was preparing a funeral, at random, Thuc Sinh came. He burst into tears. They interred the skeleton. They thought that Thuy Kieu was dead.

However, Thuy Kieu was still living. She was abducted and

brought to the palace of the parents of Hoan Thu. Of course, she did not know the owners of the palace and their scheme. In the next morning, she was summoned to a splendid hall.

One female servant came to the cell and called,
She had to follow the savant to present herself.
Along the gallery, she saw the magnificence,
Arts of architecture and decoration (1722)
Two lines of lamps were lighted through in daytime.
At the end of the hall, a lady sat in a luxurious armchair.
The lady not only asked but interrogated, (1725)
Although Thuy Kieu told the lady her true origin,
The lady pretended to be angry and reprimanded:
"Hey, headstrong girl, liar,
Wanton girl, (1729)
Either traitorous servant or infidel wife,
Immoral girl,
Ugly base, clumsy girl, (1732)
I've bought you to be my servant;
But you fantasize the noble origin.
Servants, let show the discipline of my palace;
Flog to make her know my powerful hands."
Servants from all corners loudly submitted "Yes lady."
Two male servants used a can and a whip to beat.

Thuy Kieu was maltreated by Old Mother Hoan. She was beaten to a pulp. A pair of other servants had pity on her, but they could not do anything. To refute the noble origin of Thuy Kieu, the mother changed the name Thuy Kieu to Hoa (Flower). She had to toil as a servant for the old mother.

The head of female servants had compassion for Thuy Kieu; she carefully recommended that since both Old Mother Hoan and her daughter Hoan Thu were cruel and jealous, that several servants were sycophants, to avoid worse miseries, Thuy Kieu had to conceal her noble origin as well as not to identify any relatives, acquaintances, and so forth whenever she was still under the claws of the two women.

Two months passed. Again, Hoan Thu came to visit her parents. Hoan Thu and her old mother talked about their wicked scheme of maltreatment on Thuy Kieu. The old mother had accomplished its first episode; its next one would be implemented by Hoan Thu herself. Still, Thuy Kieu did not know Hoan Thu was the wife of Thuc Sinh. Thuy Kieu had to follow Hoan Thu to Vo Tich.

Mother and daughter checked the scheme;
Then the mother summoned and said to Hoa:
"This young lady, my daughter, lacks female servants,
Followed her and work for her." (1772)
Thuy Kieu had to obey the order;
She could not know where the next corner of the hell was!

Thuy Kieu had to toil as a female servant in the castle of Hoan Thu in Vo Tich Province. Several weeks later, in one evening, Hoan Thu summoned Thuy Kieu and handed her a zither to test her musical talent:

Obeyed she played some pieces of her own composition,
Fine strings sounded sweetly in larghetto movements. (1780)
Hoan-Thu felt fond of the melodious charisma,
But her hardship was one of her cruel characteristics.

Thuy Kieu lived in humiliation, loneliness, and self-pity. She did not know which province she was dragging her rove life.

Simultaneously, Thuc Sinh thought that Thuy Kieu was dead; he stayed provisionally in the other rented house of his father in Lam Chuy and bewailed her ill fate.

Four months later, Thuc Sinh came back to his castle. Hoan Thu ordered her servants to prepare a lavish meal in the evening to greet Thuc Sinh.

The lady welcomed her husband warmly and
Told him all her fond remembrances. (1802)
The castle was specially decorated and incensed.
The lady summoned servant Hoa to greet her master.
Glimpsed at Thuc-Sinh, Thuy Kieu faltered, (1805)
Thuy Kieu realized Thuc-Sinh, the husband,
She thought to herself, "My sharp eyes prove,
Thuc-Sinh is there, I don't falsely realize.
It's so clear; (1802)
I'm caught in the net of his wife.

What a sly crone she is;
What a wicked scheme she has organized!"

Both Thuy Kieu and Thuc Sinh recognized each other, but did not dare to acknowledge each other in the situation of being a servant and a master in the sly scheme. Thuy Kieu assessed the characteristics of Hoan Thu:

"Outwardly, she smiles and talks sweetly;
Inwardly, she scheme killings without swords." (1816)

Thuy Kieu floundered. Grazing at Thuc Sinh, her mind and heart bewildered. Under the iron hands of Hoan Thu, she had to obey and bow her head downward.

On the other hand, Thuc Sinh was dismayed and upset in hallucination; his mind worried, his heart lamented. He thought to himself:

"Who engenders this tragic situation? (1825)
Whose nets, whose yokes we are caught and burden?"

Thuc Sinh did not dare to recognize Thuy Kieu, but his painful sadness made his tears spill out. Hoan Thu knew the reason but theatrically questioned him:

"Honey, you've just come home, why are you so sorrowful?"
He answer, "I'm deeply grieved by my dead mother;
Even though she died three year ago, I still

remember her."
She praised, "You show great filial piety; (1833)
But let's drink to our love and relieve this autumn tedium."

Hoan Thu and Thuc Sinh exchanged sweet toasts and lovely words. Contrarily, Thu Kieu had to stand next to the table and serve what Hoan Thu commanded.

Hoan-Thu tried to find faults to berate Thuy Kieu,
Who was forced to kneel to offer up every drink. (1838)

These deeds made Thuc Sinh shed more tears. He talked and laughed as if he was delirious, so he pleaded that he was drunk and intended to retreat to his room. But Hoan Thu was in a tantrum and bawled out.

"Slave Hoa, persuade your master to continue his cup;
Or you will be flogged." (1844)

In panic, Thuc Sinh stayed and drank. Hoan Thu talked and laughed in a half-drunk manner, but she invented another part for the drama. She told him this:

"Slave Hoa is skilled at all arts; to ease your spirit,
I order her to play some musical compositions." (1850)

Then Hoan Thu handed the zither to Thuy Kieu, who readjusted the frets and played a sorrowful melody.

Four strings groaned, lamented, and cried;
(1853)
His heart was writhed, his spirit was
wrenched.
The two listeners perceived the same way of
expression,
Hoan-Thu smiled ironically, Thuc-Sinh
sobbed sadly.
More tears be shed like streams; (1857)
His head stooped, his mind tried to control
his sorrow.

In a tantrum, Hoan Thu reprimanded Thuy Kieu that Thuc Sinh was sorrowful because of the sad melody. Hoan Thu reviled, asking why Thuy Kieu did not select a joyful composition. Thuc Sinh became more hurt in his mind.

Thuc-Sinh perceived heart-rending, (1863)
He smiled reluctantly and talked
unwillingly.

At midnight, Hoan Thuc and Thuc Sinh went hand in hand to their bedroom. Thuy Kieu came back to her cell and sobbed in pain and humiliation.

Days and nights passed. Thuy Kieu toiled as a servant. One day, Hoan Thu was curious about the origin of Thuy Kieu, so he asked Thuc Sinh to grill Hoa. Again, he was frightened because the truth could make Hoan Thu angry, but he ventured to question Thuy Kieu in a soft tone. Thuy Kieu knelt and bowed her head to write the sum of her origin and submitted.

Hoan Thu read the sum and felt partly emotional, so she said to him that Hoa was really a wealthily, talented woman but ill-fated; thus, she intended to show her mercy. According to the begging of Hoa, she agreed to give the favor. She would order her servants to build a small pagoda at the left corner of the large backyard, plant a tall Bo tree nearby, and dig a small pool to transplant lotus. Hoa would enter nunhood and pray to Buddha to reach Nirvana.

A week later, Thuy Kieu initiated her Buddhist nunhood. She wore a dark-yellow robe, ignited joss sticks, and held flowers to pledge three vows and five commands. Her nunhood name was Trac Tuyen (Witted Purity).

Thuy Kieu spent her time reciting prayers to Buddha in the mornings and prostrated under her breath in the evenings. Two seasons passed.

However, one day, to test the fidelity of Thuc Sinh and the loyalty of Thuy Kieu, Hoan Thu pretended to leave the castle to visit her parents, but she sneaked back to the castle.

Thuc Sinh did not know the snare. On the next day, he came to the small pagoda and clarified his impotence to Thuy Kieu.

"I resign myself of being unfaithful in love;
All the miseries have poured on you. (1946)
My stratagem is inferior to the one of the woman;
Looking inwardly I feel painful, speaking out
I suffocated my voice.
I've engendered misfortunes to you;
Harm your youth I've made. (1950)
My life I don't care;
I'd intention to commit suicide because of you;
But I haven't a son yet to be my heir;

In humiliation, I'm dragging my life. (1954)
This guilt I'll redeem myself in my next life."

In reply, Thuy Kieu compared herself as a boat made of precious wood that was stormed by turbulent waves. She thanked him since he had rescued her from the hell of Ngung Bich Whorehouse.

"My life writhed with the dirty mud. (1959)
If you hadn't rescued me, I've not lived till today.
You made the gallant risk; (1661)
Your deed is really an exemplary chivalry.
Unluckily, it's impossible to be your concubine."

Even though Thuy Kieu said her sincere thanks, Thuc Sinh continued to groan. Then he persuaded her to flee.

"Her acts of the past show her sly cruelty;
We cannot conjecture her scheme in the future. (1968)
When other waves of storm happen;
More miseries you endure, more sufferings I feel.
It'd better you flee away;
Our tender love has no chance to re-unify."

Turn by turn, they groaned and poured out their suffered sorrows and sad feelings. They did not know that Hoan Thu hid behind a bush nearby and listened all the details.

When Hoan Thu did not want to hear any more, she walked with heavy steps towards the two confiders. She pretended that she knew nothing about the talk. She gently smiled and sweetly asked Thuc Sinh:

"From where you've just come here honey?"
He was scared, so he lied: (1985)
"I've strolled through the garden, admired flowers,
Considerately I've come here.
Concurrently I view the scene of the pagoda,
I read the prayers which Hoa has written."

Immediately, Hoan Thu praised that what Hoa had written were quintessential, that her ill fate was pitiful, and that her talents were valued a thousand taels of gold.

Thereafter, hand in hand, Hoan Thu and Thuc Sinh walked slowly through the garden into the castle.

At the same time, Thuy Kieu stood in a big shock at the small pagoda. Then, Thuy Kieu noticed a female servant who was at the direction from which Hoan Thu had come. The servant told her more clearly what Hoan Thu knew.

"The lady was standing here and listening all the details,
His love and grieves your sufferings and thanks." (2000)

Thuy Kieu was very frightened. She measured in her mind the sly wickedness of this jealous woman and thought whether there was any similar one in this world.

"So sly and so complicated;
The more I think, the more I'm frightened.
Is she the worst devilish woman in this world,
So Thuc-Sinh has to surrender? (2008)
When a jealous woman sees her husband with his lover,
Her face is gloomy, her teeth are screeched.
Contrarily, the face of this woman is cheerful,
She speaks sweetly, she smiles tenderly.
Women express their anger in similar situations is normal,
This woman should be an extremely wicked one.
Thus, I have to resolve our life; (2015)
Mouth of tigers and venom of snakes are near here."

Thuy Kieu decided to flee. Nonetheless, she thought that because she was alone in the strange territory, she could be hungry and thirsty. Thus, to keep at hand for eventual use, she stashed an heirloom, the small gold bell of the pagoda, in her bag of clothes and escaped in a full-moon night. She walked aimlessly and without destination.

When dawn broke, a pagoda alternatively appeared and disappeared in the distance. She hurried toward it.

A couple of hours later, she reached the gate of the pagoda. She knocked. An old monk opened the gate; his monkhood name was Giac Duyen. He invited her in. Since she was in the dark-yellow robe of a nun, he asked her whether she came alone or with her master monk. She lied that her master monk lost the way and would probably come a couple of days later.

Since she had the bell and knew well many Buddhist prayers, the old monk trusted her even though no master monk came later.

Nonetheless, a month later, a connoisseur in antiques visited the pagoda. The old monk Giac Duyen showed the visitor the bell. The visitor said that the bell looked very similar to the one of Hoan Thu family.

In the evening, Monk Giac Duyen asked Thuy Kieu about the origin of the bell. She confessed the truth and told him her whole miserable story. Although he became frightened, he had pity on her, so he tried to arrange a refuge for her. He remembered Bac Aunt, a Buddhist follower who lived on the other side of the river and often came to the pagoda to pray. The monk asked Bac Aunt to give Thuy Kieu a refuge. Bac Aunt agreed, and Thuy Kieu followed Bac Aunt.

Unfortunately, what the monk did not know was that Bac Aunt was a girl trader like Ma Giam Sinh; although there were some differences between them.

On the one hand, Ma Giam Sinh paid three hundred taels of gold to buy Thuy Kieu, but he was a prurient man who deflowered and slept with her in a period of two months. At the same time, she was forced to be a courtesan for him to get the equivalent amount of gold, then he sold her to the brothel Ngung Bich.

On the other hand, Bac Aunt was a woman. She paid nothing, but procured the antique bell in gold; she would sell pretty Thuy Kieu to a whorehouse to get an amount of gold.

Bac-Aunt was secretly joyful at the beauty
and charm;
She would sell Thuy Kieu with a high price.
(2090)

After several days, Bac Aunt said to Thuy Kieu that since she had stolen the bell, the heirloom of the Hoan Thu family, no one dared to let her dwell in one's house. Moreover, she was alone in this strange land. With these two reasons, the best solution is to marry his nephew Bac Hanh in Chau Thai, a faraway province from Vo Tich.

"You should do what I've just
recommended;
After the wedding, you'll move to Chau-
Thai.
There is no one who knows who you are,
There you'll be free and safe. (2110)
If you won't do what I've recommended,
Miseries will come to you, implication will
come to me."

The words of Bac Aunt made Thuy Kieu disappointed and sorrowful. However, she was in desperation.

"I'm in stalemate, so I've to follow your
recommend;
But I don't know his stature or his
characteristics,
Or his situation, or his opinion, or his
intention. (2121)
I'm afraid of falling into a mouth of a
tiger."

Immediately, Bac Aunt pledged that her nephew Bac Hanh was a good person and would be a husband of fidelity. On the next day, she left the house to Chau Thai.

Four weeks later, she came back with a man who she introduced as her nephew. The house was decorated. Some neighbors were invited. Thuy Kieu had to be the bride. The bridegroom and the bride knelt before the altar of the tutelary guardian and ancient Lares to take vows of fidelity.

A week after the wedding ceremony, the couple boarded a boat for Chau Thai. It anchored in the harbor. Bac Hanh said to Thuy Kieu to stay in the boat, and he went away. An hour later, he came back to the boat with another man. At that moment, Thuy Kieu did not know that the other man was the pimp of Chau Thai Whorehouse, that he came to see how pretty she was to value a price, and that he paid Bac Hanh an amount of gold to get her.

When a horse cart came to pick her up, Bac Hanh had already sneaked away.

The horse cart stopped at the flowered-bed front yard;
An old crone came out and guided her into the house,
Urged her to prostrate before an altar which stood
The pale-and-dense eyelash statue, the talisman of brothels.
She knew what kind of the house was; (2149)
But she was incarcerated like a bird in a cage.

In sorrow and disappointment, Thuy Kieu lamented her ill fate and groaned in self-pity.

"Damn, the ill-fate of the pretty and talented girl
She unbound herself; now she is rebound so easily! (2152)
The world is full of snares and traps;
Pretty and talented girl is envied by both heaven and earth.

Water purified and cleansed itself,
Now it is poured mud and made dirty again. (2156)
Is it the way heaven treats the pretty and talented girl?
She tried all her efforts, but heaven doesn't forgive!
She is young; she hasn't committed any sin or guilt,
Why is she forced to live in the hell of miseries?"

Thuy Kieu knew that it was impossible to flee. Again, she submitted to work as a prostitute in Chau Thai Brothel.

Several months passed. One day, a customer from Viet Dong Province came and met Thuy Kieu because of rumors saying that she was pretty and talented. His name was Tu Hai. He was tall, virile, and excelled in the art of fighting. Moreover, he was the leader of his rebel army.

After some visits, Tu Hai and Thuy Kieu liked each other. The words, opinions, and outlooks on life that they exchanged were harmonious. He asked her to marry him. She agreed because it was a good chance to leave the brothel. He paid the ransom to the owner. Thuy Kieu became the wife of Tu Hai. She followed him to Viet Dong.

A year passed. Tu Hai decided to let Thuy Kieu stay at home and continue to lead his army to fight against the government. She pleaded to go with him, but he said that his army was still on the move, so there was no other home for her. He promised he would receive her with consideration after his army occupied some provinces.

"Better you should wait until I've successes;
I'll organize a lavish and joyful wedding."
(2128)

Then Thuy Kieu lived lonely in the house in a small town of Viet Dong province. Another year passed. Suddenly, one morning, there was boisterous brouhaha heard in the whole town with sounds of horses, gongs, swords, and spears. Ten generals of the rebel army arrived in the front yard of the house. The generals invited her to step on a procession chair; their caravan went to their headquarters since the rebel army had already occupied several provinces. Thus, as Tu Hai had promised to Thuy Kieu, he ordered the procession as the first part of their wedding.

However, Tu Hai continued his conquest. His army won all battles and occupied the southern half of the country.

In his occupied territories, he formed his own court;
It consisted of both civilian and military mandarins. (2442)
Sometimes he attacked through the whole country,
Ruined many forts, trampled many citadels. (444)
His sword swished, his rivals were faint with fright;
He despised and scorned the corruptive authorities.
He was dignified and dauntless in his territories,
Powerful and majestic like a king. (2448)

He reigned his occupied territories in five years. No one dared to challenge his powers. For Thuy Kieu, this was the only episode she lived in peace since the morning she had left the villa of her parents.

Nonetheless, after five years, the king of the country appointed mandarin Bo Ton Hien general commandant of the special military campaign to suppress the rebellion. He was an efficient strategist. He knew that Tu Hai was an able rebel leader, and the opinion of Thuy Kieu influenced Tu Hai. Thus, he combined psychological warfare with military actions. He ordered his troops stationed at the front line and began to use psychological warfare firstly. To Tu Hai, he sent a peaceful message informing that if Tu Hai cooperated with the king, he would be made duke in the royal court, and his generals would be governors in several provinces. To Thuy Kieu, he sent two royal concubines bringing diamonds, pearls, gems, emeralds, and gold as tribute. But Tu Hai suspected the real intention of Bo Ton Hien. He told Thuy Kieu.

"I myself have built my own kingdom,
Strolled and roved freely from south-sea through territories.
If I myself offer to be in their royal court, and present there, Mandarins envied, my life is not safe. (2466)
Robes and hats of a duke bind themselves together;
What a duke, backs must bend to enter, heads must bow to exit!
Contrarily, it's wonderful for me to live in my own kingdom;

With my powers, nobody knows who will win.
Firmament I poke, water I stir, earth I quiver;
No one is my superior." (2472)

Nonetheless, Thuy Kieu was gullible; she trusted the contents in the message of Bo Ton Hien. Additionally, the tributes and the seductions made her yield. Furthermore, she had endured so many miseries, so she compared herself as a water fern that drifted in currents. She visualized that if Tu Hai would be a duke, she would be duchess; both of them would have honor and fulfill their loyal duties to the king. In addition, she could look for a chance to return to her native province to visit her father, mother, and brother. Also, she could go to Lieu Duong Province to visit her sister, who was the wife of her former lover Kim Trong; they had probably children. With these hopes, she advised Tu Hai to surrender.

"Since the day you've risen up in arm, (2493)
Piles of bones have heaped as high as your head.
In history, you will be considered as rebel leader only;
No one will praise you but hate. (2496)
In the contrary, if you cooperate with the king,
Both of us will have high honor and status."

Her sweet words made Tu Hai yield. He invited his rival generals to his headquarter to plan cooperations. Therefore, the defensive tactics of his headquarters were revealed. Thereafter, Bo Ton Hien lied that the king agreed to make Tu Hai duke and

Thuy Kieu duchess. Then both sides arranged a cooperation party in the headquarters of the rebels.

On the day of the ceremonies, Tu Hai and his rebel army were inattentive in their defenses. Suddenly, Bo Ton Hien burned a big firecracker to signal his troops; immediately, his troops sprang the surprised attack. Tu Hai had to fight several rival generals.

Surrounded by many enemies, Tu-Hai fought alone,
Ferocious tiger could not beat a flock of foxes.
His bravery ended when his soul left his body.
Although he died, his body stood straight, (2520)
Steadily like a block of stone, firmly like a pillar of bronze.
His rival shook his body, but it did not stir. (2522)

Thus, the army of Tu Hai was defeated, the rebels ran in utter disarray, and their defensive fort was destroyed. But the body of Tu Hai still stood straight; two soldiers of Bo Ton Hien escorted Thuy Kieu to the body. She cried bitterly in regret.

"Your courage and smartness are in excess;
You're in this plight because you've consented to my words.
I repent for what I persuaded you;
I cannot live in this situation of shame and suffering; (2532)
Wait for me; I follow you to the Elysium."

Thuy Kieu attempted to butt her head to the wall nearby to commit suicide, but one soldier immediately drew her back. At that very second, the body of Tu Hai fell down. Bo Ton Hien heard the news; he ordered a soldier guiding her to meet him.

Thuy Kieu said to the mandarin that though his victory was the result of his psychological warfare and military tactics, her persuasion was a substantial part in making Tu Hai surrender. She pleaded him two favors: giving permission to inter the corpse of Tu Hai and to let her return to her native province. However, Kieu had approved only the first favor.

In that afternoon, Bo Ton Hien commanded his troops to organize a celebration for their victory. During the banquet, he was drunk. He ordered a soldier to guide Thuy Kieu for him. He doted on her prettiness and charm; he handed her a zither to play some musical compositions.

Her music sounded like some wind
groaning, rain sobbing,
Cicada lamenting, and gibbon bewailing.
(2571)
Her fingertip blooded upon the four strings.
Even Bo-Ton-Hien was in tears despite his
victorious mood.

Her fingertip bled upon the four strings because one of them snapped at the last note of the last composition. He asked her who the composer was. She answered that she herself had written these ill-fated compositions when she had been in her teenage years.

"Now the ill-fate is effective into my life (2577)
You know for sure, you make my life miserable."

After the music, the longer he gazed at her beauty and charm, the more he was over head and mind for sex desire. He took liberties with her.

"You and I have predestined love tie, (2581)
Let's join in wedlock similar to a zither
having new strings."

However, she refused by saying that she could not be a wife of any man anymore. Again, she pleaded for his permission to let her return to her native province.

"My life is miserable in misfortunes; (2583)
I've responsibility for the death of the man.
Like a withered flower, only discards rest on
me;
Like a snapped string, my heart breaks
pitifully.
Open your generosity, give me the favor,
Grant me permission to return to my native
province."

Unfortunately, Bo Ton Hien was not a generous man; he was a toadying-to-superior-and-suppressing-to-inferior guy.

He regained his senses at dawn and remembered his acts of liberties with Thuy Kieu. He worried about his honor:

"I'm a high-rank mandarin of the royal court;
My superiors mind, my inferiors watched.
(2592)
I can't be suffered as a womanizer;
To resolve this pitfall, I should have a
scheme."

To cover this problem of fame, Bo Ton Hien imposed a dictatorial decision on Thuy Kieu. He compelled her to be a concubine of the tribe chief who was going to leave his troops and return to the tribe in a faraway province. A wedding party was organized on the very day, and it lasted until dusk. Another misery was poured on Thuy Kieu. She sadly thought sarcastically:

"The match-maker fairy did the utterly
nonsensical work,
Took wedding threads and bound her with
a random man." (2600)

After the wedding party, Bo Ton Hien ordered a bridal cart immediately picking up the bride to the barge of the tribe chief. The bridegroom was deeply drunk and soundly slept. The barge passed the turbulent river that night.

At that dark night, outside the barge, the storm roared, waves crashed, and thunderclaps boomed. Inside the barge, Thuy Kieu groaned dolefully in tears. She remembered her happy childhood with her parents and siblings, felt hurt for her miseries that began on the day her father and brother had been tortured by the constables, pondered her ill fate, and decided to commit suicide.

"Merits inherited from parents are futility,
talents are in trashes.
It's better my corpse being rolled in waves,
buried in sand, or Drifted in immense sea
to indentified horizon.
Where will I live; where will I die? (2608)
Who has the right to destroy love and
marriage?
Who has the right to bind a woman with a

man?
Why is my life so miserable?
One more day I live, one more misery I suffer. (2612)
Without meaning, without purpose,
Why do I continue to drag out my life? (2614)
Hundred of miseries have poured on my life;
My death will end my ill-fate full of miseries."

He wrote all the thoughts in her desperate letter and put it under her pillow. Then she went out to the deck and sprang downward onto the turbulent river to commit suicide.

When the tribe chief and his men realized that Thuy Kieu had sprung downward, they tried to rescue her, but their efforts were in vain.

Injustice, corruption, cruelty, and despotism of the feudal authorities engendered miseries, resentments, and deaths of so many victims. In the case of Thuy Kieu, her beauty and talents were supplemental causes.

It was a pity for the precarious and fragile file;
Prettiness and talents could be the causes of the miseries.
Though the termination of their life was sad, (2641)
Living to endure more miseries was sadder.

Fifteen years passed. From the day Ma Giam Sinh had bought Thuy Kieu at the villa of her parents to the night she sprang downward onto the waves in the turbulent river to commit suicide, fifteen years passed.

Monk Giac Duyen was a bodhisattva of compassion and altruism. He often thought about the fate of Thuy Kieu after she had left his pagoda to the house of Bac Aunt. He inquired of some Buddhist followers what happened to her; they told him that she married Bac Hanh and went to Chau Thai Province. However, the monk perceived something wrong happening to her, so he let his disciples run the pagoda and traveled around the large country to inquire what happened to her. The more he inquired, the more he discovered that her life was full of miseries.

One day, on a mountain, he met a fairy and asked about the destiny of Thuy Kieu. The fairy explained her misfortunes as well as her blessings. The fairy concluded that her misfortunes were going to end, and she would receive blessings thereafter. Also, the fairy foretold to the monk the exact section of turbulent river and the time that Thuy Kieu would spring downward to commit suicide.

The monk was joyful in his mind with the explanations. He determined a plan to rescue Thuy Kieu. Then he went from one section to other section until he arrived in the very one the fairy had told him of.

The monk built a temporary pagoda of
dried bamboos,
On a side of the hill at the west border of
the river. (2698)
Then he engaged five fishermen with their
boats and nets,

Told them the place and the time the
incident would happen.

Monk Giac Duyen discovered Thuy Kieu. She was still in a coma. The monk called her for a couple of minutes, and she herself gradually resuscitated.

On the next day, Monk Giac Duyen engaged some local inhabitants to build another small pagoda on the other side for Thuy Kieu, and she led a Buddhist nun life there.

As traditions required, Kim Trong mourned his dead father for three years. Thereafter, his mother and siblings took care of the worship house of the family in Lieu Duong for him. He came to Que Huong Town to look for Thuy Kieu, but he saw only a dilapidated villa and its desolated surroundings. Some neighbors told him the stories of disasters that family Vuong had endured: the injustice suffering, the selling of Thuy Kieu to have gold to recue Vuong Father and Vuong Quan, the poverty of Vuong family, and their going to an unknown province to earn their living.

After several weeks of inquiries, Kim Trong went to the city where the Vuong family was living. He reached the front door of a shanty and tried to call the name of Vuong Quan, who ran out from the shanty. They recognized each other. Kim Trong entered the shanty to met Vuong Father, Vuong Mother, and Thuy Van. All the three sobbed bitterly. They talked about the filial duty of Thuy Kieu and the entrusting of Thuy Kieu for Thuy Van with the duty of being the wife of Kim Trong. On the next day, Kim Trong and Thuy Van took their vows of fidelity; the family had a simple ceremony for the marriage.

Kim Trong helped the family to renovate their dwelling from a shanty to a house. Then Kim Trong and Vuong Quan reviewed what they had studied. They both succeeded in the next competitive examination.

With high achievement their futures became bright. (2861)
Their fames spread from the royal capital to their native town.

They were appointed governors to two side-by-side provinces. They both tried to find out where Thuy Kieu was. More and more, they revealed the miseries that she had burdened. The last detail they knew was that she had committed suicide at the section of Turbulent River.

The whole family came to the section of the river. They built an altar and planned a week of praying for her spirit to be free from all sufferings.

However, on the second day of their praying, Monk Giac Duyen passed and saw the name and the picture of Thuy Kieu; he told them that she was still alive. They cleared the altar and followed the monk to her pagoda.

Thuy Kieu told all of them that Monk Giac Duyen had saved her life. They all prostrated to thank the monk. Vuong Father begged his permission for Thuy Kieu to come home for reunification, but she refused.

"I'm used to the food of Buddhist nuns,
Love the color of Buddhist clothes. (3044)
The fire of love is quenched in my heart.
It's better for me not to come back to rose dusks."

She said that she was very happy because everyone in the family was healthy, and she asked them to let her continue her nunhood in the pagoda.

However, Vuong Father explained that lives existed thanks to the harmony between the heavens and the earth. Human beings should live harmoniously with nature and one another to have better lives.

"If you live as nun-hood in pagodas to the end of your life,
You can't fulfill your duty of daughters and vows of fidelity.
Thanks are to Buddhas your life is saved (3055)
We'll build a special altar at home to worship all Buddhas."

After listening to the teaching of Vuong Father, Thuy Kieu pondered a while and decided to reunite with her family. She prostrated to thank Monk Giac Duyen and left the pagoda.

They led Thuy Kieu back to Que-Huong, the native city of Vuong family. They restarted their reunited lives in their very own villa, which they had repaired and renovated in the previous month.

Then they organized a small but cozy wedding for Kim Trong and Thuy Kieu on the next Saturday.

However, in the night after the wedding celebration, when Kim Trong invited Thuy Kieu to fulfill an important part of marriage together for their first lovemaking consummation, she gave two reasons to refuse:

"The part of my past life was dirtily smeared, (3101)
I'm not worthy of being your spouse any more.
On the other hand, I've cleansed myself by

the living
in the pagoda,
Let me continue that way of living as a nun
at home."

However, Kim Trong explained that her fulfillment of filial duty was more precious than her virginity. Why she behaved frigidly to him when he loved and esteemed her more than fifteen years ago.

With the sincere love and esteem of Kim Trong, Thuy Kieu agreed to begin all activities and meanings of their happy marriage.

All members of Vuong family were joyful,
(3135)
They witnessed the harmony and happiness
of Kim Trong, Thuy Kieu, and Thuy Van.

Their descendents inherited their harmony and blessing thereafter.

Although *The Tale of Thuy Kieu* (1802) is only a fabricated story, it reflects some corruptive societies in this world. Also, it reflects numerous miseries of young women who are victims of swindlers and sex traders in this world. Unfortunately, many victims do not have happy endings like the protagonist, Vuong Thuy Kieu, in the tale.

Poet Nguyen Du ended this epic literary work of 3,254

poetic lines with the humble conclusion in the last two lines:

> *These simple words were collected from countryside.*
> *Hopefully they make readers entertain in a pair of hours.*

However, Nguyen Du is really a celebrity in the world. Also, he could be the first supporter of the Women's Rights Movement.

Selected to Be Brides by Foreigners

The Show

"Wow! All of them are beautiful like nymphs, similar to the characters described in Greco-Roman myths such as Helen, Athena, Hera, Venus, Rhea, Hestia, Dionne, Aphrodite, Persephone, Gaia, and so forth," a young man over twenty years old from a western country said in his low voice.

"Yeah, they're charming, similar to the most beautiful women in the history of my country like Tay Thi, Duong Qui Phi, Dieu Thuyen, Vo Tac Thien, Tiet Dao, Trac Van Quan, Ban Tiep Du, Vuong Chieu Quan, Ta Dao Uan, and so on."

A forty-year-old man from an eastern country expressed his agreements.

"Do you know their ages?"

"Oh, you haven't read their short autobiographical life stories? They're from eighteen to twenty-six years old. I think some of them are sixteen but use forged identifications."

"Do you think this country has more beautiful women than many other countries?"

"Perhaps, I know a lot of things about matchmaking clubs and situations of bride candidates. You should know women who register in matchmaking clubs have already been chosen by matchmakers. Iterant matchmakers seek every corner of this country to find out beautiful women as you call them nymphs. They tell nymphs visualizations of bright futures in foreign countries if nymphs married foreigners. Nymphs believe them."

"Do all the bride candidates still have virginity as the ads of matchmaking clubs?"

"No and yes."

"What do you mean?"

"You're a very simple man."

"I'm twenty-five years old but have no experiences with women."

"Are you so? Each girl has a hymen which covers the entrance of her vagina. Normally, her hymen is not torn before her first sexual intercourse. It's called virginity. Normally, at the first sexual intercourse, her hymen is perforated, so some drops of blood ooze out. Thus, in some cultures, brides must prove their virginity by showing some drops of blood on towels under their buttocks after their first sexual intercourse with their husbands. I say normally because, in many cases, hymens of girls were torn by her strong movements such as bad falls, strong washes, and so forth before they have their first sexual intercourses.

"To answer your question on the virginity of the bride candidates, my estimation is that half of the women still have natural virginities, others have artificial hymens."

"You're a man of knowledge. Give me explanations about artificial hymens."

"The branch of beauty surgery today uses modern technology to make many artificial parts to change bodies of human beings. Hymens are simple things. Other easy works are the surgeries to make vaginas of women smaller."

"Can a selected candidate deny being a bride of a man who selects her?"

"It hasn't happened yet. Let me explain complicated situations. Since this country has been invaded, its bad fate rolled its people in misfortunes, and the great majority of them become poor or destitute. High and middle classes of the former society are pushed down to the bottom. Their properties are taken by the invaders. Former officials and officers endure agonies in labor camps. Their families live in miseries.

"When a beautiful or pretty woman registers as a bride candidate, she owes the matchmaking club an amount of money of exorbitant price for bad quality a la mode clothes, cheap jewelry baubles, nasty local perfumes, and so forth for the show. Then the cost of body examinations of physicians adds to the amount. If she needs surgeries for an artificial hymen or a narrower vagina, her debt becomes much higher. If she refuses to be the bride of the man who selected her, she must pay her debt immediately. Unfortunately, she cannot. Thus, she consents to be his bride, signs a marriage certificate, and lets her fate drift although she feels he is a bad guy."

"After signing a marriage certificate, her debt is forgiven, isn't it?"

"No, from the country of the man selected her, she must send money to her parents to pay in installments. Her parents are the hostages of the matchmaking club."

"I am a good man and want to be a good husband. I seek a good wife."

"Me too, my wife died ten years ago. For several years, I haven't been able to find a harmonious woman to marry as my legitimate wife because in my country there are more men than women, so I come here. Two women that you and I select will be lucky. It's sorry, a half of the bride candidates fall in hands of bad men who will make the lives of the women they selected miserable."

"Why do you know that?"

"I explain what I've mentioned. My country was very large in the last century. Now, it is divided into four separated and independent parts: one large country and three small ones. I live in the small part with the name Dahilo. There are a dozen million more men than women in all those four new independent countries. From which lots of men come to this country to seek women. I witness a half of the women having from normal to bearable lives. Unfortunately, another half of the women have miserable lives. I myself witnessed one man who sold a beautiful woman from this country to another man. Some months later, he had a more beautiful woman also from this country. There are even ads with photos of beautiful women of this country, prices, guarantees, and so forth in some websites. It's pitiful for lots of women of this country. They are snared into colorful nets but full of venom inside."

"It's sorry for them. By the way, before entering this hall, I saw you converse with several men in your language. The four new and independent countries still have the same official language, don't they?"

"Yes, they do."

"Why do so many people, including these beautiful women, crave to leave this country?"

"After the invasion, the rulers consist of invaders and their collaborators, about 20 percent of the population. They treat the governed unfairly and punish the defeated cruelly, so the great majority of the people crave to flee or immigrate. However, few of them have gold and means to flee. Very few of them have relatives who are living in other countries to file visas for them. In reality, though the majority of the people adapt to survive under the rule of invaders, they seek opportunities to leave. To marry a foreigner is an opportunity."

"You know so many things about this country. I think your purpose is not only to find a legitimate wife."

"You're not wrong. I'm a historian. My main purpose is to find a legitimate wife, but in this occasion, I carry out fact-findings on this society after the invasion. I've been in this country for six months. This is the ninth show I've watched. The cost of attending a show is not a matter for me. I'll select a woman to marry in the next show. I'll stay here with her a pair of days. Thereafter, I and she will fly to my country."

"Many thanks. I wish you select a good woman in the next show."

"Our conversation made us distracted from the first part of the show. You can select a woman in this show or any next one. Good luck to you too."

"Ms. Santolina, you're fantastically beautiful, but our matchmaking club admits candidates from eighteen to twenty-six years old only. You're thirty-five! We know the liking of our customers. They intend to select beautiful but young candidates. The younger the hotter."

"Let me have a chance. I don't owe you money, like the others. I pay all my costs. I promise I'll quit after the second show, which I take part if I won't be selected."

With the conditions, Santolina was admitted to take part in two shows. Before the show, like other candidates, Santolina was elaborately made-up and pervasively sprayed with perfumes in the antechamber or closed room opening to the showroom.

Every man had the right to select a woman who he considered his nymphet. Quite contrary, all women had to let their fates drift.

It could happen that one bride candidate was selected by more than one man, however. To solve this possible dilemma in advance, an elder man had the priority. It was the rule that men had signed before they entered the showroom.

The show had three parts. Each part lasted from twenty to thirty minutes. There was a break of fifteen minutes after each part for the bride candidates to prepare, and they were made-up in the closed antechamber.

In the first part of the show, the candidates wore model dresses and glittering jewels. The dress of each candidate had a different color from others. A special matchmaker chose the color suitable for the skin of each candidate. Each of them had a number pinned at the front and the back of her dress. Santolina was in blue; she looked like Cinderella in the fairy story. Her dress was pinned number 38; it was her number in all parts of the show. The candidates walked with deliberate steps to and fro as well as turned slowly around before thirty men from six foreign countries five times. The women tried to prove that they had the charm and suaveness of their gaits and appearances. Then they sat on the chairs facing the men.

In the second part of the show, the bride candidates wore bikinis. Santolina was in blue again; she looked like a mermaid from her head to knees. Again, the bride candidates walked with deliberate steps and turned slowly around before the men like in the first part. They tried to show their attractive features.

In the third or last part of the show, the candidates were totally nude. Their breasts were made-up with their nipples in light-rose color. Their mons pubis or mons veneris were left with pubic hairs because some men were influenced by their culture belief that a man who had coitus with a woman without pubic hair on her mons pubis would meet unluckiness. Again, the nymphs walked with deliberate steps and turned slowly around before the men. The candidates should expose their seductive prettiness and the sexual jewels of their real bodies.

Then the bride candidates came back to the closed antechamber, wore again their dresses of the first part of the show, and waited for results. Their psychological moods were complicated and contradictory paradox; they wanted to be selected and not to be selected.

If a bride candidate was selected, which man selected her? What kind of a man was he? She knew nothing about him, from his personality to his numerous relationships and connections, his characteristics, behavior, outlook, family, country, language, and so forth.

If a bride candidate was not selected, her aspiration to escape the unfair, cruel, and dictatorial authorities was still unfulfilled. Then she should participate in another show, and her debt to the matchmaking club would be higher.

Nonetheless, the candidates did not have to wait long. After a quarter, a matchmaker entered the closed antechamber and gave them results.

"Hi, ladies, exactly one-third of you are selected. I don't read the names of the selected but the numbers slowly. Listen carefully, okay? Numbers 2, 6, 10, 13, 16, 19, 20, 24, 26, 28,

29, 30, 38, congratulations! Those who are not selected can leave now. The selected come back to the showroom. Each of you stands separately to greet your bridegroom. You don't know him, but he knows you. He's your husband."

The unselected walked desolately out the room in silence and melancholy.

The selected, with their numbers still pinned on their dresses, reentered slowly the showroom in worry and confusion. Santolina was one of them.

As the matchmaker had recommended, the selected stood separately from one another in the showroom. They were in puzzlement.

The men needed only several seconds to reach their nymphs; they embraced, hugged, caressed, and kissed. The brides floundered and were stunned in the first minutes, then they embraced their so-called bridegrooms like actresses performing their roles on stage.

Thirty-five-year-old Santolina was selected by the forty-year-old man. After their embrace, he greeted and introduced himself.

"Hi, Santolina, I know your name and something about you since I've carefully read your life story. My name is Bachmon. I'm forty years old. In looking at my appearance, you can guess my race. I come from Dahilo, an independent country recently separated from Chensanh. Probably, you've known Chensanh. It was a large country. Now it is divided into four independent countries: Chensanh, Mahong, Lucdo, and Dahilo."

"Hi, Bachmon, you speak rather well our language. It's a positive use to understand each other. I understand and speak your language a little. By the way, a matchmaker complained before us that you're a tough nut because you had watched nine shows but hadn't selected any bride candidate. Why do you select me today?"

"I've intended to select you just after I'd read your short life story. In the show, I realized you're prettier than your photo."

"I didn't stick my beautiful photo. I don't want to have a man who marries me because of my beauty only."

"The main reasons I selected you are your age and your education as you've written in your short life story."

"Bachmon, I'm not a virgin. I married once. Sorry, I didn't write the two details in the life story."

"I don't expect you to be a virgin. I married once also. My wife died ten years ago. We didn't have any children. Can you tell me about your marriage?"

"I had a lover. However, I married another man. It's a tortuous detail. I'll tell you about my lover. Our love began in our last year of high school. Then we studied together in the Faculty of Social Sciences. Three years after, he received a scholarship from the government of Unto Blumen, the most developed country, for two years of studies. When we said good-bye, he told me that he would return after two years, and we would arrange our wedding. But ten months later, I received his letter written that he had an accident. His right leg was amputated, and he urged me to seek another man to marry. I wrote him six letters telling him that I loved him and decided to marry him no matter how handicapped he was. Unfortunately, I received no replies.

"Three years later, I married another man because of the will of my parents. Though I hadn't loved him before, I did my duty as his wife because he was nice. You do know the very long and ferocious war in this country. Most young men had to join the army. Like other wives of soldiers, I lived in the anxiety of losing him on any day. Only six months after my wedding, the war ended with the ignominy of our side. When he heard the surrender of the commander in chief from the radio, he committed suicide."

"Why do you register to marry a foreigner?"

"Because I'm still young and beautiful, at least two crass men of the victor side have boorishly flirted and cunningly harassed me; they have often intimidated and disturbed me and my family. Fortunately, I am living with my parents and my younger brother in one house, so they haven't been able to rape me. I abhor these authorities and want to leave this country."

"In your life story, you didn't mention children. If you have, I can file visas of exit for them."

"Thank you, I don't have any children. The marriage was too short."

"Do you owe the matchmaking club any debt? I can pay for you tomorrow."

"No, I've already paid all my debts so I can deny being the bride of a man if I realize him to be a bad guy."

"I'll try to be your good husband. I hope we'll live in harmony together."

"You seem to be a good man. But excuse me for saying the truth. As I know, half of the men come here to find women because they have one or some problems in their countries."

"You're right. You've probably known there are more men than women in all four new countries: Mahong, Lucdo, Chensanh, and Dahilo."

"I don't mean that. I concentrate on innate and inherent problems, for instance mental sickness, body defect, criminal addiction, sadistic behavior, and so forth. Although they have problems, they can pick up beautiful women from this country!"

"I should confess that even though the beauty of a woman is not the main purpose of my selection, I'm proud of having a beautiful wife."

"It's normal. I don't reproach that. I'll take care of my beauty for my nice husband."

"By the way, according to your life story, you studied sociology but may not work on the field of sociology."

"Yes, I got BA diploma on sociology seven years ago. Then I was in charge of the two-page part "Socio-Economy" of the magazine *Pragmatic Economists* in the period longer than four years. Unfortunately, the invaders won the war. Like all other public and private offices and organs, the victors occupied the office and materials of the magazine publication. The office became a branch of their political newspaper. The director of the branch kept me and some technicians to tutor his inferiors. A year later, he sent the technicians to labor camps, except me. He guaranteed to keep me as his employee. In spite of the miserable salary, I had to type several hours every day. Then they began to have errors, so I quit the job."

"You also wrote that you can play piano."

"Yes, not of a standard of a musician, but I can play rather well."

"Wow, you're a talented woman. By the way, I've been in this country for six months, carried out fact-findings on this society and, uh, watched shows, ten shows, as you know. I understand the unfair and sly systems which the victors organized to get priorities, to misuse authorities, to punish the defeated and their families, to subjugate and submit the governed. By the way, do you stay in this hotel with me tonight? We'll go to the administration office tomorrow morning and sign our marriage certificate."

"Please, let me come back home to say good-bye to my parents and my brother. I'll come here early tomorrow morning and go with you to the administration office for our marriage certificate. I'll sleep with you after we've our marriage certificate. Oh, what's the number of your room?"

"Number 25, oh, I should present myself to your parents and your brother. I invite everyone for dinner in the restaurant at the first floor tomorrow evening."

"They'll come. Of course, they want to know who and how you are. Thanks for your nicety."

"You're welcome!"

Suddenly, three female voices called Santolina from one direction.

"Santolina!"

"Santolina!" "Santolina, please wait!"

Santolina and Bachmon looked to the direction of the voices. Three selected women and three men of the same race of Bachmon were coming. When they stood in a circle, they shook hands, and each woman introduced herself and her man.

"My name is Brassia. Cotat is my husband's name. He tells me that though he is in Lucdo, Mr. Bachmon is in Dahilo, the two countries are neighbors. A part of Lucdo borders is adjacent with Dahilo. He is of the same race and speaks the same language of Mr. Bachmon, and his hometown is Desung in Lucdo. Please, Mr. Bachmon, give me your address so I'll be able to contact Ms. Santolina later."

"My name is Tarda. My husband's name is Gakho. He tells me that he lives in the town named Cangro in Mahong. Dahilo and Mahong are neighbor countries. Mahong, Lucdo, and Dahilo speak the same language. Like Brassia, please, Mr. Bachmon, give me your address so I'll able to contact Ms. Santolina later."

"My name is Vanda. Tomorrow, I'll fly with Doty, my husband, to his hometown Nikot, Chensanh. As he says, it also speaks the same language. Please, Mr. Bachmon, give me also your address. I want to contact Ms. Santolina later."

Bachmon wrote his address three times and handed each to the three young women. They said thanks and read the address in low voices.

"Mr. Bachmon Khuatnon, 12389 Datlanh Avenue, Comay, 64125 Dahilo."

Bachmon thought of the necessity to inform them of something about the town he was living in, so he said, "Comay, a city with one million inhabitants, lies in the eastern beach of Dahilo. Dahilo is a new independent country separated from Chensanh, like Lucdo and Mahong. Thus, each new independent country has a part of its borders adjacent to the former large Chensanh."

Again, the women said thanks to Bachmon. The three men shook hands with Bachmon and said good-bye. The three couples walked hand in hand towards the front yard of the hotel.

Bachmon and Santolina turned their conversation to the

schedule of their next days.

"Santolina, you can go home now, but be here at eight o'clock tomorrow morning. We'll take breakfast together. Then we go to the administration office for our marriage certificate, and—"

"And I go home again. I'll be here with my parents and my brother at six o'clock tomorrow evening for dinner, as you've invited. After dinner, they go home, and I, uh, stay here with you."

"I agree with you, honey. I'll order tickets, and we'll fly to our hometown on the day after tomorrow. Now, let's have a big hug."

Santolina in Her Husband's Country

The three-bedroom house of Bachmon was old but airy. As the director of the library of the town, he usually worked eight hours on workdays and five hours on Saturdays. He was also a member of a political party, conservative party. So he was very busy. Usually, he was not at home in the daytime and came home about ten at night.

The beginning of Santolina's time in the foreign country was grievous. She missed her parents, brother, relatives, friends, home, hometown, native country, and so on. Thus, she sobbed every day. To improve her use of Dahilo language, Bachmon bought textbooks and pronunciation discs for her to learn and practice at home.

It is presumed that neighbors discriminated her during that time because she heard them talking about and ridiculing the prevalent destitution of her native country when they walked on the sidewalk in front of the house. They talked and laughed loudly because they probably thought she did not understand their language.

After seven months of living in such situation, by her thirty-sixth birthday, Bachmon asked her, "Why are you living in sadness, honey? Try to stop sorrowing and start living. To help you have solace, what present do you want for your thirty-sixth birthday?"

"If it's possible, buy a piano for me. If not, buy an electric organ of eight octaves. It can substitute for a piano."

"Oh, I totally forgot your talent. You'll get a piano as a present on your coming birthday. Then you'd better verify your talent in a school. Public Comay College is only five miles away from here. You'll be a musician."

Since the day Santolina had gotten the good piano, she played famous classical music of celebrities like Beethoven, Bach, Mozart, and Strauss several hours a day to relax. Many walkers halted on the sidewalk before the house and listened. It is assumed they admired her talent.

A month later, Bachmon guided her to enroll in the Comay College and register in music and piano courses. After several tests, she was allowed to attend classes of the seniors.

Additionally, the college gave her twelve hours weekly to tutor piano practices to freshmen. The money she earned was nearly enough to pay for her tuition. After a year of studies, Santolina had BA in music. Thereafter, she got the job as a music teacher at a private middle school in the city. Her life was peaceful in those two years.

Then Bachmon was chosen as the candidate for the congress in the caucus of the conservative party. He won the election and lived in the capital. He came home on Sundays only. The life of Santolina became lonely.

The Story of Brassia

In one afternoon, Santolina left the middle school, drove home, and opened the mailbox. There lay a thick letter from Brassia of Desung, Lucdo. It made the rhythm of her heart faster than usual. She hurriedly took it, stepped into the house, tore the envelope, and read in silence.

Dear Santolina, I have secretly written this letter in many times between intervals, so it could have rambling parts and an abrupt end.

I describe events I did not understand during the times they were happening to me. My understanding came only after my calamitous endurances and thoughtful retrospections.

I think you still remember the evening I met you after the show. After saying good-bye to you and the others, Cotat led me to meet his uncle Chuno. The uncle guided him and me to the restaurant in the first floor for dinner.

Uncle Chuno ordered food. For drinks, I had a cup of orange juice, but Chuno and Cotat drank mixed brandies. In the middle of the meal, Cotat spoke nonsense, his eyes turned red. The uncle reviled him.

"You're drunk with alcohol. Go upstairs to

our room and take the medication."

Cotat gave up the dinner and went upstairs. Probably, he took some tranquilizers, lay down on one bed, and slept. There were two beds in the room.

In the restaurant, uncle Chuno and I continued to eat and drink. He stared at me and praised my prettiness. He also said that Cotat selected me because of his advice, that I had to stay overnight in the room with Cotat because I would go to the administration office early in the next morning to sign the marriage certificate with Cotat. The reason was that the afternoon of that day was the last flight of their booked plane tickets to their hometown Desung in Lucdo.

After the dinner, I follow the uncle to the bedroom. As my logical thought, Cotat was going to be my husband, I had to lie on the bed with him because the other bed had to be reserved for Chuno.

I entered the restroom, changed from my dress to a nightgown, and came out. Chuno signaled me to lie on the bed with Cotat but next to the wall. At that time, Cotat was in deep sleep, and his position was at the aisle or at the side of Chuno.

The uncle turned the lights off. I rolled my body to face the wall. My sleep came some minutes later.

Sleeping in darkness, I felt a man take my nightgown, brassiere, and slip off. I was totally nude. He turned my body with my face upward; his hands fondled my body from breasts to vagina. Then his body moved up, lay on my body, and we had intercourse. It was painful for me. But I thought that it was Cotat, who was going to be my husband, so I tried to be silent to let him fulfill his sexual desire. The coitus lasted about ten minutes. Still in darkness, I felt the man leave the bed and step to the other bed.

I groped for my slip, bra, and nightgown, but I found only my nightgown, put it on, and tried to sleep again.

After only one minute, while I was still lulling myself to sleep, the other man from the other bed crossed the aisle, lay beside me, took my nightgown off, moved his body up, lay on my nude body, and tried to make intercourse again. I cried relatively loud to protest because I thought it was Uncle Chuno.

Immediately, the lights were turned on. The man lying on my body was not who I thought. It was Cotat, not Chuno. The damned uncle had already deflowered me, as he had planned. He had just misused my body and sexual organs to fulfill his sexual desire. It was him who turned the lights on and reviled me.

"A wife may not refuse her husband having sexual intercourse. Cotat is your husband, okay?"

Then Chuno turned the lights off and lay on the other bed. In this situation, I had to let Cotat have intercourse with me. It lasted only a pair of minutes.

After suffering two consecutive unwilling sexual intercourses, my mind was in deep grief; my eyes were full of tears. A thought of escape flashed through my mind, but the debt I owed to the matchmaking club and other intricate consequences immediately appeared in my mind. Thus, I let my ill-fated destiny drift.

The plane landed on a small airport in Desung, Lucdo, in the evening of the next day, Saturday. A decrepit and dusty mini truck was waiting for us. The driver was a man who Chuno called Younger Brother Churem. Similar to Chuno, Churem was in his forties. Except for the driver seat, there was only another seat at its ride side, so Chuno signaled Cotat and me to climb and sit on the floor of the trunk behind the two seats. Chuno took up the driver seat. Churem took up the right seat. Chuno drove the mini truck to their house.

Their thatched-roof-and-soiled-wall house stands alone and is surrounded by paddies. Other nearest houses are about six hundred yards or farther.

Chuno parked the mini truck before their house. They led me walking around the front, the inside, and the back of their house. They guided me to go around. I observed these following things:

In the one-hundred-yard rectangular area surrounding the house, many kinds of edible tubes such as potato, taro, yam, and so on are planted.

In the front of the house, there is a water well, a cell covered by reed lattices for bathing, a basket of bowls perched on a tinny stock trellis near the well, and a stack of rice stubble.

Inside the earthen-floor house, it's not divided into rooms by wall but by reed lattice screens into three parts. In the middle part there is a narrow bamboo bed for Chuno. In the right part, there is a similar bed for Cotat. There is no electricity, but each part has a kerosene lamp. The left part is the kitchen in which there are four rickety chairs, an obsolete table, an earthen tripod, some pots, and a rice stubble sheaf for cooking.

At the back of their house, a latrine hides inside the one-yard square of mulberries.

Then they led me back to the kitchen. Chuno signaled me to sit down on one chair and told me to learn how to use a rice stubble sheaf and earthen tripod for cooking. The meal was frugal.

I perceived their poverty. Later, I learned that Chuno had sold two-hundred-yard squares of their paddies, a half of their inherited property, for the costs to purchase and transport me to their house. Both Chuno and Churem were single.

During the meal, Chuno was the single talker. At the end of the frugal meal, Chuno commanded, "Churem, take a rice stubble sheaf and spread it on the floor beside my bed to sleep. Cotat, sleep with me on my bed. Brassia, sleep alone on the other bed in the right part of the house."

I knew immediately his plan. A sorrowful regret of not escaping when I had still been in the homeland just after suffering two consecutive forced sexual intercourses came to my mind, and the regret has not disappeared.

It happened as I thought. In the first night in the house, I suffered three nonconsensual sexual intercourses. Between Chuno and Churem, I could not differentiate who was the first, who was the second, but I knew Cotat was the third. In following times, Cotat was always the last one.

In the afternoon of the next day, Churem left their house, walked to the main road about one mile far from their house, and took the intercity bus to a city four hundred miles away. He worked as a janitor in a large building there. He reserved a part of his salary to help Chuno and Cotat. He came to their house on weekends. Thus, I endured again and again three humiliations in weekends like the first night.

Half a year later, I learned some following details of their family. Twenty-four years ago, the deluge had decimated crops before the harvest time, then the consequent famine ravaged the population in the vast territory of Lucdo consisting of many areas including Desung. Most members of their family had starved, but Chuno, Churem, and Cotat had survived. Cotat had been ten months old at the time of his parents' death.

The sickness of Cotat makes him quite dependent on his uncle Chuno.

Since the third day after my arrival in their house, I must have joined the works of Chuno and Cotat within the one-hundred-yard rectangular area surrounding their house and other one-hundred-yard paddies adjacent to the area.

Usually, Chuno watched or kept himself near me to prevent my attempt to escape. In reality, in this strange land, I have had no idea about ways and know only some words of their language. So I have thought that a young and beautiful woman like me has easily been incarcerated by worse rapists. Therefore, I have not thought on any attempt to escape but prayed for a miracle.

One day in the eleventh month, a fifty-year-old woman transported an over-eighty-year-old man in a rickshaw to this house. Chuno ordered me to let the old man suck my breasts! I protested, but he intimidated me. I had to submit. The old man sucked consecutively my two breasts in a quarter of an hour.

Nothing flowed out from my breasts.

However, the woman transported the old man to this house on the following days. The man sucked as I have just written. To my surprise, from the tenth day, milk has flowed out from my breasts. For sure, Chuno has earned from my milk.

The woman looked at me with pity and sympathy sometimes. So I tried to converse with her in all opportunities. With my broken words in their language and our body languages, I could gradually understand more and more necessary details of the family of Chino and the ill fate of the very woman.

Her name is Tirana; she is forty years old, though she appears older. Here is her life story in short:

Her parents and her two brothers died in the famine twenty-four years ago. She was then sixteen, and her sister Tyba was fourteen. While they were lying on the road near the dead bodies of their dears and were going to die, a married old couple carried them home and fed them, and they survived. After the famine, Tirana and Tyba stayed in the house of the rich benefactors and worked as nannies for two little children of the married couple.

About a year later, the woman asked Tirana to be her husband's concubine because she had problems in her sex organs. Tirana knew that it was illegal but thought about their earlier rescue from starvation and agreed. The woman enticed her to drink a cup of secret medication liquid for her not to have any child with her husband.

Nonetheless, the man became greedy. He attempted several times to rape Tyba. Thus, Tyba escaped from their house and fled to a place Tirana did not know of.

In reality, the man treated Tirana as a sex object, and the family considered her as a servant only. This very man has sucked my breasts for two months. Tirana has intended to escape. However, she has hesitated because of the thought that her sister could only contact her through the address of their house.

Santolina had been in Comay, Dahilo, for nearly three years. She had taught music at the middle school for one full school year. On the last day of the first school year, she drove home at midnight because of the celebration. It was relatively dark. When she parked her car at the front of the garage, she saw the appearances of two women sitting flat on the ground before the front door; they both looked toward her car. She stepped out and realized that one of the women was Brassia. The two compatriots embraced each other and burst into tears.

Some minutes later, the two compatriots calmed down. Brassia introduced the other woman, Tirana, to Santolina.

Santolina unlocked the front door, guided the comers into the house, and said, "Be fully relaxed. My husband, Bachmon, is not at home. Since last winter, he has spent his time in the capital and rarely comes home. He is now an important politician for the conservative party in this election campaign."

Tirana showed Santolina a small piece of paper and said in an emotional voice, "We reached here thanks to the help and guidance of my youngest sister, Tyba. Here are her address and phone number."

"Oh, the city is not very far from here. It's about three hundred miles."

"Please call her. She will be very happy and will come here to pick me up."

"It's over midnight. Let her sleep. I'll call her tomorrow early morning. My vacation begins today. I can help you more than calling her."

"Thank you."

"I made some warm food ready for both of you. Then take a warm shower and sleep on reserve beds in the next room. I'll push my bed there. But sleep for your health. You're tired. We'll confide tomorrow."

However, they could not wait for tomorrow. They were eager to tell and listen. At the first minute on the bed, Tirana began to tell Santolina their story.

"A lot of positive conditions came unexpectedly. My sister, Tyba, who I had not known dead or living for a long period, sent me letters at the address of my neighbor.

"Oh, she is a good neighbor. Everywhere, there are good people and bad people. It can happen in some countries. There are fewer good people than in other ones. The great difficulty is that bad guys disguise themselves as good ones. We should differentiate.

"After some contacts, she sent me money triple the cost of a plane ticket because she thought I had to bribe some guy. She urged me to escape as soon as possible. But I'd pity on Brassia and wanted to help her to escape with me.

"At that time, I'd already had my passport, but the passport of Brassia was kept by Chuno. Another matter was that we did not know whether we'd to have visas to fly from Lucdo to Dahilo. Luckily, my neighbor helped us have information from the Dahilo consulate.

"I tell you the information in short: Lucdo, Mahong, and Dahilo have just received independence from the large country Chensanh. Thus, citizens from the three new countries do not need visas to travel from one country to another."

"The task of Brassia was to steal her passport. I told her that men were usually in deep sleep after sexual intercourse at night. She had to act when the chance came. She had success."

"You handed two passports and money to your good neighbor who bought two plane tickets. Then you make a tryst and sneaked to your neighbor, who drove you to the airport."

"Exactly right."

"Lucdo is ruled by a clique of dictators. Some people come here, register at commission offices for refugees, and are accepted as refugees. Both of you should do the same. But to have jobs is far better. Tirana, the official language here and your mother language are the same. I'll help you."

"Thank you, Santolina. Call my sister tomorrow. She'll pick me up and do this indispensability for me."

"Brassia, you should learn the official language. I'll tutor you at home. Then you'll need a job. I'll help you. Tirana, I'll call your sister tomorrow. Surely, she'll be joyful and pick you up."

"Anyhow, we'll keep contact with one another. We're close friends, aren't we?"

"We've warmer relationship than close friends. Tirana, you and your sister, Tyba, are our great benefactors."

The Story of Tarda

In the first Friday afternoon of the second school year, Santolina left the school, stopped at the bazaar, and bought a weekly magazine. In skimming through some news, an emotion came to her when she looked at the photograph of a young and beautiful woman; she read the subtitle and the enclosed caption. "A woman was pitilessly killed. Photograph of the victim was shot three years ago."

Looking at the photograph, she perceived some features acquainted. In a hurry, she drove home. She pointed out the subtitle, the photograph, and the caption to Brassia, who immediately cried, "It's Tarda!"

Santolina stared at the photograph again. Then she read the news:

"A dead body of a young woman wrapped in a tarpaulin bag was discovered in a trash bin at a park sixty miles away from her dwelling, an apartment inside the large building in the city of Cangro, Mahong. There were bumps and bruises on her body as she had been severely whipped."

Her name is Tarda. She came from Eastnama to Mahong three years ago after signing the marriage certificate with Gakho, who is living in the apartment with a high-ranking police officer whose wife and two children are living in a faraway city.

Sometimes, neighbors heard sobs of this woman from the

apartment and thought that the woman endured unwilling sexual intercourses inflicted by the two men. But neighbors did not see her come out the apartment.

Neighbors also thought that the woman was forced to work as a prostitute since they often saw different men enter and leave the apartment within an hour in weekends.

However, nobody else dared to interfere because of the high-ranking police officer.

Santolina handed the magazine to Brassia, who read the news again in sadness. When Brassia finished the reading, Santolina said, "The evidences are clear. Do you think the authorities of Mahong will punish the two bastards?"

"No, I don't think so. I, Tarda, and Vanda are unlucky because Chensanh, Lucdo, and Mahong are ruled by bands of dictators, like our country Eastnama now! If members of their bands committed crimes conspicuously, their courts will give fake verdicts, and the criminals are escorted to prisons. But people have no time to watch whether their authorities executed the verdicts because they are so busy to struggle for their living. At any time, the criminals can change their name and take other high positions in other provinces.

Santolina, you're a lucky woman. You married a good man living in Dahilo. You're lucky because this country has democracy, and laws are respected."

"Oh, let's not mind the clique of dictators anymore. By the way, do you know what religion Tarda follows? Let's find its nearest dignitary to say a mass for her soul."

"It's a very good idea. But I don't know her religion. Let's write to her parents. I've their address. But let's not tell them why and how she died."

Bachmon was engrossed on politics in the capital, so he rarely came home.

After seven months, Brassia could use the official language

rather well, thanks to the help of Santolina. More luckily, in the ninth month, she got a job as a cleaner at the library of the city; she also got the permanent resident status and divorce certificate. Though her salary was low, she was comfy because Santolina let her dwell in the house. The two compatriots treated each other like harmonious sisters.

The Story of Vanda

The usual schedule of Santolina at the school was from eight in the morning to two o'clock in the afternoon from Mondays to Fridays. The working time of Brassia was from noon to eight in the evening from Mondays to Saturdays.

In one morning of a Saturday, Santolina received a letter of Vanda from Nikot, Chensanh. At first, she intended not to open it until Brassia got home. Then she guessed that something happened to Vanda, so she tore the envelope. In looking at the three pages of the letter, she realized the different ink colors in different parts. They proved that the letter had been written in several times in a period of some months. She could not wait to read.

Dear Santolina,

I have torn up and thrown away what I have written a couple of times. Finally, I held these papers. I have much spare time in this center, so I want to write a very long letter similar to my memoir, but I do not have ability, and my mind is not lucid anymore. Thus, I can only describe my story in simple lines on these papers.

I begin my story with my unforgettable, romantic, and chaste love.

We loved each other when we were seventeen years old and were in the eleventh grade of the local high school. I loved him because of his energy and uprightness. He loved me because of my gentleness and beauty. Our gifts were romantic verses.

We had leisured walks through the shady park or along the fresh seashore, swims in the pool or at the beach, strolls on the roads along paddies with green rice seedlings or full golden-ear rice plants, gazes at the moon from the large slab of stone in the front yard or through leaves of fruit trees at the backyard of my parents' villa.

We encouraged each other in our studies to reach to standards so we could be admitted to a university. We promised we would marry when one of us had a job.

Unfortunately, our love lasted only one year since his outlook on life suddenly changed. He was no longer satisfied with the society at that time. His ideal was not to improve or reform but destroy everything and build a quiet new society.

His family was not poor but belonged to a section of common people. Sometimes, he talked about his utopian ideal and criticized some officials including my father and several wealthy families including my grandparents. Our love cooled down. Just after the final examination of the twelfth grade, he disappeared. I had no interest to find out where he went.

When the invaders and their followers won the war, my ex-lover appeared as a victor, drove my grandparents out of their villa, and occupied it. My grandparents had to move to my parents' villa with

some chattels stashed in sundries.

A month later, my father had to present himself to the invaders and was transported to a labor camp.

Unexpectedly, a year later, my ex-lover was arrested and received a death verdict because of a fabricated reason of being a spy for the former government, but the real reason was that a puny follower like him dared to occupy the luxurious villa.

The stringent unfairness of the invaders made my family become very poor. The greatest sorrow was the agony of my father in the labor camp. Suddenly, a wife of an invader came to our house and said that if we bribed her husband with six taels of gold, he would interfere, and my father would be released within a week, and that we could promise only, but within two days after my father's homecoming, we had to hand gold, or our family would be punished severely. She gave us her address.

I had pity on my father. Without informing any member of my family, I came to her house on the next day and described our poverty and entreated her. The amount was reduced to two taels. However, from where could I have gold?

I heard of the match-making club that had lent some young and beautiful women money or gold after they had signed contracts to marry foreign men. I came to the club, signed, and borrowed the gold. My father was released. I paid the gold to the wife.

Then I took part in the show and was selected by Dotu. After the show, I met you, Brassia, and Tarda. On the next day, I flew with Dotu to Nikot, Chensanh.

All members of my family had not known my works, but after my arrival in Nikot a day, in a letter, I told them my works. That was the single letter I wrote to my family. On my part, I had not known the language of Chensanh before I came here. I have not a chance here to learn, so I have not been able to converse to anyone in this country until I came to this center.

I have endured so many misfortunes that have harmed then destroyed my life. My ex-lover is the harmer, and Dotu is a destroyer. Dotu is one in the group of four smugglers. They call themselves Stealth of Four. They have a wooden cottage in the thick forest near the common border of Chensanh and Lucdo. The forest runs through the two countries. At least, one of them is present in the cottage.

These four hoodlums confined me in the their cottage and forced me to be their sex object. There was rarely a day they did not torment my body to fulfill their sexual desires. Sometimes, all the four gang-raped me and misused my whole body to fulfill their lust.

They often turned on their computer to check e-mails or searched the Internet in early mornings. One day in the second year of my endurance, I glanced at their computer. One e-mail showed a photograph of a woman whose appearance looked like our compatriot. She was not as beautiful as me, and her age was in the late thirties. They talked to one another and contacted the other side through their computer.

On the next day, a shut-up jeep arrived at the cottage. Two men stepped out and drew the woman into the cottage. When she saw me, she said loudly, "I and my thirteen-year-old daughter were abducted six months ago. Inform my husband. The address…

hums—"

The two men grabbed her and gagged her mouth with a bit of cloth before she spoke out her address! Where was her daughter? I do not know!

The two men handed the hoodlums an amount of gold, blindfolded me, and drew me to their shut-up jeep.

According to my deduction, the hoodlums exchanged me for the woman. The amount of gold was the payment for the difference because I was more beautiful and younger.

The two bastards confined me in one room of a small house. I heard traffic noises from probably half a mile away, but I did not hear any voices of any neighbors.

The two bastards were heroin dealers. They forced me to be their sex object. When they left the house, they chained one of my wrists to the bed. Much worse, they injected heroin to my blood. They destroyed my life. After about ten months I became a heroin addict.

Unexpectedly, in one early morning, I heard noises of two strange cars at the right and the left of the house. Then I heard several loud words from one car's loudspeaker. I saw the two bastards raise their hands over their heads and step out the house.

I realized it was the police force. I cried out loudly. Hearing my female voice, a policewoman ran to me. She realized I was a victim of sex crimes. She checked my arms. She saw traces of heroin injections. Other police persons searched throughout the house and found a large bag of heroin. I was rescued, but it was too late! I was a heroin addict. I was driven to this rehab center.

After five months in this rehab center, I could converse with several natives in their language. I asked the board of directors to inform the authorities of the case of our compatriot woman and her daughter being abducted. She was confined by the four hoodlum smugglers, and her daughter was in an unknown place. Also, in this rehab center, I have tried to write this letter.

Dear Santolina or to whom this letter may concern,

Rehab Center informed you that Vanda died because of an overdose of sleeping pills last week.

We found nothing valuable except her written letter and your address near her body.

Rehab Center interred her body in the small cemetery nearby.

Truthfully,

Like other evenings, Brassia came home after eight. She greeted Santolina, but there was no answer as usual. She hurried to the kitchen. She saw Santolina weeping at the dinner table. Brassia stared round-eyed at Santolina and could not say any more words. Santolina handed Brassia the letter and said, "Vanda is dead. Read it. Tomorrow, we'll go to the dignitary of the religion and pay him to celebrate a mass for the souls of our two sisters. Let's consider Tarda and Vanda our sisters."

Turbulence Came to Santolina's Life

Bachmon became an important politician. He stayed in the capital and rarely came home. His conservative party won by a landslide. The chairman of the party would be the prime minister. Bachmon would be the minister of finance.

Nevertheless, a catastrophe came. At the appearance before the public of the Prime Minister and his cabinet, a radical of a rival party aimed his gun toward the PM and shot him. His target was the PM, but the bullets missed him and hit Bachmon. Although Bachmon was driven immediately to the hospital nearby, he died half an hour later.

At home, both Santolina and Brassia were shocked at the catastrophic news.

The government organized a state funeral for Bachmon. Santolina and Brassia were officially invited to attend the funeral as his wife (widow) and sister-in-law. A special car of the government drove them to the capital.

During the rites and rituals of the funeral, Santolina and Brassia were always walking, standing, and sitting close to each other. International presses received pictures from the ceremonies of the funeral and broadcasted or communicated in Dahilo and many other countries.

After a fortnight, all the ceremonies of the funeral were over. The special car of the government drove Santolina and

Brassia from the capital back to Comay City.

Their mailbox was fully jammed after the fortnight. They brought all mails into the house.

When they sorted the mails to categories. Santolina paid attention at the middle of an envelope on which the handwriting of her address had something familiar. She looked up at the left corner of the envelope. The sender was Trithuc, her lover who had had scholarship and left their native country to study in Unto Blumen eight years ago.

Although Santolina had forgotten after some years of trying, the handwriting strongly raised her emotions and sulky thoughts on the past: their romantic love in the senior year of high school and the next three years at the university, his saying good-bye at the airport, his non-replies to her several letters after the amputation of his right leg, and so on.

Brassia saw Santolina dumbfounded in looking at the envelope, so she asked, "Santolina, what happened? Are you okay? Whose letter is that?"

Santolina handed the envelop to Brassia and said in low and emotional voice, "Please open it and read the letter in a degree I can hear you."

Unto Blumen, July

Dear Santolina,

Please forgive me for my wrong decision of non-replies to your eight letters, which I still keep in the box on my writing table here.

In deciding so, I thought that you would find another man better than me, and I would forget you. But I was totally wrong. Your life was rolled in an unlucky harness, and I could not forget your nice sweetness. My wrong decision engendered so many losses for you and me.

Two years after my wrong decision, I wrote a letter to a friend of mine in our native country and asked him some news about you. Then he wrote to me that you had just married. I was very regretful but could not do anything.

I have been very sad because of my missing you. I have kept my promise of living as a single man until today.

Last Saturday evening, I and my nephew Trinhan sat in our living room and watched TV. In the program News in the World, I recognized you as the widow of Mr. Bachmon at the state funeral. Trinhan paid attention to the younger woman walking, standing, and sitting beside you, however.

After the broadcast, I told Trinhan the whole story of our love, our saying good-bye at the airport, your letters, and so on. Then I told him my intention to meet you, say my apology, and ask you to marry me. Simultaneously, Trinhan praised the beauty and charm of the woman beside you. On the next Monday, we contacted the consulate of Dahilo, so we know your address.

After our few exchanges, Trinhan wants to marry the woman without consideration of anything in her past if there is no present hindrance. By the way, I and Trinhan are living together in a large five-bedroom house. We are dentists. We own and work in our office.

Please, Santolina, reply as early as possible. I and Trinhan crave to fly to Comay, Dahilo, to meet you and the woman as soon as possible.

Sincerely

Even though the letter brought good news for both

Santolina and Brassia, Santolina was still calm and secretive. But Brassia expressed her spontaneous joy.

"Santolina, Trithuc still loves you so much. Accept his apology and marry him."

"How are about you? I marry Trithuc and live with him in Unto Blumen. Will you live here in Dahilo alone?"

"I've lived here in Dahilo like your younger sister. I'll be able to live in Unto Blumen like your niece."

"I understand you. Nevertheless, Bachmon died only a month ago. I'll tell them that they should wait for at least six months more. Okay, you're my younger sister here in Dahilo. After six months more, you'll be my niece in Unto Blumen."

"A period of six months is not a long time. I thank you, Santolina."

Agreements of Lobelia's Dog Vigor

Never did Lobelia's dog, Vigor, speak, but his actions and reactions proved that he totally agreed with the political side of his master, Lobelia, and her lover, Janvier.

Vigor was the present of Janvier to Lobelia for her eighteenth birthday. Vigor was three months old at that time. His coat was dark brown in his back and golden beige in the abdomen; additionally, there was a circle of straighter and longer hair surrounding his neck and two other ones surrounding his tail. Thus, he looked like a vigorous lion, and Lobelia named him Vigor. He was intelligent and bold.

When Vigor was one year old, he began to be most awe-inspiring dog in the street. In comparison with five other dogs in the neighborhood, his bark was clear and dignified since the old dog yelped like an asthma sufferer, the awkward hound neighed like a whooping-cougher, the golden Labrador uttered like a nightmare-dreamer, the roguish poodle stammered like a drunkard, and the small fox dog stuttered like a bone-choker. It was assumed that other dogs respected and enjoyed his bark since they stopped theirs if they heard his. It was similar to singers in a choir stopping their singing after a refrain to let their soloist sing verses alone. Their barks often happened in the second half of the night, from one to five o'clock.

Not only Lobelia but also her mother, Bellis, and father,

Larus, loved and esteemed Vigor like a member of their family. Vigor was overjoyed when Janvier came to visit Lobelia and her parents. It is presumed that Vigor knew he was the present of Janvier to Lobelia. He wished their love would reach marriage and they would happily live together thereafter.

Lobelia and Janvier studied in the same high school in the precinct of the capital of their country, and in last three consecutive school years, they were in the same classes. They were both seventeen-year-olds in the first half of their twelfth grade, but Janvier was three weeks older. Lobelia was charming, her oval face beautified with a dimple on her left cheek. Her eyes looked like two lily petals. When she smiled, her lips and dimple looked like a flower and a bud, and her eyes smiled altogether with her lips and dimple. Lobelia was curried by some male classmates. One of them was Megilp, but she did not like any of them.

On the other hand, Janvier was handsome and refined. Some female classmates liked him. One of them was Calla, but he ignored them. He did not intend to have a lover at his age.

However, one afternoon in the month before Lobelia's eighteenth birthday, on the way on foot from school to home, she was hit slightly by a motorcycle. She fell down, sprained her right ankle, and was faint. The driver drove his motorcycle away. Janvier saw the accident from one hundred yards behind, called the emergency vehicle, and sat beside her to the hospital. Then he informed her parents of the accident and visited her every evening. Love flourished in the week of his visiting times.

Lobelia was released from the hospital on the Friday thereafter, and on the next Monday, she went back to school. Janvier helped her for the missed week of school. Their classmates had very quick-witted intuition. After only some days, all of them knew Janvier and Lobelia a lover couple.

Another couple of lovers appeared within their class

several days later. Megilp, who had curried with Lobelia, and Calla, who had liked Janvier, became lovers. Was their love engendered by the one of Lobelia and Janvier's? Or was Calla and Megilp also a matched couple since she was pretty and charming and he was smooth-tongued and virile? Or was there another reason? No classmate could explain.

Lobelia was the single child living in the same house with Mr. Larus and Mrs. Bellis Garland. Mr. Garland was an official in the prime minister's office. He was fifty-eight years old when Lobelia was in the twelfth grade.

Mrs. Garland was a housewife and a year younger than her husband. Their country, Eastnama, endured the war of invasion from the neighbor country Kanxono since its clique of rulers with the deceitful name Revolution League (RL) thought that they had suzerainty over Eastnama. The war robbed them of their eldest son and made the second son handicapped. The eldest son had enlisted in the paratroop branch of the army in the third year of the war and had sacrificed his life in a battlefield in his fifth year of duty. The second son had been severely wounded a year later in the shelling night of the RL guys to the district where their house was located, and one shell had exploded on the roof part above his bedroom.

Lobelia and her parents were very sad. She and her mother had sobbed every evening for a month after each misfortune. Her parents groaned many times, "Why can't we have died for them?" The photo of the dead son in military uniform was put on the altar to remember him by. In this Eastnama war, so many parents thought longingly of their dead children! The handicapped son was taken care of by a religious charity in the foreign country of Fragrance because of humanity.

Eastnama War was in its fourteenth year. All families were affected by the war. Politicians analyzed the war. Writers commented on the war. Journalists reported battles of the war. People talked about the war.

The students of the class of Lobelia, Janvier, Calla, and Megilp often talked about the war in break times. Several male students discussed the war with one another, how to end the war, whether they would join the army or not.

Janvier opinionatedly said that Eastnama had to protect its freedom, democracy, and prosperity, so he would enlist in the army. If other young men did the same, Eastnama would win the war. Contrarily, Megilp found fault and denigrated the freedom, democracy, and prosperity of Eastnama; he criticized that every policy in this country was imperfect. If RL guys win the war, they would build a perfect society, a paradise for this country.

Megilp came from a village to the capital a year ago. He met a billionaire entrepreneur and told him that he was a poor high school student; he asked him for a part-time job in the capital to continue his studies. The billionaire had had a poor period when he had been a student, so he sponsored and let Megilp dwell in his luxurious villa, one block away from Mr. Garland's house. The billionaire was an itinerant entrepreneur, and he roved many cities around the country for his businesses. He had several villas in some different cities, and his family lived in the city on the beach far away from the capital. Each year, he came to the capital two or three times and stayed in this villa about ten days. Otherwise, Megilp dwelled alone in this villa as the houseman; neighbors and his classmates, even Calla, misunderstood he was a son of the entrepreneur.

Unfortunately, nobody suspected Megilp as an RL guy. At his age, sixteen, he had joined the RL. Two years later, he had been sent to the capital to infiltrate the ranks of students. Similar to many organs of the government and units of the army, in the ranks of students of high schools and universities, there were about 10 percent of RL infiltrators. They were very active. The RL infiltrators in the group of Megilp used the villa to learn instructions, allot assignments, or prepare actions. They came to the villa with schoolbags and books, so people thought that they came there to do their homework together. Two or three nights in a week, they slept there.

No, they did not sleep the all nights there, but left the villa at one o'clock to fulfill their assignments, like writing slogans on some walls, hanging their flags at some parks, spreading propaganda handbills on the streets, sabotaging some organ buildings, throwing hand grenades or plastic explosives to some government offices, assassinating someone they were commanded to, and so on. Then they went to their homes. The review of their works would be done in the next meeting.

Being the lover of Megilp, Calla was dragged into the actions of the group. After some weeks, Calla was scared and wanted to withdraw, but Megilp said, "You may not give up. The RL guys will kill you because you have known other RL infiltrators and many secrets. The organization will think you'll report to some organ of the government. Let's continue to the day of victory." Thus, Calla had no other way but continue in terrorist actions.

Calla had come from a small town to the capital three years ago to continue her studies because there was no high school in her hometown, and her father was a councilman. In the capital, she lived with her aunt's family. Her uncle-in-law was a pilot in the army. No one of her parents' family and her aunt's family knew anything about her involvement with the RL.

Lobelia's dog, Vigor, was intelligent and bold. He knew natural rules as well as common laws: Human beings ought to regulate and practice their activities by day and sleep by night. Dogs should patrol and guard their master's property by night and lie down by day but not neglect to protect the property.

The RL infiltrators violated these natural rules as well as common laws. Thus, Vigor barked at them vehemently and so did the other dogs. Vigor hated the violators who committed betrayals. They were officials or employees of the government by day but terrorists for RL by night; they were officers or soldiers of the army by day but did sabotages for RL by night. They were students of public high schools and universities by day, but they did harmful actions by night. They were traitors since they benefitted from the democratic and law-respectful side but served the dictatorial and deceiving side. They got salaries from the side that rendered prosperity to the people, but they fought for the side that brought poverty to the people.

Though the RL infiltrators were only about 10 percent in the most organs of the government, units of the army, and ranks of students, or 3 percent of the population, their sabotages and vandalism caused hugely catastrophic damages: damage in properties, damage in politics, damage in moralities, damage in the wills of fighting, and so on.

At the end of the school year, Janvier, Lobelia, Megilp, Calla, and their thirty-five other classmates graduated. Even though Janvier was among the students who had the condition to defer for his study in a university, he enlisted in the army. Simultaneously, Megilp registered to study at a faculty of agriculture. Lobelia and Calla registered to study at a faculty of nurse practitioners.

However, in their school years at universities, so many demonstrations and boycotts happened. The RL infiltrators in ranks of students misused laws that protected freedom in Eastnama to organize boycotts and demonstrations to make the rear of this country tumultuous. Students who expressed their disagreements with the demonstrations or boycotts were terrorized; students who organized the protests against demonstrations or boycotts were assassinated.

The motive of the RL infiltrators in ranks of students was to make the rear of Eastnama tumultuous. Nevertheless, the motives of other aping students were different. A part of them wanted their images to appear on TV and on the newspapers. They often held placards and were on the front lines of the demonstrations; after some demonstrations, they were entangled with both sides: the organizers and the government. As a result, they could not give up. Another part was scared of the general draft. To them, to be a soldier in this dangerous war was worse than a defeat of Eastnama. Unfortunately, in some faculties, pairs of professors supported the boycotts and demonstrations.

In parallel, RL infiltrators in fabrics, unions, and so forth also organized demonstrations and boycotts. The rear of this country was really tumultuous.

Janvier earned a second lieutenant's stripes after a year in military academy. He was transferred to the special forces unit, defending at the front line of the border. The day he said good-bye to his lover, Lobelia, her parents, and Vigor, they were very sad. Since his unit was so far from the capital, each year, he had only one opportunity to come home to meet them. However, he wrote letters to her every fortnight. In his letters, he also sent some greetings to Lobelia's parents and Vigor.

Love in Separateness

Honestly and purely I love you
In my heart and my soul.
Watching the flickering stars I remember your eyes;
Watching the strobe lights
The last Christmas images with you appear in my mind.

Unfortunately, the war has lasted so long;
When does it end? Nobody knows!
Lives in our country
Have so many vicissitudes and storms.
They hinder our happy union.

This unit is at the front line,
Has to be permanently vigilant,
Is attacked by enemies at any night,
Is shelled on any day,
Live in bunkers in most days and nights.

It is presumed that Vigor discovered Janvier's letters; he sat facing Lobelia to listen to her read his letters. In her replies, Lobelia's parents said greetings to Janvier through their daughter's letter. A couple of times, they asked her when they would marry. Likewise, Lobelia wrote letters in verses sometimes:

Fidelity of Love

Like buds open
My love flourishes only one time.
Everything in this world has an end;
So does this war.
I wait for you
When I still live in this world,
Or in my next life.

Both Lobelia and Janvier had honest and pure love, but the war hindered their future. Most young couples in Eastnama had the same dilemma. The war became more and more ferocious and bloodier. Janvier expressed more and more pessimist appraisals:

Vicissitudes harm our Love
On days, I cannot differentiate
Cicadas chirp lilting melodies or wailing dirges?
Drizzles rub persistently on earth for coolness or chillness?
At nights, I cannot differentiate
Crickets sing lullabies for living nature or dead victims?
Torrents drum on ponchos for celebration or Requiem?

Don't reproach me because
I haven't asked you to marry.
As we witnessed
Lots of young wives lost their husbands after their weddings.
So many veterans lost parts of their bodies
Have to endure handicapped lives.
My future I don't know.

To marry me means more worries for you.
To marry me means more hardness for you.
You are free,
To marry anyone
Who can render your life easier.
This sincere wish comes from my heart and mind.

The letter made Lobelia sad. She had written to him that she would wait for him all her life or her next life. Why did he write such bad thoughts to her? Didn't he know how much she loved him? It is presumed that Vigor was also sad.

Although Vigor barked vehemently for six years against the secret RL infiltrators, they attained the victory in the nineteenth year of the war. The army of Eastnama disintegrated, and its government surrendered.

Rich people were afraid of deaths and wounds more than the poor people. The rich thought that losing their beloved was worse than living under dictatorship and in poverty. Just after the RL guys gripped power, the people of Eastnama began to taste the dictatorship and poverty; the families of the former officials or officers tasted the cruelty and destitution.

Since the RL guys had all power and authority so quickly, they could not control the people immediately, so they needed volunteers who knew the people well. The former hoodlums and criminals were the most enthusiastic. They knew, in the former society, people had had contempt for them, but this new power gave them authority to make people afraid of them. They wanted to take revenge; they thought their lives were quite changed. So they became arrogant and domineering over the people to prove their authority; they worked zealously for the new powers. They harassed and denounced the people meanly and cruelly.

In the block of the street where the Garlands lived, the ex-robber named Kraut, who had been jailed for four years, was the most enthusiastic volunteer. The head guy of RL in the blocks assigned Kraut to list all former officials, officers, and their families living within the block as well as report which families still stay home and which families had fled away. Like other volunteers, Kraut enthusiastically did more work than he was assigned.

In the first month after the RL guys took power, Kraut came to the Garlands' every two days to investigate whatever belonged to the family including any news about Janvier. Vigor barked vehemently at Kraut every time he came. Lobelia had to bawl, tramp, and shoo Vigor to the backyard. Kraut expressed his anger at Vigor every time.

Megilp also came in some weekends to ask for news of his classmate Janvier. He was overbearing and vainglorious; he was on the side of the victors. He had some power and authority. On the contrary, Lobelia and Janvier were on the side of the defeated. Nonetheless, Vigor barked at Megilp very vehemently; he even snarled in an angry way. He once crouched in a position ready to spring to bite Megilp. It is assumed he expressed his detestation at the guy he had barked at nights for six years, and this guy dared to step into this house.

After the surrender, the prime minister's office of the former government did not exist anymore. Mr. Garland stayed home. He became very weak because of his sorrow and his age of sixty-four.

Three evenings in every week, the new authority of the block enforced all families to let one member at home; other ones had to gather at the end of the street to listen to propagandas describing paradise, freedom, and democracy that the RL guys would build for the people. All the details in propagandas were quite opposite to the reality. Sometimes, heaven bestowed benedictions; it rained before the gatherings. So the gatherings were automatically canceled.

Horribly, from 5:00 a.m. to 10:00 p.m., inhabitants had to hear loud broadcasts from loudspeakers bound on lampposts at corners of all streets. The broadcasts consisted of pierce, shrill, and offensive propagandas as well as victorious and extolling songs praising the emperor, the RL clique, or insulting lectures against the former government and army. Dwellers near the loudspeakers were more pitiable. These loudspeakers relayed the broadcasts from the central radio, or they read local communiqués that ordered local inhabitants to do some works such as fatigue duties.

Unexpectedly, one afternoon of the tenth day after the defeat, Vigor looked toward the street and moaned strangely. Victor had special sense to realize Janvier was coming. After several seconds, Lobelia also recognized Janvier through the window though he was in wrinkled civilian clothes, his whole appearance was dirty, his hair was disheveled, his face was gaunt, and his eyes were deep. She opened the front door; he stepped into the living room. She looked at him sadly; her eyes moistened with tears. He did not greet Lobelia but told her this:

"My unit received the command to abandon the post and withdraw to the near city, but on the way to the withdrawal, the enemies followed and attacked. A lot of my soldiers died and were wounded. Many others were arrested. My unit disintegrated. I escaped to the forest and hid in a shrub from that afternoon and the next whole night. At dawn, I walked to the road. The carnages were in front of my eyes. Many hundreds of unwhole corpses of soldiers, civilians, adults, and children lay there. Hundreds of wounded groaned, cried, or asked for water, but I couldn't do anything. Bags, motorcycles, vehicles, and many things lay about in disorder. From one bag near a corpse, I pulled out these civilian clothes, changed, and threw away my uniform. I tried to start some motorcycles. The fifth ran. En route, I saw several other similar carnages.

"With help in different ways from several good people, I arrived in the suburb of the capital this noon. I abandoned the motorcycle and hitchhiked to the street near my parents' house. From there, I walked toward my parents' house.

"However, when I came near the house I saw an RL guy who entered the house. Probably, my parents, sister, and brother are not there. Perhaps, they had fled and some RL guys have occupied the house. Now I've nowhere to go. May I stay here a few moments?"

Mr. and Mrs. Garland were there and heard Janvier's story from the middle of it. They had pity on him, but it was nearly impossible to let him live in the house. The new authorities began to control people strictly. Households consisted of only those who had registered in the address booklets of the former government; any new ones who were added to the households had to have certificates signed by heads of RL guys of districts or their superiors. Neighbors had to watch one another and report any strangers who came to which houses or any abnormal activities of other neighbors.

Mr. Garland told his wife, "Guide him to go to our son's bedroom. He has to hide there. We'll think of how to help him."

Lobelia brought some food and a drink for Janvier. She sadly looked at him in tears. Janvier sorrowfully looked down the floor.

In that late evening, Mr. Garland beckoned his wife and daughter to the master's bedroom and said, "Bellis, Lobelia, do you remember the guy who sat at the left hand of the chairman who read the propaganda in the gathering yesterday evening? He is my former colleague. His name is Licro Rongu. I didn't know he was an infiltrator. After the gathering, he told me he is now working in the district chief's office. Tomorrow evening, I'll come to his house to plead with him whether he can help us in some ways."

In the next late evening, after the talk with Licro Rongu, the infiltrator, Mr. Larus Garland came home with a hope. He told his wife, Lobelia, and Janvier, "Mr. Licro Rongu didn't describe it directly, but his words made me understand that the RL guys are hypocrites. They are extremely greedy and corrupt. They appropriate and grip real estates and belongings of the people, as many as possible. Real estates they occupy openly as everybody sees, but belongings they take covertly, and a part of them they get through briberies. The head of the district assigned Licro to be the intermediary to seek briberies for him, but he must do the work covertly. Janvier can be added to our household with two certificates: a certificate of marriage with Lobelia and another certificate of adding his name to our household. He'll ask the head of the district how much we'll pay tomorrow, and he'll tell us tomorrow evening."

The deal was arranged covertly. In the next evening, Licro Rongu came to the Garlands' house. Mr. Garland handed four taels of gold to his former colleague and had the two certificates. However, Janvier lived within some rooms in the back part of the house only.

At the lunch on the next day, Mr. Garland told Lobelia and Janvier before Mrs. Garland, "Lobelia and Janvier, as I know, you've loved each other for seven years. Now you've the certificate of marriage. Let us celebrate your wedding tonight. In front of your mother, me, and Vigor, kiss each other to prove your love."

Lobelia and Janvier stood up, embraced each other, and had a long and lovely kiss before Mr. and Mrs. Garland and Vigor. Their parents clapped lightly, and the dog wagged his tail cheerfully.

Then Mr. Garland told Mrs. Garland and Lobelia, "Try to have special dishes for the wedding tonight. A sparely frugal wedding, but the precious thing is their love."

Some drops of tears ran down from Lobelia's eyes. Janvier's eyes moistened. Were they glad or sad or both? Mrs. Garland looked at her daughter and son-in-law in sadness. But Vigor wagged his tail and moaned in joy.

Two months later, Lobelia felt nauseated and craved for sour food. Mrs. Garland explained that Lobelia was pregnant.

All the household were joyful but worried—joyful because they would have a baby, worried because their lives would meet more difficulties to feed the baby.

Three months after the victory, the RL guys proclaimed through means of the communications and lectures that they were high-minded victors. They bestowed amnesties and clemencies to all officers and officials of the former army and government, but the victors needed all intellectuals, artists, and rich people, former officials, and officers to build paradises in Eastnama. Thus, the victors asked all of them to present themselves in facilities to study the victors' policies, plans, and projects. The time limit was within one month.

Janvier procrastinated to present himself to the last day of the time limit because of Lobelia's pregnancy, but he had lived within some rooms in the back part of the house before the day. When he said good-bye, the whole household was sad; Lobelia sobbed bitterly. Vigor had some drops of tears in his eyes.

Mr. Garland was sick after several days of the wedding; he became very weak and lay on bed. The Garlands thought that Mr. Garland could not help the victors with anything, so he did not present himself.

On the day of surrender, the uncle-in-law of Calla came home, brought his family to the air base, and flew overseas. Calla refused to go with them. She had been a vanguard of RL and had used lots of her time to do dangerous actions for the victors, so she had not graduated as a nurse practitioner like Lobelia, but she expected rewards from RL and the marriage with Megilp.

A week after the victory, since the family of her aunt had left their house and fled, an RL victor came, occupied the house, and forced Calla to move out.

Calla came back to her native town to seek her parents and younger brother. However, the house of her parents was also occupied by a victor.

A neighbor told her in low voice, "Your parents, your brother, and I were among the evacuees who left the town some hours before the RL guys arrived. The evacuation was chaotic. Six miles eastward away the town, we were shelled. I saw your parents, your brother, and many others die in the carnage. I survived and returned home. Two days later, I came to the place. I saw a bulldozer was pushing the corpses down to a large hole."

Back to the capital, Calla moved to the villa of the entrepreneur and lived with Megilp. The entrepreneur had not come back to the villa since a half year before the surrender. Megilp registered Calla as his wife. He got the certificate of marriage and the certificate adding her name to his household easily. However, Megilp did so many works for the new authorities. Seven days in a week, he left the villa very early and came back at midnight. He was tired and went directly to sleep; rarely had he time to talk with Calla, who felt forlorn after the loss of her parents and brother as well as the departure of her aunt's family.

In one evening of the fifth month after the surrender, Licro Rongu visited the Garland family. Mr. and Mrs. Garland were surprised and suspecting. Vigor looked at him with his completely indifferent eyes.

However, Licro Rongu confided to them that he felt shameful because he had been an RL infiltrator who worked for the cruel, despotic, sly, and cunning RL guys.

He said, "To preserve my life, you don't and won't say to anyone else what I am going to say to you. As you know, I'm working in the district chief's office. One time, the district chief and his inferiors were gone on their official business for a week. I furtively read some top secret instructions of the RL clique to their high ranks in Eastnama. The instructions order them their ways to control dictatorially this country and its people. After reading these instructions. I understand the following:

"Experienced with their ways they have governed in Kanxono, people of that country have accomplished all the works they have planned. Nobody has had any time to think or any means to protest against them. Disobeying people have been maltreated in secret or open ways or were killed. Their families have lived in misery. Subjugated and submitted people have been distributed jobs with low to high salaries and issued few or many pieces of stamps to buy raw food and necessities depending on their degrees of subjugation or submission. Only those who had records of cruelty on disobeying people have conditions to join the ranks of RL.

"To grip powers firmly and control tightly the people of this country, they'll annihilate all possibilities of protestations against them and make all people completely dependent on them in all means of living and thinking. Turn by turn, lots of dictatorial measures are being implemented, or they will be implemented soon. Some measures will be repeated two, three, or many times if the measures are necessary.

1. Officials and officers of the former government and army, intellectuals, artists, and rich men have abilities to protest or oppose. They call all these dangerous challengers. They'll kill the challengers in unnoticeable manners, destroy the fidelity of the wives of the challengers in sophisticated ways, and bar children of the challengers from having good careers and bright futures in unfair policies. The manners to kill the challengers are the following: They deceive the challengers to present in assigned facilities. They secretly transport the challengers in groups of some hundreds into different areas in jungles of two countries, Eastnama and Kanxono, encircle the challenges there, enforce the challengers to replace bulls and buffaloes in hard works of primitive agriculture and tree-hewing. Consequently, because of mental tortures resulting from reviling insults and physical tortures resulting from hard work, meager food, unhygienic conditions, lack of medicine, the challengers will gradually die in jungles, unknown to outside world. The ways to destroy the fidelity of the wives of the challengers are sophisticated but can be described as the following: They take away means of livelihoods of the wives so the wives cannot nourish

themselves and their children, and they, the RL guys, have positive situations to curry the wives who have to submit to sexual intercourse in exchange for some means of living. They confiscate properties, rummage to take away all valuable things like gold, diamond, foreign currencies, and the like. They pressure the wives to volunteer for public works like wiping streets, cleaning sewers, dredging irrigation canals, and so on. They try to deceive and pressure the wives to move to the so-called fairylands in the jungles, where the wives and their children will gradually die because of shortage of food, lack of medication, and hard work in primitive agriculture with rudimentary tools. They try to occupy houses of the wives whose husbands are slaves in labor camps or jails, and only they, the RL guys, have the power to protect the houses. If the wives need their protection, the wives have to submit to sexual intercourse. The unfair policies to bar children of dangerous challengers from having good careers and bright futures are the following: Every applicant must have an additional curriculum vitae of many pages stating in detail the lives of parents, siblings, and grandparents of both sides as well as mentioning all relatives and friends. A curriculum vitae must be certified by a district chief or one of a higher rank. An applicant who has a parent labeled as a dangerous challenger has no chance to have a good career, get a high-paying job, or study at a university. Thus, the children of that category can only get humble jobs with low salaries, which no children of RL guys want.

2. They'll confiscate all means of livelihood.

Although they proclaim that the country belongs to the people, in reality, they are dictatorial bosses of everything in the country. All the people will be their obedient employees. They'll confiscate all farms and paddies. Raising or planting farmers or peasants will be their tenants who have to sell them products with prices they'll decide. Factories, fishing, transportation, and all other means of living will be in the same ill policies.

3. They transport as many things as possible such as industrial, technical, medical, musical equipments as well as instruments such as gears and tools, and even fixtures in public buildings are dismantled to transport to Kanxono.
4. To make the people became from poor to destitute, except the RL guys themselves, in order to be completely dependent on them, they'll implement a campaign called Beat the Exploiters in several stages. In an abrupt night, numerous houses of have families will simultaneously be occupied, searched thoroughly, listed in details of all belongings, and evaluated the total worth. Families that have belongings equivalent to a tael of gold will be judged as vampires that have drawn blood of other people; members of those families have to leave their houses with small bags of clothes for each and will be transported directly to fairylands in jungles.
5. The present currency will be worthless. They will impose a curfew on the day of exchange for new currency. On the decided day, one member of each family will bring money of the whole family to an assigned building to exchange for new money. The maximum amount of

new money each family will have the right to exchange is enough for each family to buy food for about a month. For any surplus money, its owner will receive a receipt written the surplus amount. The surplus will only harm the owner. It proves that the owner is rich, and the owner will be labeled as a vampire in the future.

6. Our culture that our ancestors have developed for many centuries will be considered the depraved one. They'll forbid our cultural activities including tiny activities like an individual singing a song lightly. They'll destroy all types of books including dictionaries, films, and so on. Replacements will be books, films, songs, poems, and so on extolling the emperor as a great saint and the RL clique as the top wisest persons in the world, praising them with a pack of lies like freedom and paradise they build for the people, as well as describing gratitude of people to the emperor and the clique."

Mrs. Garland interrupted, "Mr. Rongu, you've just told us the words *turn by turn*. Some parts have already happened, and others will come. We've already witnessed and endured a lot of these measures, policies, and campaigns."

"Oh yeah, you mean I'm saying the truth. By the way, listen to me, wives and daughters of former officials and former officers are targets as sex objects of any RL ranks. Family members of former officers and officials are targets to be insulted by the victors and their collaborators. The whole society is upside down, dull-witted guys are interested to insult educated persons now. Abstain from reaction to avoid more troubles. Lobelia, you've something lucky that other wives don't have. I mean you're still working as a nurse practitioner.

Careers of technique and medicine they lag far behind the standard of the world today, so their guys cannot replace in the next few years. Try to hold on to your job to avoid being forced to move to a fairyland. Oh, it's too late. I must go home now. Remember, do not tell anyone what I've told you. Bye."

What Licro divulged to them reassured the dictatorial policies which people already began to taste. The Garlands had to stash their last belongings worth three dozen taels of gold.

In a very early morning in the third week of the fifth month after the surrender, Kraut led six armed men to the Garlands. They pointed their guns toward the Garlands' house like they were searching for some criminal. Vigor looked straightly toward Kraut with anger and barked vehemently. Lobelia and Mrs. Garland were scared, so was Mr. Garland, who was lying on bed. When Lobelia recognized Kraut, she bawled, tramped, and shooed Vigor to the backyard. The armed men rushed into the house like they were in a battlefield. The six armed men scattered to all the corners of the house.

One armed man pointed his gun to the head of Mr. Garland and shouted, "Where do you hide weapons?"

"We don't have any weapons."

"Say where do you hide weapons or I shoot."

"We don't have any weapons."

"You're an official. Why didn't you present yourself in the assigned building like other officials and officers to study our policies, plans, projects to help us build paradises for you, your children, and other people?"

"I am sixty-four years old. I am very sick. I lie in bed. I know for sure I cannot help the new government in any way, so I didn't present myself."

"Your body is sick, but your mind is clear."

The armed man signaled his two inferiors to pull Mr. Garland up and drag him out the house into a truck parked in the street. They ignored the sobbing cries of Mrs. Garland and Lobelia as well as the bark of Vigor; one armed man drove the truck away.

Immediately, Kraut led ten youths, six females, and four males with crowbars and shovels, entering the house. They rummaged everywhere, in the house, the front yard, and the backyard. Two females dragged Mrs. Garland and Lobelia to a bedroom; the mother and the daughter had to strip in the nude. In females searched thoroughly even lapels of their clothes.

Since Vigor barked very vehemently, they told Lobelia to guide him to the cul-de-sac or somewhere else. Because Lobelia had to go working, she asked the neighbor at the other side of the street to take care Vigor for her.

At the house, Kraut and his guys, six females and four males, continued to rummage and forage everywhere, inside and outside the house. They searched thoroughly roofs, beams picture frames, walls, wardrobes, cases, boxes, bags, clothes, cupboard, dryer, TV sets, cabinet, pots, radio sets, refrigerator, pans, bowls, and so on. They dug floor tiles one by one in the house, in the front yard, in the backyard.

Until late in the evening, they found no weapons, no valuable belongings, and no traces of anything that they could judge as opposing or protesting the new powers. Sycophant Kraut lost an opportunity to add his records with the new authorities.

He angrily shouted at Mrs. Garland, "Where do you hide it?"

Mrs. Garland answered, "We hide nothing."

The RL guys used human powers and means to protect their authorities and powers as well as dredging and damaging people's belongings and properties more than all their other plans including producing and manufacturing.

Since Lobelia was busy with their career, Mrs. Garland went to several offices to ask some information about her husband, but each office told her to go to another. She was told to go around and around back to the offices she had asked.

After many days, Mrs. Garland gave up in sorrow. She and her daughter Lobelia thought that Mr. Garland was tortured to death and was buried somewhere like the RL guys had done with many other victims in the past several decades.

Unexpectedly, in an afternoon of the sixth month after Mr. Garland had been dragged away, Mrs. Garland received a letter telling her to go the address of the jail in the fourteenth district of the capital to pick up her husband.

With joy, she left her house immediately. After some procedures in the front room of the jail, a man pushed a bed into the room. Mr. Garland lay half-alive and half-dead on the bed. A small truck transported them home. Mr. Garland was carried into the house and on his bed. He lay in a coma. Mrs. Garland moaned in tears, so did Vigor.

In the evening, Lobelia sobbed when she came home. Mrs. Garland and Lobelia were joyful though there appeared some bruises caused by tortures on Mr. Garland's body. They consoled each other that he was not dead and buried somewhere like many other victims; they would try to find medication and herbs to treat him. Victims of the RL guys had to be silent, or they were added some more fantasized guilt, so they often consoled themselves not being behaved worse.

In parallel, what people in other countries considered the rights they automatically have, in Kanxono and Eastnama, the RL guys bestowed these rights drop by drop as their favors.

After several months of the victory, the whole society of Eastnama was totally changed. There appeared five different social classes. The highest class consisted of the RL guys coming from Kanxono. They had authorities, powers, issued houses, cars, and means of livelihoods, satisfactorily rationed means of living as well as numerous other prerogatives and privileges. About 10 percent of the population were in the daily-necessity class. They consisted of native Eastnama who had worked or supported RL guys during the war. They had means of livelihood equal to their situations in former society plus some privileges. They were often vainglorious to lower classes.

About 20 percent of the population were in the poor class. They were obedient or submitted employees of the authorities. They lived in inadequacy. About 40 percent of the population were peasant-and-farmer class. Their paddies and farms were confiscated. They became tenant peasants and farmers. They had to sell their products with dirt-cheap prices. Their lives were worse than the third class. The harassed class consisted of families of former officials and officers of about 30 percent of the population. They lived in anxiety, and most of them lived in destitution.

The victors created different systems of public shops. The special system supplied luxurious and qualified goods for the first class. Other systems sold things from a pound of potatoes to a dozen of nails to other classes according to stamps. Numbers of stamps were issued based on classes, and local authorities had powers to cut down stamps of anyone in lower classes. Additionally, goods for these classes had bad quality caused by different forms of corruptions.

Parts of goods were smuggled out to sell in black markets with much higher prices, so was raw food. Thus, the parts of raw food that were sold in public shops were sprinkled with water to make them heavier; consequently, they would mold or rot. Certainly, the authorities were behind these huge smugglings.

Ruddily plump and smartly dressed guys were the RL victors and their family members.

Contrarily, the majority of the people were scrawny and gaunt; parts of them wore mended clothes. The victors extirpated successfully all possibilities of protestations and oppositions. Days and nights, the people thought and worked for food and goods only. However, in public, people had to show pretend euphoria and happiness on their faces, in their words, and their activities since they were taught again and again that they were emancipated, their yokes were thrown away, and their shackles were cut by RL liberators. Those who did not show their pretend euphoria and happiness were considered as opposing or disobeying elements; they would be harassed or sent to labor camps.

Lobelia worked in the hospital, so family Garland was in the third class. She was issued stamps for her old parents, herself, and her newborn baby, Jasper. There was nothing for dogs, Vigor and all other dogs. The Garlands had to share their food to Vigor. It made their lives more difficult.

The RL guys won the war after their fighters had spent two decades of arduous, dangerous, inadequate, and deficient conditions in the jungles or hidden places. Thus, they decided to compensate themselves and a small part of their collaborators, to destroy all seeds of opposition and disobedience, to grip absolute authorities, to punish their enemies, to submit and subjugate the people. To attain these purposes, they implemented publicly and secretly numerous unfair policies, rules, measures, and methods.

Generally, each victor tried to get a house; the higher rank tried to have the better house, more prerogatives, and more privileges.

The victors, most of them had hidden in the jungles for many years, flirted, intimidated, or coerced the wives and girls of the former officials and officers of surrendered government and defeated army to let them fulfill sexual desires.

These women endured numerous pressures and miseries under the victor's powers and authorities. Their lovely husbands or fathers endured agonies in labor camps. Their means of livelihood were taken away, and they could hardly nourish themselves and their children. Worse, the majority of them lost their houses. Thus, they and their children lived forlornly in destitution.

The victors used their authorities and prerogatives to trick the miserable wives and girls. For example, the victors could vaguely promise to mitigate their ill-treatment or aid in some ways like to help their husbands or fathers in labor camps, to help the very wives or children. If the promises did not work, the victors could show their authorities to ill-treat in some more despotic extent. Thus, a part of the wives and girls were in a stalemate and reluctantly gave their bodies to the victors to fulfill their lust.

Megilp, became a VIP within many blocks of the streets surrounding the luxurious and spacious villa he was dwelling. In one way, he was vainglorious and overbearing because he was flattered and beseeched by so many local inhabitants with the hope he wrote recommendations to some administrations for their employment to avoid being enforced to leave their house in the situations of each members having a bag of clothes and move to fairylands in jungles. He was engrossed and enthusiastic in voluntary works because the new powers made so many changes which frightened and puzzled the people who often came to someone they had known before the victory like him to entreat for help. Thus, seven days of every week, he left the villa very early in mornings, came home at nights, and tiredly went directly to his bed. Calla felt more and more forlorn. Why did he behave his pretty lover in this way? The vain gloriousness was seated in his heart and mind.

The RL guys had already governed Eastnama for two years; the people were already under their firm grips. They did not need the help of native followers and volunteers in their authorities anymore, so they began to eliminate most these native followers and volunteers who they did not trust. There were about one million of eliminated guys. They denounced these guys with different guilts like undermining their prestige, disturbing the order of the society, spying for some shrapnel of the former government, and so on. Most of the guys in second class were eliminated.

Licro Rongu was accused of receiving many bribes! He was arrested and imprisoned in a jail, his house was inventoried and confiscated, and his family members were transported directly to a fairyland.

Kraut was accused of undermining the prestige of the new government. He was arrested and transported directly to a labor camp.

Nonetheless, the situations of Megilp and Calla were complicated. Megilp was in the RL middle rank; Calla moved to live with Megilp several days after the victory. Megilp automatically occupied the luxurious villa of the entrepreneur because he had dwelled there, and his name had been in the address booklet of the villa for seven years before the victory. Misfortune came to him because several higher ranks were jealous of his villa; one among them was the director of general department of police. The victors had the unwritten principle: a higher rank gets a better house.

The director ordered his one inferior who secretly hid some small flags of the former government at a corner of the front yard of the villa, and he reported to the general department of police. The villa was searched thoroughly, and the obvious evidence was the flags. Megilp was arrested, tortured, accused of organizing a scheme to overthrow the government, and imprisoned.

The villa was immediately issued to the director. Seeing that Calla had no other place to move, the director exchanged views with his wife, and they agreed to let Calla stay in the villa. But the real motivation of the director was not compassion but the beauty and charm of Calla, who was much younger than his wife. Furthermore, Calla had features of nobleness and elegance because she came from a former middle-class family; his father had been a former councilman.

Living in the villa, Calla was in a stalemate. When the wife of the director was not at home, Calla had to let him fulfill his sexual lust. The director was a concupiscent devil; he aggressively asked her to do shameful sexual actions.

Labor toilers in the camps had died about 20 percent to the end of the second year after the surrender because they had to endure reviling insults, hard work in primitive agriculture, and tree hewing with rudimentary tools, meager and moldy food as well as lack of medication and hygiene, and the tendency of their deaths in the next year increased. The miserable situation happened partly because most of the fruits of their labor had to be delivered to organs of the government.

It occurred that several toilers, during their labor, sneakily took some bites of raw food like potato, yam, beet, maize, or beans. Their wardens were surprised and cruelly beat them with their rifles' butts, in some cases, to death. Miraculously, the insects and worms that the toilers caught during their labor helped them survived.

On the other hand, the RL clique realized that while tenant farmers and peasants were not working hard, the products from labor camps delivered to the organs of government were noticeably substantial. Thus, the RL clique decided to use the families of the toilers to nourish them in order to decrease the deaths of the toilers. The clique gave their families permission to send parcels of dried food, clothes, and medication every semester.

Praiseworthily, the parcels proved the beautiful and great love of the wives, children, and parents of the labor toilers. Although they live in poverty or destitution, the majority of them still stinted themselves on food and clothes in order to send or bring some necessities to their loved ones who were more miserable in camps. Pitifully, a part of the wives and parents were in very destitute situations, so they could not do the same.

In the evening, Lobelia came home, like other days, after working; she received the first notification to send a parcel of dried food, clothes, and medication to her husband, Janvier, after two years and twenty-eight days without any information about him. She was joyful; he was still alive. She remembered vividly the moment Janvier had said good-bye to her, her parents, and Vigor. She had been pregnant then. She watched their seventeen-month-old son, Jasper, who was learning to talk.

"Mom, where's Dad?" Jasper asked her this same question many times.

"There." Again and again she pointed to the photograph hung on the wall. The photograph of Janvier and her had been shot on the day she had been released from the hospital ten years ago.

Seeing the notification, Vigor came near Lobelia and moaned; he felt that there was some information about Janvier on it.

Hearing the moaning, Mrs. Garland came out from the kitchen. Lobelia handed the notification to her mother.

After reading, she said joyfully, "He's still alive. I've heard about notifications in the market three days ago. People have said that families of any dears in camps don't receive notifications within these days. They should think that their dears are dead and buried in jungles. People said that the most necessary for a dear in the camps now are a pot of salty crushed fish paste, a warm jacket, and quinine pills. I'll help you in preparing a parcel. I'll go to tell your dad about the notification. He'll be joyful too. Yeah, Janvier is still alive."

After half an hour, both Lobelia and Mrs. Garland reread the notification and realized that there was no real address of the camp in the notification but a PO Box only.

However, they sent two parcels in the year, and Lobelia got two small pieces of replies in which there were some handwritten words of Janvier.

Early in the next year, Lobelia received the notification with another PO Box. There were hundreds of labor camps. Each year, from every camp, a half of the toilers were transported to other camps. They were replaced by the toilers from other camps, and the newcomers mingled with those who stayed. The aim of RL guys was to make the toilers not trust one another. The toilers could not know who the spying terriers of the wardens were.

Two other parcels were sent to the new PO Box in another year; Lobelia got two similar replies like the last year.

After two years of sending parcels, the RL clique gave permission to two members of each toiler's family to visit and bring necessities to the toilers every six months, but the members had to have the written permission of their local authorities. In reality, nearly all the families had only the ability to visit once a year.

However, the journeys through the jungles or marshes to the camps were full of risks, dangers, and hardships. In addition, there was a strict rule limiting visits to fifteen minutes. The visitors and toilers had to sit at two opposite sides of the tables or stand apart to talk; touching was not allowed. And the mean and cruel wardens sat nearby or walked to and fro in the middle to observe and listen all to the visitors and the toilers. So the visits became tragedies of lies. Additionally, many kinds of dried food were cut to pieces to inspect whether there were any forbidden things hidden inside.

In the first month of the fourth year after Janvier had presented himself to the victors, Lobelia received the notification to visit and bring necessities to her husband. The notification guided that the name of the camp was Xo Freedom in the Bunden area, and its nearest small town was Mota. At first, she thought she would bring three-and-a-half-year-old Jasper with her in the visit in order to let the father and the son know each other; after reading the address in the notification and after looking for the location on the map, Lobelia found out that the camp was in the vast muddy jungle northwest of Eastnama, so she prepared to go alone. She and her parents estimated the cost of the visit was high, and her parents sold the antique ironwood table in the living room for the costs.

Lobelia had to prepare for three works before the visit: (1) to apply to the local district office for a written permission, (2) to apply to the director of the clinic where she was working for five days off, and (3) to buy the necessities consisting medication, dried food, and raw food. Mrs. Garland helped her in many ways to keep processed raw food still edible after some months.

Lobelia applied for permission in the local district office to the receptionist. He said that she would come on the next day. But on the next day, he said that the head of the office had not signed. She understood what it meant, but she went to work. In the evening, her mother told her that one man from the office had arrived in their house and said if she wanted the head of the office to sign the permission, she should hand him a ring of gold. The mother handed him a ring. In the next morning, Lobelia went into the office, but the receptionist said that the permission was signed, but she should go to his house in the evening to get it. Lobelia was thinking whether the receptionist asked for sexual intercourse or bribery. In the evening, her mother brought a small amount of money to the house of the receptionist and got the permission. In the new authorities, the higher ranks asked more substantial briberies but only through lower ranks who could be scapegoats if corruptions would become scandals.

For the five days off, it happened also tortuously with two similar briberies.

Like all other area activities, the tickets for interregional busses to Mota were sold for formality's sake from the windows in three hours and were cleaned out. But in all corners of the bus station, tickets were covertly sold with tripled prices. After buying a ticket in the black market, Lobelia elbowed with others to step into the decrepit and dirty bus. Some cried because their bags or wallets were snatched away by stealers. Lobelia reached inside the bus, but she had to stand. Passengers and baggage were jammed.

However, the bus started at 6:00 a.m. Passengers prayed in their mind for their safe arrival in their destinations. Halfway through the trip the bus took a rest for half an hour.

The bus arrived in Mota at 8:00 p.m. At the bus station, Lobelia noticed eleven other women who also came there to visit and bring necessities to their husbands. They greeted one another. They were tired and hungry. A man invited them to their inn and said that a rowing boat would transport them from the inn to the camp. They followed him. The inn was a shanty on stilts at the border of a muddy jungle. There were no beds, but there were hemmed sedge mats, decrepit blankets, and mosquito nets for them. They could not sleep. They were worrying and felt strange. Mosquitoes surrounded the nets like anthills; they buzzed like some flowed flutes. Bugs from the mats bit them and sucked their blood. Some wild animal screamed horribly outside the inn. So they decided to remain awake all night. Every woman had a story of oppression and several experiences to share to the others.

"All RL guys are professional liars. They're trained to lie," one woman began. "Lying became their inherence. What they said are opposite to the reality or the truth. Oh, sorry, we also must lie in public. We can say the truth only with our trusted guys in privacy. People must lie in public. Foreigners cannot understand people must lie to escape punishments."

The second woman continued, "Our dears in camps are instructed on how to write letters to their families. Their wardens check what were written and sent for them. So our dears must lie. Only necessities that laborers ask their families are true."

The third woman added, "The chief of my local quarter harasses me for sex. At first, he tried to meet me anywhere I was to flirt with me. Now, he comes to my house, intimidates me, and tells me directly, if I don't let him have sex, he'll report bad thing to the camp where my husband is laboring. My husband will be executed. Um, my neighbors advise me not to make him shameful. He'll take revenge meanly."

The fourth woman asked, "My case is similar. I'm harassed by the controlling policeman of interblocks. He flirts and says that I'm still young and beautiful, that he knows the policies of the government, that the RL clique never releases the former officials and officers, that I'm waiting in vain, and so on. I witness most victors demand wives and daughters of the surrendered government or defeated officers to let them fulfill their sexual desires. Can anyone among you say the reason?"

The fifth woman explained, "Though they are victors, the majority of them had just either eradicated illiteracy or finished elementary schools. Others hid for years in jungles. The male victors are very interested to have sexual intercourse with the wives and daughters of the former officials and officers of the surrendered government and defeated army because these women still have features of nobleness and elegance of the middle or high classes of the former society.

"Both of you are in the dangerous situations. It's difficult to escape their claws. Nearly all young wives whose husbands toil in camps are in similarly caddish claws. But I'll tell you some experiences of others. When you see him, if you live with a parent, call your parent to accompany you wherever you are. If you've a child, tell your child to hold your hand to accompany you wherever you are. If you don't have a parent or a child living with you, beg one old woman among your relatives to come to live with you."

The sixth woman asked, "My situation is in similarly caddish claws. I've a six-year-old son. He accompanies me when the caddish guy comes. However, once the guy came at night and knocked at my door and said that there were some suspected things in my house, so he came to inspect. My son slept so deeply and knew nothing. I was lucky that night, some neighbors were curious in watching whether there were some illegal things in my house."

The seventh woman said, "Oh, you tell all of us one solution: neighbors. Beg and foretell our neighbors if any guy comes at night, you'll speak loudly and make loud noises. Neighbors will pretend to be curious to watch."

The eight woman maintained sadly, "Young wives of former officials and officers are objects of lustful guys who have authority and power as well as tricks and means. Thus, lots of the wives have to submit their bodies to the caddish guys in order to survive. Don't reproach them."

The eleventh women talked about being harassed in sex and lots of other issues like being asked to donate their house, being compelled to clean sewerage, having some pounds of raw food taken away because policemen said that the raw food was smuggled, and so on until 5:00 a.m.

Suddenly, one woman screamed, "He-help!"

Another woman cried, "Faugh, a snake!"

A cobra slithered at one corner of the floor toward a mosquito net. Immediately, the inn owner appeared with two flashlights. He pointed the lights directly into the eyes of the snake. The snake halted and withdrew.

In the early morning, the women took some pieces of dried food for breakfast. Then they paid for the night and the transportation of the rowboat to and from the inn to the camp. The inn owner guided them down to the rowboat. Two peasants rowed the boat on some small and natural canals. They saw many kinds of wild animals including chimpanzees, a pair of pythons, some crocodiles, alligators, and many types of snakes: copperheads, cobra, black-and-white-ringed kraits, yellow-and-white-ringed kraits, endorphins, and colubrids.

At 10:00 a.m., the boat stopped. The rowers pointed at the direction of the camp and said, "The boat cannot reach the camp. You've to slog forward two hundred yards. We'll wait for you here until 4:00 p.m. Good luck."

"Heaven, have pity on me!"

"All my life, I haven't slogged once."

"I haven't too!"

Nearly all the women said similar words. But they had no other choice. They stepped down. Mud was under some inches of water. Some snakes swam away. The rowers handed them their bags. Horribly, a flock of leeches ambushed them. The women sobbed, but all their hands were busy with their bags. The leeches stuck fast to their legs and sucked their blood. On their way, some women fell down. Their bags were soggy. They burst into tears.

When they reached the border of the camp, the leeches were full of their blood but still stuck fast to their legs. They threw their bags down and tried to yank the leeches out, but they could not since the leeches were like greasy elastic bands.

A warden in the watchtower said loudly, "Hey, women, there're six pots of lime with chopsticks in front of you. Take the chopsticks and apply a little bit of lime at the mouths of the leeches."

They did what the warden had said, and the leeches fell down to the ground.

A camp ruler from the cottage with its name Welcome Guest House came and guided them into the cottage. Another ruler signaled them to sit down on the earthen floor. Each woman registered her name and the name of her husband. One ruler brought the list away. The older ruler began his lecture:

"We, the liberators, are the top intelligence of human beings. We are building a paradise in this country for all of you and your children.

"Your husbands committed many crimes against the people. They deserve to be executed. But we grant them clemencies. But they have to labor to show their concrete repentance and to redeem their past actions.

"You have to encourage them to study well and labor well. You have to tell them that everyone at your home is healthy and everything is well so their minds rest in peace to study and labor.

"You may not sob nor burst into tears because to sob or cry means you indignantly resent us. Each of you and your husband may not touch each other because to touch expresses obscene acts. If any of you or your husband violate any regulation I've said, we'll stop your visit immediately, and your husband will be punished later. Do you understand? Now, wait here. Your husbands will come."

After haft an hour, twelve scrawny slaves in mended clothes accompanied by four wardens with rifles walked toward the cottages. Each woman stared and tried to recognize her husband, but they could not because all the slaves had the appearance of scrawny beggars. The toilers entered the cottage. Finally, the women realized their miserable husbands. They had to bite their lips to prevent their sobs.

The women were invited to stand in a horizontal line along a rope. Then each toiler was allowed to come and stand at another rope opposite his wife.

One ruler bawled his command, "The mutual contact begins."

Some pairs could not talk but continued to stare each other. Other husbands asked questions and heard lies.

Between the two ropes, another ruler walked to and fro to listen to what was said and to watch what gestures were done.

Fifteen minutes passed quickly. The ruler gave the other command, "The contact ends. Hand your presents." Each woman handed her two bags to her husband. Some wives tried to rub briefly their husbands' hands.

Then the toilers had to show all the pieces of presents for the inspection. All cans had to be opened. Several other pieces such as sausages, cheese, and so on were cut to two or three parts.

Thereafter, the toilers repacked and carried their presents. They walked back to the path but to the opposite direction. Their wives peered at them, but it presumed that their husbands were not allowed to look backward.

After the visit, the women slogged back to the rowboat. They were exhausted. They remembered they did not have lunch. But they had no bags anymore to carry. They reached the boat at 4:00 p.m. There were three pots of lime in the boat for them to get rid of leeches. They got back to the inn at 6:00 p.m.

The inn owner said, "You're probably very hungry. Hand me some money for your dinner. Oh, I'm sure you cannot buy tickets back home from the windows tomorrow morning. If I buy them in the black market for you now, they're much cheaper than you'll buy them tomorrow. So together, each of you hand me..."

The wives realized that their blood was sucked from all directions; they were inflicted from all social strata. For example, in the inn and the mud, their blood was sucked not only from above and around the nets by mosquitoes but also from under the hemmed sedge mats by bugs and from the mud by leeches.

Lobelia came home on the next day at 9:00 p.m. She was very exhausted. Jasper embraced her and sobbed, but Vigor wagged his tail joyfully. Mr. and Mrs. Garland asked her how Janvier was. She visualized her husband as a scrawny and ragged beggar but answered, "He's okay." She did not want to make her parents sadder.

After Megilp had been arrested and the director of the general department of the police owned the luxurious villa, Calla became the victim of the lustful director. Four months later, she knew she was pregnant.

Calla told the director, "I'm pregnant, probably two months."

He commanded, "You must have an abortion. I myself will drive you to the abortionist not far from here and pay the cost."

"No, I won't, never."

"If you don't, you'll be kicked out to the street. You'll be more miserable. On other hand, I'll be reduced to a lower rank because of my low ethical standard."

"All of you've no ethics. All of you've bad conduct."

"But in public, every one of us behaves as a guy of high ethics."

"All of you are deceivers, liars, and hypocrites."

"Yes, our hypocrisies, deceptions, lies, slyness, cruelties, and despotism helped us winning the war. Now, to grip firmly power and authority, we must continue to use them.

Our hostile influences in the world have said that democracy, freedom, equality, compassion, and charity have been won. We've proved that they have been wrong."

Misfortunes continued to pour on Calla. A kangaroo court of the victors judged that Megilp had committed the high crime of treason against the new government and gave him the verdict of death penalty.

The governmental committee that executed the verdict wanted to have the heart, kidneys, and some other organs of Megilp to buy to its connected hospital, so it invited Calla, whose name was in the certificate of marriage with Megilp, to its office. The office asked her to sign on a form of donation. In the totally puzzled and disappointed situation, she did not read but signed on the form.

On the way back to the villa, a car hit Calla and her bicycle. She died at the very place.

Passersby murmured, "It's not an accident. It's a despotic killing. The young woman is pregnant. Two victims are dead in one killing."

Several minutes later, an ambulance transported her corpse directly to a cemetery.

To the toilers in labor camps as well as their waiting wives and families that were inflicted by the new society, the time had passed so slowly. They felt that six years were as long as six decades. In spite of destitution or poverty, the wives endured hunger to spare something to send then bring some necessities to their husbands in labor camps. Their love overcame all hardships and dangers.

Janvier had toiled in three different labor camps for six years. Lobelia had sent him four parcels in the first and the second camps as well as carried out two visits in the third camp. All these camps were in their country, Eastnama. But the third notification for the visit made Lobelia and her parents more frightened; the address of the fourth camp called Xo Prosperity was in the highland jungles of Kanxono.

All different steps required before the visit happened similarly to the last two times. The journey in the wagon for coal of the train then truck for pigs to the inn at the border of the jungle was harder with jostling and robbing.

In the inn where they'll stay overnight before crossing the jungle to go to the labor camp the next morning, Lobelia and ten other wives greeted one another. Mosquitoes were above and around the nets, and bugs were under the hemmed sedge mats. They cannot sleep, so they shared their stories and experiences to one another:

One woman began, "The war ended six years ago, but the people of Kanxono are still even poorer in comparison with our people after six miserable years, but the RL clique led them fighting in the war, and they won."

Another woman explained, "Oh, these people had no other way, they had to fight. My dear, you haven't understood yet! Six years under the totally dictatorial rule and absolutely state-owned economy are not enough for you to understand?"

The third woman said, "The victors intend to kill silently all officials and officers of the former government and army and destroy sophisticatedly their families."

The fourth woman maintained, "Still live, still to fight. The controlling policeman of my interblocks is using pressure with his intention to sleep with me. But I'd rather die than betray my husband and children."

The fifth woman expressed, "Anything I did to earn something for the living of my two little children and me was considered illegal and taken by the controlling police of my interblocks: selling used clothes, baking and selling glutinous rice, and so on. Once I told him that he took away all my means of living, we would die in hunger, but the bastard answered me that to die in hunger was our problem, not his."

Listening to the stories and experiences all the night, Lobelia thought to herself, "Lots of the wives are in more miserable situations than mine since I live with my parents and still have a job, so my burden and coping with the infliction and harshness are not as heavy as theirs."

Early in the morning, while the women were eating some pieces of sweet potatoes for breakfast, the inn owner told them, "The camp is in the jungle about fourteen miles away from here. The roads are very slippery and complicated. You have to climb on two bamboo footbridges. Losing your way is possible if you have no guide. Furthermore, you're all women, it's easy to be robbed, raped, and killed. Similar things happened four times in the past. I advise you to hire six highlanders waiting outside the inn to carry your bags and guide the way."

The women agreed.

On the way, they had to overcome dangers. They saw many different wild animals including some ferocious ones like snakes, tigers, leopards, and so on. One highlander told them about the visit:

"Rules for visits of this camp are similar to many other ones. All of you will sit at one side of the long table. Each husband will sit opposite to his wife. At each head of the table, a ruler will sit to observe your gestures and listen to your words. Of course, you must lie. But if any one of you needs to inform your husband of something like a member of one's family died, she should sit in the middle. Others should help her by talking a little louder."

"Let me sit in the middle," said one woman. "I'll tell my husband that our son was dead because his schoolteacher guided his class picking up empty cans in the field, a mine exploded, and our son died."

"No, don't tell him," advised another woman. "It'll make him more disappointed, and both of you'll gain nothing."

Lobelia murmured to the woman near her about the highlander, "In this shifty society, there is still an honest and helpful guy."

"Be careful," murmured the woman in the back, "there are various sophisticated ways of deception and tricks. It could be the way he lures us to confide in him or divulge something. Be not so simple in trusting anyone."

After three applications of Lobelia for the days off to visit her husband, the victor with the nickname Six Fast, the head of the employee office, was interested in her. He flirted with her in the clinic and sought her in the Garlands' house on weekends.

Every time Six Fast came, Lobelia held Jasper's hand wherever she went. At the same time, Mrs. Garland followed him and conversed with him. She used details that she had heard from lectures or radios to pretend respect for his emperor, clique, and himself.

Quite oppositely, when Vigor saw Six Fast, Vigor expressed enmity toward the flirter. He barked vehemently and snarled angrily. Lobelia had to bawl, tramp, and shoo him to the backyard. It presumed Vigor felt irritated.

Unfortunately, regret happened when Six Fast came for the tenth time. Vigor crouched, sprang up, and bit the left ankle of the flirter. His pants were ripped, but he was not injured, thanks to the thick khaki cloth. Both Lobelia and Mrs. Garland were scared. They shooed Vigor to the backyard and begged for his forgiveness.

With wrath, Six Fast left the house with many words of intimidation, "You'll be punished. This dog must die."

The whole household of the Garlands were anxious. After analyzing all possible consequences, in that evening, Mrs. Garland brought one tael of gold to the house of Six Fast for the tribute and begged for his forgiveness again.

After the incident, Lobelia talked to Vigor, "You harm us so much. You're brave, but your reaction is selfish and lacks sagaciousness. It means nothing to this new regime. Your reaction caused us a big loss."

Vigor seemed very regretful. That evening, he did not eat anything. In the following days, he ate quite a little.

Vigor did not bark after the incident. He often lay under the wooden divan in the living room. Jasper was a seven-year-old little boy. Mr. Garland was paralyzed and on his bed. Mrs. Garland and Lobelia were so busy and had so many anxieties, so they had no time to notice Vigor. They forgot him.

Some days later, Lobelia asked her mother, "Where is Vigor? I haven't seen or heard him since the day before yesterday."

They looked at each other. They called him, but there was no Vigor anymore to come out. They concluded that Six Fast had sent somebody who had caught him. They loved Vigor, but it was his ill fate. They were sad, but they had to accept his fate.

Two days later, on a Sunday, a stinky odor emanated from a corner of their backyard behind the big jar. There were lots of flies flying up and down. Vigor lay dead there. Lobelia, Mrs. Garland, and Jasper used a jute bag to wrap the dead body of Vigor and called a rickshaw to transport it to the rice paddy. They bought a large bundle of rice stubble, made the pyre, and burnt it. They prayed and talked to his spirit:

"Our love dog Vigor, may your spirit go to the garden of real happiness outside this world. Vigor, it is easy for you to decide to leave this society full of deep sufferings, anxieties, and resentments since you are not bound by relationships. You are free now. We, human beings, have so many relationships, so many duties, so many responsibilities. We may not end our lives as easily as you have. You're lucky. We aren't. We can't forget you, Vigor. Please remember us as we remember you. Adieu."

In sufferings and resentments, the time passed slowly. Being a wife of a former officer laboring in camp, Lobelia had to work harder than other colleagues at the clinic to keep her job and not to be forced to move to a fairyland.

One evening, Lobelia came home after a hard workday. Immediately, Mrs. Garland showed her then read a letter from Fragrance Embassy with unexpected information:

Attestation,

Dear Mr. and Mrs. Garland,

Your handicapped son in Fragrance needs a member of your family.

Based on humanity, Fragrance Embassy to Eastnama will issue an immigrant visa to one member of your family. If he or she has children under fifteen years old, the children may accompany him or her.

Joy and worry came to Lobelia with the news. She thought to herself, if her mother went to Fragrance, she could not simultaneously work the hard job in the clinics and do all three duties to her sick father, to her husband in camp, and to her little son, Jasper. On the other hand, if she went to Fragrance, similar hardships would happen to her mother.

"Lobelia, I know what you are thinking. But we may not miss this golden chance. For the future of little Jasper, for your future, for chance to ask humanitarian organizations of the world to help Janvier, you must go. We still stash some taels of gold. We will bribe for your visa of exit. Your father has the same decision as mine," said Mrs. Garland.

"But I cannot abandon my husband, Janvier, in the labor camp!"

"Not abandon, Lobelia. I'll find a relative to help me. We'll try to advise Janvier secretly. I think he'll agree. If you stay in this country, we cannot do anything but endure sufferings and die slowly in sorrow and resentment. Be courageous and wise, Lobelia."

Women Victims of the Pirates

"Hee-haw hee-haw hee-haw hee-haw hee-haw! Hee hee hee hee!"

The louder and longer the children laughed, the more self-pity and shameful Miltonia felt. Her nephew and niece are watching a comic film in which the protagonist is a gentle and mild pirate. She thinks to herself, "Was there such a gentle and mild pirate in the last century? Weren't pirates wicked robbers in the open seas?" To her, any plot that changes barbarous, wicked, or cruel guys into mild ones to make fun commit a kind of brazen action: making fun of the sufferings of others. Will Hitler and the Nazis, Stalin and the Bolsheviks, Pol Pot and the Khmer Rouge, or the terrorists who attacked New York on September 11 be funny characters in the future? If the last ones would be, the audience were extremists.

The pirates, the painful images caused by the brutal and wicked pirates have not been able to be eliminated from her mind. The pirates killed the men and raped the women in the boats. The pirates shipped eleven women from the age of fourteen to thirty-seven including herself to wild and isolated islets. There the pirates oppressed and humiliated the women as their sex slaves.

To avoid the film and the laughter, Miltonia left the living room for her bedroom. She lay on her bed and tried to calm down her mind, but the images of the past twelve years reappeared turn by turn.

Miltonia began to attend history classes at the Faculty of Social Sciences as a freshman after the celebration of her nineteenth birthday. In the next school year, she was a sophomore; her youngest sister, Muscaria, was a freshman at the same faculty and had the same major.

The ferociously bloody war in her country, Eastnama, was in the fifteenth year. In all faculties, there were two hostile sides: pro-defensive groups and anti-defensive groups. Each side had about 10 percent of the students and 5 percent of the professors. The rest were neutral.

The pro-defensive groups opinionated that the war was the catastrophe engendered by the invasion from the neighbor country Kanxono commanded by a clique called the RL, which stood for the deceitful name Revolution League. Since more than 80 percent of the RL soldiers were sent from the neighboring country Kanxono, if the RL clique gave up their dream of suzerainty and withdrew their soldiers, peace would come.

The anti-defensive groups opinionated that the society of Eastnama was not perfect and that soldiers who came from the neighbor country Kanxono were liberators who helped the people of Eastnama to raise up their arms to overthrow the government and to build a paradise similar to Kanxono. Thus, all social classes in Eastnama had guys who collaborated with liberators. The anti-defensive groups were extremely active and aggressive. They organized demonstrations, boycotts, and sleepless nights with anti-defensive songs. In their boycott days, any student who dared to enter classes would be covertly disturbed later. They assassinated many prominent students of pro-defensive groups.

All the neutral students and professors waited and watched

passively. Probably they were afraid of the aggressive acts of anti-defensive groups, which would not keep their lives safe.

Miltonia and Muscaria were two daughters of Mr. and Mrs. Miscanthus, who had no sons. Mr. Miscanthus was a professor of civilization at the Faculty of Social Sciences. He was an RL sympathizer. His paper handouts often consisted of some small details of his anti-defensive opinions. Nevertheless, he did not talk about politics at home with his two daughters.

Although Miltonia studied history, she loved music.

She could sing well and accompany it with a guitar when she or someone else sang. Her love for music made the rapprochement between herself and the anti-defensive group of the faculty. To sing in the sleepless nights had some allure as bonfires where young students could relax like the camping nights in her times of lower schools. Also, Muscaria joined her elder sister.

At the first time she brought her guitar to a sleepless night, the whole group greeted her ardently; she harmonized with them spontaneously.

In sleepless nights, most of the songs were sung in chorus. All the joiners clapped their hands at their rhythm. Simultaneously she accompanied them with her guitar. All the songs had anti-defensive meanings, but they were not an issue with her. She felt that everybody in the group admired her talent and prettiness, and that made her proud.

The Faculty of Social Sciences had about four hundred students in each school year. Although the anti-defensive group had about thirty students, they changed the whole political aspect of the faculty. The government was careful in handling the anti-defensive group because they were protected by rights to express their opinions guaranteed by the constitution and defended by the international presses. Therefore, outsiders misunderstood that the majority of students were on the side of anti-defensive movement.

While the anti-defensive group was being active and aggressive, contrarily, the pro-defensive group was timid and unorganized, especially after its two consecutive leaders had been assassinated in the twelfth and thirteenth years of the war. Therefore, activities of the pro-defensive group had only fleeting effectively on 80 percent of neutral students.

Summer vacation came. The anti-defensive group of the Faculty of Social Science was invited by the anti-defensive group of the Faculty of Natural Sciences for a week of camping together. During the days, Miltonia made an acquaintance with Cercis, a student of physics. Cercis played guitar better than Miltonia. The guitarists were admired by all campers.

Cercis was a sophomore at the Faculty of Natural Sciences. He was the first child of the multimillionaire couple Mr. and Mrs. Cyclamen, who had two sons but no daughters. Cercis's younger brother Cleome was a freshman in the same faculty. They were RL sympathizers.

To the campers, the purposes of the week were relaxation and recreation, but to the two leaders of the two anti-defensive groups and their superiors, their purposes was to push the groups to be more active and effective in making the rear of this country more tumultuous. A superior named Third Thunderbolt appeared unexpectedly one evening. He analyzed the imperfect society of Eastnama at the time, then he visualized a paradise society after the victory of the RL. He advised campers to join RL. He strongly emphasized that only RL guys would have bright futures. Later, after the victory of RL, it was revealed that Third Thunderbolt had been the secret commander of political proselytizing. Miltonia, Muscaria, and lots of other campers became RL sympathizers.

After the week of camping, Cercis came to the Miscanthuses' house on weekends to tutor Miltonia in music and guitar. Love between them came a few months later.

For the twentieth birthday party of Cercis, he invited not only his lover, Miltonia, but also her sister, Muscaria. As a result, his brother Cleome and Muscaria fell in love with each other at first sight. It was the romantic party for both couples, Cercis and Miltonia and Cleome and Muscaria. Under the circumstance, the anti-defensive activities influenced gradually but strongly Cleome and Muscaria.

Before the war, Dr. Cyclamen had been the richest man in the city. He had inherited the large pharmacy in the center of the city, the luxurious villa behind it, and the scenic real estate of a half square mile in the suburb at the border of the beautiful lake. At his age of thirty, he had married the pretty queen of the city of the year. One and a half years later, the pretty queen had bore Cercis, and one year later, she had bore Cleome. At the age of fifteen, Cercis had already witnessed the ferocity of the war.

The RL guys secretly recruited manpower from all organs of the government and units of its army, or their guys infiltrated into the organs and units. As a result, there were 10 percent of them everywhere. They had discipline; they were very active and clever. They achieved their aims.

One female employee named Sauerin in the pharmacy of Mr. Cyclamen was an infiltrator. She was the inferior and sex partner of Third Thunderbolt. In the sixth year of the war, in a private conversation with her boss, she directly said, "Be calm, Mr. Cyclamen, I'm an RL member. If you divulge this to anyone, all members of your family will be in danger."

"No, I won't. It's your privacy. We have nothing to do with it."

"You don't understand our aim. The RL needs your help, very big help. You may not refuse. The safety of your family is in our hands."

"What you say is similar to an ultimatum or a verdict. What a help do you need?"

"Before I describe our project, I warn you not to tell my secret and our project to your wife and children. Probably they cannot keep the secrets. Think about the safety of your whole family. It is in our hands. Remember, our guys are in all units of this army and organs of this government.

"Our million fighters in jungles and battlefields, sick and wounded, need large amounts of medication, but we're seriously short of them. We'll hand you our money to build a medication fabric on your half-square-mile real estate. Since you've the estate, try to contribute one-fourth of the capital. We'll hand you the other three-fourths. Um, the products in the future will be divided into two. You'll sell your half anywhere you want. Another half will belong to us.

"Think and prepare procedures for the project right away. You can ask my opinion at any time I'm working here."

Sauerin told Mr. Cyclamen the decisions of RL like a commander. He had to do all the things for the safety of his family.

Although the people of Kanxono, the country of the invaders, lived in poverty, the RL clique, who ruled it, had monies and means to do anything they wanted.

The medication factory began to be built four months later, then it began to produce medication a year later. Outwardly, Mr. Cyclamen performed as the boss, but inwardly, Sauerin decided everything in the factory.

While Mr. Cyclamen was worrying about the control of the RL over the safety and property of his whole family, his two sons became RL sympathizers and were enthusiastic on activities of the anti-defensive movement. Eastnama was in a chaotic circumstance. In these families, parents did not dare to say the truth to their children. In other families, their members did not trust one another. In other families, siblings were in the hostile sides that fought against each other.

Secret Commander Third Thunderbolt instructed his three inferiors, the secret boss, Sauerin, of medication factory, the leader of the anti-defensive group at the Faculty of Social Sciences, and the leader of the anti-defensive group at the

Faculty of Natural Sciences, to coordinate in selecting two students for two different missions of the RL.

He said, "True, about 10 percent in manpower of our enemies' army and government are our infiltrators. In their ground troops, we've already a general. In their air forces, we've already a colonel. But in their navy, we've only noncommissioned officers, sergeants and lower ranks. It's nearly impossible they'll be promoted to be high officers and generals. Thus, among our anti-defensive groups, select at least one male student who'll enlist in the navy officer academy of our enemies in the next recruitment. On another issue, the issue of studying-abroad-student proselytizing, Fragrance is the country where the large number of students from Eastnama are. They've to be organized in more effective demonstrations against their own government. But our student infiltrators there haven't done their jobs of proselytizing well. Select at least two students and send them to Fragrance to strengthen our student infiltrators there. Sauerin, you'll finance for these two selected students."

After some days of pondering and exchanging opinions among Sauerin and the two leaders of the anti-defensive groups of the faculties, Cercis was selected to enroll in the navy officer academy, Muscaria and Cleome were selected to study abroad in Fragrance.

Since Cercis had passed the second year of physics at the Faculty of Sciences, the navy officer academy admitted him without necessary tests.

Muscaria and Cleome went to Fragrance to study as private students. Officially, the billionaire Cyclamen financed his son and his son's lover for their studies.

Worry and sadness came to numerous couples in this long and bloody war. Miltonia and Cercis had the same psychological situation. The navy officer academy was about four hundred miles far from their native city, so they had to live far away from each other.

In the night before the day they said good-bye, the heavy

rains and strong winds turned to torrent and storm. On the very day, the second day of August, though the torrent and storm weakened, the sky was still dark. Shrubs stooped down; their leaves were tangled. Trees lost a part of their branches that scattered everywhere on the ground. Several big trees were uprooted and fell down. Water puddles were at the two edges of streets. The sudden coldness and wetness caused misfortune to categories of animals living in nature; some dead birds lay on the grass.

Miltonia, Muscaria, and Cleome drove with Cercis to the inland airport to say good-bye to Cercis, who flew to the navy officer academy. The moment was full of emotion. Miltonia sobbed. The eyes of Muscaria and Cleome moistened. Though Cercis was an RL sympathizer, he felt unsafe in going to the war, so he confided with his love, Miltonia:

"I step into this dangerous and bloody war today. Sincerely I'm afraid of death since sudden deaths often come to young guys like me in the war. Next week, Cleome and Muscaria fly to Fragrance to study and execute the mission of student proselytizing. We don't know when they'll return. None of us know when we'll meet one another again. None of us know how our futures are. This war is the turbulent current of life. Like a piece of water ferns, each of us was drifted in the current. It is impossible to escape."

"We can't our own futures nor can we stand outside the war," interrupted Miltonia. "But don't talk about that any more. I'm afraid. Today, I say good-bye to you. Next week, I say good-bye to Muscaria and Cleome. Alas, it happens in my life, so many farewells, so many separations!"

Miltonia sobbed more bitterly; Muscaria shed tears. Cercis's and Cleome's eyes moistened. The good-bye was sad, like in a funeral.

Deaths from both belligerent sides were high. Although the deaths of the government side was one-tenth in comparison with the invading side, the total number reached about three hundred thousand after sixteen years of war, and disabled veterans were fivefold. The government needed new soldiers to fill the positions of the dead and the veterans. Therefore, the schedule of four years in the navy officer academy was shortened to two years.

Cercis graduated and got the second lieutenant rank in the navy. He was sent to take up his duty in the cruiser named *Sea Hunter* under a major commandant and five other navy officers. In the cruiser, he secretly worked with other three infiltrators including Gavit, who was in the low ranks at the cruiser but in the high ranks in the invader side. In other words, in the navy of the government, Cercis was a second lieutenant, and Gavit was a sergeant, but in the invaders' rank, Cercis was in a lower rank and was secretly commanded by Gavit.

In verses Cercis sent to Miltonia, his lover, it seemed that he changed his mind and knew he worked for the wrong side, which harmed their native country:

Circumstances of the Ocean

Ocean is usually gentle and calm,
Suave and beautiful,
Gives freshness and healthfulness,
Unfortunately, when there appear
Earthquakes or hurricanes,
Like monsters or devils,
They force the ocean become devastators and killers.

Miltonia also expressed the similar confusion about her anti-defensive activities as well as actions of those who worked for the RL in her replying letter:

Our people are gentle and good mannered,
Live in the prosperous and fertile land,
Protect and help mutually in compassion.
Suddenly, they sowed utopian promises
Wage the ferocious and bloodshed war,
Like monster and devils,
They force many of us become devastators
and killers.

However, both Cercis and Miltonia did not have the courage to turn to the right side because they knew they were secretly spied on by some secret infiltrators. In reality, Sergeant Gavit secretly reported the shaken opinions of Cercis and Miltonia to his superior Third Thunderbolt.

Cleome and Muscaria arrived in the airport of Fragrance's. They were greeted by a group of ten students studying abroad headed by Heperis, the leader of anti-defensive students. They reached their rented multi-room villa and had dinner. During the meal, Heperis stood up and said the following:

"Cleome and Muscaria, you're welcome to our group. You'll know every one of us by name in the next few days. As we know, our first duty is to attract and drag people, especially students, of all nationalities into anti-defensive demonstrations. Our compatriot students must be cores. All compatriot students must join to some extent in our actions. Many of them work to finance their studies. We'll give them money higher than their wages so they'll give up their jobs to join our actions. The embassy of Kanxono here hands us all the money we'll need.

If anyone doesn't join us, we'll secretly disturb them. We'll exchange opinions how to disturb in different concrete cases. Until now, our intellectual proselytizing has had successful results. At least two famous philosophers and several prestigious professors express anti-defensive opinions. Some high-ranking dignitaries of a religion joined our demonstrations. These have huge effects in the politics of the world.

"On the area of media, we don't need to proselytize but automatically receive huge successes because of two reasons:

"First, even though the atrocities of our side are much more severe than the ones of other side since our terrorizing actions lie in our policy to deter the people not to work for the other side and force people to work for us, but we do atrocities covertly and destroy traces. Photographers and reporters can't have proofs to illustrate that the atrocities are ours, so our several atrocities are depicted as the ones of the other side, and some cases are even in their national textbooks.

"Second, the medium of the world has professional and technical talents of selecting sensational news, scenes and stories that make their readers and watchers shocked and interested to buy their newspapers and magazines or watch their programs and films. Those are the points of their successes. Objectively, readers and watchers in the world are very interested and extremely shocked at atrocities done by the other side. Furthermore, their photographers or reporters may receive awards or prizes because they find out atrocities of the other side, not ours. Thus, they crave to find out the atrocities of the other side. These harm the other side very much."

Cleome and Muscaria tried to fulfill all assignments of the leaders. In every weekend, they organized anti-defensive demonstrations, press conferences, and workshops in the capital of Fragrance. They attained their purposes since many newspapers, televisions, and radios reported their activities.

Another matter, the Eastnama government, which had sent its own students to study abroad, was pitifully embarrassed because of the disloyalty of its own students. The movements of the anti-defensive rose in its own country and abroad made it puzzled. While fighters of invaders were drastically fighting until they would attain final victory, opinions of the world want to end the war; it meant that the defenders had to surrender.

Eastnama was attacked not only in battlefields but also from many other fronts such as sabotages and vandalism of infiltrators, anti-defensive movements in the world and in every Eastnama country. In addition, with the exhaustion of the people who endured the war too long with the deaths and disabilities of their family members, the army and the government of Eastnama became weak in the nineteenth year of the war. After some strategic mistakes of the highest commandant of the army, commanders of one-third of its forces stopped fighting. Some weeks later, the head government surrendered. Soldiers of all ranks were sad and disappointed. Many of them committed suicide. Many others fled overseas, especially the ones in the air force and navy because they had the means to flee. About a million people also fled with boats.

However, the cruiser *Sea Hunter* has a different fate. Sergeant Gavit, the higher-ranking infiltrator, commanded Lieutenant Cercis, the lower-ranking infiltrator, that when the officers met in the command room, he had to open the latch of the door and signal him and three other infiltrators to plunge into the room.

It happened like Gavit had planned. Four infiltrators with loaded weapons plunged into the room and forced the six officers to raise their hands and turn their faces to the wall. Instantly, the infiltrators shot the four officers but spared Cercis and the commander. The infiltrators forced the commander to give his order that the cruiser return to the sea base of Eastnama. The four dead bodies were thrown down to the ocean. At the sea base, four other battleships were in the same fate as the *Sea Hunter*. But all the defeated soldiers, including officers, were allowed to go home.

The invaders attained the final victory. They proclaimed through all means of medium that they were high-minded victors. They bestowed amnesties and clemencies on all officers and officials of the defeated army and surrendering government. However, all intellectuals, artists, and rich people as well as former officers and officials had to present themselves in facilities to study the victors' policies and projects to help the victors build paradises for both Eastnama and Kanxono.

Therefore, about one million of the categories presented themselves in the assigned facilities. Among them were tycoon Cyclamen as a rich man and Professor Miscanthus as an intellectual. Also, Second Lieutenant Cercis had to present himself. The victors were all deceivers. At night, the victors secretly transported the deceived to different slave camps in jungles scattered in two countries of Eastnama and Kanxono. Professor Miscanthus, Cyclamen, and Second Lieutenant Cercis were among them. They were transported to three different camps.

Miltonia lived suffering with two burdens and duties for two slaves in the camps: her father, Mr. Miscanthus, and her lover, Cercis. Their works of the past for the RL meant nothing after the victory. Like other young women in the defeated side, she was also a sexual target of two victors: the controlling policeman of her interblocks and the vice chief of her local quarter. The two caddish guys used different tactics: crass flirtation, promising help, and harassing intimidation.

Since Professor Miscanthus had anti-defensive and pro-RL records in his former lectures, he was released from the labor camp in the second year. He applied to return to his former career as professor of civilization at the Faculty of Social Sciences. But the victors required him to study their politics in six months and pledge to teach their political viewpoints and outlooks. The professor consented to study and pledge.

Nonetheless, in the second month of his teaching, he decided to speak out his resentments before his students:

"My dear students, what I said in the last month are lies. In this society, everyone must lie before other people to avoid trouble, to have a job, to be promoted, and so on. But all the things I say now are true.

"As you know, before the victory, 90 percent of the people lived in adequacy in Eastnama, and some 12 percent lived in richness. There was everything in the free markets.

"After the victory, this country has had two abundances: the pictures of the emperor smiling at everybody and slogans extolling the victors. They are hung everywhere, at all vestibules and in all rooms of public buildings, at all the parks, corners of the streets, in all private houses. Contrarily, the confiscation of farms, paddies, factories, and so on make all other things be in severe shortages. They are sold based on stamps in public shops but only for formality's sake.

"Why does the emperor smile? Does he smile because 50 percent of the people find themselves in dire need of food and clothes? Does he smile because the other 40 percent of the people live in poverty? Does he smile because we, the instructors or professors, measure and weigh carefully two yards of cloth, some pounds of potatoes, a pint of sauce to ration impartially?

"Why does the emperor smile? Does he smile because children and women become smugglers everywhere in the country? What do they smuggle? One smuggles a pound of meat, the other a kilogram of sugar, the other a dozen pounds of raw rice, and so on.

"Why does the emperor smile? Does he smile because his network of policemen are intertwined everywhere in the country? They not only arrest non-subjugated but also take smuggled goods, like a pound of meat, a kilogram of sugar, regardless of the bitter sobs of the smugglers who are scrawny children or gaunt women.

"Why does the emperor smile? Does he smile because his deceitful, sly, and cunning strategies helped his followers become the victors, who now have absolute power and authority, who live off the sufferings of the majority of the people and take the properties and belongings of the defeated?

"Why does the emperor smile? Does he smile because his above strategies still bring great success to his followers after the war? For example, a million intellectuals, artists, rich people as well as former officials and officers obediently present themselves to enter the slave camps.

"Why does the emperor smile? Does he smile because the victors harass the wives and the children of the slaves as well as destroy the fidelity of many wives?

"Now I tell you another issue. I was laboring twenty-three months in two different camps. I dare to say they're slave camps in which the victors have killed talents absurdly and barbarously. I've lots of things to tell you.

"After I had heard on the radio the announcement that the victors need help of all intellectuals, artists, rich people as well as former officers and officials of the former army and government to build a far better society. All these categories had to present themselves to study the victor's projects and policies. They all had to bring the course fee of four hundred Eastnama dollars for one month. Thus, a million men of the categories who presented themselves thought that they had to study the victors' projects and policies in one month.

"I presented myself one early morning at the facility that the victors decided for intellectuals. There I met all sorts of intellectuals: scientists, professors, doctors, architects, lawyers, engineers, and the like. We had to stand or sit on the two lines along the street and wait for our turn to register and pay the fee to the victors. Several of us even worried whether they were accepted to study. I had to wait until 2:15 p.m. for my turn. It was one of many greatly successful and skillful deceptions of the victors. Like other categories, intellectuals were enthusiastic in registering and paying to enter slave camps.

"How could the incident be explained? Either the victors were skillful and clever, or we were silly and stupid—or both. Was there any other explanation?

"The slaves have been ill-treated both mentally and physically.

"Slaves have been insulted and taught utopian or propagandist dogmas by the rulers who had committed them to memory because most of them had just either eradicated illiteracy or finished elementary schools. Slaves have had to write down again and again enough wrongs to deserve to be slaves though many wrongs they had not done. They have had to tell stories of all members of their great families of father's and mother's sides of five generations though many details they haven't known. They have had to spy on one another and report any suspected or counter-revolutionary words and activities.

"Physically, there have been only two kinds work for the slaves: primitive agriculture and tree-hewing with rudimentary tools. In the history of human beings, it is the first time it has happened that slaves have had to labor in hunger. Their families have had to send food, clothes, medication with the hope they would survive. But their families have lived in poverty or destitution, so their help has been limited, and about 10 percent of slaves have died in undeserved misfortunes each year.

"Laboring in hunger has been the most terrible and drawn-out misery of the slaves. I tell you some examples from many horrors I witnessed in the camps. The first case, while pulling up earthnuts in the harvest, a laborer, Engineer Khoso, quickly put several tubers into his pocket. Unfortunately, the warden nearby caught him, ran toward him, and beat him with a rifle butt. The laborer died in the field half an hour later. The second case, while walking along the maize field, at the turn, a laborer, songwriter Binan, quickly broke a bulk. Unfortunately, the warden at the end of the line caught and shot him. He died some minutes later. The third case, while slaves were watching a propagandist film in the front yard of the row of shanties on a Saturday evening, a laborer, former sculptor Matmang, sneaked into the kitchen and stole a boiled egg. Unfortunately, a warden caught and shouted loudly. Four other wardens ran, surrounded him, and beat him from all corners. Since he was scrawny, he fell from one warden to another like a volleyball. After the beating, two other inmates carried him to his plywood sleeping panel, but he died that night.

"Being beaten and shackled in isolated cells or conexes (empty metal cartridge trunks), which made slaves die, were not rare in the camps, it happened often to the slaves with mental disorders. Laboring in the mentally and physically miserable conditions as well as knowing the complicated misfortunes of their families outside, many slaves had mental disorders. But the wardens judged that the those slaves faked madness. They beat and shackled them from one foot to two feet and two hands in isolated cells in several days, weeks, or months based on what those slaves had raved about, especially words or activities though absurd but touching their emperor of Kanxono, their RL clique, or their authorities. Most of those slaves died in the cells.

"Another issue I tell you is the studying policies in universities. My colleagues from Kanxono praise the rejecting policy toward children of former officials and officers to universities. In my opinion, the victors either fear that their children from their country Kanxono cannot compete against young generations of this country, Eastnama, or they expect their children will continue their dictatorial and despotic regime. Thus, they implement their injustice and discriminating policies.

"Several of my colleagues have confided to me the same mental affliction that I have endured. Present judges, directors, or chairmen have come to our house and said that they registered to attend our subjects in universities. But they will have no time to attend classes. Thus, in the next two, three, or four years, we must write doctorates for these guys to get a masters or PhD diplomas, and we'll be rewarded. If we don't finish what they command, we'll be punished.

"We inquired and know the truth: Even though they were appointed and are present judges, directors, or chairmen, they finished only from the eight to tenth grades, so they are lacking indispensable diplomas, and they want to have them in the next two, three, or four years."

Then it was time for the break. When Mr. Miscanthus was going to leave the classroom, a student came near him and said in a low voice, "Professor, I came here from Kanxono, the country of the invaders. Based on the stories of my parents and my own experiences, I think what you have just told the students are true. But no one gets anything from your speech. It will harm you and your family for sure. Even though the people of Kanxono have been angry under the sophisticated and mean-minded cruelty and despotism for many decades, they haven't been able to do anything successful against the dictators. It has been dangerous to trust anybody since a denouncer could be one's nearest neighbor, best friend, gullible child, or infidel spouse. Therefore, the majority of people in Kanxono have lived in subjugated situations to survive. The minority worked in submitted situations to get some low positions with privileges. Some sly individuals have attained high positions. They have been cruel but dull-witted and loyal to the dictator clique that have usually admitted them to be in police forces in low ranks or wardens, as you have witnessed.

"Professor, if there were no 10 percent of Eastnamans who worked as infiltrators for the invaders, this country wouldn't have lost the war. Why did you have anti-defensive and pro-RL opinions in many years during the war and now you speak out the miserable truth?"

"I've just said, either the invaders were skillful and clever, or I was silly and stupid, or both. I thank you for what you've just said. Oh, I have a break now."

Professor Miscanthus left the classroom for the break. However, never did he come back. Some students murmured to one another that they saw him being arrested a couple of minutes later.

Mrs. Miscanthus and Miltonia heard the news that Mr.

Miscanthus had been arrested from a student some hours later.

In the next several months, the wife and the daughter went to many police offices to ask for information about him. One police officer answered that he had to be reeducated in an unrevealed place for a long period. But some neighbors whispered that he had been killed and either buried in a jungle or put into a jute bag with a brick and was thrown down a river. But the two women believed that he still lived and was incarcerated somewhere.

After the victory, the RL guys were very clumsy in economy. Nearly all factories came to a standstill, so did the pharmaceutical factory of Mr. Cyclamen. Thus, Mr. Cyclamen was released from the camp after three months to manage the factory. Although it was active again, the quality and quantity of the products were much lower than the ones in the days before the victory. Mr. Cyclamen earned the salary as a lowest worker.

Then the Beat the Exploiters Campaign was mobilized in the thirtieth month after the victory. The victims were those who had owned valuable things before the victory, such as factories, plantations, businesses, and shops including very small ones, though all of them had already been confiscated, as well as those who had villas or large houses as well as those who were suspected of stashing gold, diamonds, and so on.

In one night, dwellings and real estates of victims were suddenly occupied by groups of several guys; some of them were armed. They rummaged, listed belongings, and evaluated values. Simultaneously, from all means of medium, the victors condemned the victims as vampires who had drawn the blood of people. Then the dwellings and real estates of the victims were confiscated to be either public offices or bestowed to members of RL guys.

The villa of the Cyclamen had the same ill fate. At 3:00

a.m., a group of ten young guys, two among them armed, rummaged everywhere inside and around the villa. They climbed on the roof, dug the tiles, foraged wardrobes, clothes, TV sets, radio sets, pans, bowls, cases, boxes, bags, pots, picture frames, the dryer, cabinet, cupboard, and so on. They also searched thoroughly the bodies of Mr. and Mrs. Cyclamen.

Late in the evening, after several minutes of reading the whole list of inventory, the head of the group spoke out his verdict to Mr. Cyclamen:

"This villa and all the things here are confiscated because you exploited labor of other workers. Since you are still working for the pharmaceutical factory of the liberators, you and your wife may live in the cabin at the corner of the backyard there. We're fair because the majority of workers in this country have similar housing like this cabin. You've two hours to move your living necessities there."

All throughout the day, Mr. and Mrs. Cyclamen were sorrowful and anxious. They did not eat and drink anything. But he spoke out his resentment after hearing the verdict:

"We had donated our properties and talents to support you for seven years during the war. We have continued to serve you until today, but you are ungrateful blackguards. Our son Cercis had worked for you as an infiltrator in the former navy for three years, but you forced him to labor in camps. You're ungrateful and inhuman. All of you are wicked bastards, cruel scoundrels."

Mrs. Cyclamen quickly used her hand to cover her husband's mouth. She could not speak a word but sobbed bitterly.

The head of the group spoke:

"These are not your property. They belong to all people. You used your talents to exploit the labor of workers. Your son Cercis has an unstable and imprecise standpoint. He has to labor to stabilize his mind. Now, do you want us to move your living necessities to the cabin, or do you want us to send you back to the camp?"

Within two hours, the desperate husband and wife moved some of their clothes, some towels, pans, bowls, dishes, a raw rice pot, a table, a bed, a nightstand, a blanket, some cover sheets, some photos of their family, and several other sundries.

The victors continued to pour misfortunes on the Cyclamens. Ten days later, the high-ranking family of the victors moved into the villa. All the four members of the family tried to annoy the Cyclamens. The members did not want the presence of the Cyclamens at the backyard.

The Cyclamens dragged their lives in physical and mental sufferings. One of them was that they could not buy means for trips to visit and bring necessities to his son Cercis in labor camps. They had entreated help from Miltonia, his lover.

In many days, Mr. and Mrs. Cyclamen exchanged views on how to escape the miseries. They finally agreed with each other that the best solution was to go abroad. They hoped that their son Cleome in Fragrance could file immigrant visas for them.

However, they knew that the dictators had already built intertwined information systems to check words and activities of who the dictators did not trust. To meet or call any foreigners was totally prohibited. Contact with any Eastnaman living outside the country by mail was surely examined. If they described the truth of being miserably ill-treated, the victors would judge that they had indignant resentment, and the punishments would be more severe. In addition, their applications for immigration or visas of exit would be difficult, if not impossible. According to the experiences of many people, even dishonest praises for the victors had some positive effects, similar to good credits in applying for something in the future. Thus, they wrote a mild letter to their son in Fragrance:

Dear Cleome,

We congratulate you and your brother, Cercis, since both of you worked for the side of the victors. We proudly congratulate ourselves since we supported the same side.

Since you decided to stay in Fragrance and your brother, Cercis, is studying in the camp, a necessary step to stabilize his viewpoint, the villa has become too large for us. Thus, we let the high-rank family of the city live in our villa, and we moved to the cabin at the corner of the backyard.

Dear Cleome, both of us are in the late fifties, but we haven't lived in any foreign country for a day. Our final aspiration is to live in Fragrance for several years because both of us have friends in the country. Please, Cleome, file visas for us. We hope that our aspiration will be fulfilled soon.

Love,
Your parents

Dear Father and Mother,

Congratulations on your important support for the victors in many years during the war. In reality, all the members of our family are among the victors. We are joyful because we attained success, and our dangers are over.

Dear Father and Mother, your support in the past and the victory today can be compared to your planting fruit trees in an orchard and caring for them for several years. Now the trees have reached your goal, and you are enjoying their fruits, shades, and other benefits. Furthermore, no other country is as beautiful as ours. Therefore, dear Father and Mother, stay in our country and continue to enjoy the success you built from your hard work.

I haven't returned to our country because I love Muscaria, as you know. She does not want to return to our country, but I am persuading her. When she agrees, I will inform you.

Respectfully,
Your son Cleome

PS: I hope we will organize our wedding in Eastnama in the very city I was born.

"Lives under these rulers are absolutely complicated," said Mr. Cyclamen sadly to his wife after reading their son's letter. "Not only media and communications extol the rulers but also private conversations and letters. Though people endure numerous sufferings and miseries, they only dare to mention it indirectly, similar to secret codes. Hearers or readers should decipher to understand. Sorry for us, our Cleome in Fragrance does not understand our miserable and resentful situations."

"Only the people who have lived under these rulers realize secret codes and try to decipher," said Mrs. Cyclamen. "Outsiders, even our son, understand only simple meanings."

"Can we directly describe to him the victors are sly dictators, they act like plunderers, our properties were appropriated brazenly, we and the majority of our people are living in misery, his brother is among one million of former officers, and officials, intellectuals, artists, and rich people are laboring as slaves in the worst conditions. If…"

"I know what you want to say more. If he returns, he can be either be a slave like his brother or a plunderer who takes a house of another family. We don't want both cases, but we may not describe clearly. It's dangerous for all of us. We'll try to find another way, to flee for example."

Cleome and Muscaria had struggled enthusiastically for the RL in the capital of Fragrance from their arrival to the eleventh month after the surrender of the Eastnaman government and the disintegration of its army. Although their studies in universities had been distracted by their political activities, both of them had graduated: Cleome as an electric engineer and Muscaria as a bank accountant. They did not return to their native country but stayed in Fragrance and got jobs in the capital. Cleome worked in an electricity company, and Muscaria worked in an international bank.

After several months under the rule of the victors, Eastnaman living abroad were informed by two opposite kinds of news about circumstances of the great majority of the people in their native country.

News on radios broadcasted from their country and information distributed from embassies and consulates gave euphoric images and descriptions. The great majority of their people lived in happiness and comfort.

Quite oppositely, stories and photographs of fleers from their country described agonized and desperate lives of slaves in camps as well as destitute and imprisoned lives of people in their country.

Cleome believed the first kind of news. He thought that his parents were rewarded by the victors because of their support during the war and that his brother, Cercis, was studying the victors' policies in a center and would be put in an important position later because of his record of working as an infiltrator in the former navy.

Contrarily, Muscaria believed the second kind of news. She knew that his father was laboring in the camp like a slave, that her mother and sister, Miltonia, were living in destitution, especially since one refugee, Miltonia's former classmate, had met her and told the detailed miserable situations of her father, mother, and sister.

After vehement discussions, quarrels, and wrangles on their different perceptions about what was really happening in their country, Cleome and Muscaria separated, and never did they meet each other again.

Then the bank that Muscaria was working for transferred her to Unto Blumen, where the majority of her compatriots resettled after their native country had lost the war.

In Unto Blumen, Muscaria met several former classmates. Among them was Salix, a young male student who was studying the last year for his MD degree. They loved each other and married a year later.

Disappointed with Cleome, Mr. and Mrs. Cyclamen sought another way to flee. After a month of pondering, Mr. Cyclamen said to his wife, "I remember Miltonia mentioned to me on one occasion something about fleeing this country. The majority of the people in this country want to flee after several months of tasting the despotic rule of the victors."

"I also remember that occasion. We'll change views with her. God bless her. She loves Cercis. She is arduously grueling because of love."

"Two decades of war engendered millions of miseries, losses, and destructions to five generations of the people in this country. People wanted to end the war, but the victors have created more miseries for the majority of the people.

"These are the intentions of the victors to make people either submitted or subjugated and be their obeisant servants in various ways to attain their ambitious goals."

Before as well as after Mr. and Mrs. Cyclamen moved to the cabin, Miltonia often visited them on weekends, sometimes together with her mother, to share their miseries with one another. The Cyclamens told her about their asking Cleome to file visas for them and told her about his misunderstandings and refusals. Then they asked her whether she knew any ways to flee the country.

"The majority of the people of the country hate these dictators and want to leave this country for any country having freedom," she said. "But they have no chance, so they either submitted or subjugated.

"Furthermore, when the dictators know anyone who wants to leave, the dictators consider them as traitors and push them down to the bottom of this society. But there are still several millions of people who still stash gold and decide to risk it. Unfortunately, tricksters emerge everywhere, and their tricks are diversified. The deceived do not denounce to the authorities because both tricksters and the deceived would be put in jails."

"Can you tell us some legal and illegal ways of leaving this country and several tricks of tricksters in each way?"

"As you know, only those who have relatives in foreign countries have chances to leave legally if their relatives file and get visas for them. However, tricksters say that they have acquaintanceships with officials in some embassies. The foreign officials would issue visas if they were paid amounts of gold. Those deceived hand gold to tricksters and wait, but never do they get visas.

"Another trick is fabricated exoduses to some large countries in the free world. It is presumed that this trick originated from someone in the authorities because many of the deceived hand gold and applications altogether at some villas in large cities. For sure, authorities know these deeds, but this is one of their ways to get gold."

"We know about fabricated exoduses. We and our close married friends discussed about those exoduses three times last month. They're among the deceived."

"One illegal way is to pay guides who lead you on roads, rails, and jungles through the neighboring country to the next free country. It's extremely dangerous, and chances of success are one in ten. Most guides abandon risk-attempters somewhere on their way when they meet any danger. About half of risk-attempters are arrested on their way, transported back, and put in jails.

"Some details I am going to tell you are from the murmurings among my friends: On this way, risk-attempters must cross borders and sneak through a multi-sector country before reaching a free country. But there have been different sectors of belligerent militia groups. Attempters have been robbed and beaten cruelly again and again. Females from teenage to seventy have been raped and maltreated in their sex organs by the whole militia groups again and again in every sector. Those militia groups have been more fiendish than ferocious animals. They have raped before others including the victims' children, husbands, and brothers. They have bound the male members of victims and forced them to look at the painful humiliations. They have beaten and shot any male members who have had any acts of protest. The more agonizing the raped have groaned, the more severely they were maltreated. Pretty females have been forced to stay in their sectors and continue to be their sex slaves.

"In other parts, risk-attempters have died because of land mines, snakes, thirst, hunger, or being shot by militia groups intentionally or unintentionally."

"Oh my god, we won't attempt those ways. Death, we can accept, but being raped in painful humiliation, we cannot bear. However, how about fleeing by boat? So many people have murmured about the way. Lots of families have left their house secretly, and armed guys have occupied their houses on the very next days."

"Yes, another way of fleeing is crossing the sea on boats, not ships, to some neighboring countries, but the percentage of success is not higher than fleeing on roads, though the costs are higher. A half of failures have happened because of being disclosed in one of many processes. The other half of failures have happened because of falling into traps of swindlers who have deceived in two sorts: non-relationship with authorities and relations to the authorities. I can only mention some of the numerous manners."

"I mentioned some deceiving cases of non-relationships with authorities: Swindlers have collected gold and say they would buy boats, but they haven't. other swindlers have pointed at any boats on rivers to any members of deceived families and have said they have been ready to flee. They have collected gold, and made appointments for fleeing moments, but the boats do not belong to them. Other swindlers have owned boats, but the boats have disappeared before the appointment moments.

"I tell you some deceiving cases having relations to the authorities: Local authorities on coastal regions have collected gold, bought boats, and arranged all processes for the risk-attempters, but they've put delayed-action bombs camouflaged somewhere in boats before the starting moments. On the open sea, the bombs have exploded, 99 percent attempters have been drown within several minutes. Only 1 percent have held on floating pieces, and waves have pushed some victims onto beaches. Other authorities have received briberies and promised that the authorities were not to be in the agreed places where fleers have embarked and moments boats started, but they haven't kept the promises, or they have informed coastal patrollers who have robbed and shot boats sinking or dragged boats back to seaside and arrested. Furthermore, there have ships and boats of pirates in the open seas."

"All the ways are hard and dangerous. But we cannot endure the yokes of these dictators. Death is better than life. Let's try to find a boat owner who is preparing to flee."

Contacts to find means to flee were risky. If a contact was disclosed, both sides were arrested and sent to labor camps. However, within two months, Miltonia contacted a trustable boat owner who was preparing for his whole family to flee. She told Mr. and Mrs. Cyclamen:

"People have fled across the sea for three years, so boats have become rarer and rarer. Experts who have some knowledge to steer boats across the sea become scarce. The boat owner told me he intends to steer his boat but has only some experience on rivers and no knowledge about the sea. If Cercis steers his boat, Cercis and his four companions will not pay anything for the journey. This offer is a chance for you, my mother, and me to flee."

"But how about your father, Professor Misanthus? Do you've any information about him?" Mr. Cyclamen asked.

"We asked so many police departments. They only spoke in tortuous words. They had probably killed and buried him somewhere. It's their common way to terminate seeds of oppositions. My mother and I abhor these authorities and want to flee also. But the great difficulty is how to help Cercis escape from the camp and how to lead him to the appointed place at the moment of embarkation."

"All organs of these authorities are full of corruption. Of course they receive bribes in secret conditions," said Mr. Cyclamen to his wife and Miltonia. "You can disguise yourself as a peasant and pretend to work near the camp to observe and deal with a warden who takes bribes and pretends in some way to let Cercis escape. Of course, all processes are dangerous. Cercis has to disguise himself as a peasant or an employee, so he needs clothes and a forged ID."

"The owner knows a source that makes forged IDs and other papers. Clothes for Cercis, I can prepare. If he comes some days earlier, he can hide in the boat."

"I know one special case. The family of a laborer openly petitioned and secretly bribed for his homecoming to join the services in the funeral of his deceased father. The petition was accepted, and he was at home in two days."

"Don't think like a muddledheaded person, honey."

Mrs. Cyclamen said, "For these contacts and preparations, women are less observed than men. Stay home and make your spirit ready to flee."

After a week, the boat owner told Miltonia the appointments of the embarkation place and departure moment of the fleeing, an evening of a middle day of June. There was one month to prepare. But the escape of Cercis seemed to be not succeeded before the appointments. Suddenly, in the early morning before six days of the appointments, Mr. Cyclamen lay dead in bed. In his sorrowful farewell letter, there were some portions:

"I take twenty-three tablets of —— to leave this world. I ask everybody to respect my peaceful departure.

"For five years in the war, my whole family, I, my wife, my sons, Cercis and Cleome, had supported and worked for the RL to gain their goals. After victory, we have still worked for the victors. Unfortunately, Cercis is still in the camp because of misunderstanding.

"My single petition to the authorities is to let my son Cercis come home to join all services of my funeral in three days.

"To my dearest lovers, I leave this world peacefully to the world without hostilities, competitions, and feuds, so don't lament, bewail, or grieve."

However, Mrs. Cyclamen groaned and was in tears. Miltonia and her mother, Mrs. Miscanthus, sobbed sadly.

Four guys of local authorities came and inquired the death of Mr. Cyclamen. They read the farewell letter. As the tradition of this country, dead bodies stay in their homes, and their funerals start from their homes. On this occasion, the three women entreated the inquirers two favors: to write a recommendation for them to apply a petition to the labor camp for Cercis to come home as the wish of the deceased and give permission to Miltonia and her mother to stay a week with the widow. With a small bribery to each inquirer, the women got the two favors.

On the next day, Miltonia and her mother began to prepare the funeral to help Mrs. Cyclamen. Mrs. Cyclamen boarded the bus to the city near the camp where Cercis was laboring. After six more hours in an ox cart through the jungle, she reached the cottage of the camp rulers at five o'clock in the evening. At that moment, only the director of the camp was there. After some words of greeting, she handed her petition and bribery. The director quickly inspected the bribery. An aspect of satisfaction appeared on his face, then he read the letter of recommendation.

"Your petition is approved." said the director. "Cercis will have three days off at home for his father's funeral. I write permission for him right now and send a warden to call him to come here. But going through the jungle is always dangerous in late evenings. Here are two hammocks at the two corners. Both of you can sleep here and leave at any time tomorrow."

"We thank for your generosity and solicitude. As you advice, I and my son sleep on the two hammocks, and we'll leave early tomorrow morning."

In the very evening after the funeral, Miltonia, Mrs. Miscanthus, Cercis, and Mrs. Cyclamen entered the boat safely at 11:00 p.m. Together with other fleers, they hid under bundles of firewood.

"There are already fifty-six fleers in the boats," said the wife of the boat owner. "We wait for other twenty fleers, and we'll depart at three early morning."

"It's already tightly packed," said one woman. "Are there still other twenty? Why do you do this?"

"So many friends and relatives entreated us. It's so difficult to refuse. If there's freedom to leave, 80 percent or more people will go, even many men and women worked for them in the war."

"Them, them, them deceived so sophisticatedly."

Another woman said, "Only after the war, people know who they are, how they are. Now, let's have pity on one another."

"It's easy to be disclosed if a small child cries. Here are soporific tablets. Please, parents, make every small child take one."

Adults were worrying. Another family of four members embarked at two o'clock at the night. Suddenly, the boat owner entered with scariness on his face at two o'clock.

"My son has just been arrested by a group of local armed guys at the place about two miles far from here. We must depart immediately. All of you squat or lie down. Everyone must be silent. Where're you, Cercis? Yea, yea, you're here. I steer about two hours to the open sea. Then you steer. We substitute for each other."

Immediately, the boat quickly left the river-watering place. It skimmed over the rolling waves. Except for the boat owner and Cercis, fleers felt nausea. After about half an hour, several vomited. After two hours, more fleers vomited. Stinky sputum and phlegm puddles spread on their clothes and bodies. They lacked fresh air though they were in an open gulf. They were seasick. Some asked the boat owner if they could climb on the deck but were refused.

"Still in the area of coastal patrollers. They can surely realize fleers through binoculars. Try another two hours. Cercis, steer for me."

Cercis corrected the direction. He checked the compass in every few minutes. After two other hours, he shouted, "We're beginning to enter international territorial waters." Several men shouted for joy and climbed up to the deck. The boat owner told them to throw the bundles of firewood onto the sea. The sunlight on the sea was not as dazzling as the one on the land.

Many fleers asked for water; several asked for food. But the owner told his two assigned men to deliver very limited.

He commanded loudly, "This journey has to last at least six days. Be thrifty. If we aren't, many of us will die of thirst or hunger. You're the men of discipline. Be tough. Everybody will benefit from your toughness. Do all of you hear me?"

Only the two men said yes. Others agreed but were too tired and seasick to say anything. The majority of them lay in the hold of the boat.

The dusk brought bitter coldness to the open sea. All

fleers withdrew into the hold except the two steering men, who were on the stern of the boat. They exchanged shifts to steer and sleep, talked to each other on the direction, and mediated how to reach the country they intended to land.

The sun emerged. The fleers left their country longer than one day. Suddenly, a woman in the hold sobbed loudly. Her four-year-old daughter had died sometime in the night. Her four-year-old son cried thereafter. Everybody felt sad. There were murmuring prayers. An hour later, the father wrapped his dead daughter in a towel, climbed on the stern, and threw her to the sea.

Unfortunately, more and more miseries happened. In the second night, four other children died. Many mothers entreated to increase rationed water to their children. The two assigned men consented. But children continued to die.

On the fourth day, there was no water left. Some men soaked their bodies in seawater, their hands held firmly on the side of the boat. One man cut the artery at his wrist and put the wound onto the mouth of his small child who sucked his blood. Some bewailed. Others prayed. Others lay motionlessly, shut their eyes, and waited for death. Others prayed for their lives after death in another world.

At noon of the sixth day, on and in the boat, there were still twenty-five males from fourteen to sixty years old, eleven females from thirteen to sixty years old, and eight children under nine years old. But they all were tired or exhausted because of thirstiness, hunger, and seasickness.

Suddenly a point appeared at the horizon on the sea. It became larger and larger. It could be a ship. The appearance of the presumed ship engendered some hope of being rescued in the minds and hearts of most fleers. Most of them stared at the direction of the point in silence.

"It can be a boat like ours," Cercis conjectured. "Or it's a small ship of pirates." His statement not only terminated the hope but also caused scariness.

The ship came nearer and nearer. Catastrophically, the

worse misery was coming. It was the ship of pirates.

These pirates were the savage sea devils! Bared trunks, painted bodies, axes in hands, the pirates yelled barbarously and sprang onto the boat and attacked the men, who fought back weakly and hopelessly with wood slats or iron tools. The females and children were too weak and scared to react. The pirates beat and slashed the heads of some males. Blood and brain spread on many places. The pirates kicked some among twenty-five half-dead males down to the sea.

Thereafter the ten pirates raped the ten females except the oldest. Several pirates continued to rape the second victims the second time. The females groaned pitifully especially the ones who suffered the humiliation the second time. Then the pirates rummaged everywhere to rob gold, diamonds, and valuable objects. Then pirates forced four pretty females to bring their bags of clothes and step onto their ship. The pirates dismantled the motor of the boat and threw it to the sea. One pirate called another ship of other pirates through his electronic equipment. These pirates left the boat.

About two hours later, the other ship of the other ten pirates came. These pirates were the same devilish type. The pirates yelled and laughed savagely and sprang onto the boat. There were seven women and seven children on the boat. Five men lay half-dead. The pirates ignored the children. All the pirates raped.

Some of them repeat the crimes, so several women suffered the humiliation two, three, or four times. Then the pirates forced three young women including Miltonia to bring their bags of clothes and step onto their ship. The pirates steered their ship a dozen of yards far away from the boat, then the pirates steered the bow of their ship to hurtle speedily and straightly toward the boat. The boat broke into parts. Some victims fell onto the sea. Others held firmly on some planks. Then pirates steered away.

Miltonia and two other female victims were shipped to an isolated and wild islet in the open sea. Two pirates led them into the islet. The track was between lots of half-green dried shrubs and under a few canopies of almond trees. After walking about two hundred yards far from the coast, they saw a shanty under the canopy of the lush almond tree. Two lines of perennial citronella and cockscomb plants surrounded the shanty. The two pirates stood before the front door and bowled them to enter the shanty. The victims hesitated in some seconds, then they pushed the front door and stepped in. The two pirates turned back to their ship.

At the sight, Miltonia and two female victims saw four pretty women sitting on several pieces of tarpaulins spread on the very thick layer of dried grass and leaves held inside the rectangular log frame. Behind the large frame, there was the narrow one for some bags of clothes on the left, a jute bag of raw rice, a pot of cooked rice, several bowls, and spoons on the right. At the left corner, there were a jar of water and some mugs.

"Oh no, three new victims," one woman sitting in the middle said. "We're in one miserable situation. Let's behave ourselves as sisters. Put your bags there. What are your names?"

"Miltonia."

"Stipa."

"Lonicera."

"Sorry, you're probably hungry, thirsty, and tired. Here are cooked rice and salty fish. Sorry, we've no boiled plants today. Here is the bucket of water. Eat and drink something. We'll tell you lots of things, but not now. If I'm not confused, today is Friday. There are still four days before we endure the humiliation again. Ah, all of us eat dinner now."

Miltonia asked after the dinner, "Where is the toilet?"

"Look at the back door at the left corner, open that door, and you'll see the open-air commode. Look at the other back door at the right corner, the small puddle for our drinking water and all sorts of washes."

Miltonia, Stipa, and Lonicera ate and drank a little bit. Then they went outside to the commode, walked to the puddle of water, turned round to the front of the shanty, stared at the twenty-six mounds of earth, and thought that the mounds should be the twenty-six tumuli of twenty-six victims like them. Then they opened the front door to step in. All four women urged them to lie down. They told them to try to sleep.

"All of us try to sleep," the same woman said. "If any one of us utters inarticulate sounds in her sleep, any other one who doesn't sleep at the moment has to wake the dreamer up. Experience tells us that most of our dreams are nightmares."

However, Miltonia could not sleep. The fearful images on the boat replayed in her mind. Her eyes were soaked with tears. Stipa, lying next to her, uttered something. She shook her co victim up. The similar situation happened to other pair of her co victims. A pair of hours after, she was half-asleep until the next morning.

The sun set. They got up and took boiled rice and water again for breakfast. The same woman told Miltonia, Stipa, and Lonicera, "My name is Rosma. I'm thirty-seven years old, the oldest victim among us. If I'm not confused, the pirates have incarcerated me in this islet for two and a half months. Abrieta is sitting in front of you. She has been here for seven weeks. Primula and Weigela have been here for thirty-three days."

"Why haven't you collected a small stack of dried branches and grasses and set fire to signal to any ship on the sea to rescue you?" Miltonia asked.

"We've thought about that. But in reality, very rarely a passerby ship has been on this bay. Furthermore, the pirates warned us that if they discovered any trace of such thing, they would beat us to death. But we've prepared. Dried twigs and grasses have been behind several shrubs. Whenever we see a ship, we collect and set fire within a few seconds. To be rescued is the single reason we haven't committed suicide."

"Are the twenty-six mounds in front of the shanty the twenty tumuli of the victims like us?"

"The answer must be yes. When Genista, Hosta, and I were forced to arrive in this shanty, twenty-one mounds have already been there. The twenty-second and the twenty-third are the tumuli of Genista and Hosta. The twenty-fourth and twenty-fifth are the tumuli of Betula and Thuja. They came here on the same day with Abrieta. The twenty-sixth is the tumulus of Deuzia. She arrived in this shanty on the same day with Primula and Weigela."

"You don't know the twenty-one victims who had died before you came here, but tell us, what made Genista, Hosta, Betula, Thuja, and Deuzia die?"

"Different causes. Genista and Hosta died after we had come here seven days. I think, what happened on our boat were similar to yours. Then pirates shipped us to this shanty and left this islet. Each day, we stood in front of the shanty several hours and looked toward the sea. On the seventh day, they returned. When we saw their ship, we ran for away from this shanty and hid in shrubs. After some hours of searching, they set fire to lots of shrubs. We couldn't bear the scorching hotness, so we ran out. They dragged us to this shanty. I conjectured one of them their boss and pretended to like him, so I was raped by him only. But both Genista and Hosta were raped by some of them.

"Then the pirates boozed brandies and talked smutty words. I shut my eyes and faked to be asleep. After two hours, the pirates stared at us and realized Genista and Hosta lay dead. Blood ran out from their mouths. Our two co victims had bitten their tongues to commit suicide."

"It is a way Genista and Hosta chose to escape this misery. How are the case of Betula and Thuja?"

"We don't know all the animals in this islet. We've seen several different kinds of birds including albatrosses and seagulls. They're good-natured animals. But there're also dangerous animals, especially snakes. We've seen cobra, rattlesnakes, copperheads, and black-and-white-ringed kraits.

"Whenever we remember the night, we still feel the

fright. Two cobras slithered inside this log frame and attacked us. The cobras bit Betula and Thuja. We dismantled some logs and drove the cobras slithering away. Sorrowfully, for Betula and Thuja, they were dying before our eyes, but we couldn't do anything to save their lives.

"The pirates came on the next day, one of their seventh days, to fulfill their sexual desires. Then I asked them to bring perennial citronella and cockscomb plants here. You do see the two lines of the plants surrounding the shanty. Snakes are afraid and shun away from both perennial citronella and cockscomb plants."

"I didn't know that snakes are frightened of perennial citronella and cockscomb plants. But how about Deuzia's death?"

"As you know, the pirates have incarcerated us here and given us only some bags of raw rice and a pair of pots of salt. The lack of vegetables has caused problems for our digestion.

"So we have sometimes picked some sorts of wild grasses or tender buds and leaves which we have thought edible. One time, all of us vomited because of poisonous buds. Primula suffered the worst. She died that night."

With the hope to be rescued, Rosma, Abrieta, Primula, Weigela, Miltonia, Stipa, and Lonicera continued to endure the misery.

However, one time, the ship of the pirates came not alone but with another ship of another pirate bandit. The pirates of other ship led three pretty women to the shanty. There were altogether twenty pirates of the two ships that time. The pirates raped the ten women they boozed brandies and chat obscene words. The pirates of other ship talked about their exchange of three new women for three on-the-spot ones. The victims were sorrowful and anxious in hearing what the pirates talked about. They looked one another in tears.

When the pirates left, they called Lonicera, Primula, and Stipa to follow them. These three women victims were exchanged to be sex slaves for the other bandit. All the women, those who left as well as those who stayed, sobbed sadly like the three were going to a scaffold. Those who stayed and the newcomers looked at the leavers until the two ships were very far away. Then they stepped back to the shanty and continued to sob until they were half-asleep.

Some hours later, when all of them woke up and began their dinner, Rosma said to the newcomers, "We're in the same misery. Let's consider one another as sisters. My name is Rosma. Miltonia and Abrieta are sitting in front of you. Weigela is at my left side. Now tell us your names and why you're forced to be in this misery."

"My name is Yucca."

"My name is Ruscifolia."

"My name is Forsythia."

"I think our cases have been similar to yours. I say so because we fled from our country in different boats. In a similar situations, the pirates attacked our boats, killed men, raped women in our boats, robbed, forced pretty women to their ships, and destroy our boats to kill all the rest."

"The pirates incarcerated us and some other beautiful women in the islet and maltreated us as sex slaves," Forsythia continued. "You're here, it means that there are at least two bandits of pirates who incarcerate women in two separately isolated islets."

Some days later, in the evening, the sky was dark and low. Rains became torrents. Winds blew stronger and stronger. It was a typhoon. All four corners of the shanty were wet. The women were cold. They lay very close one another and took all the things which could cover them. They had a sleepless night. They waited impatiently for the dawn.

Suddenly, the women heard the steps of some guys coming nearer and nearer. Then they heard their voices of men. They listened and realized that the men could not to be pirates. All of them cried for help and ran out. The men were four marine soldiers who did not believe their eyes at first.

Two soldiers said loudly, "Mermaids, mermaid."

But Miltonia said more loudly, "No, we are normal women. The pirates imprisoned us here. Please rescue us."

All the women entreated the soldiers, "Please, rescue us."

The marine soldiers led the seven women to their cruiser, which hid behind the islet to avoid the strong winds and gusts of the typhoon. Then the women were shipped to a refugee camp in the country nearby in the free world on the next day.

In the refugee camps, the seven women wrote letters to their relatives in different countries in the free world. Their relatives applied to their government for resettling visas for them. Miltonia wrote to her sister Muscaria in Unto Blumen. About two months later, all the women had visas, but each of them got a visa from a different country. Joy and sadness were mixed in their minds and hearts. They promised to contact with one another and try to call upon free countries to rescue the women still incarcerated in the isolated islets.

Miltonia was welcomed to Unto Blumen, the country of freedom and prosperity. At the international airport, Muscaria, her husband, Salix, their little daughter, and their littler son picked her up. She reunited with her sister after six years of separation with so many losses, sufferings, and changes.

Already living in Unto Blumen for two years, Miltonia has still obsessed with miserable images. She has asked Muscaria this same question many times: "Have you written to the government to call upon the government to rescue the victims in the islets?"

"Miltonia," answered Muscaria, "I've written not only to the government but also to many congresswomen and congressmen as well as editorial offices of newspapers and televisions. More I've not been able to do. Try to forget the past. There are many clubs of our compatriots in this district. Join some. I'll lead you to school to relearn your career or learn something else. I'll tell the children to watch films in their own bedrooms. Try to throw away the sorrows and start a new life."

"Thank you, Muscaria. I'll try to follow your advices."

In one Saturday morning, Muscaria received a letter with the sender's name, Cercis Cyclamen and the receiver's name, Miltonia Miscanthus. Immediately, she called and handed her sister the letter. The whole family was joyful. Miltonia cut the envelope and opened the letter but was very emotional, so she asked Muscaria to read for her:

Dear Miltonia,

For three years, I have sought your information from any compatriots I met and through many magazines in our mother language, especially the first year after the catastrophe, but I received none.

Recently, I met a compatriot group who traveled to this country from Unto Blumen. A woman in one club with you gave me your address.

When the boat broke into parts, I and four other held firmly on five different planks. All of us were very exhausted because of hunger and disappointment. I shut my eyes, prayed in my mind, and waited to be sunk.

Unexpectedly, I heard noises of a motor resounding from afar. I opened my eyes. I saw a freighter coming nearer and nearer.

A sailor climbed down a cable ladder, swam, and rescued me. In the freighter, I told the crew that there were still four others in different planks. The sailors sought other planks, but they found nobody.

I am living in this democratic and prosperous country in three years. It is a good country. However, there are so few our compatriots living here. You and your sister's family try to file immigrant visa to Unto Blumen for me. Or will I travel to Unto Blumen and we will organize marriage there?

I am waiting for your decision.

WOMEN VICTIMS OF THE PIRATES

Payments for the Visas of Exit

"Again, your life stories are not clear! Mr. and Mrs. Nitrogen, we may not issue visas to anyone with unclear life stories. Do you want to rewrite, or each of you is interviewed separately?"

"Sirs, each of us has written life stories four times. We have nothing to hide. Please, tell us one procedure of yours which help us."

"Okay, we will interview. Mr. and Mrs. Nitrogen, all members of your family, you yourselves, your sons, Laurus and Maulus, your daughters, Lunaria and Mathiola, will be here 4:00 p.m. on the next Monday. You've a week to prepare."

Thus, the fifth interview between the official and family Nitrogen consisted of six members in the visa services office lasted only fifteen minutes.

Back home, Mr. and Mrs. Nitrogen conversed about required briberies to get visas of exit, about the RL officials took briberies only through intermediaries and about imposters pretending to be intermediaries:

"To offer briberies are indispensable condition to be issued visas. Rumors say that these guys were allowed to have only small parts of briberies. They had to deliver other substantial parts to their superiors. They were guys of six to the one and half a dozen to the other. They were in one system. None of them could reveal or denounce others because revealers or denouncers would be punished. Damn, the man who took our two taels of gold as the first part of our bribery is probably a swindler. Plunders, corruptions, tricks, extortions, and so many other ugly things happen everywhere!"

"Those are the reasons that make us and millions of our people crave to leave this beloved country. What a misfortune, native people must pay to leave. But foreigners are free, and many of them took their pets with. Native people aren't worth as pets of foreigners."

"Honey, I think, in the coming interview, an RL official will talk tortuously, and we will know a real intermediary."

In the afternoon on the appointed Monday, all members of family Nitrogen arrived in the visa services office half an hour before 4:00 p.m. and sat in the waiting room. Then they were called into a closed-door room in turns not one by one but in pairs: Mr. and Mrs. Nitrogen, Laurus and Maulus, Lunaria and Mathiola.

It was a special interview. Not one but two interviewers were in the room. The interviewees did not need to answer or say anything but to listen to the interviewers. To Mr. and Mrs. Nitrogen, the interviewers propagated and intimidated:

"RL liberators make revolution to bring freedom and equality to the people of this country, but you decide to leave. Your decision is an act of counter-revolution. Nonetheless, RL has benevolent policies towards all kinds of people. If all members of your family are reasonable to do what we guide, and you'll get visas of exit. We'll tell your children what they must do, and you may not hinder them.

"If you violate what we tell you, prisons and labor camps are the places all of you will enter. There are pieces of paper and pens on the table. Write down the name of this man and his address. You have to contact him as early as possible. Act before Friday."

To the pair Laurus and Maulus, the interviewers lectured about duties of young men and intimidated them:

"You're re twenty-two and twenty years old, but you haven't fulfilled your military services of your labor services. You're guilty of opposing the revolutionary government. You deserve to be sent in prisons or labor camps. Contrarily, you applied for visas to go abroad. How can we issue visas to you? But our RL doesn't need counter-revolutionaries like you.

"Nonetheless, if your family fulfills duties or payments in other ways and if you don't hinder other members of your family to do duties or payments, you'll have visas. We think you've enough brain to understand what we say."

To the pair Lunaria and Mathiola, the interviewers told miseries of families that fled illegally on foot through jungles and by boats on seas:

"Our visas are blissful favors. Those who have visas to fly abroad avoid so many agonies which illegal attempters meet with. About 80 percent of illegal fleers are deceived, tricked, or arrested. Our visas are the guarantees.

"What happened to attempters who cross jungles? Survivors told that many among them died because of snakes, hunger, or thirst. Bandits in the jungles barbarously beat them. Bandits searched everywhere of their bodies. They fished into mouths, anuses, vaginas and robbed. Bandits raped women, even twelve-year-old girls. Some bandits took twigs to stab into vaginas of the victims. Bandits killed husbands, fathers, or men who had any acts to protest the barbarities. Bandits forced beautiful women and girls staying in the jungles to be their continual sex objects.

"What happened to fleers in boats on open seas? The combination of seasickness, thirst, and hunger made a part of them die. In addition, pirates of different ships made them miserable. Pirates robbed. Pirates killed men and threw their bodies out to the seas. Pirates raped women and girls. Pirates shipped pretty women and girls to deserted islets to be their continual sex objects.

"Lunaria and Mathiola, those are the prices illegal fleers have to pay. However, only a small part of them can reach other countries. With our visas of exit, your parents, brothers, and you are safe from all those miseries. But we don't issue six visas for nothing. You must pay one thing. Lunaria and Mathiola, you're very beautiful, so both of you must do the following thing we mention."

"My gosh"—Lunaria understood the meaning of the thing RL officials asked—"I'm eighteen years old. I can sacrifice for my family. But my younger sister is fifteen. Please exempt her from the payment."

"Girls at the age of fifteen already have physical bodies ready to do the thing we mention. Furthermore, our superiors once watched you both and told us that both of you are beautiful, that they want to do the thing with you and your younger sister as payments for your family. You must fulfill the requirement before your family gets six precious visas. Since our superiors decide, it cannot be changed.

"Lunaria, Mathiola, is it right in Saturday afternoons, you've meetings at your local district hall to study political issues, and in Sunday mornings, you also come to the place to receive assignments for fatigue duties?"

"Yes, we must be there at two o'clock on Saturday afternoons and at eight o'clock on Sunday mornings."

"Good, one of us will come to the place and pick up at the time in Saturday evenings. You'll be exempted to study politics on all the days we pick you up. Keep all the details of this payment in secrets. Don't tell anyone including your parents and brothers. If you reveal something, all members of your family will be severely punished. We think you understand the importance and keep everything in secret."

Mr. Nitrogen was bursting to have visas of exit, so he

came to the intermediary's house in the evening of the day after the sixth interview. The host greeted him cordially, then he explained his case apologetically:

"Call me Buffalo. Don't misunderstand me. All of us are defeaters. ~~We lose everything from spirits to materials: freedom, countrymen including members of your family and mine are defeaters~~. We lose everything from spirits to materials: freedom, country, democracy, future, friends, and jobs.

"They are the invaders. To prevent resistances, they make people poor, so days and nights people calculate and do only for living, nobody has means or times to think about resistances. They throw former officials and officers into jails or labor camps, dispossess properties and anything worthy like gold and money. Wives, girls, and sons of jailers and laborers live in destitution, adversity, and intimidation, without jobs, so lots of the wives and girls should offer chastity or virginity to them in exchange for something for living, the sons can get only unrewarding works. They drive families they dislike to dirty ghettos or barren areas.

"It's clear they are in highest positions, so authorities and powers are absolutely in their hands. They confiscate all means of living and become bosses. The highest careers and most lucrative jobs belong to their family members then their followers though they are neither intelligent nor skilful. Our pure talent countrymen are in low positions. Families of former officials and officers are in the bottom.

"They are the appropriators. They flagrantly occupy numerous private properties. They implement numerous unjust laws and policies to rob properties of others. For example, they are only guys who may buy houses and jewels, so our people should sell these ones to them with the prices of one-hundredth of real values.

"As you realize, our people, not in hundreds or thousands but in millions, leave this beloved country. Rich people are the first leavers. We look around, already a half of our neighbors are families of the two organizations of invaders with deceitful named RL or RA, which stand for Revolution League and Revolution Army.

"The guys in the visa service office coerce me to do this dirty and dangerous work. It's dirty because applicants hand me gold with resentments like I myself force them to hand briberies, but I also confess to you, they give me 3 percent of each bribery. It's dangerous. I know some cases, RL guys arrest the very intermediaries they appointed to show off that they are clean. Furthermore, robbers often watch when I've guests. I can be murdered at any time.

"You've gold and successfully stashed it. So you can pay for the promised visas of exit. My family also wants to leave this country, but I don't have gold like you. I'm trying to scrape on small pieces gradually to have two taels of gold for my son to flee."

"Mr. Buffalo, I understand you. But I'm sorry. How many taels I must hand you for the six promised visas? It is late now, eight thirty already."

"Oh, each visas costs two taels. Twelve taels altogether for six visas. They said that you must pay before Friday."

Mr. Nitrogen had already estimated the prices. Thus, he handed twelve taels of gold to the intermediary, said goodbye, and stepped out the front door. Anxiety and puzzlement blended in his mind. He had just spent the last part of the hidden treasure of his family for the hope.

He left the house. He rethought the circumstances the intermediary had depicted; all were true. But talking about such things with a stranger was very abnormal at the time. RL and RA have policies to reward those who denounced suspected actions and dissatisfied words of others. Many betrayals had already happened, so people were serious and careful even with friends and relatives, in several cases with their family members also.

He went to the street. It was very dark. Lampposts were still there, but bulbs were stolen. Suddenly, he remembered one verdict illustrated in newspapers and broadcasted from radios:

A man in the street was executed because he had stolen two tires of an RL member. Then a comparison appeared in his head: RL and RA guys were unpunished even though they had stolen public properties valued in millions. Additionally, they had implicit rights to hold private properties openly and take briberies secretly.

He hurried to home. He knew that his wife and four children were waiting for him for dinner and for a result. "Hope" is the only word he could say to them, but he has nothing to prove or show even a receipt or a piece of handwriting on paper.

After the last interview, all members of family Nitrogen became persons of very few words and contemplative. The parents thought that their children had the same worry. But Lunaria and Mathiola had the quite different anxiety. They felt very sorrowful about the humiliation they would suffer. The dinner lasted much shorter than the ones in the past. Lunaria and Mathiola cleaned the dishes in silence and went to their bedrooms.

Mathiola entered Lunaria's bedroom, locked the door, and asked her elder sister, "Lunaria, have the miseries and agonies really happened to attempters crossing the jungles and attempters using boats on the seas as the interviewers said?"

"Yes, radios from foreign countries have broadcasted lots of similar stories told by survivors. People in this country can hear those stories from radio sets but must be in secrecy. If an RL or RA guy knows, punishment will be consequences. But our countrymen continue to leave. They feel that living under these dictators is worse than deaths. By the way, do you understand what the interviewers require us?"

"We must consent them to drive us to some house and rape us. Lunaria, I'm anxious. Can we refuse or inform any other authorities?"

"If we refuse or inform any other authorities, the getting-out plan of our family is ruined. Furthermore, we can be judged as slanderers since they're all in one dictatorial system, they take sides with one another. Worse, unexpected miseries will come to our family."

"Lunaria, the interviewers mentioned about their superiors. Will each of us be raped by more than one man?"

Lunaria could not answer. She sighed deeply and stayed in silence.

On Friday, three days after Mr. Nitrogen had handed gold to the intermediary, one high-ranking guy of RL came to the house of the Nitrogens. The guest began the conversation with the full praise for the immigrating plan of the hosts:

"You're wise. You're going to immigrate to Unto Blumen, the most prosperous and advanced country in the world. Your children will have bright futures and will be happy. Paradise is there, not here. You're going to leave this country. Sell this house to me for ten taels of gold."

"Oh, excuse me, our house has the value of two thousand taels of gold. How can you tell us to sell it to you for ten taels?"

"Either you get about ten taels or nothing. Only high ranks of RL or RA have permission to live in this area with spacious and roomy houses. In two or three years in the future, inhabitants of his area will be moved to another suitable area. After your leaving, this house will be issued to a family of high rank as I've just said. I like this house, but I'm not sure I'll be issued this house, so I pay you ten taels and move in. The house has five bedrooms, doesn't it? Either you let me use two bedrooms and you can stay in three other ones until you leave, or I can exchange a smaller house in another area for you."

"O my god, we're so confused. We cannot know how to answer you now. Please, let us be in peace until we leave."

"I sincerely want to help your family. You had better select my first advice. If you choose the second and move to another house, its local authority will ask you to prove your ownership, and you don't have any proper proof. You'll be repelled from it and become homeless. A lot of your countrymen exchanged smaller houses and became homeless. Moreover, you need to stay here because the visa services office will use this address to contact you. Think about my sincere help. Tomorrow I go far on official business. I'll come here after two weeks. Bye."

When Mr. Nitrogen was sure that the high-ranking RL was far away, he sighed deeply and said to his wife, "Robbers say benevolence and righteousness. They are all bandits in one system but in different groups with numerous ways of robberies. Their banditries are sophisticated.

"Experiences of other leavers teach us that only when we are in a plane, and the plane takes off, we are sure we escape from this hell."

Young people were required to study politics in Saturday afternoons and did fatigue duties in Sunday mornings. However, during the studies of politics, several studiers could be called out for special assignments, which came out of the blue. Others did not know what kind of assignments but did not dare to ask.

In the Saturday afternoon after the six interview at the visa services office, Lunaria and Mathiola came to the local district hall to study politics. Fifteen minutes later, the lecturer called them out to present themselves at the corner of the front yard. They were very sad. They knew what was going to happen.

A jeep transported them up to a hill into former castle of a billionaire who had fled to a foreign country on the day the invaders had come. The castle was then used by a group of high-rank RL males as their recreation center after the invasion. In reality, it is their hedonistic center. Social evils happened here on weekends.

Two RL men guided Lunaria and Mathiola to the large

waiting room and pointed the two last chairs to them. Ten young women were already sitting there in sadness; none spoke.

A minute later, a man brought a tray of twelve portions of fast food and handed each woman one portion. Then he looked back and realized that no woman began to eat. He glowered at them, intimidated them, and coaxed them.

"You should finish your fast food in ten minutes. Those who don't finish will have heavier tasks. You've surpassing things to be proud. First, the selections mean you're beautiful and charming. Second, you're partners are top, erudite, and noble men in the world. Third, you're special guests at this elegant center. Fourth…"

The man left the room. Each woman tried to finish her portion, but could not. They hid the leftovers in the trash can at the corner.

Fifteen minutes passed. The second man entered the room. He coaxed the women again as if all these officials had learned the same lesson. Then he sorted the women into two types.

"Ladies, who of you haven't slept with any partner, in clearer words, those of you who haven't had sex with any partner, stand at my left hand. Those of you who have had sex with any partner, stand at my right hand."

Eleven women including Lunaria and Mathiola stood at his left hand. They were young, from fifteen to nineteen years of age. Only one woman stood at his right hand.

Unexpectedly, she cried, "I am thirty years old, married, and have two children. Why do you drive me here and coerce me to do this miserable work? Drive me home. We'll pay more in gold."

"Be proud, lady. Our high-ranking superior selected you because you are so beautiful and charming. He has passed through lots of young ladies. Now he wants an experienced one and selected you. Act wisely. Apply your experiences. Make him satisfied, and you will be home early. If you don't obey, your family will be punished. Follow our rules.

"I am an old matron. How many times must this old matron come here to do the miserable work?"

"Be cautious in your words. This is honorable work, No lady has a chance to come here more than ten times. Go through that corridor and enter room number 4. If you need a pill, it's in the small box on the nightstand. Be cheerful with him. Let go."

"Hi, young ladies, I call each of you by name and tell the number of the room. Go along the same corridor, you'll find it. Each of you must take a pill. You two, be cheerful with your partners."

Walking in the corridor, Lunaria approached her younger sister and whispered in her ear, "Try to make things reverse what he entices. Make the rapist bored with you. They are all professional enticers and liars. They hide skillfully their cruelties and tyrannies. Don't trust any one of them."

A quarter later, three jeeps came with twelve abusers. In the parking lot, one of them spoke up:

"Dear High Superior, what type of flowers do you enjoy today? Teens or virginal women are always attractive, aren't they?"

"I've enjoyed different types, deflowered several teens, fulfilled my desires on lots of young women from fifteen to twenty. Today, I select a special meal, a thirty-year-old woman, and expect her experiences."

"Oh, you're really a skillful connoisseur. Do you mean the beauty is married and has a child?"

"It's not a matter whether she has children. She comes from a noble and wealthy family of the former society. She is the wife of a former minister who is now in our labor camp. She doesn't know when her husband will be released. Uh, we don't know either, do we? She wants to bring her two children abroad without her husband."

"Dear High Superior, we're perfectly wise. We defeat our enemies, but we don't kill them. We detain them in camps to labor for us. We take not only their possessions and estates but also their daughters and wives. We destroy everything of them. Gradually, they will die in camps."

The twelve abusers entered the waiting rooms. The second man, one of the inferiors, was still sitting there. He stood up and spoke:

"Dear Superiors, all your love partners are in the rooms as your assignments. These ones are mild. Do you remember the last women two months ago? They protested loudly on the first day, we had to bind their limbs and used rods to make them calm."

"Very good. Four of you are here today, aren't you? Similar to past times. When any of us leave the rooms, you may enter there to get pleasures from their beautiful bodies. Ah, at least two of you must be on guard so you can exchange with one another, understand?"

"We thank you for your favor, High Superior. Be convinced of the security here to enjoy the best pleasure. Your safety is our first priority."

The twelve abusers entered their wanted rooms. Then noises of taking off clothes rustled, thuds of falls plopped, creaks of beds whizzed from the rooms.

Some minutes later, from the rooms, female wails cried out painfully, and female sobs groaned imploringly, female entreats resounded emotionally.

Suddenly, male oinks and chuckles like pigs echoed from one room. Then and then similar oinks and chuckles sounded from others.

More than an hour passed. Turn in turn, the women haggardly walked back to the waiting room and sat dazedly at the table.

Several minutes later, the second inferior came back to the room. He glanced at the sad faces and pronounced the same lesson:

"Some of you felt painful because it was the first time. It won't happen again in the next and next times. Think about the benefits you and your families procure. With visas, all members of your families including yourselves will leave this country safely. Without visas your families can attempt other ways and suffer lots of miseries.

"If your families attempt to cross jungles, deaths cause by snakes, hunger, or thirst can happened. Bandits in jungles would rob and kill your fathers, brothers, and lovers. They would barbarously rape you, your mothers, and sisters, and they force you and your sisters to stay in the jungles to be their continual sex objects.

"If your families attempt to flee on boats across open seas, the combination of seasickness, hunger, and thirst could make you or any members of your families die. In addition, pirates would rob you. They would kill your fathers, brothers, and lovers. They would cruelly rape you, your mothers, and sisters. They would ship you and your sisters to deserted islets as their continual sex objects.

"Now, I ask you. Any one of you think that what I've just said are not true, raise your hands."

The women thought on the dictatorship, despotism, and unfairness that caused millions of their native people to leave everything behind and risk their lives to flee, but they sat still.

"Okay, you'll be joyful to come here in the next and the next times, won't you? Who want to go home by busses now, raise your hands. We transport you to the bus station not far from here."

All the women raised their hands.

In the bus, Lunaria gently pulled Mathiola's head to her shoulder and consoled her.

"They're succeeded invaders. They took public booties openly and personal booties secretly. It's pitiful for lots of beautiful women like you and me. Mathiola, calm down. We hope all members of our family will leave this hell soon."

Beautiful Women as Personal Booty

The majority of visitors of the library were students of two universities in the city. They came here to search documents or have convenient seats to do some works for their studies. Truly, some young people came here to find lovers.

Formosa and Japonica, two female students, were close friends. They often came here together. They were twenty years old. They were studying world literature at the Faculty of Letters. They had appearances of prettiness, charm, and suavity. Similarly, Alder and Fergus, two male students, were close friends. They often came here together. They were in the early twenties. They were senior students. Alder was studying at the Faculty of Architecture. Fergus was attending at the Faculty of Medicine. They were gentle, elegant, and handsome.

Their romantic love began in the precincts of this library. Alder liked Formosa, and Fergus liked Japonica at first sight. Each gentleman tried several times in nearly one year to converse with his dream lover but failed since the ladies were bashful and shy. But the two gentlemen continued to seek an opportunity.

On a serene Saturday morning of May, the weather was very beautiful. Formosa had an artful soul. She called Japonica to go out to stroll with her around the flower garden of the library. After two rounds of walking, the two ladies sat on a bench facing some small bushes of roses. While Japonica was watching the scene, Formosa composed and jotted down a poem:

A Beautiful Morning of May

At the flower garden,
In the beautiful Saturday morning of May,
The air is fresh and pure,
Flower buds smile,
Other flowers are show off their colors,
Tiny leaves shoot out their wings,
Drops of dew perch on boughs and leaves,
Breezes come by again and again,
Leaves raise themselves higher in greetings,
Several bees embrace the pistils in the flowers for honey,
Some pairs of small butterflies flying round and round,
Birds twitter somewhere nearby,

The serene nature attracted lots of visitors who came out to stroll for fresh air and gaze the scene. The two gentlemen were also among the strollers. They walked slowly. At random, they saw the two ladies. The gentlemen did not miss the good chance.

"Good morning, ladies. It's beautiful this morning," the gentlemen greeted.

"Good morning, sirs, yes, May is the month of flowers," Japonica replied.

Alder asked an allowance to sit down. The ladies blushed, but heaven gave them the special sense of knowing who liked whom, and each lady tacitly agreed with the selections. Thus,

Japonica stood up. She gave up her seat to Alder. Formosa inched a little leftward to make room for him. He expressed his thanks and sat down. At the same time, Fergus invited Japonica to the other bench nearby. Each pair conversed spontaneously and harmoniously about their present studies, future plans, and current events longer than an hour. Before they said good-bye, each pair agreed to meet each other again at the same place and the same time on the next Saturday.

Their tryst became more and more romantic. Love emerged between each pair. They were harmonious lovers. They were in the age of love and marrying. Each pair of lovers planned that they would marry after one of them would graduate and have a job. The two pairs hoped that they would organize their weddings together.

One and a half years later, the two gentlemen graduated, and they had good jobs some months later.

The two pairs organized their weddings together on the Saturday of May. It was the anniversary they had gotten to know each other in the garden of the library. The two couples lived happily thereafter. Their houses were in one district, one block far from each other. Their close friendship continued.

Human beings have waged many wars in this world, and the results of wars have not been changed. More men than women of both belligerent sides have been killed, but lots of women have been raped during the evolution of wars. Then after every war, men of this victorious side have procured many booties. Their leader has become a king or emperor with extra powers and rights. His inferiors have been issued properties in different forms, have held high positions with prerogatives, taken defeated men as servants, and misused defeated women as sex objects to fulfill their lust.

Eastnama, the native country of the two couples, was prosperous. Its people lived peacefully thanks to the help of its government in two decades. Unfortunately, the RL of its neighbor country Kanxono obsessed the thought that they had suzerainty to rule Eastnama, so they decided to invade it.

In comparison between the two countries, Kanxono was very poor, and its people lived in miseries under the dictatorship of the sly and despotic totalitarianism of the clique. Nonetheless, the RL clique that waged the war of invasion used very strange strategies and tactics as well as unusual characteristics and behaviors, which the government and the army of Eastnama could not analyze and understand. Therefore, the invaders controlled more and more territories and their inhabitants. Only one-third of the inhabitants could flee to cities controlled by the government of Eastnama, and they had to leave behind their properties and belongings.

In general, rich people are afraid of deaths and injuries much more than destitute people. The Eastnama war caused deaths, wounds, atrocities, destructions, and numerous other bad results in the country. It presumed that the soldiers the RL clique sent to fight for their war were not afraid of deaths of wounds. Most of them fight to death. Were they brainwashed? Or did they have no other way? Or did they crave to have rewards that the RL clique had promised? There were consecutive waves of battles during two decades of the war. In each wave, a hundred thousand soldiers of the invaders died; however, the RL clique sent another hundred thousand to replace them. The RL clique had no pity on the soldiers or their families. Nevertheless, there were no protests against the war from the families of these soldiers or from the people of Kanxono since they were afraid that the clique would make them more miserable.

Additionally, for their tactics, the RL clique applied the strange abilities like living in underground tunnels or secret places and acting or fighting at nights and so on. In daylight, they dug underground tunnels or secret places. Tunnels were usually dug under forests; secrets places were usually dug under stables or pigsties. At night, they crawled out to terrorize people to work for them, or collect taxes, or attack posts, and so on. People called them ghosts because they appeared at night and disappeared in daylight.

Also, the RL guys used the unusual characters such as deceitfulness, cunningness, bloodthirstiness, and slyness. They had been using these characters to take and grip powers in Kanxono successfully, so they were applying the same despotic rules during the war. Although the society of Eastnama was prosperous and democratic, it was not a perfect society. They lied that if they win the war, they would build a perfect society. Anyone who told the real circumstances in Kanxono or expressed doubt would be arrested at night and vanished from this world.

The RL guys were very smooth-tongued, so about 10 percent of the people in Eastnama trusted them and became their followers or collaborators. These trustees were either gullible or craving for power. The RL clique began the war in jungles and countrysides. In regions that they controlled, all people had to work for them. Those who did not work for them would be murdered, and their families would be in disaster. Anyone who did not want to work for them, one's whole family had to flee to regions controlled by the government.

The RL guys did numerous sly acts. For example, when they wanted to destroy a temple, they shot from the temple and ran away. The army of the government destroyed it. For another example, when they wanted to kill a family, they hung their flag on the roof of the house of the family. Aircrafts of the army bombed the house.

The RL guys stringently forced everyone in regions they controlled to join teams that they organized. Ones had to watch one another. One had to report suspected words and activities to them to avoid being punished as accomplices.

The Eastnama war became more ferocious, bloody, and

destructive. The RL guys applied cleverly and skillfully strange strategies and tactics as well as characteristics and behaviors, so they won many battles though the casualties of their side was tenfold higher than the ones of the army of the Eastnama government. They controlled more and more separate regional territories. On maps, these regional territories looked like tabbies on the fur of a leopard. The war spread from jungles to forests and regions in countrysides and cities after more than a decade.

To defend themselves, the government of Eastnama had to order a general draft. Men from eighteen to thirty-five years old had to join the army. Students could defer to study, but they had to pass their school year exams. Of course, the draft could enforce only men in regions that the government still controlled. The draftees were sad, but most of them thought it was a necessary measure to protect their freedom and prosperity, so they accepted it. Both Alder and Fergus were twenty-six years old, so they had to join the Eastnama army. The two couples were very sad. They had just married five months earlier. However, the two young men had to leave their young wives and join the army although none of them knew when the war would end. Alder composed these verses on the day he said good-bye to his young wife:

I Could Not Answer Her

In the precinct of the library,
I met a sweet and suave lady.
Formosa, the name of the beautiful flower species.
Formosa, the name of the charming lady.
Our love began in the morning of May,
Then we married and have lived happily.

Our happiness has just lasted six months

however.
Who have disturbed the happiness of others?
Who have deceived others?
Who have sought prerogatives on calamities of others?
Who have murdered others because of different opinions?

Who have waged wars to fulfill their ambitions?

Spanning in more than a decade,
Our country has deeply engulfed in the war.
All young men must participate as draftees or enlistees.
They use their abilities and energies,
Not to build and construct but to kill and destroy.
Who impose these unjust and unrighteous compulsions?

In the past as well as today,
Guys have gone into wars,
Few have returned!

In the afternoon of November,
Red leaves from branches were falling down;
I say good-bye to my young wife,
Leaves groaned, she wept;
Scarlet sunlight expressed similar sadness.
She asked the date of my return.
I cannot answer her.

The husbands left in worry and fretfulness. The wives looked at them in sadness and sorrow. The trees at the sides of the streets stood dolefully and dazedly. Some birds perched quietly and baggily on stripped branches.

After a year in the military training center, both Alder and Fergus got second lieutenant rank in the army, but each of them was sent to a different military unit in a different region. Alder was transferred to the engineering corps and was assigned as commander of the platoon in an engineering battalion stationed in the coastal plain four hundred miles northeast from their home city. Simultaneously, Fergus was transferred to the medical corps and was assigned as assistant for a doctor in the medical committee of the armor squadron stationed on highlands five hundred miles southwest from their home city.

Both of them were very busy with their duties because the war became very ferocious, bloody, and destructive. From the day they left the military training center, they did not meet each other, but they wrote to their wives monthly and vice versa. Each wife also received some photos of her husband in military uniforms.

At the home city, Formosa and Japonica became closer friends. They visited each other more frequently and shared news of the war and letters from their husbands. Formosa showed some more verses from Alder:

Her Letter

Our love is so beautiful, she writes:
Believe her fidelity, must I;
When bees still make honey,
Her lover is only me;
In distance we are separately,
notwithstanding,
In love we are deeply attaching.

When there appears moonbeam,
I read her letter.

When there are several stars,
I read her letter.
When lightning bugs perch on leaves
nearby,
I read her letter.

Although the moonlight is not bright,
I can read because I have read it at
daylight.
Although the starlight is not bright,
I can read because I have read it at
daylight.
Although the lightning bugs' light is not
bright,
I can read because I have read it at
daylight.

When he had short times, he composed some lines though he was very busy.

The military unit of Second Lieutenant Alder had to rebuild roads, bridges, and so on that were destroyed by the RL guys. To the RL guys, destruction was an important part of their strategy. The RL guys destroyed again and again the projects that had just been rebuilt.

Exotic Dreams

In the cabin of the truck,
I dreamed I was a king seating on a throne.
You had just seated beside me as a queen,
Then you went somewhere nearby,
To make a tour of inspection around our
inner city.
You came back to the next hall

To instruct a committee to organize a royal party.

During the project at the seashore,
I saw the blue water,
Looked like the color of your eyes.
I saw the curls of waves,
Looked like the locks of your hair.
I saw the foam on the tops of the waves,
Looked like the white flowers
In the front yard you took the loving care of.
I heard the music of a mermaid singing
On the sea at the farthest horizon,
Similar to the song you had sung many times,
The song of love.

Each young wife and husband lived in two different faraway places, so they missed each other very much. The separation inspired them to have romantic imaginations that each of them wrote in letters or composed as poems, such as the ones of Alder. They missed each other very much, but to come and go from one city to another or from one region to another was risky since the regional territories controlled by the RL guys were though separate but throughout the whole country like tabbies on fur of a leopard.

Though RL guys were in separate territories, they secretly contacted one another at some deserted spots. They stopped vehicles to coerce passengers to listen to their propagandas and pay taxes to them. They force young men to forests to work for them, they took all medication, and they killed soldiers of the government if there were any who were on leave and disguised as passengers to go home.

Formosa missed Alder very much. She decided to make a journey to visit her husband. It was a risk; the roads connected from one region to another were not safe because the sabotages and stops of the RL guys. For passengers, only inter-region buses were used. Trains of the country were useless since numerous sections of railroads were undermined. No one dared to drive personal cars through the roads since the RL guys would condemn those passengers as rich and held them as hostage for ransom.

Formosa left her home for the journey in a morning. Roads were bad. Some sections were dug by the RL guys at the night before, and they were quickly repaired by engineering corps the next morning for temporary use, so vehicles moved slowly. In one section, they had to stop to wait for the repair. Thus, after ten hours, the bus in which Formosa boarded had gone only two hundred miles.

Suddenly, at one spot, a crew of ten RL guys appeared and stopped all the vehicles of both opposite directions. They called each other and one another co liberator and co liberators. All passengers were gathered. Six co liberators stepped up into the vehicles and rummaged. Simultaneously, the passengers were escorted away by four other co liberators to a place under a canopy of foliage. The place was about one hundred yards far from the road in the forest.

One co liberator was waiting for them in the place. After some words of greetings, he read four papers of a propagandist lecture. The first part of the propaganda described his home country Kanxono as a paradise in which his people had extremely happy lives in wealthy and freedom. Its second part depicted virtues of his emperor in Kanxono, who was a great saint who sacrificed his whole life for his country and people. The emperor had no time for himself. He had no wives nor children. He kept his celibacy. Thanks to his reign, the paradise was built in his Kanxono country. Thus, the RL guys followed the emperor's example to serve people rather themselves. Its third part explained the situations of this country Eastnama that the prosperity and freedom were only affected ones. Thus, he and his co liberators sacrificed their happy lives in Kanxono to arrive in this country, Eastnama, to help its people fight against the army of the government. The co liberators would succeed; they would build a paradise like the one in Kanxono for the people of Eastnama. The last part of the lecture was an appeal for support. Urgent and concrete support were the contribution of all jewels the passengers were wearing as well as cash the passengers brought on their journey. After the contribution, the passengers would go back to their vehicles. Whoever did not contribute all the cash would be held and escorted to the deeper place in the forest.

After the lecture, the co liberators singled out four passengers and searched throughout their bodies and wallets. All other passengers were scared, so they handed all their jewels and cash to the liars.

At that moment, the six co liberators who had rummaged the baggages in the vehicles came to the place. One of them held the baggage of Formosa, murmured some words to the ear of the lecturer, and handed it to him.

The very lecturer or propagandist called, "Who has the name Formosa?"

In fear, Formosa raised her right hand. He ordered her to stay in the place, then he spoke loudly to the other passengers to go back to their vehicles to continue their journey.

When the other passengers were out of sight, the lecturer thrust his hand into her baggage and took out the photo of Alder in military uniform.

He asked her, "Is the man in the photo your young husband?"

Knowing that it was impossible to deny, she nodded and shivered. He signaled to one co liberator who escorted her into the maze of the forest.

After about an hour of going on foot, the guy and Formosa reached to a place with three thatched cottages under a large canopy of foliage. The guy led Formosa into one cottage in the middle. She was shocked at the first sight. On a low bamboo bed with its two back legs fixed to the two pillars of the cottage, a young woman sat quietly. Her left ankle was locked in a small and one-yard-long chain, and the chain was locked to the left pillar. Beside her there are two bottles of water and some dry food. Just behind the pillar, there is an open commode. She looked at Formosa sadly and said nothing. The guy signaled Formosa to sit on the right corner of the bed. Her right ankle endured the same ill fate as the left ankle of the young woman. Then the guy went away.

After the guy had left the cottage, the young woman introduced herself and told Formosa her story.

"My name is Celandine. I'm seventeen and a half years old. I've been detained here and been the sex object of the head of the squad for two years. His alias is Sixth Conqueror. All men here have aliases, and they use only aliases."

"Is Sixth Conqueror the guy who reads propagandist lecture?"

"Yes, he is. He wears neither stripes nor medals, but he is an authoritarian. In the cottage at the left, thirty-five-year-old Marigold and, in the cottage at the right, thirty-seven-year-old Pansy are my co endurers. They chain us when they go away.

"They come back in the afternoon and unchain us, then we are allowed eat together and talk to one another what they allow in normal voices. Simultaneously, they eat nearby, but four of them are on guard at the four corners of this large canopy, and they relieve the guard after every two hours. After meals, each of us must return into the decided cottage and be sex objects for them. Sixth Conqueror uses his authority to monopolize sex acts on me because I'm younger than Marigold and Pansy, my two co endurers, who are sex objects of the others in two other cottages.

"But you're here today. You're so pretty, noble, charming, and elegant. Sixth Conqueror is greedy of both virgin girls and pretty women as I once heard his inferiors murmuring to one another, so the situations can be changed. They also murmured that the great majority of women in their country, Kanxono, are plain in their appearances because of shortage of nutrition from their births to present time and manual labor from dawn to late evenings. Thus, they are happy with their situation of not living in Kanxono but fighting in this war in Eastnama since they have good food to eat, pretty women to fulfill their lusts, and so on. Usually, they sleep and have sex acts on us by turns during the time from afternoon meal to one o'clock the next morning. Then they chained us and go away to do their actions for another day."

"Are all of them from Kanxono?"

"About 80 percent of them are from invader's country Kanxono. And 20 percent are either hoodlums or gullible guys of this Eastnama country."

"What you say are quite opposite to what he has read from his propagandist lecture!"

"Oh, quite opposite. The truth is absolutely opposite what they propagandize. I tell you only what I've heard from their private conversations. Their emperor has usually at least four beautiful and young women to fulfill his sexual desire. Additionally, many virgins are recruited by his body guard team for him to deflower. Except for the families of the RL clique, their people live in poverty, so there are girls who are ready to exchange their virginity for something. There are also fans of the emperor. They're proud to be deflowered by him. To follow their emperor's example means to learn how to conceal evil acts and activities and deceive people cleverly like him. To do these works, the RL clique establishes their special system that propagandizes for him and for themselves. Its concealment and deceit have great successes. Though their people live in poverty, a half of them believe that their emperor is the great living saint, and their poverty is engendered by natural calamities and belligerent foreigners. Those who do not believe must be silent. Anyone who expresses disbelief will be punished severely, and one's family will live in miseries."

"Why do you say that Marigold, Pansy, and you are sex objects of them, are they nice anytime when they make sexual intercourses?"

"Never, all of them are greedy, stinky, egoistic, and concupiscent. We're only their sex slaves, nothing else. We detest them. It is presumed that they exchange their sexual act experiences. They all coerce us to do different smutty acts to fulfill their lust. The nice and love relationship between lovers becomes a disgusted yoke."

"For two years, you haven't been pregnant, but if a pregnancy comes, what will happen?"

"They distribute contraceptive drugs or pills. It is assumed that some organs of our government sell medication including the contraceptive drugs and pills to the RL guys. They straightly say many times that if anyone of is pregnant, she must be killed and buried. Like their emperor, they must conceal their evil acts and deceive people cleverly. Two months earlier, thirty-year-old Marjoram was pregnant. She disappeared. Probably, they escorted her to somewhere in the forest, killed, and buried her. They are so barbarous."

"There are some rumors saying that the RL guys are ghosts and that they have magic of devils. You've lived with these guys and have been sex objects to them for two years. Do you have any appraisal?"

"It's a complicated issue. The rumor says so because the RL guys appear in hamlets, villages, suburbs, streets to propagandize, collect taxes, recruit gullible guys, coerce people to work for them, execute those who do not fulfill the work they assigned before other people, and punish their families at nights. They force people to dig roads or damage facilities at nights. They attack units of our army or government at nights. They abduct employees of our government at nights. They disappear before dawn. Where are they in daylight? In countryside, they hide in forests nearby. When our army carries on some strategic military movements in areas they hide, they creep into underground tunnels in forests. In towns or cities, they live in underground tunnels in daylight. Normal people will die because of lack of oxygen in the tunnels, but they can live in the tunnels for weeks or months when our army operates above their secret tunnels. In short, I've these appraisals: Though they're human beings, they've schedules and habits of ghosts, and they are imparted with magic and evils of devils."

"What are the causes they incarcerate and force Pansy, Marigold, and you to be their sex objects?"

"Both Pansy and Marigold have husbands in our army of the government that these guys fight against. In journeys to visit their husbands, these guys rummaged and found photos of their husbands in military uniforms in their handbags. I think your case is similar. Mine is different. Let us drink some water, and I'll tell you.

"Our family was a have one. It consisted of my parents, two elder brothers, and me. We lived in the faraway-from-road village that was protected by the twelve-soldier squad of our army. Three years ago, in a dark night of April, a platoon of the sixty-six RL guys attacked the squad.

"Calamities came to my family. In the very night, my two brothers slept in the post of the soldiers because they had celebrated the birthday dinner of a soldier who was their friend. After fighting about four hours, all the soldiers of the squad and my two brothers sacrificed their lives. The RL guys occupied the village and buried the fourteen corpses in one single hole. During the first day of their occupation, we heard that RL guys were planning to punish those who had worked for the government. Because my brothers died in the post, my father led my mother and me fleeing to the nearest city controlled by our government.

"We were homeless scavengers. We lived from the pile of garbage there. Our lives in the city were miserable. After several months, I pleaded my father to return to our village and promised to do anything I can to help my parents. In dilemma, my father agreed, and we returned. However, one part of the RL platoon stationed in our house. Its commander was and is Sixth Conqueror. He allowed us dwelling under the right eave of our house.

"In the evening of the next day, he summoned me alone into our house. He was the only man in the house. He had sent all his inferiors outside to guard or do something else. In the light of the kerosene lamp, I saw he doted on me. He said that so many women of Eastnama are beautiful, that I'd sex appeal and glamour of a teen of fifteen. He told me that, in the next morning, he and two other commanders of two other sub platoons would have a session with their higher commander, Fourth Quick, of the platoon to decide the fate of my parents, that the commander had had intention to execute both my father and mother because the evidence of my two brothers in the battle. Then he said that as he had arranged, one of his inferiors had just led my parents to the house of our neighbors, that if I consented to be his sex partner, he would rescue my parents and give back the house to my parents. His words made me scared, but in such situation, I said to him that I consented.

"Immediately, he held me firmly. After some minutes he stripped off my clothes. I'd not been nude before anybody. I was very shameful. He rubbed me both from back to front especially on my breasts. Then he took off his clothes, pushed me to lie on the bed, ordered and told me how to do smutty acts. Oh, I'm shameful. I cannot tell you these details and those next details. Then his thing entered. Ugh, ugh, ugh, aahoohoo! I was only fifteen. Ugh, aahoohoo! It was not one that night but three. It was very painful.

"The next morning, he went to their session. What was the issue in the session, I didn't know. What he said to me about the intention of his superior on the fates of my parents could be his lies to have me. They're all clever deceivers trained in professional schools. In that evening, this RL platoon split to separate sub platoons and moved. He ordered me to go with him. We moved all the night and came here. I've been his sex object until now.

"Then he realized that he could not be the only man having sexual intercourses. His inferiors wanted it too. Thus, after several days, they escorted Marigold and Marjoram to the other cottages. Some months later, they escorted Pansy to the cottage. Today, you're here."

"Why didn't your parents try to seek you?"

"I thought about my parents many times. I didn't know whether they were executed. I didn't ask him because I knew he wouldn't say the truth. Furthermore, when the RL guys executed anyone before other people, their purpose was to scare the people. But their usual way was different, they invited victims to follow them at nights and the victims vanished from this world. Never did their families dared to mention about the victims to the RL guys. If my parents are still living, similar to other people, they won't dare to mention about me."

"You've been here for two years. Have You, Marigold, or Pansy ever made an attempt to escape?"

"Any attempt to escape is a deadly risk. Three-fourth is death, and only one-fourth is life. First, the chains are locked to the pillars when they are away. To break the pillars, the single way is to set fire to the cottage. I hid matches below the bed, but the cottage will be ravaged before the pillars fall down. We'll die in the blaze. Second, this forest is a maze to us. I've no idea which direction leads to a road. We can be caught again. They'll maltreat us worse. Furthermore, we can be killed by snakes, wild animals, lack of water, and so on. Third, there are also other RL units in the forest, they'll catch and suspect us as spies and torture us, and we'll be the sex objects of other RL guys. Um..."

Chok-chok-chok-chok. Chuht-chuht-chuht-chuht.

Chok-chok-chok-chok. Chuht-chuht-chuht-chuht.

"Heavens! Celandine, who's shooting?"

"The RL guys. I can realize the explosions from their weapons."

Dap-dap-dap-dap-dap. Shess-shess-shess-shess.

Dap-dap-dap-dap-dap. Shess-shess-shess-shess.

"Good heavens! Celandine, what now?"

"From our army. Formosa, can you differentiate the different explosions? It's a battlefield here! We're going to die. Ugh, no, we can cry for help. If the cottage is on fire, try to push the pillar down. The chain will slip out. Run away, throw yourself down to a lower place, and cry for help. Our army will pass here."

"We'll try together, Celandine."

Shhhsssseeeiiig, boom, shhhsssseeeiiig, boom, shhhsssseeeiiig, boom.

"The cottage fell. My chain is loose. Yours is too. Run away."

"Blood! Celandine, you're injured."

"I can slither out and—run away. Run away."

The instruction of Celandine saved Formosa. The skirmish lasted about twenty minutes. Then several soldiers of the army advanced to the canopy. They heard the cry of Formosa from a lower place and let her come out. They found Celandine lying dead in a shrub in front of the cottage. Also, they found Marigold and Pansy lying dead in the other cottages. Three young women died, one survived as Celandine had estimated, "Three-fourth is death, and only one-fourth is life." The soldiers had shot and shelled toward the direction of their enemies, but the women had been chained by the RL guys in place! That war was full of twist and turns. The soldiers cut off the chains for the survivors and the dead. They called military means of transportation. Formosa and the three corpses arrived in the nearest city before dusk.

On the next day, the army organized a small and simple funeral for the three dead victims on two days later. The husbands of Marigold and Pansy were there. Formosa followed their caskets to the cemetery. Their graves were filled up. She said adieu to them in tears.

Formosa contacted Alder. He got a week of leaves. He

boarded a flight for the city. She told him all the details of the hellish experience and the appraisals of Celandine, her rescuer. The couple spent a week there together, but she was still in sadness. Then she boarded a flight for their home city, and he boarded for his unit.

At the airport of their hometown, Japonica greeted and drove Formosa to her home. Formosa told Japonica all the hellish journey of herself and humiliated cases of Celandine, Marigold Marjoram, Pansy, and the appraisals of Celandine. Japonica wrote all the details to Fergus. They warned one another not to make any similar risk but boarded flights from one city for another only.

The war became more and more ferocious. Even though the deaths of RL guys was a tenfold higher than the ones of the army of Eastnama, their emperor and his RL clique did not care. Their soldiers fought to death since their families in Kanxono were in the despotic hands of the emperor and the RL clique. In Eastnama, more and more territories in countryside were under their control. More and more people of Eastnama were forced to work for them. Even people in several suburbs of some cities were harassed at night.

However, every six months, Alder had a week of leaves to spend time with wife, Formosa. Fergus and Japonica had the similar time. On the day of the third anniversary of their marriages, Japonica and Fergus had then a one-year-old son named Prunus, and Formosa and Alder had then a two-month-old daughter named Fruticosa.

Unfortunately, little Prunus was sick of petechial fever. Hearing the news, Fergus was worrying and restless. He asked his superior and got a week of leaves, but the airport of the city had been attacked and shelled in the night before. Air traffic control station was ruined; lanes of airstrip were badly holed.

The airport was temporary useless.

However, Fergus was worrying and restless. He decided to disguise as a seventy-year-old poor farmer to board inter-region buses. He dyed his hair white, drew wrinkles on his face, and wore tarnished clothes of farmers. But these deeds were observed by his driver who was an infiltrator. In the most organs of the Eastnama government and units of the army, about 10 percent were RL infiltrators. They were dangerous and harmful spies. When the driver of Fergus drove him to the bus station, he secretly informed the driver of the bus that Fergus was a surgical doctor in the army. Bus drivers who drove through the territories controlled by the RL guys had to work for them.

About forty miles away from the city, the bus was stopped by an RL guy and did the following acts: gathered passengers to propagandize and collect taxes, rummaged baggages of passengers to search anything linking with the government or army, and collected medication.

Then one liberator came to Fergus and said, "You are not an old farmer but a young doctor. Our division needs you. Stay here."

He ordered the other passengers to go back to their vehicle.

Fergus was blindfolded and was guided to go on foot. About half an hour later, the liberators took off the blindfold, and he was handed over to another crew. They walked some hours in the jungle and reached an area with several cottages under canopies of big trees. Fergus conjectured the place was the headquarters or rear of an RL division. A liberator guide led him into one cottage where a wounded liberator was lying on the bamboo bed. Standing beside the bed was a beautiful woman in fatigue; she was in her early thirties. The guide saluted the wounded respectfully and introduced Fergus to the wounded.

"Second Thunder, here is doctor of medicine of the other side's army." Then he told the woman, "Ninth Medic, he'll help you to operate our Second Thunder." Then he went to the front door and guarded it together with a pair of other soldiers.

The woman told Fergus, "Some shrapnel has been deep in the chest and abdomen of Second Thunder since the day before yesterday, but I haven't known how to take it out. Luckily, you came here today. Please help us with all your heart."

"I cure anyone who is in danger with my ability and conscience as I vowed before the statue of Hippocrates, the originator of medicine, without thinking of who my patient is. However, the lack of medication and equipment here make the operation risky. I know I am your prisoner here. I know I must do this operation. I know I must risk my life. Let us begin. Help with what I ask you."

The operation lasted two hours. The shrapnel was taken out. Second Thunder slept deeply thereafter. All of them thought he would recover. The guide told Ninth Medic to go back to her cottage. Also, he led Fergus there. There were two bamboo beds in the cottage. The woman sat on the right bed.

The guide told Fergus to sit down on the left bed and said, "Our division needs you, so I have to chain you to this pillar to prevent you to escape."

Then he left the cottage. Ten minutes later, another liberator brought food and drinks for the woman, and Fergus and left the cottage.

The woman began to converse in a low voice:

"Dr. Fergus, I thank you. If you aren't here, I'm in trouble. They force me to operate, but I can't. I didn't study medicine at any school. Oh, my story is long. You'll get my story part by part. Second Thunder and Ninth Medic are only aliases. My real name is Depda. He is a brigadier general, commandant of this division. He and I are from the same native village in Kanxono. He's ten years older.

"He was born in a poor family. I was born from a rich family. When he was very young, he followed RL clique and became an important RL guy. He didn't come back to the village in a decade. He was promoted to higher and higher ranks. Then he was close to the emperor, the sly and deceitful emperor. When I was an eighteen-year-old, he came back and asked my parents to marry me though I disliked him. Being refused, he was at enmity with my family."

"He wanted to marry you because you were pretty, didn't he?"

"Probably it is the reason. In Kanxono, pretty women are few since the RL clique has taken power. People including women have been in shortage of nutrition from their births. Later, being adults, they have worked hard from dawn to late evenings to fulfill the duties the RL guys assigned.

"However, both I and my two-year-younger sister, Deptam, are pretty. Second Thunder took revenge on my family. He recommended the body guard team of the emperor to bring both us to the emperor. Then he entreated the emperor to have my sister and give me for him. The emperor agreed. Men around the emperor envied him. At that time, the RL clique decided to wage this invasion war. He pleaded the emperor to fight in this war. He was promoted to general and commandant of this division, and this division crossed the common border from Kanxono to Eastnama fourteen years ago. In sum, he had coerced me to follow him and be his sexual object since the day the emperor let him have me."

"Why and how have you related to medicine?"

"Both sides of this ferocious war have had dead and wounded in battles. But your side has military hospitals and transportation means, so the wounded are bought to the hospitals and the dead to their families. Contrarily, our side hasn't had hospitals and means of transportation, so the light wounded are helped forward or carried by other fighters to rears like this one. Ill fates came to the heavy wounded. They were shot by their co liberators to death and buried together with the dead in large holes.

"The rear here has duty of curing the wounded, but we severely lack equipment and medication. We use herbs and insects of the jungle adding to our medication. Our crew of medicine here consisted of me and two other male nurses who, after middle school, had studied at a nurse school for six months. There were so many wounded, so I helped them. After several years, I did the works better than the two men, so they said that I learned medicine in pragmatic fields and elected me head of the crew."

"You've hated him. Why haven't you escaped?"

"Sigh, in Kanxono, the RL machines control stringently all individuals: where they live, where they go, where they sleep, whom they meet, and so on. Those machines also control all materials even the tiny things like a needle, a yard of thread, a bowl of rice, a cup of sauce, and so on. No one can live outside their hands. Differently, in Eastnama, everything is in free markets, but I've no job, no relatives, no acquaintances, no friends. How can I live? Furthermore, the clique usually sends their agents to assassinate escapees because they think escapees have known secrets and reported to your government or army.

"However, I want to escape. Can you help me? I'm married and have a son."

"One characteristic of the RL guys is suspiciousness. If you escape, they'll sentence that I'm your accomplice, and I'll be severely punished. If I help you, I must also escape. Can you sponsor me before your government?"

"I'll try all my best to help you. I promise."

"Okay, I'll risk my life. I've a key of the chain under my bed. Now try to sleep for some hours. We'll start by two. I'll unlock the chain. Be silent and follow me."

Depda and Fergus left the rear and reached near a small military post beside a road before dawn. After half an hour of mutual signs and shouts at the top of their voices, they were allowed to enter the post. Thereafter, a military car picked them up to the city nearby. They presented themselves and wrote their incidents. The commandant of the army there issued identity cards and commanded his inferiors to give them meals and two separate rooms to stay in overnight.

On the next morning, the commandant invited Fergus and Depta to take breakfast with him.

After the meal, Depta told the commander, "Since I'm a

defector, I know that RL guys sentence me to death for sure. I want your side to win this war. It presumes your side doesn't conceive the strangeness of the other side."

"True, we don't understand the strange strategies and tactics as well as characteristics and behaviors of our enemies. We appreciate your analysis."

"Those strange strategies and tactics as well as characteristics and behaviors can't be easy to analyze. Or they can be partly explained only through several details from the Old Testament:

"At the beginning, Almighty God created nine ranks of angels. All of them were unseen, smart, and mighty. Lucifer was in the first rank. Michael was in the second rank.

"However, Lucifer revolted against God and waged the war in heavens, and a half of disloyal angels followed Lucifer. They formed their evil legion. They challenged the powers of God.

On the other hand, Angel Michael was loyal to God and fought bravely against the evil legion. Another half of Angels loyal to God such as Cherubim, Gabriel, Raphael, Seraphim, and so on followed Angel Michael. They formed their holy coalition and fought against the evil legion. The holy coalition fought very courageously in many battles, and the holy coalition defeated the evil legion.

"After the war in heavens, God punished all members of evil legion. God created hell and incarcerated them there. They became devils, Lucifer became Satan. The names of some other devils were Beelzebub, Dagon, Horus, Iris, Moloch, Osiris, and so on.

"However, where was hell? Hell, in which the devils were detained, was in the deep underground center of one planet in universe. As a result, the devils were accustomed to underground lives.

"How was hell? Hell was very stinky as a vast latrine and utterly dark as incessant night without lights. As a result, the devils could easily live in stinky places and usually chose dark hours at nights to fulfill their actions.

"How were the devils? The devils were cunning, sly, deceitful, cruel, bloodthirsty, barbarous, distrustful, jealous, envy, and greedy.

"When God created human beings, the devils were very jealous of human beings' happiness. Then the devils pleaded with God to let them test the loyalty of human beings. God allowed and opened the gates of hell. Thus, the devils came to this earth. They tried all their abilities to make human beings as harmful as possible to avenge their lost war in heavens. Their first success was the temptation in Eden. The temptation made Eve and Adam disobey God. The couple ate the forbidden fruit, so God punished the couple. After the sin, all descendents of the couple have inherited bad consequences.

"The devils did not stop after their first success. They've continued their harmful works in this world. They've dragged a part of human beings as devilish followers working for them. This bad part of human beings have scattered everywhere as bad guys, robber gangs, and so on. Usually the devils imparted their devilish followers with their abilities of mightiness, smartness, and habits for strategies and tactics to harm good part of human beings. Since the devils could pretend to be angels to deceive human beings. Their devilish followers could pretend to be good guys to deceive.

"Calamites happened to any country that were ruled by groups that had devilish characteristics."

"We thank for your profound analysis. Please, tell us concrete circumstances in your native country, Kanxono, in the past and present under the rules of RL clique."

"The RL clique was cunning. To procure powers, they promised the people cleverly that when they were in powers, they would bring prosperity to the country and freedom to the people. Unfortunately, when they were in powers, all their works were opposite to their promises. They governed with dictatorial, despotic, and counterproductive rules, so the country became poor, and the great majority people lived in poverty or destitution. RL guys were lustful and corruptive.

For example, their leader, the emperor, had permanently four beautiful women in his palace to fulfill his sexual desire in privacy. But they all behaved in public as men of virtues and values. Anyone who mentioned about their lustfulness and corruption would be attributed a fabricated crime and punished severely.

"The RL clique was deceiving. They pretended skillfully to be nice and honest, so lots of the people fought against their rivals to let them grip power. Additionally, they used different methods from enticements to punishments to brainwash able persons who did not follow their dogmas. If their brainwashing works did not succeed, they secretly disposed those persons. When they were in power, they unmasked their real character of despotism. They suppressed cruelly all the people and their families that did not obey them.

"Two parallel conditions required to join RL ranks and to have a high position and prerogatives were total loyalty to the clique and cunning cruelty to the governed people. The purposes of the clique were to make people absolutely dependent on them for living and know only their dogmas. In implementations, the RL clique distributed all positions, jobs, prerogatives, and privilege not based on talents, ingenuity, or diligence but on loyalties, sycophancy, or cruelty to non-subjugated people.

"The RL clique was sly. They often used other people to carry on their cruel plans. They forced tamed intellectuals to destroy untamed ones. They divided people in social classes. They urged the poor class to kill the rich class. Those who did not execute their orders would be ruined by their punishments. Thus, everyone had to obey them. Furthermore people had to be dependent on them for all means of living.

"The RL clique was bloodthirsty. They murdered not only able persons who could challenge their powers, patriotic persons who criticized them, the haves who could be independent on their rationed means of living but also those who did not work for them.

"The RL clique was distrustful, so they organized multi-spying systems. Any word or action which violated their dictatorial rules was reported. Each system was afraid that if it did not report, other systems would report, and they would be punished as accomplices or for concealing guys. Additionally, to make their powers absolutely secure, all suspected were murdered or incarcerated.

"The RL clique was jealous, envious, and greedy, so they were very angry with the prosperity of this neighbor country Eastnama. After a decade of their reign, they were sure that the people of Kanxono were submitted and obeyed what they required and commanded, they started this war. The clique promised that the people of Kanxono would receive all the things in Eastnama after their final victory and that the more one fought decisively, the more substantial reward one would received.

"Sir, now you see most guys that the RL clique have sent here fought fiercely like mayflies in this war of invasion. They've thought that there are numerous precious things in this country they can loot after their victory. They plan to take beautiful palaces, castles, mansions, and villas to live in this country.

"How will Eastnama be if they win? The RL clique will make the people of Eastnama become poor and will have to work hard for meager means of living as the people of Kanxono. The clique will enforce some millions of men of Eastnama to toil in slave camps in conditions with shortage of food, hygiene, medication. The clique's plan is that these men will gradually die in camps. The clique knows that wives and children of toilers will have no chance to survive unless they were submitted.

"In conclusion, the principles of RL clique are to make

peoples poor, dull, and frightened, so the governed have to submit in order to buy rationed means of living to survive and know only what the group propagate. Those who express their disbeliefs will be murdered and their families will live in destitution. The clique will collect all means of living, so the governed have to work hard as employees from dawn to dusk for the clique and then work hard at home in late evenings to have enough means of living, so the governed have no time to think anything different from what the group tell them. Also, the governed absolutely have no means to challenge the powers of the clique."

After the conversation, the commander issued two seats in a military plane for the home city of Fergus. A week later, little Prunus had recovered. Fergus flew back to his unit.

In the city, Depda dwelled in the Women Defector Center of the government and had permission to visit either Japonica or Formosa in weekends. After several weeks, Depda came to Formosa's house more frequently than to Japonica. The three women, little boy Prunus, and little girl Fruticosa often ate dinner and played joyfully together at Formosa's house on weekends. In some occasions, they took photographs together inside the house as well as at the backyard and front yard.

Unfortunately, the joyfulness lasted only six months. In a Sunday evening, when Depda stepped out the front door of the house, two men on one motorcycle passed by. The man on the backseat fired four shots on her chest. She fell down and died immediately. The man was a specialist assassin. He threw a small board with the words The Verdict of RL on the Traitor beside her body. The motorcycle and the men disappeared quickly.

In the funeral, Formosa, Japonica, Fruticosa, and Prunus sobbed. They were sad like they lost a close member of their family. After the funeral, Formosa wrote in her diary:

Women Victims of the War

Guys maltreat other people,
Wage the war,
Seed hostility is
Children of devils.
Guys prevent others to do against their good wills,
Oppress, tyrannize, kill,
Destroy the happiness of others become
Disciples of devils.

I witnessed the women victims;
Depda, Marigold, Marjoram, Pansy, Celandine
Were misused as sex playthings.
They lost freedom and dignity.
I felt their sufferings and miseries.
I saw them die in pain and agony.

There are thousands of other women victims,
I do not know their names and their cases.

Their emotion is a natural character of human beings. Only disciples or children of devils are heartless and do evil actions.

Deaths, sufferings, and destruction have happened in every war. This war has dragged out in Eastnama for nineteen years. The RL clique did not care about the millions of deaths in both sides. They did not give up their thought of suzerainty although the deaths of their side were tenfold higher. They were human beings but had mightiness, power, habits, and characteristics that devils had imparted to them.

The soldiers of the RL clique fought to deaths because of various reasons: Most of them avoid being the cause that made the RL clique punish severely their families consisting of parents and siblings. Another part of them expected rewards that the RL clique would bestow to their families after their deaths. Other part of them craves numerous precious things in Eastnama they would have if they won this war. Other part of them were brainwashed; they believed that the RL clique would build paradises in both Kanxono and Eastnama.

Contrarily, the people of Eastnama loved their lives. This war made more and more families lose their dears: husbands, fathers, mothers, sons, daughters, brothers, sisters, and friends. They witnessed the funerals with young wives and small children, followed the coffins covered with national flags. They saw the casualties of civilians dead, wounded, or injured by mines, spike traps, stray bullets, and so on. They met more and more war-disabled young men who lost parts of their bodies. Thus, their support for the fight against the invasion and occupation of the RL guys decreased. They thought that to live in destitution and under dictatorship were bad, but deaths or disabilities of their lovers were worse. As a result, Eastnama lost this war after nineteen years of fighting against the invasion and occupation of the RL guys. Its government surrendered, and its army disintegrated.

The RL guys were greedy, cruel, and despotic but sly and cunning. They proclaimed their lectures through all means of media and communications that they were high-minded victors. They bestowed amnesties and clemencies on all officials of surrendering government and officers of defeated army, but the victors needed help from all intellectuals, artists, rich people, former officials, and officers to build paradises in Eastnama, so the victors asked all of them to present themselves in assigned facilities to study the victors' policies, plans, and projects. About one million in the categories were deceived and presented in the facilities.

In the decided night, the RL victors shut off all sources of electricity of capital and cities. The victors secretly transported the deceived to slave camps in jungles where the deceived had to labor very hard in primitive agriculture and tree hewing with rudimentary tools in the conditions of meager food, lack of hygiene, and drinking water as well as severe shortage of medication, regardless if the deceived were professors, architects, engineers, pilots, pharmacists, and so on. The purposes of the RL clique were to kill these deceived gradually and silently in the jungles.

Alder and Fergus were among the deceived. Alder said good-bye to his young wife, Formosa, and five-year-old daughter, Fruticosa and presented himself in the assigned elementary school. Fergus said good-bye to his young wife, Japonica, and six-year-old son, Prunus, and presented himself in the assigned high school. Like other deceived, Alder and Fergus were transported to two different labor camps.

The then RL clique controlled all means of activities in the whole Eastnama, from important fabrics to tiny things like a needle, a yard of cloth, from large paddies to a bowl of rice, and so on. The prosperity of Eastnama disappeared after some months under their rules. The subjugated could buy rationed meager means of living. The more who were submitted, the more they were rationed. Those who were not subjugated or submitted had to die or live in destitution.

In the first week in every slave camp, each of the deceived was handed either a cleaver, a sickle, or a hoe to cut trees, bamboos, and elephant grasses or alang plants. They had built some cottages, beds, and tables for the rulers of the camp as well as a kitchen and rows of shanties for themselves. On the first day of the following week, they had to write full confessions on their guilts, guilt of fighting against the RL, guilt of preventing people supporting the RL, and so on. They had a whole day to write. They wrote and handed respectfully again and again their confessions many times to the rulers of the camps, but the rulers said that their confessions lacked sincerity and details.

In reality, the rulers meticulously compared the confessions whether there were any details different to one another. In the late evening, the rulers collected their last confessions and gave each of them a bowl of rice cooked from rotten raw rice and a mug of water scooped from the brook nearby.

In the slave camp named Xo Paradise, Alder wrote his confession with contents citing that despite his architecture career, he had to join the former army like other young men because of the general draft of the former government, that he had never gone to battles and not shot a single bullet toward the RL guys for seven years in the former army, that his works had been repairing roads and bridges for the people to go from one province to another and transport goods from one place to another, that his works had been useful to all people. Thus he was not guilty.

After several collections, the rulers of the slave camp called him to their bureau.

One of them said angrily, "Do you want to make fun to us? Do you know we're the liberators of the people? You must confess your guilts to labor. If you don't, we'll form a court here to execute you. Go back to your plank and write your confession that you built roads and bridges on which the tanks and military vehicles of the enemies moved to fight against the liberators of the people, that you are worthy to be executed, that the liberators grant clemency to spare your life, that you labor to show your repentance for your guilts. Go and write."

Alder wrote what the victors required.

Simultaneously, in the camp named Xo Liberty, Fergus wrote his confession with contents citing that despite being a civil doctor of medicine, he had obeyed the general draft to join the former army, that during seven years in the army, he was treating and curing the sick and wounded soldiers of both sides. Concretely, he had operated a severely wounded general of the liberator side whose alias was Second Thunder in the jungle six years ago. Thus, he was not guilty.

After some collections, Fergus was called to the bureau of the slave camp.

One liberator told him, "Your confessions are unacceptable because of two reasons: it doesn't have enough details and your denial of your guilts. For example, you didn't write the highest grade you had finished in your school."

"Sir, I'm a doctor."

"I know you're a doctor, but which grade in middle school or high school did you finish? I take my brother Sixth Stilt for an example, he finished the eighth grade. Then he came and fought to liberate this country. His duty was curing and nursing wounded and sick liberators. With his courage, experience, and seniority, he was promoted to higher and higher ranks. After ten years, he was promoted to doctor of medicine. Just after our victory, he took over the hospital and is the director of the hospital in the large city not far from here. Hmm, in short, he studied eighth grade in school. He is a doctor now because of his experiences in curing and nursing in rears of battlefields.

"Hmm, on the matter of your treating and curing of the sick and wounded soldiers of both sides, I must explain also. You treated and cured soldiers of your side, so they could continue to fight against us: big guilt. You treated and cured soldiers of our side, so they lost chance to be heroes of Kanxono and Eastnama: big guilt. Do you hear me? Go to the corner and do what I command."

All the slave laborers reproached themselves because they had been so gullible and had presented themselves to be slaves. Deaths began. They committed suicide because they could not endure the ignominiousness from the repeating insults and absurd labor. They died because they tried to escape. They were shot to death or wounded and dragged to the yards before the rows of shanties where the wounded cried to death since the rulers wanted to warn other laborers. They died because of the accidents of the dangerous labor. They died because of the serious lack of food. They died because of their sicknesses and serious lack of medication. The death rate was about 10 percent yearly.

And the dead were buried in the jungles. Their families did not know anything about their deaths. If the world outside knew some famous scientists or politicians who died in slave camps, the RL guys informed that they had committed suicide.

Simultaneously, in the capital and cities, the wives and children endured other cruelties and miseries. The victors tried to fulfill their greedy desires. They wanted to compensate themselves for the years they had lived in dangerous conditions in the forests or the underground tunnels and to take revenge on the deceived, their former rivals who had fought against them. They occupied and owned properties of the deceived. Wives and children of the deceived had to be servants of them in many ways to survive. Worse, a half of them lost their houses because the victors occupied the houses and threw them out to the streets, so they became homeless or went to the countryside to built small shanties and be destitute there. There were no clear policies and rules for occupying and owning the houses. Thus, any RL victors of any place did what he wanted, and the victors supported one another in their actions of occupying and owning the properties, houses, and servants as well as maltreating wives and children of the deceived.

Also, the victors tried to fulfill their lustful desires. They wanted to compensate themselves for the years of shortage of women in jungles or no women in underground tunnels and to take revenge on the deceived who had fought against them. Of course young wives and girls of the deceived were their victims. Since these wives and girls were in the situation of being maltreated by the new rulers and their husbands or fathers were in miserable condition in the labor camps in the jungles, the victors could vaguely promise to mitigate their maltreatment or to help with something. The young wives or girls could reluctantly let their bodies be used by the victors to fulfill their lust. Contrarily, if the tactic of promises did not work, the victors could intimidate to maltreat the victims more severely or to report something imagined to the rulers of the slave camps where their husbands or fathers were laboring. The young wives or girls could reluctantly let their bodies be used by the victors to fulfill their lust. Furthermore, the victors could show their stuff to maltreat in some crueler extends, the young wives or girls could reluctantly let their bodies to the victors to fulfill their lust. There were no clear policies and rules, and the victors took sides to one another.

About 10 percent of the families in Eastnama had members who were collaborators of followers of RL clique. They had economic lives as equal as they had had before the defeat of Eastnama, but most of them became scapegoats a year later. Other families became poor. The families which had members in labor camps lived in destitution and desperations.

Most of the victors targeted properties, houses, and women in areas they were assigned to occupy. However, a small part of them tried to find out the houses of women who they had some relations with them. For examples, Sixth Conqueror tried to find out where Formosa lived. He hated Formosa because her presence in the forest where his squad had stationed on the day he lost Celandine, and his inferiors lost Marigold and Pansy. Similarly, Second Thunder sought where the wife of Fergus lived, he wanted to take revenge on Fergus, who had instigated Depda running away.

Like other victors, Sixth Conqueror was clever in his words, he promised Formosa to help her husband in the labor camp and protect the house not being occupied by others.

After a month in the labor camp, an unexpected good luck came to Fergus. Director Sixth Stilt of the hospital in the city not far from the camp asked his brother Fifth Stick to escort Fergus to the hospital. Dr. Sixth Stilt wanted to know how physicians of Eastnama treated and cured sick and injured patients because the most patients who were examined by physicians of victors, including him, were scared and escaped the hospital.

Five days after the arrival of Fergus in the hospital, an important event happened to the victors. Their emperor died. Many high ranks of the RL in Eastnama had to come back immediately to Kanxono capital and stay there for four weeks to mourn and attend his funeral. Among them were General Second Thunder and Dr. Sixth Stilt.

Fergus did not miss the golden opportunity. He left the hospital that evening. With the identification and other proofs of being an employee signed by Dr. Sixth Stilt, he came safely to his home. Japonica and Prunus were overjoyed and embraced him, but he urged Japonica to quickly take all their jewels and gold they had stashed. They put them into a small bag. In a hurry, they led little Prunus to the house of Formosa. Unfortunately, Formosa and little Fruticosa were not at home at the moment. Japonica took a piece of paper and wrote some words of good-bye and promised to contact and help her friend whenever it would be possible. She slipped it into the slit of the front door. In hurry, they walked to the bus station and boarded one bus to the town on the coast. There they paid a boat owner who helped them to the international territorial waters. They hoped that a foreign ship would rescue and ship them to a country in which they would resettle and enjoy a real democracy and freedom without deceptions, lies, and so forth as the RL guys implemented in Kanxono and Eastnama. Luckily, they were rescued.

Pitifully, Alder, Formosa, and Fruticosa still endured waves of miseries. Like the youngest wives whose husbands labored in the slave camps, Formosa was the sexual target of two victors since she was still pretty and charming although her age was in the mid-thirties. During the first month after the victory, Sixth

Conqueror often came in the evenings to flirt and promised to help her husband in the camp as well as herself and little Fruticosa. He promised to protect the house and not let it be occupied by others.

In the second month, another victor, Fourth Quick came to Formosa's house. His original purpose was to find Sixth Conqueror because former inferior had abducted fifteen-year-old Celandine away from her village ten years ago. He had also craved for having sex with Celandine, but his inferior stole his thunder. His jealousy purposed to punish his inferior, but he used the pretext of the forceful and statutory rapes of Sixth Conqueror. However, when he met Formosa, he had also passion for her beauty and charm, so he had additional purpose. He eliminated his inferior from the competition to get Formosa.

When the rivals encountered each other in the house of Formosa the second time, Fourth Quick reprimanded Sixth Conqueror, "You committed serious crimes."

"What?"

"You abducted fifteen-year-old Celandine and raped her. You can't deny."

"Not few RL guys had sexual intercourses with teens, even our emperor in Kanxono did that, you know for sure. Why do you condemn me only?"

"Yes, our emperor did, but only a part of our RL guys knew, and the very great majority of the people of Kanxono didn't know, and peoples in the world didn't know. To them, our emperor was a great saint with perfect virtues and values. Several books have already described him a great saint. In the future, the next generations in Kanxono and Eastnama will continue to consider him a great saint, even sculpt his statue to adore him. The issue was the compulsion of concealment. You had to conceal your crimes, but you didn't, you couldn't. The villages knew your rapes. You must be punished."

"But Celandine was dead."

"That made your crime more serious."

Suddenly, two inferiors of Fourth Quick appeared with weapons. They bound the hands of Sixth Conqueror, escorted him into a military jeep, and drove away.

After the incident, no one knew where Sixth Conqueror was.

However, Formosa still lived in harassment and sorrow. Fourth Quick came very often to intimidate her. Additionally, she had to sell valuable things gradually in order to buy meager food to survive.

In one evening, a ragged woman handed Formosa a small and dirty paper with these hand-scribed words on it:

"Your husband was perhaps dead. He and his two close friends had escaped from the camp. A month later, we found two skeletons in the jungle five miles far from the camp. We brought the skeletons and buried them on the hill about thirty yards south far from the fence of Xo Paradise camp. One of the escapes succeeded. But we do not know who."

The words were from a co slave in the camp, where Alder labored. The news made Formosa desperate. At that night, she mixed coal powder with oil in a bowl and crushed the mixture on her face to make her face dirty. Before dawn, she led her five-year-old daughter Fruticosa, left her house, and went to an unknown destination.

Deptam was free. Her sexual submission ended after the death of the emperor in Kanxono. She came to Eastnama to search for traces and whereabouts of her elder sister Depda. After some weeks of inquiries, she found out that her eldest sister had often come to the house of Formosa and little Fruticosa in a period of six months before being assassinated in front of the house. She arrived in the city and was guided to visit the grave of her elder sister. The former government had interred the corpse of her elder sister. Then she came to the place where her elder sister had fallen down bloody after being shot. She sobbed bitterly for several minutes.

However, Formosa and little Fruticosa had left their house three days before, and it was occupied by Fourth Quick. She required the head liberator of the district to issue another house for Fourth Quick and let her live in the very house in which she had some memories about her elder sister.

She was eager to search Formosa and little Fruticosa to come back to live with her. Thus, she wrote an announcement that appeared in the Saturday and Sunday newspapers:

Dear Formosa and little Fruticosa,

I am Deptam, younger sister of Depda. I am living in your house now and try all my best to help you. Return to your home. I am waiting for you.
If anyone knows mother Formosa and little daughter Fruticosa, please, tell them this announcement. Those who bring them home will receive a liberal reward.

However, did Formosa have the newspaper, or did she read the announcement? Could anyone realize Formosa after her face was changed? Did the mother and the little daughter still live, or were they dead?

Wandering as beggars, Formosa and Fruticosa were hungry and haggard. Very few people gave them food because the people lacked in food for themselves.

One late evening, Formosa led her little daughter back to their house. Standing in the front door, Formosa realized that someone was inside, she immediately thought it was Fourth Quick, so she led her daughter to turn away.

Suddenly, the front door opened. A joyful female voice spoke out:

"Oh, you are. This is your house. Turn back. Come in. I'm waiting for you."

The voice of a woman made Formosa surprised, and she turned back. Deptam ran to the mother and daughter, held their hands, and led them enter their house.

While the returnees were washing, Deptam prepared a spare meal. Then the mother and daughter ate appetizingly.

Little Fruticosa had a good sleep after the dinner, but the two women remained awake and told each other their whole stories.

At the end, Deptam said, "Formosa, you and Fruticosa have at least two hopes. The first one, your husband can be the successful escapee, who's now living in a free country. The second one, your close friend Japonica and her husband living in either Unto Blumen or Fragrance are ready to help you. In the present, RL guys need persons who can use simultaneously three languages like you to help them in their embassies. I'll interfere, you'll work in one of the two embassies. Little Fruticosa will go with you. When you reach the country, try to find out your husband or your friends and try to escape and stay there.

"As for me, RL guys respect me now. But in the future, they'll be able to turn their behaviors and treat me badly. So when you succeed, find a means to signal me. I'll also fly to the place you live in and ask your help."

Secret Scores for Admission to Universities

"Professor, all the last three school years, I passed the final examinations with excellent scores, why may I not automatically continue the study of my final year but must do this competitive examination again?"

"Tulipa, you were studying at this Faculty of Nurses in three school years. You do realize lots of changes here after our country was invaded. Similar to all other organs, directors and managing boards come from the invaders' country. Their professional knowledge and skill are poor, but they show their imperious authority. To us, they instruct many antiscientific and ludicrous works, but we must follow. To students, they require futile and absurd works.

"Tulipa, your written competitive exam has high scores. The assigned time and date for your oral exam is ten o'clock tomorrow morning. One guy among managing boards is your examiner. I can do nothing to help you. 'Good luck' are only words I can say to you."

"Thank you, professor."

Tulipa left the campus. Puzzle and anxiety were full in her mind. She thought on the meanings of the word *changes* the professor had implied. The real implementations of the invaders were suzerainties, despoilments, and punishments. They occupied and controlled everything. Only air and sunlight they cannot occupy. They systematically doomed the whole people. They despotically incarcerated not only the officials and officers of the surrendered government and defeated army but also artists and intellectuals in prisons or labor camps. Family members of prisoners and camp laborers were despoiled all means to earn their livings. To recruit collaborators, they handed out favors to some despicable guys who denounced their native people.

She thought of her classmates and schoolmates of all four grades. There were 120 students consisting of freshmen, sophomores, juniors, and seniors, but nearly all of them were females since most males did not want to work as nurses. Then and again, she passed the houses of the parents of several students. The houses were occupied by invaders, and she did not know where the families of her schoolmates had gone. Sometimes at random, she encountered some other classmates in streets, but their appearances were changed: youthful and upright attitudes were replaced by anxious and careful cautions because nobody knew who the collaborators were or who denounced others with the hope of getting something from the victors.

She thought of her parents and younger brother. Her father was a former corporal of the defeated army. Though he was not incarcerated in a prison or labor camp, he could not find even a low-paying job because of his life story. Her mother who had owned a kiosk of kid clothes, but the kiosk was confiscated. She was also jobless since her life story had the implication of her husband. Her brother was a graduate of high school with honors, but he had no chance for admission to a university or get a normal job. His only chance was to join the Youth Volunteer Union, which went to reclaim virgin soil with rudimentary tools like hoes, shovel, and so on in jungles, but it was sorry that volunteers earned even not enough food for themselves. They needed support. They got dry food, clothes, and medication from their families. They received only the promise that after two years, they would get fair jobs suitable to their talents. For the livings of her whole family, her parents had to sell gradually furniture of their house then jewels of her mother. With stingy thriftiness, however, her mother's last jewel would be sold in the next eleven months.

She thought of herself. She knew her parents and brother were expecting her to finish her last school year at Faculty of Nurses and would get a job to help them. Their expectation made her worry. She perspired when she reached her home's front door.

She entered the house. His father and brother looked at her face to conjecture a result.

But her mother asked directly, "Did you pass the examination? You're intelligent, so it isn't difficult to you, is it?"

"Mother, I passed the written part. The oral part will be at ten o'clock tomorrow morning, and the examiner is a guy from the invaders' country. You know the present authorities don't need intelligent or talented persons but collaborative or loyal ones. I'll try all my best. But don't expect me to do what I cannot do."

"Honey, our daughter says the shifty reality of this present society. Let her calm down. Our ill fates go with the miserable destiny of our country. Tulipa, go to the kitchen, some pieces of cassava are there for you." Then the father murmured to the ear of the mother, "If it is necessary, we can terminate our lives with rat poison."

Tulipa came to the faculty before ten o'clock in the morning of the next day. It was the assigned oral exam day for all former students—freshmen, sophomores, and juniors—who wanted to continue their study and had passed the written part of the exam.

However, only seventeen female students, about one-fifth,

were in the campus for the oral exam. Where were the others? Hadn't they passed the written exam? Or had they fled abroad? Or had male students joined the Youth Volunteer Union? Tulipa felt lonely and nervous when she realized that other sixteen examinees were former freshmen and sophomores. She was the only one of former junior grade.

In previous years, for oral exams, each grade had been assigned a different day. All students of the grade had sat at one corner of the lecture hall, and the examiner had sat at the opposite corner. The examiner had called the students turn by turn by name to come and sit on the chair opposite the examiner for one's oral exam. After a week, the results had been posted up before the hall.

However, the invaders promulgated numerous changes that year. Changes made the whole people quite dependent on them, changes offered them privileges, changes gave them prerogatives, changes assisted them easily to abuse, and changes showed their authorities, changes caused their victims to have no chance to protest but to submit to their abusers.

At ten o'clock, one guy from the managing boards came to the doorframe of the hall and said loudly, "You'll be called turn by turn to the next room for your oral exam. Close the door of the room when you're inside, so no questions and answers are heard from outside. The results will be posted up here one week before the beginning of the school year. By the way, you should come to this faculty every Saturday afternoon to study politics."

Then he went into the next room. He was the examiner. Tulipa was the first oral examinee being called. The examiner stared at her from the top of her head to her toes. Then he slightly intimidated and slightly enticed her, "I have read your life story. Your father is a former under officer of the army that we defeated, isn't he?"

"Yes, sir"

"During the war, did your father, mother, you yourself, or your younger brother have any work that supported our side?"

"No, sir"

"Sorry, your ethical situation has only negative points. You are disqualified on the study in the next school year, your final year, to become a nurse. But don't worry. If you follow my counseling, it will make you qualified. We're in the group consisting of six members from different organs of the present government. Come to our address and we'll help you how to rewrite your life story, then the high-ranking public security agent in our group will certify your new life story. Take the piece of paper and pen on the table. I'll say our address for you to write down. You had better come in Saturday afternoon. It's a golden opportunity. We're ready to help you. If you come, you're exempted from the study of politics. If you come, you'll surely be admitted to the senior grade.

"Tulipa, we'll assist you to come there. From the street of your house, take the bus number 38 eastward to the last station. A beige van with the national emblem will wait for you there at two o'clock. Don't worry. We'll recognize you."

Tulipa put the address paper into her shirt pocket and left the room. When she reentered the lecture hall, several sophomores and freshmen surrounded and asked her about what kind of questions the examiner requested. But she had only one short answer: "He checked my life story."

The answer made them anxious. Everyone of them probably had some unsuitability to the new government in their life stories.

Then one examinee said to the others, "I know her house. She is the unique student of former junior grade. We can later come to her house and ask for necessary advices."

Tulipa left the campus. She felt embarrassed when she remembered the stare of the examiner and the address paper in her pocket. She understood what would happened if she came to the place. She trembled when she imagined some probable obscenities of the six guys whom the examiner had mentioned. She felt sorrowful on the miseries and stalemate of her family. She pondered whether or not she come to the place. She thought anxiously whether the group of the six guys really help her to have fruitful result as the examiner had promised if she boldly sacrificed her virginity. She worried when she thought that they would probably require her to come there more than one time.

Again, she thought on the miseries and the stalemate of her family. She try to seek for another way to rescue her family, but she found none. Thus, she decided to risk but not let anyone of her family know her sacrifice and humiliation. She tried to regain composure and entered the front door of her house.

Her parents and brother looked at her. She knew she had to say something about the oral examination:

"The results will be posted up at the faculty one week before the beginning of the school year. They have so many ways to ill-treat the people. Daddy, mom, on Saturdays, I should be present in the Faculty of Political Studies. I'll leave at one o'clock."

By one o'clock in the afternoon on Saturday, while Tulipa was preparing to leave the house, she heard some knocks at the front door. Through the front window, she realized three female students she had met in the lecture hall at the Faculty of Nursing. She understood immediately that their circumstances were similar to hers. She stepped out. One of them introduced:

"Hi, Tulipa, we're all former freshmen. Ajuga is my name. Briza is at my left hand. Chusquea is at my right hand. We come here to take the same bus with you."

Tulipa said in low voices:

"I think you understand where we go and what will happen there. But if my parents or my brother ask you, let say we go to the Faculty of Political Studies."

The three students nodded. They entered the house and drank some pure water. A pair minutes later, they went together to the bus station not far from the house. In the bus, they all sat silently in meditation.

At the last station, they stepped down from the bus. They saw two other young females sitting on a bench and watching at them. The two sides immediately realized they were schoolmates. They quickly ran toward one another and emotionally embraced one another. One of the two introduced:

"We're former sophomores. Romneya is my name. Saccharata is my best friend. We've just come here from the bus number 39."

They had not to wait long. Several minutes later, the beige van came. The examiner sat in the front-right seat. The driver pressed a button. The right-side door opened. Likely being hypnotized, the students stepped into the van and sat silently in the six seats behind the two men.

The van ran eastward. After ten miles, it turned right upward to a hill and stopped in the yard of a wooden house. It was the rest house of a former hunter group. When the students were following the two men toward the front room or waiting room, Saccharata held Tulipa's hand to slow down behind the others and murmured:

You're our eldest sister. Please, represent us to ask them to keep their promises. Also, ask them other necessary questions."

The front room was airy. A large table stood in the middle of room. Twelve chairs surrounded the table, but four men had already sat on the four ones facing the front door. The four men stared at the students from one to another.

The examiner pointed to the six chairs opposite the four men and told the students to sit down. Then the examiner and the driver took two seats next to the fourth men. The examiner pulled out a paper from his pocket, gave the students orders, and stated to his superiors:

"I read your name one by one, stand up to present yourself to my superiors. Ajuga, Briza, and Chusquea: nineteen years old. Romneya and Saccharata: twenty years old. Tulipa: twenty one years old.

"Dear superiors, these beauties are former students of Faculty of Nurses. They want to continue their studies. But their life stories have some unsuitability to be readmitted. So they come here to ask our help. I think we've ready to help them if they have something to exchange. Their presence here without gold or the likes implies what they have already agreed the thing to exchange."

"Sirs, my name is Tulipa. Because I'm the eldest, my schoolmates want me to ask you to keep your promises, we mean the surety for us to continue our studies until we obtain our objective diplomas."

"Of course, as I said in the room of the faculty, I read your life stories. All of you have similar obstructions: your fathers are either under officers of the defeated army or low-ranking officials of the surrendered government. You should change only this part in your life stories, either you'll describe that your father dodged the drafts of the former government and hid somewhere, or you can fabricate some similarities. For other parts, you can rewrite the exact sameness.

Now, it's time for you to do your duties to get scores for your oral examination. Each high official here selects one of you, and you go with him into a bedroom to make love. Be spontaneous. It's a joyful work. If you have no idea, do what he tells you. I think it lasts more or less than half an hour. If he asks you to make love the second time, do it with joy, he'll tell me and you'll get more points.

To make you feel confident, I present the four high officials sitting before you. Opposite Saccharata is Director General of Hospitals in this capital. After your graduation, he can help you workplaces where you want. In lovemaking you can him Two Phit. Opposite Romneya is the vice president of the national press. In lovemaking, call him Three Rot. Opposite Chusquea is vice chief of the police department in this capital. He'll certify your life stories. In lovemaking, call him Four Xep. Opposite Briza is head of Faculty of Nurses. You will see him in the faculty. In lovemaking, call him Seven Vem. I'm secretary general of Faculty of Nurses as you know. In lovemaking, call me Nine Phet. The van driver is the manager of this property. He is on guard outside. I and he will exchange positions later. In lovemaking, call him Ten Dot. If you forget this special name of your partner, ask him in the bedroom. Contrarily, in this house, we call you beauties, okay?

"After lovemaking, you can come here and write your new life story. But don't hurry, you have nine more Saturdays to write. It's two fifty now. We have three hours. The van will transport you and reach the bus station before six."

"Sir, there are eleven Saturdays before the beginning of the next school year, but how many more Saturdays we have to come here."

"I've mentioned. I explain clearer. The minimum points for your oral examination is 100. Every Saturday you come here and do your duty, you get 10 points. Some of you who will make an extra second time or third time in any Saturday will get 5 points more for each time. Believe me. The more points you get now, the more benefits you will have in the final exam of the next school year, a condition to get good jobs. Beauties, everything is explained to you. No more questions.

Dear superiors, it's time for each of you to select one of the beauties. Mr. Vice President of the national press, it's your turn to select first.

"Ah, you've already selected. You've discerning eyes. These six beauties are really six attractive and charming nymphets. I suggest. Let's each of the beauties go into one room. None of them knows which room belongs to whom. Then we enjoy her selection."

"Dear Mr. Director, dear Mr. Vice Chief, dear Mr. Head of Faculty, please, give your words."

"Excellent."

"I agree."

"Me too."

"Beauties, do you hear? Each of you goes into one room. The six rooms are along the verandah at my right hand."

At first, the six young students looked one another and hesitated. But after a several seconds, they slowly followed one another to the verandah and each of them stepped into one room.

Waiting in the front room, the five men commended the selection and arrangement of "Nine Phet" and talked about their booties.

"Hey, it isn't a matter I call you Nine Phet, and you call me Two Phit here, is it? Three Rot is right. They are all beautiful and charming. After our victory, we procure different gains not only material treasures like the valuable estates but also pleasant fulfillments like young nymphets. I think they still have virginity. To deflower is a precious enjoyment, isn't it?"

"Call me Seven Vem. There is a belief saying that a man deflowers a virgin will procure fortune thereafter. But in our case, our victory brings us gains including having virgins to deflower."

"Call me Four Xep. Each of us gains many things. But in each organ there is some different preciousness that is easier for victors there to take than other victors in other organs. For example, high schools and universities are the places teen girls and young women gather. So there are surfeits of beauties for victors there to select. By the way, many more former students at Faculty of Nurses may continue their studies. Why only six these beauties do duties, Seven Vem?"

"There are some different ways for them to do their duties. Like your organs, most of them must donate us gold, money, or diamonds. Of course, all the ways are carried out in secrecy. For example, at this time, the parents of these beauties think their daughters are studying politics or doing fatigue duties somewhere."

"Dear Superiors, the beauties are ready. They're waiting for us. Can anyone of us know which nymphet is on one's bed now? Lets come to enjoy the most amazing pleasure in our lives."

"Nine Phet, you may go first because you'll be on guard

to exchange for Ten Dot. However, we've three hours. Enjoy your best."

"Thank you"

Except Ten Dot was on guard, each of the five men went to his room. Male voices of "aha" or "oho" expressing agreement or surprise intoned, and male instructs or requests murmured from the rooms.

The noises of taking off clothes rustled, thuds of falls plopped, retching of throats choked, creaks of beds whizzed from the rooms.

Suddenly, female wails cried out painfully, female sobs groaned imploringly, female entreats resounded emotionally from some rooms.

Ten minutes passed the first oink like babble of a pig sounded from one room. Then and then other similar oinks echoed from others.

Half an hour later, turn in turn, the female students came sadly back to the waiting room and sat dazedly at the table. Some glanced at the basket and the stack of their useless life stories in the middle on the table, but none of them do anything.

An hour later, Nine Phet, the examiner, appeared. He looked around all the sad faces and said:

"Some of you felt painful because it was the first time. It won't happen again in the next and next times. Think about your future study and your family situations to continue this beneficial work. At the same time on every Saturday, the same van will come to the same bus station to pick you up. Now, you have nearly two hours before the van transport you to the bus station. As I said, you can rewrite your life story today or next or next Saturday. If you don't want to write today, you can chat with one another."

The examiner left the room. Nevertheless, no students wrote or talked. Some drooped their heads on the edge of the table. Others looked aimlessly through the window.

The third Saturday, the third day of their humiliation came. Like two previous times, when Tulipa, Ajura, Briza, and Chusquea stepped down from the bus at the last station, they saw Romneya and Saccharata were sitting on the same bench. However, this time, there was a teen girl between them. They stood up to greet one another.

Seeing Tulipa, Ajura, Briza, and Chusquea looked inquiringly at the teen, Romneya told Tulipa and three others the reason of the presence of the teen:

"Tulipa, here is Nitida, daughter of our neighbor family. Her father was arrested two days ago because he was one of the organizers of a boat ready to flee out this country. Her mother asked me whether I know a high-ranking man in police branch in order to bribe for her husband's release. She said that the earlier his case is bribed, the easier it's solved. I told her about the vice chief of the police department at this rest house. But Nitida eavesdropped our conversation. Today, she follows me. I try to persuade her to go home, but she doesn't take my advice."

"How old are you, Nitida?"

"I'm fifteen years old."

"You're too young to decide. Do you know what happens when you meet the man in the rest house?"

"I must let him use my body to have sex, but I sacrifice what I can. I beg all of you, let me rescue my father. They're torturing my father to find more organizers."

"Are you the single child of your parents?"

"No, I've an eighteen-year-old elder brother, but he joins Youth Volunteer Union last week. He is now in the jungle to reclaim virgin soil."

"My eighteen-year-old younger brother joins Youth Volunteer Union last week also. Do you know the name of the company your brother is serving?"

"YVU-19C."

"The same company of my brother. Probably, your brother and mine have already known each other."

"If not yet, we'll write them to make them friends, won't we? Excuse me, You're my elder sister, so your brother is an elder brother of mine."

Suddenly, the students turned their eyes toward one direction. The appearance of the beige van at the corner of the road interrupted their conversation. Then the bus stopped at the same parking lot. This time, the examiner was not in the van.

The students walked to the bus; Nitida followed them. The driver looked fixedly at Nitida. When she began to step up into the van, he stretched straightly his hand to halt her and asked successively:

"Who are you? What do you want? Why do you step up? Do you know where this van go?"

Both Romneya and Tulipa reacted oppositely to their own persuasions to Nitida for returning home some minutes earlier. They besought the driver to let her sit in the reserve seat. He consented but his face had a fretful sign.

The van reached and stopped at the front yard of the rest house. When the students and Nitida entered the waiting room, the examiner was there. He looked fixed at Nitida but pointed a chair for her to sit down and asked:

"Who are you? Why do you come here?"

"I...a...I...a...I...my name is Nitida. My father is arrested. I want to meet Mr. Vice Chief of the police department to entreat his help. Please let me a...an...a..."

"Ok, he'll come here in several minutes. Say directly to him what kind of help you want from him, okay?"

About ten minutes later, Two Phit, Three Rot, Four Xep, and Seven Vem entered the room. Nine Phet talked to them about the newcomer immediately:

"Here is Nitida. She said that his father is detained, so she comes here to entreat Mr. Vice Chief for help."

All eyes looked at Nitida. Four Xep presumed to be

interested and supercilious. He directly said to Nitida, but he intentionally let all others hear him:

"The situation of your father and what kind of help he needs should be explained in privacy. Walk along the veranda at your left hand and enter the room number four. I'll be there in a pair minutes."

There were six rooms of six abusers, but six students plus Nitida equal seven. Thus, Nine Phet told them:

"Each of you go to one room except Tulipa. Hey Tulipa, you're beautiful, but the others are younger than you. You stay here in this waiting room. In spite of staying here, you have ten points like the others. If any of us wants two beauties in one desire, he'll call you. Now, I go to my room to know which one is my beauty today."

About a quarter later, from the waiting room, Tulipa heard groans probably from the room number four. She closed her eyes in sadness.

From that day, Nitida and Tulipa became close friends. They behaved each other like sisters. In Saturday evenings, after the suffering of humiliation, Nitida went with Tulipa to her house before coming home. Also, their brothers in YVU-19C became close friends thanks to their contacts.

On their fifth Saturday of humiliation, a warm day in summer, Nitida wore a jacket. In that evening, when the two close friends were in the Tulipa's house, she asked in a soft quiet voice:

"Nitida, why have you worn the thick jacket in this warm day? Have you hid something in it?"

"Last Saturday, the vice chief of the police department said that he's only the second man at the departments, that when my father is released, I must bring him two taels of gold to bribe his superior, if it is not done, my father will be arrested again and his situation will be worse, and that I must do it in secrecy. Yesterday, my father came home. My parents handed me two taels of gold, and I hid in the jacket."

"They are robbers. And did you do it in secrecy?"

"Sorry. When I passed the room number 3, Three Rot, vice president of the national press, looked fixedly at my jacket and pulled me into his room. He pressed the pocket and knew the two taels of gold. He told me to stay with him. But at the moment, Four Xep, the vice chief of the police department, entered the room and said that I come to the house to ask his help, so I belong to him only. The two men quarreled in a minute. Then Four Xep pulled me to his room number 4."

"Their quarrel can be a problem for you later. But you can do nothing. Ah, it's only a conjecture. Be calm. By the way, how is your father?"

"Half death. But I think, he'll recover."

"I'm angry. You've to pay both in sex and gold. Nitida, how many more Saturday afternoons must you come to the house?"

"He told me this afternoon that you, the students, should come there five more times. I must do the same."

"All of them are bastards."

On the next night, Sunday, at two o'clock, while Tulipa and her parents were still sleeping, they heard someone knocked at their front door. They were frightened because they thought that the police came to arrest someone of them as this organ had usually done. But it was Nitida. Her face had some joyful appearance. She talked immediately:

"Did you hear the radio broadcasting from Fragrance, a country with freedom like Unto Blumen? My brother and yours sent their words to us and you. They fled to the neighbor country. In the refugee camp, a representative of Fragrance interviewed and allowed them to resettle in the country since their fathers are former under officers in the former army."

"At what time their words were broadcasted?"

"At midnight. My father said that they'll be broadcasted once more time at midnight tomorrow."

Tulipa led Nitida to her bed. The two lay silently and thought about wishes that their brothers would hopefully do for them. The final wish was that their brothers would file visas for all members of their families to get out of the hell they were enduring.

Ten weeks of ignominious sufferings passed. The six students were admitted to the Faculty of Nursing again. Nitida attended the ninth grade at her local high school. They were all busy because of their political and professional studies at schools, fatigue and secure duties for local authorities as well as familial errands and chores for their parents. They had no time to talk or visit one another.

Three more months passed. One early morning, at the Faculty of Nursing, Romneya showed Tulipa a newspaper and pointed to the news that they guessed it was written by Three Rot, vice president of the national press:

Statutory Rape

A beautiful fifteen-year-old female teen
was raped many times. Nitida is her name.
She is pregnant in the third month now.
As she reveals, the rapist is a high-ranking
policeman. So it will be very hard to accuse
him.

Tulipa and Romneya felt deeply sad and anxious, sad on pitiful Nitida and anxious on their possible entanglement.

In the afternoon of the very day, knotty misfortunes began to happen to Tulipa and Romneya: four policepersons arrived in the Faculty of Nursing to arrest the two students.

In the provisional jail, with many forms of intimidation, the police tried to coerce the two students to confess that they had enticed Nitida to sleep with the man for money. It used only the words "the man" and never revealed who he was. In other words, it coerced them to confess they were two madams. But they flatly refused. After a day, the police realized that it needed only one victim because its arrangements to lay simultaneously the blame at the two students in this case seemed to be an absurd story. So it released Romneya. And it continued to detain Tulipa.

A week later, Tulipa was taken to a farcial court. A prosecutor read with stumbles the so-called Nitida's statements confirming that Tulipa had enticed her to sleep with the man for money. Then, with difficulty, the judge read the verdict of four years in labor camp for Tulipa. The trial ended after quarter of an hour.

The justice of the victors left the man untouched. Several days after the verdict, some guys saw the vice chief of police and the vice president of the national press boozed together in the villa of the latter.

In the labor camp, Tulipa was not in a misery situation in comparison with the great majority of her inmates. Her mother sent or brought dried food and necessary needs every month thanks to the money her brother sent from Fragrance and the presents of Nitida's parents as her mother told.

The first mention about Nitida engendered Tulipa hate. But her mother explained that her hate meant she did not understand the slyness and cunningness of these authorities. So Tulipa calm down.

The time in the labor camp slowed to a crawl. The happiest hours for camp laborers were the visit times of their family members. Like some previous months, at nine o'clock in the morning on the last Sunday of the seventh month, Tulipa was called to the front cottage to wait for her visitors. At ten o'clock, from a distance, she saw her mother walking near a female figure that she guessed Nitida.

At the beginning of the meeting, Tulipa and her mother greeted each other joyfully. But Nitida stood silently in sadness. Realizing that, the mother guided Tulipa and Nitida to a far corner of the yard, sat on the ground, and conversed in very low voices.

Tulipa greeted, "Hi, Nitida. How is the baby?"

Immediately, the mother interfered, "I forgot to tell you. She had an abortion at the later third month of the pregnancy."

"Tulipa, I'm sorry for the statements the prosecutor read at the trial," Nitida confided. "The police intimidated me that night. At dawn, one policewoman put the paper on the table and told me to sign. I didn't read but signed. I'm sure the police added the statements on the very paper. I'm very sorry about that."

"Nitida, you don't have any fault at all. We're the victims of these sly and cunning authorities."

"Tulipa, do you remember the night I lay on your bed? We had the dreams that our brothers will file visas for all members of our families to get out of this hell. Our dreams were only wishes. But now, our dreams become true."

"What do you mean?"

"We have the letter from my brother informing that he and your brother have already filed visas for our two families to immigrate to Fragrance."

Submitted to Work As a Spy

My name is Nhutien Vitin. Lots of people say to me that I am very pretty and charming, and I know they say the truth. Probably, you will have the same conclusion after your reading of my story.

According to my conception and perception, all women want to be beautiful, but only a small part of them procure their wishes. In all generations and in all countries, there appear several very beautiful women.

Today, most beautiful women benefit by having beauty. There are lucrative careers and jobs for beautiful women such as models, advertisers, and so on. The more beautiful an actress is, the more famous she becomes. Surely, beauty is the first condition to apply as candidates in competitions for Miss National, Miss International, and so forth. These women are lucky.

Contrarily, in this world, there are still beautiful women who are coerced to work for egoist interests of unrighteous men. These women must consent to have sexual intercourse with men who have powers or monies. In other words, these women must do ignominious works, which render their lives from unhappiness to misery. These women are in the unlucky categories.

In my case, the men of the dictatorial clique have inflicted many sufferings on me including working as a spy for them.

I was told that both my paternal and maternal ancestors had settled in Kanxono country for many past centuries. The great-grandparents of my father had reclaimed a vast coastal area of virgin soil and become wealthy, then they had founded the prosperous town on their own soil. Their children and grandchildren had been industrious bosses or managers though they had inherited the wealth. On my mother side, my grandfather had been an ingenuous technician and resourceful businessman. He himself had built power looms, borrowed gold from my paternal grandparents, established a weave factory, and succeeded. Since the two families had lived in the same town, their relationship had had positive opportunity to engender chances for their children becoming close friends.

During the childhood and teenage of my father and mother, they were learning same classes from kindergarten to the end of their high school though my mother was seven months younger. Call my father Manhky, my mother Nangthi. They loved each other sometime in their high school period with celibate love. The two families knew their love and urged them to marry, but they agreed with each other that they would marry later just after their attainment of some degrees from universities.

After their high school graduation, both his and her parents encouraged them to study in a foreign country. They chose a university in the capital of Unto Blumen, the most developed country at that time. He studied construction engineering; she studied the official language of Unto Blumen. However, their love was so ripe, they organized their marriage after only two semesters. All members of the two families were in the capital of Unto Blumen to celebrate their wedding.

After a year, my sister, Binhquan, was born. Two years later, my brother, Phonghai, was welcomed to the world. My maternal grandmother arrived in the capital of Unto Blumen to help my parents. But two years later, it was my turn to be brought into the world.

Thanks to the diligence of my parents, the wholehearted help of my grandmother, and the financial support from my grandparents of both sides, my father got an MS and my mother got an MA a month before my second birthday celebration. But after the celebration, my grandmother left Unto Blumen back for Kanxono.

However, my parents stayed in Unto Blumen after they had graduated because of the advices from my grandparents of both sides: Kanxono had been in a war for four years and it was in ferocious situation at that time.

"The present circumstances in Kanxono are not good for you, especially for your children. This will end, and you can return home thereafter."

This was the small quote from the letter of my paternal grandfather.

Some months later, my father got a job in a construction company, and my mother got a job in a cultural center. For us, in daytime, my sister was in an elementary school, my brother was in kindergarten, and I was in child care.

Based on what I heard from my parents, I tell you something about my altruistic grandparents, the cruel war, and their involvements in the war.

(The last name of my paternal grandparents is Vitin, and the last name of my maternal grandparents is Donso.)

My four grandparents of both sides were the generous philanthropists. They pooled money to donate one-tenth to the cost of the national library in the capital of Kanxono. At their hometown, they financed several important projects such as the series of schools from the preschool to the high school, the library, the recreation center, the hospital, and the public nursing home. In addition, their altruistic works expanded directly to the poor in their hometown. For example, they supported free lunch for children of the poor in the schools.

The dynasty that had reigned Kanxono since the beginning of the century had consisted of only dull and antediluvian kings. When many countries in the world had already developed thanks to sciences and technologies, those consecutive kings had ignored all the means and chances of developments although they had received warnings of many clear-sighted citizens from inside and outside the country.

During four decades, many countries in the world were implementing their reforms, but the last king of Kanxono did not follow the trend. Therefore, my two grandfathers exchanged views with each other and wrote nearly fifty reforming proposals in agriculture, industry, education, diplomacy to the last king of the dynasty, but he opposed all.

At the same period, a group of sly guys formed a clique. Then the clique established the so-called Revolution League, raised the so-called Revolution Army, and started the war from their first base in a dense jungle. The RL promised many interesting and excellent things such as prosperity for all the people, free education for all children, equality, freedom, and so on. Their promises were ideological wishes of the majority of the people including my grandparents of both sides. Therefore, from the beginning of the war, my grandparents not only secretly supported RL and RA in many ways, but also agreed their sons, or my uncles, joining the RA, uncle Anhvu of my father side, and uncle Manhdan of my mother side. The RA fought the first battle sometime in the year my elder sister was born in Unto Blumen.

My grandparents secretly supported the RL and the RA twice than they paid taxes to the government of the king. Additionally, they let RL cadres hide themselves and cover their antigovernment handbills in their villas when they had activities in the area.

Unfortunately, the war in Kanxono became ferocious

and dirty. From the sixth year of the war, RL clique decided to use two parallel strategies: fighting against the army of the government (AG) and destroying industry and infrastructure. Therefore, that country became worse and worse. Miseries happened everywhere. On the other hand, in territories RL or RA controlled, all inhabitants, adults and children, had to support them. Young guys had to join RA. Whoever had any suspected words or activities against them were executed openly or secretly. Additionally, RL guys snuck through territories controlled by the government to assassinate or kidnap its officials.

When RA had already destroyed and damaged lots of material and technical bases as well as parts of infrastructure, AG had to spread out in small units to protect the people, infrastructure, and bases including my grandparents' factory. RA usually concentrated tenfold units to assault small units of AG, which suffered many losses.

In the tenth year of the war against the government, RL clique had the confidence that they would win the war. Thus, the RL clique gathered themselves in a secret session to confirm their original goal of dictatorship that was opposite to the promises they openly propagated. They viewed the ideologies of the important guys in their RL and RA as well as their supporters and collaborators. They divided them in two large categories. Those who would join their dictatorship were in their category of loyalists; those who would possibly oppose their dictatorship were in their category of betrayals.

Persons of prestige, elite, high education or wealth in RL or RA could challenge their powers, so RL clique classified them as subcategory of inner enemies. The clique secretly decided to kill inner enemies before the end of the war. The ways of killings were sophisticated and different, and one of them was the series of kangaroo courts formed in their controlled territories. They decided to annihilate all of their rivals. In that campaign, they killed nearly all of their possible challengers or rivals.

If their possible challengers were not living in their

controlled territories, they abducted their victims to theirs.

They either killed their possible challengers secretly or formed kangaroo courts in open markets or fields at nights, delivered diabolical verdicts, and immediately executed their victims cruelly at the very places. To hide their despotism, they used some types of the poor or illiterate peasants and jealous or greedy-for-fame workers to carry their killing campaign.

Misfortunes began to pour on my whole large family: My grandparents of both sides were in their subcategory of inner enemies. First, they had slyly killed my uncles Anhvu and Manhdan, then they abducted my grandparents to their territory.

In the case of uncle Anhvu, they gave him responsibility to be a trainer of landmine-detonator remover. They said to him, "You have to practice at least two hundred times before you train others." Thus, he practiced and practiced alone in the field. In the sixth day, a loud explosion BOOM occurred. He died in a heartrending scene: his body was torn apart at the place. (Later, my father told me that it was not an accident, but they camouflaged a delayed-action mine nearby.)

In the case of uncle Manhdan, they promoted him to head of a commando crew. In a raid, while the two sides were firing against each other, his commander shot him from behind. (Later, his best friend told my parents the secret.)

However, my grandparents of both sides had not known the secrets of the killings. They continued to support RL and RA until they knew the slyness.

Then in a night of that winter, some RL guys abducted my four grandparents to a territory they controlled. They incarcerated my grandparents and several other pairs in a house. They formed kangaroo courts in the field next to the village and dragged the victims pair on a row trials in the late evenings. The arms of the victims were bound together behind their backs above their elbows. It was sarcastically called bound like wings of angels. They hung labels Counter-Revolutionary at the chest and Inner Enemy at the back of each victim who was forced to kneel all the times during the trials.

My grandparents on my father side were on their trial a night before my grandparents on my mother side. The cruel scenes of trials and executions were extremely barbarous.

The court consisted of two tables wedged together in the field. A dozen of blazing torches were at two sides of the tables and corners of the court field. A male RL guy sat in the middle as the main judge. Two peasants sat at his right and left sides as co judges. Six other RL guys and RA soldiers armed with guns walked around the perimeter of the court field. A dazed crowd of peasants squatted a pair of yards far from the tables and facing the judges. Four other RL guys without guns blended in the crowd difficult to differentiate.

To begin the trial, the main judge signaled everybody, except my knelt grandparents, to stand up and sing a song praising RL and RA. Then the judges sat down. The crowd squatted down. The men with guns stayed standing. The main judge read a lecture extolling the head of the RL, his lofty sacrifices, and elevated virtues like a great saint, so he would be an able and clear-sighted emperor in the future. He and his RL clique would bring prosperity and freedom to the people of Kanxono. The lecture also appealed to the people to help him and his RL in elimination of the so-called enemies of the revolution consisted of not only outer enemies but also inner enemies like my grandparents, who were forced to kneel before the crowd. The way he read proved that he had just eradicated illiteracy.

After the lecture, the main judge shouted several slogans. Some extolled RL and RA; others insulted their inner enemies. His right fist was raised in the air on each slogan. The dazed crowd repeated each slogan and raised their rights fists like the judge. The four cadres, who blended in the crowd, watched the crowd. Anybody in the crowd who had any sign of pitiful emotion was noticed and would be in troubles later.

Then the denunciation began. From the front row of the crowd, a woman stepped out and stood in front of my grandparents. Surprisingly, the woman, the accuser, was the former cook of my grandparents' family. She performed what she had been trained:

The accuser pointed her forefinger near the foreheads of my grandfather then grandmother and said, "Male and female landlords Vitin, do you remember me?"

My grandfather answered softly, "Yes, ma'am, you are Mrs. Degat, our former cook."

The accuser shot back, "Oh, you still remember me, but do you remember the day you expelled me from your house for no reason?"

My grandmother spoke softly and emotionally, "Why can you fabricate such a false story? We were treating you like my cousin. We paid your salary every month. The day before that day, your sister had come to my house. In that night, she and you discussed in your bedroom whether you would join the Revolutionary Army with her. In the next morning, you—"

Suddenly, a cadre in the crowd shouted loudly, "Down with landlords Vitin." All the cadres stared into the crowd. Immediately, the whole crowd shouted the same, "Down with landlords Vitin. Down with landlords Vitin. Down with landlords Vitin."

The main judge raised his right hand to make the crowd still. The co judge at the right read guilts written on the paper on the table before him. The co judge at the left read other guilts on another paper. All the three judges had probably just eradicated illiteracy.

There was no lawyer for my grandparents, no one dared to say anything contrary to what had been read. My grandfather attempted to explain something two times, but his voice was overcome and drowned by the shouts, "Down with landlords Vitin. Down, down."

As the RL clique had cleverly planned for their whole killing campaign, this denunciation did not last long to avoid nervousness for the illiterate accuser, to prevent uncontrollable emotion for the crowd, and to conceal the dullness of judges.

The main judge raised his right hand to make the crowd still. Then he slowly read the verdict of death sentence written on the paper.

An RL guy in the crowd clapped his hands loudly. Immediately the crowd did the same. Then he began to sing songs describing their victory over their so-called outer enemies and inner enemies, clapped for rhythms. The crowd sang and clapped along with him. (The crowd had to gather to learn their songs some evenings before the row of trials.)

Two other RL guys dragged my grandparents out about six dozen yards away. Two executers were ready at the place. They pushed my grandparents down on the ground, raised their scimitars, and slashed the heads of my grandparents off. Blood sprouted out to the clothes, labels and ground. They put the dead bodies and heads in a large jute bag, threw it into an ox cart, transported to a place faraway, buried it, and left no traces.

In the next evening, the kangaroo court opened the trial against my grandparents of my mother side. The same labels, blazing torches, wedged table, armed RL and RA guys, and mingled guys in the crowd. Several workers were in the crowd. In that evening, the three judges were workers, not peasants, and the accuser was one former worker of my grandfather's factory.

Some items before the accusation were the same ones: the same extolling lecture, the same slogans. Others were the similar ones: gestures of the main judge, the stares of the cadres to the crowd, the repeats of the crowd.

Then the denunciation began. From the crowd, the man, the accuser, stepped out and stood in front of my grandparents. He performed what he had been trained:

The accuser, with his right forefinger pointed near the foreheads of my grandfather then grandmother, said, "Male and female industrial exploiters, do you remember me?"

My grandfather, soft and shaken, answered, "Yes, sir, you are Mr. Saybiti, who worked in our factory four years ago."

The accuser spoke in a louder voice, "Oh, you still remember me, but do you remember the day you dismissed me for no reason?"

My grandfather answered softly, "Why can you say that? You were dead drunk with alcohol so many times in the workplace. It was impossible to let you continue to work because of your safety and—"

Suddenly, an RL guy in the crowd shouted loudly, "Down with exploiter Donso." All the RL guys stared into the crowd. Immediately, the whole crowd shouted the same, "Down with exploiter Donso. Down with exploiter Donso. Down with exploiter Donso." They used this way to stop words of victims very places in the campaign. Victims had no right and no chance to defend themselves.

The main judge raised his right hand to make the crowd still. The co judge on the right read the guilts written on the paper on the table before him. The co judge on the left read other guilts on another paper. The main judge read the verdict of death sentence written on the paper.

An RL guy in the crowd clapped his hands to praise the verdict, then he sang songs describing their victory over the so-called outer enemies and inner enemies, clapped for the rhythms. The crowd sang the clapped along with him.

Two other RL guys dragged my grandparents out about six dozen yards away. Two cadres armed with rifles were ready at the places. They pushed my grandparents falling down on the ground and shot at the close range to the heads and chests of my grandparents. Blood sprouts out to the clothes, labels, and grounds. They put the dead bodies in a large jute bag, threw it into an ox cart, transported to a place faraway, buried it and left no traces.

The killing campaign lasted longer than two years. Nearly all of their possible challengers and rivals were killed. Although parts of people knew the slyness of the head of the RL clique, RL and RA were already too strong. The AG could not reverse the situation.

However, the whole Kanxono country was trembling. Thus, members of RL clique gathered themselves in a session to pass an admission that the killing campaign was wrong, and the head of RL performed a sob to apologize to all victims' families. They broadcasted the admission and sob on radios and TVs. But no guys in RL or any ones else were removed from their positions or punished because of the killing campaign. The sob and admission were only the shameless deceits to make people calm. They stopped their open campaign but continue their secret killings. Most of the people living Kanxono knew the deceits. But peoples outside the country still believed what RL clique propagated.

A year later, RL and RA won the war. The head of RL became the emperor with title Baxaoke, and the members of RL clique shared all top positions of authorities, their loyalists were their inferiors. They built their dictatorial system as they had decided a dozen years before when they had started the war. To grip firmly powers, they used despotic and mean rules to govern Kanxono.

However, RL clique continued to propagate to peoples outside the country that Kanxono had high standards of democracy, freedom, equality, and prosperity. The real miserable lives of the people in the country were sophisticatedly and skillfully concealed. While the people inside Kanxono were enduring the hardships and miseries under the despotic dictatorship, peoples outside the country still believe the propagandas.

My parents in Unto Blumen knew vaguely that my two uncles and my four grandparents were dead but had no further news to understand why and how the deaths had occurred. We were doleful. They were eager to come back to Kanxono to seek the truth.

In one afternoon, my parents received a letter of the very emperor Baxaoke from Kanxono, who had been the former head of RL. Inside the envelope, there were also visas for all of us: my parents, Binhquan, Phonghai, and me. The dishonest but warm explanation of the emperor about the deaths of my grandparents and uncles made my parents deeply moved. My mother sobbed because of both the dead and the words of explanation of the letter:

Republic of Kanxono
Equality, Liberty, Happiness

Emperor Baxaoke of Kanxono to the Vitin family

Dear Mr. Manhky Vitin, Mrs. Nangthi Vitin (maiden name Donso), Binhquan, Phonghai, and Nhutien,

I personally send all of you affectionate regards and best wishes from myself as well as from all members of my cabinet.

The images of you are in my heart and mind since you are dear citizens, lovely sons and daughters, and talent treasures of loving Kanxono.

I appreciate the sacrifices of your brothers for the success of RA. Nevertheless, I feel great anguish in retrospection on the blindly mistakes that several silly followers did in the period of the war that I did not expect, especially the mistakes that made many of our good citizens dead. I am very regretful that your parents are among the dead. I apologize to you all.

The war is over now. Please, forget the anguish of the past and think about the future. Kanxono, your beloved native country, is eagerly longing for your return. Surely, this country will be much better if able persons like you contribute talents, skills, energies, and efforts to rebuild. That being so, I ordered the Ministry of Foreign Affairs to issue visas for all of you. I expect and will greet you at your return.

Sincerely yours,

Emperor Baxaoke of Kanxono

My parents read the letter and the visas many times. Though all the five visas had the signatures and seals of the Minister of Foreign Affair, they had two anomalies: no photos of us and blank spaces on the lines for our dates of births.

After some months of discussion, my parents decided to return to Kanxono. My sister, Binhquan, brother, Phonghai, and I were too young, so we were dependent on the decision of my parents. Everyone of us stuck one's photo and wrote one's date of birth onto one's visa. My father and mother were both forty-five, Binhquan was sixteen, Phonghai was fourteen, and I was twelve at the time. We mailed the visas back to Kanxono. A month later, we received the visas with all necessary details.

To move from Unto Blumen to Kanxono, my parents had lots of preparations and works such as informing of leaving their jobs to their bosses, noting of ending the rental to their house owner. Additionally, they bought some diamonds and transferred their money to the national bank in Kanxono. Binhquan, Phonghai, and I were sad to say adieux to our friends.

At the airport of the capital of Kanxono, a group of ten RL guys cheerfully greeted us. They put garlands of flowers around our necks and shot photographs. A bus drove us to a barrack in the suburb. The barracks was guarded with strict security precautions by a group of RA soldiers.

When we stepped down on the yard, several civilians standing on the balconies of the buildings at the left and right sides looked at us with sorrowful and pitiful eyes, but my parents, sister, and brother did not notice.

The RL guys led us to enter into the waiting room in the main building facing the gate. They locked the door. They asked us to take off all adornments such as jewels, watches, and so on that we were wearing and put them on the table.

Then three RL women led my mother, my sister, and me to the small room with its door giving on the waiting room. They ordered us to take off our clothes and put on the table. They inspected our mouths, their fingers thrust into our vaginas and anuses to search whether any precious things were stashed. I felt very painful and humiliated. I saw my mother and sister were pale and trembling. Thereafter, they handed their clothes to us to wear. When we stepped out the small room with dizziness, my father and brother were shocked because of seeing us pale in quite different clothes.

Then two RL men led my father and brother to the same small room. Probably, they did similar inspection and search on my father and brother. A quarter later, we saw my father and brother stepped out the small room, they also were pale in different clothes.

After half an hour of waiting, a high rank of RL came and gave a propagandist lecture to my parents:

"Welcome to Kanxono,

"RL is very glad to see you return to this native country to contribute your talents, skills, energies, and efforts to rebuild this country.

"The purposes of our emperor and RL for Kanxono are equality, happiness, and freedom. Equality is the first priority. RL is implementing equality. As you know, the great majority of our people are still not enough means of living including food and clothes. There are no equalities if you wear luxurious clothes, decorate your bodies with jewels, have money in a bank. Thus, we confiscate your whole baggage. Don't worry, RL issues you new clothes and other necessities in the ten bags at that corner. Here are your food stamps for one month. Respect all the laws RL has promulgated, so RL can give suitable jobs to you and permission to your children to go to school.

"Now, take the ten bags we issue you. An RL friend will lead you to a car. It drives you to your new dwelling."

We did not speak about their inflictions, but we all knew we were already shackled in their huge cage. If we protested, they squeezed their shackles tighter, so we followed their decisions. In the car, my mother, my sister, and I melted into tears. My father and my brother sat in a daze.

We arrived in a building of two floors for twenty families. Our dwelling was one rectangular room of six yards wide and twelve yards long on the second floor. There were one bathroom cell with one commode, one sink, and one bathtub inside, but there was no running water. All the families had to use buckets to carry water from the fountain in the front yard.

In the bags they had issued, there were three sedge mats, three blankets, and three mosquito nets. We had had to sleep on the floor several months before my parents could buy some secondhand furniture: three beds, two tables, six chairs, and several other necessary sundries in different occasions.

No dwelling rooms had kitchens, but there was the collective kitchen at the end of each floor. Since cooking in the collective kitchen had consequences of tetchy frictions and inquisitive eyes, nearly every family made a small fire stove in a corner of its room and bought kerosene or coal in black market for fuel.

The lack of conveniences in the room was only a small part of the huge troubles in our lives. The other small part was happening within the perimeter of the building.

Seven days a week, from five o'clock in the morning to ten in the evening, the loudspeaker at the lamppost in the front yard relayed piercing broadcasts from the central radio. It began with loud shouts of morning exercises at five o'clock, then the rotations of extorted news, propagandist lectures, and shrilling songs extolling the emperor, RL, or RA lasted until ten o'clock in evenings.

They classified inhabitants in groups based on ages and sexes. There were five groups: elementary children, teens, young adults, male seniors, and female seniors. Members of each group had to gather in a room for one meeting in one evening for every week to hear their brainwashing lessons of refined liars.

In the meetings of elementary children, two or three RL guys taught children to sing songs extolling the emperor, RL clique, and the so-called heroes. They told children precious virtues and miraculous actions of the emperor.

Schedules in the meetings of teens were similar to the ones of children. In addition, they told teens embroidered stories of the so-called heroes and encouraged teens to be ready to sacrifice for the emperor and RL clique when they needs.

In the meetings of other groups, their RL guys read propagandist lectures and news similar to the broadcastings from the radio, or local RL guys informed fatigue duties such as cleaning around the building and within the precinct in the following Sunday or holiday. These fatigue duties usually lasted about four hours. But young adults could be asked to go to a field in the country to work like peasants on a whole day. Each member would be asked to comment on works of others in the next meeting.

It presumed that no family made friends with any other. The dwellers only greeted one another diplomatically at the staircase and the yard but did not visit one another's rooms. No one trusted anyone because of many complicated reasons, which I could partly understand only after many months of living in the building.

However, an exception happened to family Cungthe and ours. The family had also been gullible and deceived. They had come back from Fragrance to Kanxono six months before us. Mr. and Mrs. Cungthe had the same age of my parents. Their son, Sekho, was a peer of my brother, Phonghai, and their daughter, Thira, had the same age as me.

In the early morning on the second Sunday after our moving in, Mrs. Cungthe came to our room for the pretext of calling my mother to go together to the fatigue duty. Based on the experiences of her family living within the cage and in the shackles in the six months, she told my mother in low voice many useful experience and advices in half an hour. Thanks to the broadcasts from the loudspeaker in the front yard, outsiders did not hear:

"I saw you move in last Wednesday. After nearly a week, how do you feel?"

"Very anguished and inconvenient! We feel we're living in a cramped condition. They've dispossessed not only our property and belonging but also our freedom, happiness, and future of our children. Why were we so gullible?"

"Believe me. Many buildings near here are much worse. Example, the building on the other side of this street has no commode in each room. Inhabitants have to share stinky and dirty two-compartment latrines at one corner of its yard.

"They are wonderful deceivers. Intellectuals and elites also believed them and entered their cage. We led not only our lives into this hell but also the lives of our children."

"My husband and I were also deceived. It was our stupidity. Our children had no idea. Damn, the people are so miserable. Why are there no demonstrations against them?"

"Oh, I heard some. After four months they took powers, a pair of thousands people gathered in Central Park to protest their pauperizing policies. Their RA units blockaded all the surrounded streets. Then they invited some presumed leaders of the protestation to negotiate. But those leaders never came back. After two days without water and food, others demonstrators gradually and automatically left the park. They're much clever than other governments in the world. They didn't need tear gas, smoke hand grenades, cudgels, clashes. Reporters had no evidence or proof of suppression.

"Now, the people are absolutely dependent on them. They

control all means of livelihoods from cities to countries. Only those who are submitted or fake to be submitted are given jobs to get tickets to buy what they ration. They calculate meanly even tiny things like a pot of sauce, some needles, several yards of threads, a pound rice, a yard of cloth. Two inhabitants may buy a pot of sauce. Three inhabitants may buy two needles yearly. Each inhabitant may buy twenty-six pounds of rice monthly, each inhabitant may buy two yards of cloth yearly."

"Oh, I understand clearly today! They killed our four parents and all the haves to annihilate all persons who had means to challenge their powers. Now, they are in powers, they lure intellectuals into their cage. Then they implement these policies to make the people deeply dependent on them, so everyone must be submitted to work obediently for them. No challengers. No rivals. No protests. They're so clever. They organize perfect dictatorial systems."

"Right! The people don't have the means nor time to oppose or protest them. The people spend all the rest of their energies and time for the issue of how to have enough food and clothes. You see, when someone visit one's relatives, one should bring one's own raw food. It's so difficult for one's relative to entertain one a meal."

"Can we have any ways to flee? Have you tried to go back to Fragrance?"

"Damn, only officials can get a visa to go out. You see, anyone who is absent one's home even a night must have an official permission paper of one's local authority. Then one must have show the paper to the authority of other local where one overnights. No house owner dares to let any other overnight without a permission paper. Gradually, you'll understand the reasons."

"They have lectured us about equality. How are the lives of RL guys? I see the people are scrawny, but RL guys and members of their families are plump."

"The truth is quite contrary to what they promulgate, write, broadcast, and say. In public, they behave hypocritically as they're the guys of integrity, frugality, and virtues. However, in reality, they are the guys of stealing public properties, corruptions, cahoots, and grafts in every organ. They silently confer on themselves numerous privileges and prerogatives, so they have lavish lives in luxurious villas. Most of them are promiscuous. Many males are polygamous. Each wife and her children dwell in a separate villa and have a high standard of living."

"I see the inhabitants here have the frigid attitude to one another, no family makes friends with other ones. Why?"

"Oh, haven't you known they have organized many independent and overlapped systems of informers among the people in the whole country to watch one another? Each system of informers has to tell them any suspicious words or activities. If there is any sneaking suspicion word or activity, all of the system tell them because each system thinks that if it does not tell them, other systems do, and it will be attributed guilts of being accomplices or protectors.

"Don't trust any outsider, even a child. Be careful with your relatives, friends, and acquaintances. In several families, husbands or wives spy their spouses, children denounce their parents. One can be tested whether one is really subjugated or submitted by different tricks. For an example, a spy can backbite something about the emperor, RL, or RA. If one responds warmly, one is trapped. Other example, an informer sticks a protesting slogan in a latrine which one often uses, and the spy hides somewhere to watch. If one doesn't tell them the slogan, one is snared."

"What happens to one if one is accused of having any dissatisfaction, protestation, or noncooperation?"

"Destinies of the people in this country are in the hands of RL guys. They hold all powers now. They use all means to protect their powers. They give good jobs and high positions to those who protect their powers. Their prisons or labor camps are the places they punish those who have words or actions of backbite, disagreement, protestation or some similarity. Total numbers of prisons and labor camps are higher than the ones of schools and hospitals."

The conversation lasted nearly half an hour. Other members of the female adult group gathered in the front yard and were ready to begin their fatigue duty. Mrs. Cungthe and my mother rushed downstairs and joined them.

Four weeks later, after many applications, Binhquan, Phonghai, and I went to Revolution School, a combination of middle and high school. My sister was in eleventh grade. My brother and Sekho were in the same class of ninth grade, I and Thira were in the same class of the seventh grade.

Then my parents got jobs. My mother worked as an interpreter in the ministry of foreign affairs, and my father worked as an engineer in the road and bridge department.

In every school, there were two well-organized groups of students, most of whom are children of RL and RA guys. The groups were parts of the teenage and youth unions, two efficient informer systems. Other informer systems in schools were the representatives of classes, union of teachers, and secret agents of the police. Suspicious words or activities of teachers, staffs, or students were informed to the authorities.

Half of the subjects had the contents relating to propagandist politics. Some students artfully and shamelessly extolled the emperor, RL clique, and their embroiled heroes. The main goal of the education was to form students to be loyal to the emperor and RL clique. The more a student praised the emperor and RL clique, the higher degree he or she got. Sciences and technologies were the secondary matters.

My sister, brother, and I witnessed and faced lots of unreasonable and unfair ways. Though I am the youngest, my patience was better than my sister and brother, who often confided to each other at our homeroom about ridicules or troubles of schools to relax or seek consolations:

"I don't know whether the heads of these high school students are brainwashed and rammed with propagandas or they are sycophants who try to get high degrees in schools today and train themselves in order to become deceivers to join RL to procure important positions in society tomorrow."

"This way of live has happened not only in schools but everywhere in this country. But what are special things?"

"Childish things! But I was surprised. They were written by high school students, and the teacher read it before our class as good examples.

"The other extolling piece states that the emperor has worked hard, but he has put all his salaries to an account, and the whole money has been used to buy candies and cookies for children of this country on Independence Day every year. It's miserable. Children of this poor country have some candies and cookies only two or three occasion, but they should express gratitude to the emperor and RL guys.

"Tetchily, the teacher asked me whether we had candies and cookies in Unto Blumen to eat like children in this country. I must have shaken my head promptly."

"What, you've been contaminated by their way of lying after only some months?"

"No, I didn't lie. My shaking meant I didn't answer. If I said the truth that we had enjoyed the prosperity and freedom in Unto Blumen, I would be accused some guilts as counter-propaganda and sent to a labor camp."

My sister was right. If we could not extol them, we had to shut our mouth. A word of complaining on this country or praising on any other country would be a guilt.

Another example happened in my middle school. In a cleaning, a ten-year-old male student put the picture of the emperor from the wall down to the floor to wipe spider's web at the wall. He was accused the guilt of not respecting the emperor and sent to a labor camp. There were thousands teens in labor camps scattered in jungles. Boys had to work hard as adults. Girls were victims of sexual abusers. There were no verdicts for camp laborers. Every year, camp directors wrote comments on behaviors of laborers and sent it to the ministry of interior. A labor could be released thanks to the comments.

Since we could not be sycophants nor liars, we all got low degrees though our points in sciences were high.

Working in the Ministry of Foreign Affairs, my mother often interpreted questions of foreign journalists and answers of officials. She knew that all words of her interpretations were recorded, so she had to be exact. But at home, she frequently confided to my father about false news and deceiving issues that she had interpreted:

"Many foreign journalists have been so gullible. They haven't understood that interviewees haven't dared to say the truth. Moreover, officials have disguised as objects to be interviewed. The journalists have written what they have been deceived on their newspapers or magazines."

"Honey, we ourselves were gullible in Unto Blumen, so was the family Cungthe in Fragrance, so were other families coming here from other countries. Only living under this covered duress, we've understood the sophistries of unseen yokes forcing all the people to be either subjugated not to protest against these dictators or submitted to work for them."

My father faced more tetchy and dangerous situations. Although he was an engineer, all his superiors were RL guys with crassly professional knowledge, but they frequently showed their authorities with irrational instructions, and he had to explain their wrong details in their instructions. They consented but were unsatisfied. Additionally, they often stole materials, so constructions had risky safety.

Inferiors knew the corruptions of their RL superiors, but no inferiors dared to denounce since all previous denouncements against RL superiors had backfired.

Five years passed. The new emperor and his RL clique were controlling all means of livelihoods; they managed cleverly and successfully the lives of the people. In other words, people were absolutely dependent on them and had to obey them to have just enough means of living. Then they unanimously decided to invade their neighbor countries to impose their suzerainty. The most prosperous neighbor Eastnama country was their first target.

The ways they started the war of invasion was similar to the ones they had started the war in their own country, Kanxono, two decades earlier. Their propagandist and deceiving purposes were noble, but their concealed and real purposes were like the ones in the Ancient and Middle Ages: plunders, powers, and women. More women in Eastnama were pretty and elegant because of its prosperity.

Back to our family, we lived in humble circumstances dependent on my parents' salaries consisting food tickets and two very small amounts of money. My sister had low degree of her high school, so she was not allowed to attend any university. She applied at many organs for a paid work but only the textile factory gave her a job as lowest rank worker. She accepted it since she did not want to be a burden of my parents.

The war of invasion of the emperor and RL clique to occupy Eastnama was in the second year when my brother finished high school studies. He was in the worse situation in comparison with my sister. He had no chances not only to attend a university but also to get a job. Sekho, son of family Cungthe was in the same situation. The RL clique implemented the policies causing stalement to young men, except their children. Thus, young men had to join their invasion troops. Single and young women lived in less difficult circumstances but were encouraged to join the troops also.

My brother and Sekho discussed with each other and went together to join RA. After four weeks of training, their unit was sent into the war. The emperor and the RL clique sent a half million soldiers to Eastnama every year to fulfill their dead soldiers of their RA in their invasion.

Misfortunes poured to our family when the director of the organ, where my father worked, stole more materials for the project of a local office building than previous cases. My father denied to execute the design of the project since it would be in jeopardy to fall down. The direction intimidated my father and said that not my father but he himself would be responsible. Thus, my father listed all the rest of materials and asked him to write down his words of responsibility below and signed. The director did what my father asked.

As my father had estimated, the cracks of the building appeared just after a week of completion. The very director accused that my father had stole and sold the materials in a sneaking black market. My father was arrested and tortured.

The director's words of responsibility and signature meant nothing. Nobody in the organ dared to raise his voice to defend my father although many among the staff knew who the stealer was.

The room of my family was rummaged in every corner and place. But there was no money or anything precious for them to find.

Under these rulers, arrestees had to admit guilts and were sent to labor camps. Any arrestees who did not admit guilts would be chained in dungeon cells to deaths. Since my father did not admit the guilts which they accused, they chained him in a dungeon cell. There were full of miseries in dungeon cells and labor camps, but the ones in dungeon cells were much more horrible. Our family was in agony.

My brother and Sekho had gone to the war for fifteen

months. Like other families which had members in the war, we knew that casualties of RA side were high, but we did not receive any news about our dears from the war.

Suddenly, in one afternoon, I saw Sekho walked into the front yard. His two arms were lost and his skin became darker. I called my mother, we rushed to our front door and waved him. But he ignored.

In that evening, Sekho, the nineteen years old handicapped, came to our room. We could see him clearer: arms lost to elbows, scars on his face and neck, dark brown skin. He looked like a weather-beaten forty-year-old man.

He told us in a low voice, "Don't say to anybody what I tell you, or I will be punished. I came back to this capital last week, but I'd to stay in the barrack to study politics before going home. I studied how to lie to everybody. In general, I must conceal the terror, the danger, the hardness, and casualties I faced and witnessed. Contrarily, I've to embroil our glorious feat of arms, brave actions, help of companion-in-arms, and so on."

"Families which have dears in the war have visualized the negatives you've said. Contrarily, we've been hackneyed with the embroideries we've heard in stories and songs broadcasted in political lectures as well as from TVs and radios. Sekho, please, can you give us some news about Phonghai. We burn with impatience."

"Oh, I'm sorry. To understand Phonghai and my duty, I should summarize the ways our troops have fought in the war. We've avoided to clash with other side in daytimes, so we've hidden in jungles or underground tunnels in daytimes. We've selected posts of our rivals and gathered our human forces tenfold more than theirs and attacked them at nighttimes. We've mounted lightning attacks within three hours, withdrawn very quickly, and hidden again.

"Despite our selections, our casualties have been tenfold higher than theirs. Since we haven't had means to transport our wounded and dead, the heavy wounded, who haven't been withdrawn, have been shot to death and buried together with the dead.

"Before we've opened fire, our commandos have tied plastic explosives on backs, slithered toward the posts, put the explosives at concertina fences, attached fuses connected with strings, and slithered back. To begin the attacks, some of our officers have jerked the strings to made the plastic explode."

"We know, commandos have faced more deathly possibilities: mines and shots of the rivals."

"You're right. Phonghai and I were selected to join the commando team of the regiment. I was injured because of the mine of the rivals. I could run in the withdrawal, so I survived and came back here."

We knew that my brother was still in suffering-and-death war. Sekho's visit lasted round half an hour. Again, he asked us not to tell anyone what he had said. Then he left. A contradictory feeling happened, we had craved to know news about my brother, but we became sadder when we got some.

Their invasion war was in the third year. Probably, casualties were extremely high. Since the emperor and the RL clique needed millions of soldiers to send to their war in Eastnama, they made the living circumstances more difficult to young males. As a result, nearly all young males enrolled in RA. Simultaneously, they also encouraged females to volunteer to join RA for their implicit purpose: comfort of their officers and their so-called heroes.

Their ebullient encouragement happened when I and Thira were in the first week of twelfth grade in Revolution School. Both of us were seventeen at the time.

In one morning, the group of six smooth-talking RL females arrived in our school and entered every class to entice female students. They lectured that their war was a sacred one, that to go to their war was saving mankind, that the RL clique would issue benefits to volunteers and families. Then they let the students ask questions. Most of their answers intentionally drew back to their lecture: sacred and saving mankind war. But

I tried to ask a question relating to the concrete situation of my family.

"My father is in a prison. If I volunteer to join RA, will my father be released after some weeks or one month?"

"If you love your father, volunteer," answered the head of the group. "He'll unify with your mother within four weeks and have a job within three months."

Then they distributed the volunteer forms to female students. Thira murmured to me that she volunteer with the purpose that the RL clique would give her parents better lives. I thought that I had to rescue my father from the prison. Thus, Thira and I fulfilled the forms, signed, and handed them to the group.

Both my mother and Mrs. Cungthe cried bitterly when they knew we had signed the volunteer forms. My mother exchanged views with Mrs. Cungthe how to cancel our enrollments. After an hour of discussion, Mrs. Cungthe said, "There's only one hope. Let's write petitions explaining that our daughters have not been eighteen years old yet and send them to the headquarter of RA."

My mother reprimanded me, "Nhutien, we lost many things and fell into these miseries because of their honeyed words and cunning deceits. But you're still so gullible! You still believe them. Do you know they used most females in the war to fulfill sexual needs of their officers and embroidered heroes? Their male guys are in jungles many years without women, so to sleep with women is a great compensation or a huge reward."

My mother sent the petition for me to the headquarter of RA. Mrs. Cungthe did the similar petition for Thira.

After ten days, my mother received their reply together with an enclosed paper. The reply told that I would be released on my very first day in RA if I was really under eighteen years old. The enclosed paper contained information of the building and day I had to present myself. Mrs. Cungthe received a similar reply and an enclosed paper.

In the morning on the Monday we had to present

ourselves, my mother and Mrs. Cungthe accompanied me and Thira to the building. It was guarded. We were halted at the gate. After checking papers, two cadres invited me and Thira coming inside, but the two mothers had to stay outside. We said good-bye. The mothers sobbed like their daughters were going to the dead world.

The gate was closed at six in the afternoon. No ranks of RA mentioned anything about our chance of being released because of our seventeen years of age. In the very evening, we were driven to the women's military training center. Some hundred female volunteers like us were already there. The course was named Course W-5.

Our schedule of first month in the center consisted of touching personal weapons, watching films teaching how to use those weapons and victory films, physical exercises, and self-embellishments. In the following month, another type of films which they called romantic and lovemaking films were added to the schedule, but these films contained many smutty scenes which made us shocked.

In one early morning of the Saturday, we were roused and specially commanded to embellish ourselves.

At nine o'clock, we were informed that the emperor and several high-ranking officials of RL and officers of RA would visit the center. We had to muster in lines. A quarter later, the emperor and his ten-man entourage arrived. The commandant of the center introduced 356 female volunteers to them. They walked from one line to other lines and viewed every one of us. The commandant and a general accompanied them. Again and again, they stopped before someone among us and told the general to jot down one's name; mine and Thira's were in the list of eleven selected.

At lunchtime, there were rumors saying that those whose names written in the list were beautiful, that I was the most beautiful one, that Thira was the second, and so on.

In that afternoon, eleven limousines owned by most powerful men came to pick up the selected females of W-5. I and Thira said good-bye in tears. I was guided to the limousine of the emperor and Thira to another limousine of another powerful man. We never met each other thereafter.

The palace of the emperor was guarded with strict security precautions. It consisted of four large luxurious halls and a dozen of expensively furnished rooms. I was guided to one bedroom with bathroom at a corner. I felt very lonely and puzzled since I knew I was the sex object of the emperor. Also, I was restless with a thought whether my sacrifice would bring any benefits as they had promised.

At six o'clock in that evening, a woman knocked the door and brought a meal into my bedroom for me. She was in the forties. She introduced herself:

"Call me Mrs. Aide. Happy birthday to you. You're eighteen years old today. I bring a special meal and cake for you. Tomorrow, you'll eat in the dining room."

"Thank you, ma'am. I totally forget my birthday because of worries and puzzles."

"I've duty to inform you. The emperor comes to this bedroom this evening and sleep with you. It's a precious present for your eighteen birthday. Many young women dream of this but they can't have. In the women's military training center, you watched romantic and lovemaking films, let imitate an actress to make the emperor satisfy. If you don't act, bad consequences will come to yourself, your parents, your sisters, and your brothers."

"My father is in prison. I have only one sister and one brother. My brother is fighting in the Eastnama war. I volunteer to join RA to exchange benefits as recruiters explained, and our most important benefits is my father being released. They promised our father will be released within a month. Ma'am, does this regime keeps the promises?"

"I inform you what I'm commanded. More, I may not.

But I can personally advise you some things: in your situation here, at least, you agree to let him fulfill his sexual desire. In this palace, there're usually four young ladies. In present time, there're four other beauties like you, one of them hasn't reached fifteen years old. They've to do the same works like you. You're here today, one of them probably leave tomorrow. I don't know how the other forbidden villa is, but here, to prevent any rumor that the emperor has a wife, no lady stays here long. People must say that he is a great living saint, he uses all his mind and time for this country, and he keeps celibacy all his life. I hope you understand these words. Now, enjoy your meal."

The woman left my bedroom. The meal was delicate dishes, but I could eat only a little bit.

At ten o'clock, the fifty-year-old emperor stepped into my bedroom. In spite of knowing in advance, I trembled. He was not as gentle as his pictures hung in million places in the country or as nice as depictions in lectures and newspapers but greedy of sexual desires.

Whatever had to happen, occurred. He asked me doing a lot of sexual acts to stimulate him. I felt nauseated, but I had to do. He moaned in pleasure. Contrarily, I suffered pain in both mind and body. It was hate-making. Then he spread a white towel under my buttocks. The highest painful point was the moment his cock trying to prick my virginity. I attempted to push him away, but my hands were too weak.

When the hate-making was over, he checked the white towel. A few drops of blood lay on it; the proof of my virginity was deflowered. He seemed to be satisfied. But I felt self-pity.

The time passed with my endurance of humiliation. In a morning of the tenth month, I was guided into the open cabin under the canopy at the left corner of the front yard of the palace to meet my mother. She and a supervisor sat on the two different benches opposite to each other. When my mother saw me, she stood up and ran out. We emotionally embraced each other. Tears ran down from our eyes. The guide came into the cabin and sat near the supervisor. After two minutes, our emotion relatively calmed down, we sat on the bench, my mother asked:

"We miss you so much. All of us speak of you every evening. In ten months we have no news from you. Why don't you write home? Are you happy?"

"I miss all of you, too. Is dad at home, and how is he? How is Binhquan? Do you have any news from Phonghai? Have you been better since my enrollment in RA?"

"Dad is working for the subdivision of construction. Your sister is in the same job. We think your brother is fighting well in the war. Your father and I receive some more tickets monthly than our colleagues and can buy more raw food and necessities."

The visit lasted half an hour. On the matter of my happiness, I evaded to answer the question of my mother because the presence of the supervisor and the guide. I could not lie to my mother. But I thought what my mother said about the situation of my father and the more tickets for raw food and necessities were true. Those were the real benefits of my sacrifice.

Two years passed. At the beginning of every semester, a new beauty came, on old one left. My period of submission to the sexual desires of the emperor came to an end.

Four days before my leaving turns, Mrs. Aide told me, "Thanks to your service, your parents have some benefits. This regime always issues benefits to those who fulfill their duties. Contrarily, it always punishes severely those who refuse to do the duties it trusts. I think you know the normalcy, most females in RA are sent to the war in Eastnama to comfort either some high officers or heroes. I think you're intelligent and experience to understand the vague meaning of the word comfort.

"However, your case is special, the day before yesterday, the director of the espionage department had a formal interview with the emperor. They agree that you're very beautiful and attractive. So they'll use you to infiltrate into a high general ranks of the enemy army, the army of Eastnama, to work as a spy. I think somebody will pick you up to the secret espionage training mansion on Monday.

"Benefits to your parents will be great. They promise they'll issue a villa, a car, and many other benefits. In sum, your parents will live like middle officials of this regime. If you refuse, severe punishments will thunder down on yourself as well as your parents. Of course, your siblings will be impacted bad consequences."

"I appreciate your information. I know my life will bristle with dangers, but I cannot escape my destiny."

On the next Sunday morning, the director of the espionage department drove his limousine to the palace and picked me up. He was about forty-five years old. On the way, he said that the emperor had discerning eyes, that I had amazing beauty and charm, and that he could not wait until Wednesday.

I knew immediately what he wanted. However, in my situation, I had to accept my fate. I thought about the eleven most powerful men, the emperor and ten others. They used their powers, inferior staffs, and public means to fulfill their greed rending unfairness and miseries in the society.

The limousine reached the espionage training center, standing alone on the hill about a dozen miles far from the capital. Two guards saluted then opened the gate. The limousine stopped in front of the vestibule of the mansion. I heard voices of several men and women playing bowls in a hall, but they did not know my arrival.

The director guided me to a luxuriously bedroom with convenient furniture including a double bed and a brandy shelf. On the table near the self, there were already two dishes of hot meal. He invited me to sit on a chair.

He sat on the opposite chair and said, "This is your bedroom. All other nineteen trainees sleep in two large dormitories, one for the group of nine females and the other for the group of ten males. But I treat you specially."

"Why don't you let me live in the same rules and regulations like the others in this center?"

"Oh, you know the reason: mutuality. You have to treat me as nice as I treat you. I'll sleep with you on Wednesdays and Saturdays. But today is an exception. I cannot wait. After this meal, each of us drink a cup of brandy and we make love."

"Brandy makes me intoxicated. A backfire will happen, and I can't do what you want."

After the meal, I drank a cup of soft drink. He emptied a cup of brandy and led me to the bed. He took off all my clothes and stared at my beauty without moving his eyes. He kissed my sexual organs again and again. Then he took off his clothes and asked me doing sexual acts to stimulate him. He moaned in pleasure. Contrarily, I felt nauseated. Then he pressed me lying down. What had to happen, occurred. He called it lovemaking. To me, it was hate-making.

An hour after his fulfillment of sexual desire, he urged me to take a bath. Then he led me to the hall and introduced me to other trainees of the course named Es-6-Spies. Then he left to the mansion. I began to join activities and schedules like others.

No, I did not join all regulations like other trainees. Two unusual things for me were to sleep in the special bedroom and to be the sex object of the director in the evenings of Wednesdays and Saturdays.

The schedules of trainees consisted of various and complicated subjects belonging to the espionage branch. There were also a pair of subjects for the female group only and another pair for the male group only.

A pair of particular important subjects for females were greedy desires of men in powers. The special desire of lots men in powers was to appropriate young and beautiful women. Thus, tactics to bewitch men in powers of the rival side was an essential item. From the tenth week, romantic and sexual films with smutty scenes were added to the schedule of female trainees. After every film, there was a discussion of effective scenes and analysis how to ape them. The woman trainer emphasized again and again:

"If you don't have orgasms, fake it. Most of the actresses in the films don't have orgasms. They fake it. You should fake at least one orgasm in each time of lovemaking. Great effectiveness will come. You'll spare much energy and labor."

The trainer was right. Every time after my fake orgasm, the end of a hate-making comes much faster.

During my period in the center, the director was monopolistically appropriating me for his sexual greed. Other female trainees, however, had to practice what they learned from sexual films with several high officials who came in Saturday afternoons to fulfill their sexual desire.

Twenty months of the espionage course ended. Within three days, except me, other trained spied left the center. They were on the ways to different espionage teams called clusters in cities or capital of Eastnama.

After a week, in the Wednesday evening, the director came to my room with a sad feature on his face. After the hate-making, he said, "This is the last time I sleep with you. I may not keep you here anymore. The emperor orders me to send you to Cluster 36 in the capital of Eastnama. A coup d'état has just occurred there. Within a month after the coup, our forces in Eastnama occupied 40 percent of the land and controlled 30 percent of the population. Additionally, 10 percent of its people in the territories controlled by the government of Eastnama work for us. Lots of them are billionaires, multimillionaires, intellectuals, and artists including professors, writers, journalists, and music composers. We have formed Revolutionary Government (RG) consists of several of them as our tool to oppose their government and to attract more people to follow us. The slogan of the Revolutionary Government to appeal to Eastnama is "If you are patriots, contribute your parts to terminate the militarists. The results are very good. Thus, our future victory is bright.

"In our enemy side, the new group in power consists of many generals. Several of them are greedy of beautiful and young women. With your unsurpassed beauty, some of those generals will dote on you. As a spy you'll help a substantial part to reach our victory. Be always loyal to us. Your parents are in our hands.

"Prepare. A young man named Dadang Tynan, who has records of having a plot to assassinate the emperor of four years in prisons, of breaking the prison, will come here tomorrow. He'll act as your lover, lead you to the destination, and apply asylums there for you both."

The director handed me my ID card and a paper of curriculum vitae. Then he left the room.

I read the ID and the life story. Except my name and photo, other details were changed. I felt puzzled and bad. I would soon live very far from my parents and sister. During the days in the center, although I did not have freedom, I had the consolation of living near my dears. Going to Eastnama meant farewell. I sobbed bitterly in despair.

"Be always loyal to us, your parents are in our hands."

The intimidating words haunted me. My parents were their hostages. I visualized the man named Dadang Tynan, a core of RL clique, young but experienced in the espionage. He would be my superior not lover. He could be sexually greedy as the emperor and the director. Of course, the records of the plot of assassination, years in prisons, and breaking the prison were only counterfeit acts.

After a month in the refugee camp, Dadang and I got refugee status. Two days later, he and I applied for jobs at the luxurious club named Crystal Club and got jobs, Dadang as a cook and I as a waitress. The owners of the club were Mr. and Mrs. Clog, a billionaire couple of Eastnama, worked for RL guys. They were wise in businesses but gullible in politics. They were deceived by unrealistic and utopian ideals of propagandas as my grandparents had been deceived in Kanxono five decades earlier. Why on this world, there have been so many guys deceived by RL clique?

After the military putsch, the generals asked the owners to conferred Crystal Club for high officers and high officials.

Most patrons were men, and nearly all of men visited the club without female partners. The owners knew main rarity likings of the customers: booze, dancing, and women. Thus, the club had fundamentally about thirty women taxi dancers and twenty waitresses. Plus some dozen taxi dancers were in reserve. All women were beautiful. Their ages in IDs were from eighteen to thirty. However, as I knew, a dozen of them were sixteen or seventeen but used forgery identifications. Some taxi dancers and waitresses were spies and several others were sympathizers of Revolutionary Government, the tools of RL clique.

Really, the owners were keen of their business. Half of the men came to the club because of booze then women. Another half came to the club because of dancing then women. They themselves drove public cars. After boozing or dancing, each patron paid a price for his selected taxi dancer or waitress, used the public car to pick her up to his intended place, and fulfilled his sexual pleasure. All the patrons were high ranking and well-known in the army or government of Eastnama, so they paid generously the women, and no women complained about maltreatments. The women usually came back to the club by cabs in the next early morning.

Why did these beautiful Eastnama women do these works? After inquiries, I realized there were three types: The first type consisted of beautiful women whose parents were in the territories controlled by Kanxonoist forces. They were in the similar situations like mine. Later, I discovered that the invaders had a strategy of using young and single women as their informers. They held parents of the women as hostages and coerced the women arriving in the capital, cities, or towns which were still controlled by the Eastnama government as fleers from the battles. The beauties applied for jobs at luxurious clubs or bars where officers or officials were customers. The non-beauties came to house of officers and officials to beg for work as servants with very low salaries. I estimated that there were half a million women as servants.

The second type consisted of the women living in the

territories controlled by the government of Eastnama but were deceived by unrealistic and utopian propagandas, so these women worked willingly as spies or informers for the invaders.

The third type consisted of materialistic women. These women knew how to get high tips and were clinking with plenty of money.

Though Cluster 36 Spies took 50 percent of all incomes of the club from the owners and the women, the women were still satisfied with the money they had. Later, I knew secret agents of Cluster 36 Spies covertly collected money as revolutionary taxes from many billionaires and multimillionaires in the capital. I thought other cluster also collected money in other cities and towns.

When I presented myself to take up my job, the head of the Cluster 36 Spies, a middle-aged woman with the fake job as a cashier. Her name was Cordata. It was not her real name because she came from Kanxono. She gave me her command:

"You're a queen of beauty. The purpose of the emperor and his cabinet is using you to bewitch some generals, but you should try to bewitch Major General Gallop, leader of the coup d'état. It's my decision. He often comes in Saturday evenings. Though only minority of high officers and officials are greedy for women and bribes, this general is one of them. Hide in the room 23 until the general comes. You do know well what a young and beautiful woman should do to bewitch a man. You also know what work a spy must do. I'll bring food and drink for you. Here is the key. One moment, well, by the way, well, Dadang wowed before the picture of the emperor and espionage branch that he wouldn't sleep with you. In this matter, I'm convinced you rather him. Can you confirm that?"

"No, he didn't sleep with me. He didn't even cuddle with me."

"He is a spy of a firm stuff. He deserves to be promoted as my aide. As for you, be loyal to us. Remember your parents are in RL hands. Tomorrow is Saturday. General Daffodil Gallop will probably come. Now, you can go."

On the next day, at six o'clock in the evening, Major General Gallop himself drove a military jeep into the club. Its owners greeted and invited him to a special table in a small and separate room reserved for him.

Cashier Cordata told me to carry a tray consisting of a dish of braised aborigine and beans with minced beef, a dish of fried chicken, and a dish of stuffed pancakes and followed her to the table. She introduced me to the general:

"Nhutien, twenty years old. She hasn't contacted any customer. We reserved her to meet you. If you like her, she'll serve you, only you."

General Gallop did not answer the suggestion but said some words of thanks and gestured Cordata and me to sit on two opposite chairs. But Cordata excused herself and went away.

I sat down and glanced at his complexion: scarred face, spared moustache, and twisted-out-of-shape mouth. Some estimations appeared quickly to my mind about him: age of over fifty, mind of mediocrity, and greed for power and pretty women. I was also surprised how the man could be promoted as major general and the leader of the coup d'état that overthrew the legal president of the prosperous country.

On the table, there were already a bottle of brandy, a bottle of mineral water, two pairs of cups, and some other pairs for the meal. Unexpectedly, he mixed brandy with soda in a cup and put in front of me. I refused, so he exchanged a cup of water for me and said like a lady's man:

"You're a princess of beauty and niceness. But your name tells me you're not a native of Eastnama, are you?"

"I, my sister, and brother were born in Unto Blumen. We all lived there until I was twelve years old. But my parents were deceived by RL clique, carried us and all our belongings to Kanxono. There, they dispossessed everything of us including clothes. Then we lived in poverty and under the duress of the dictatorship. I fed a hope of fleeing out from the miserable and destitute country. Last two months, Dadang and I forded the frontier, crossed the forests, and reached the refugee camp."

"Have you gotten refugee status?"

I showed him my refuge-status card. He glanced on it in a second and told me to put it into my pocket. Then he invited me to eat with him. During the meal he asked me questions about my life in the period I had lived in Unto Blumen and the years I passed through in Kanxono. I told him the truth in the period in Unto Blumen and the five years in Kanxono, but I concealed my enlisting in RA, two years in the emperor's palace, twenty months in an espionage training center, and the benefits given to my parents. However, I told him about my brother, Phonghai, who was forced to join RA, was sent to fight against the army of Eastnama in the war. He said he knew the majority of soldiers in RA were forced to fight like my brother.

The meal was finished, but he continued to drink the brandy. It presumed he was intoxicated because he grumbled about politics of the war with me:

"The emperor and his RL clique don't build Kanxono to become as prosperous as Eastnama but wage the war of invasion. They're barbarous dictators. They implement policies to make lives of their people absolutely dependent on them, make their people obey what they command.

"The RL clique are best deceivers in the world. They're so sly in establishing their Revolutionary Government ruse consisted of gullible intellectuals. Those intellectuals don't know that people in Eastnama will be as miserable as people in Kanxono if we lose this war. Their propagandistic slogan 'If you are patriots, contribute your parts to terminate the militarists' is really their sly strategy. Songwriters, poets, and writers, and so on express patriotism in works like songs, poems, and writings, and so many people sing and read the works. We cannot forbid them even though these works implicit appeals to our people to follow them.

"By the way, you've experiences of living under the dictatorship which engenders poverty and miseries for the ruled people. You can help us something important. I invite you to my office building. I'll arrange a suitable job for you."

After the meal, he told me to ask Mr. and Mrs. Clog to the table, and he talked on the issue. Of course, the owners, collaborators of RL clique, consented to let me go with the general immediately. I took my bag of personal chattels and went with him to his car.

In the car, I did not call him general but Daffodil, and he seemed to be satisfied. Arriving in the office building, he guided me to a bedroom with all luxurious conveniences.

He gestured me to sit on the bed and explained, "There are six bedrooms like this in the building, but my family lived in a villa four blocks away from here. In addition, at the end of the backyard, there are ten apartments for guards, but a woman secretary dwells in one apartment, and the next one is still vacant. You will dwell there. Tonight, you sleep here with me. You do know the works the women of the Crystal Club should do, don't you?"

"I have lost my virginity. I was raped on the way of fleeing. But I don't know how to make you satisfied."

"I don't expect your virginity. Do what I tell you. Anyhow, take a white towel and a pill in the drawer of the bedside table. The bottle of water is on it.

"I should admit I'm infatuated with your beauty. I know, in poor countries, there are also some beautiful women, though fewer than rich countries, but you're specially beautiful. Oh, I remember, you was born and were living Unto Blumen twelve years."

Then the matter of sex began. I faked not to have any experience and did what he told me. Sexual acts like ones with the director of the espionage center in Kanxono happened again. I faked having an orgasm. After the sex, he slept soundly. I lay on the bed and heard him snore, and the guards changed shifts. I knew there were secret documents in the building, but I did not dare to go out the bedroom.

The general arranged a job for me as a helper of the woman secretary, and my dwelling was the apartment next to hers. Two nights a week, I had to go to the bedroom in the building to be his sex object. But it was the best chance to work as a spy.

The war became more and more ferocious. The deaths of Kanxono side reached ten million. The deaths of Eastnama side were one million, but the wounded soldiers and injured civilians became handicapped reached three million. Thus, the military government of Eastnama promulgated the draft of young males from eighteen to thirty to have soldiers for its army, and a law requiring all its citizens had to get visas of exit before leaving the country. The promulgation engendered lots of unfairness. For example, wealthy families bribed to get visas of exit for their sons to leave the country. Most of them went to Unto Blumen or Fragrance, the two wealthy countries.

One afternoon, the general told me that my brother, Phonghai, was wounded and was treated in the Third Field Hospital four hundred miles away from the capital. I felt pain all over my body and mind. He realized my pain, so he consoled me but said something about the grief-stuck issue I had known:

"You should be happy, your brother is saved. Our enemies usually killed their wounded since they don't have means of transportation and hospitals in Eastnama. Your brother was lucky, he lay near our side, so we transported him to our hospital."

"Why do you know he's my brother?"

"He informed his identification to our officers: his name, birthday, birthplace, period of fifteen years in Unto Blumen, being coerced to join RA and sent to fight in this country, as well as names of parents and siblings."

"What wound does he endure?"

"I don't know exactly. One moment, I commanded a helicopter to transport him from Third Field Hospital to Military Central Hospital eleven miles near here. You can visit him in the evening. Come back to your apartment and prepare. A soldier will drive a military jeep to pick you up at six, okay?"

My brother lay on the bed. His right foot was amputated. Two other wounds were on his body. The female nurse who took care of the room spoke her surprise to my brother:

"What a guy you are! Soldier of RA speaks fluently Unto Blumen language, has a beautiful sister working in the building of the most powerful general.

"Wealthy families are preparing to send their sons to Unto Blumen. I know the multimillionaire family Bonanza wants a tutor fluent in the language of the country for their daughter and son. If you want, I'll introduce you to them."

It was really our luck if it would happen because we would live not far from each other. Furthermore, he could avoid returning to the unfair, hypocritical, and duping society in Kanxono.

Six months later, he recovered and looked okay with his right-foot prosthesis in spite of his lightly limping gait. Thanks to the introduction of the nurse, Mr. and Mrs. Bonanza hired him to tutor Unto Blumen language for their children. They knew his difficult situation, so they picked him up to their compound.

Mr. and Mrs. Bonanza had two children, a daughter, Fenella, twenty-two years old, and a son, Rheum, nineteen years old. They both studied technology at the Faculty of Sciences, Fenella as a junior and Rheum as a freshman. The Bonanzas treated my bother nicely. They let him use one bedroom in the same building they dwelled, and he shared most activities like a member of the family.

As I advised, my brother applied for a refugee status. After only ten days, he got it thanks to the intervention of General Gallop. Then my brother applied to study Unto Blumen language at the Faculty of Letters of the same university Fenella and Rheum were studying. After some tests, he was admitted to attend in the junior class.

An unexpected love emerged between Fenella and my

brother. It was Fenella who firstly expressed her love. After five months they were in love, she asked her parents to organize a simple wedding.

The billionaire couple Mr. and Mrs. Clog, the owners of Crystal Club, were among two hundred guests of Fenella-Bonanza and Phonghai-Vitin wedding party.

At the end of the party, Mrs. Clog passed by me and said in a low voice, "Cordata asks me to tell you to do your duty. Nearly six months of going in and out the office building of the general, you haven't got anything. Try to meet Cordata to have tiny utensils like a camera and a tape recorder."

After the wedding, the Fenella-Phonghai couple moved to the small house at the left-hand side of the compound. It was the place I met Cordata to receive tiny utensils, then in many following Sundays, I handed her many photos and tapes of military campaigns and meetings of the general council.

Fenella did not know my spying actions, but my brother did. However, he ignored it because of the safety of our parents and sister. Furthermore, he knew that RL guys did not kill him because his house was the place to hand secret copies and records.

Some tapes recorded wrangles of the general council over corruptions of several generals including General Gallop to have money to fulfill their greed. Their corruptive deeds were various. Some of them were selling weapons, ammunitions, and medication to RA as well as receiving bribes from different backgrounds.

After two years of working as a spy, I knew lots of secrets. I assessed that, sooner or later, Eastnama would be lost to the hands of the invaders. Thus, I advised Fenella to urge her parents to sell their compound and arranged for their whole family to leave the country as early as possible.

Billionaire couple Clog bought the compound including furniture with the price of fifty million. I did not know exactly, but the money could be from Cluster 36 because agents of the group acted freely within the compound thereafter.

All members of family Bonanza, including Phonghai, got visas from the Unto Blumen Embassy. But they could not get visas of exit. Mrs. Bonanza told me the difficulty, and I asked General Gallop for help. He explained the situation I understood in a perfunctory manner that the organ that issued visas had to share money to a dozen of officials and officers including himself. If he interfered, he would be misunderstood that he alone took briberies stealthily. Finally, the family had to pay five hundred thousand for the five visas.

I was at the airport to say good-bye family Bonanza. My brother shed tears before his wife, parents-in-law, and brother-in-law. I perceived his sadness run high at the moment of saying good-bye because of my misfortune.

Territories that the Eastnama government controlled shrank smaller and smaller. Consequently, more and more people of Eastnama had to work, pay taxes to the so-called Revolutionary Government, the tool of RL and RA. People in those territories from teens to forty years had to carry arms to fight against the army and government of Eastnama.

In the month RA of RL clique attacked the capital of Eastnama, half of the generals and officials, one-fourth of them were corruptive ones, deserted and fled to many foreign countries, but most of them to Fragrance or Unto Blumen. Also, I fled to Unto Blumen as a refugee since I worked in the building of General Gallop.

Clean and patriotic generals and their many inferiors committed suicide before RA units flooded over their positions. The ones who did not commit suicide were cruelly and barbarously revenged later. Their families were meanly and sophisticatedly punished.

Among one hundred million people of Eastnama, five million risked their lives to get means to flee when their country was lost to the hands of invaders. They reached many countries, but the majority of them arrived in Unto Blumen and Fragrance. The fleers were treated as refugees. Then they became naturalized citizens and had all rights like other citizens in the countries.

I arrived in Unto Blumen and lived in refugee camp. After one month, I received refugee status since I had worked in the building of General Gallop.

RL clique were very clever. They foresaw that many former officers and officials of Eastnama in foreign countries could regroup and sneak back to Eastnama to fight against them. Therefore, many spies of RL clique infiltrated the five million fleers. Their plans were to sow division and suspicion among patriotic fleers. Whimsically, the spies of the RL clique were also granted refugee status. Several spies of Cluster 36 Spies were among infiltrators in Unto Blumen.

My brother, Phonghai, sister-in-law, Fenella, three-year-old niece, Fuchsia, and two-year-old nephew, Pacifix, picked me up from the camp after I had received the refugee status. We were together after nearly five years of separation. Every time I looked at my niece and nephew, I remembered my cheerful childhood in the very country Unto Blumen. Sorry, the gullibility of my parents had led all members of my family into miseries.

Both Phonghai and Fenella had studied printing. Thanks to the money of Mr. and Mrs. Bonanza, they owned a print shop and a house of five bedrooms in the western suburb twenty miles far from the center of the capital. I lived with them in their house. I followed their advice to study printing. Then I worked in their print shop as a manager.

In Eastnama, after the succeeded invasion, RL guys implemented sophisticated and mean punishments on former officers and officials including handicapped veterans of defeated army and surrendered government. Also, RL guys imposed injustice and discriminating policies on their families. In parallel, they imposed counter economic policies that gave them prerogatives and engendered poverty to other social classes.

Thus, fleers from Eastnama in foreign countries formed different organizations to oppose or protest against RL guys, who were called as backward dictators. There were some armed squads as volunteer troops that snuck to Eastnama and fought several clashes. There were a pair of consecutive governments in exile. There were plenty of newspapers and magazines that exposed wicked policies of RL clique. There were hundreds of associations that collected monies in many countries and sent to Eastnama to help objects of pity.

After five years of happy living with my brother's family, with my peaceful studying in college, and working in the print shop, the former head of Cluster 36 intimidated and coerced me to do unwilling activities again.

In one morning, Cordata appeared at the door of the print shop. I felt anxious, but she expressed gladness. After some mutual words of greetings, I invited her to step inside and sit on the chair at my table. She spoke on her subject immediately:

"We thank for your works in the past. They contributed a part to our victory. In return, your parents and sister in Kanxono are still living in the villa and enjoying the standard of middle officials. Thus, you must continue to work for us."

"You won the war and have everything. I've already fulfill my duty. For my parents and sister, I inform you, my brother and I have already filed visas. Please, let me forget and end all works involved with you. Let me have a purely ordinary life of a civilian."

"Your parents and sister won't have visas of exit so you must continue to work for us, and your parents and sister continue to have the benefits."

"Does the RL clique prepare to invade Unto Blumen? Are my parents and sister your hostages? What kind of works I must do in this country? Must I use my beauty again to fascinate a high official or officer of the government or army of Unto Blumen?"

"No, no, no, the RL clique cannot send soldiers to invade this country. Our work here is quite different.

"On the one hand, we form some organizations to implement secret instructions and resolutions of RL clique. We make full use of freedom and democracy of this country to fulfill our duties. If our rivals disturb us, they'll violate laws and be in troubles. There are native persons including lawyers who defend freedom and democracy will support us.

"On the other hand, we infiltrated into anti-RL organizations to know their plans and their leaders, to lure their members to harm their organizations secretly, to sow division and suspect among themselves. To cover, infiltrators may fake to involve in their activities like spreading anti-RL writings, joining anti-RL demonstrations, and so forth. Your works that you'll do here for us are not dangerous nor difficult. Dadang Tynan will meet you, and you'll work together with him."

Therefore, I reluctantly worked for Cluster 36 Spies again. Dadang and I acted like a couple. We joined the most important anti-RL organization. Because of our dynamic activities, Dadang was voted as vice chairman of the anti-RL organization. We were often invited to join many activities of other anti-RL organizations, so we could report to Cluster 36 Spies lots of their plans and activities.

Among hundreds of anti-RL organizations, a pair of political ones did some harm to the fame of RL in the world. Their activities were to organize demonstrations or to write motions to a government which hinder diplomatic policies of RL clique. Others organizations were harmless though they had plans to celebrate anniversaries of the past with anti-RL opinions in speeches and placards.

All organizations and associations raised monies and sent it to Eastnama to help their objects of pity. Nonetheless, these monies made RL clique wealthy and their regime strongly stable as Cordata herself once noticed:

"Activities of anti-RL organizations in foreign countries harm RL 10 percent but benefit RL 90 percent. Yearly they send nearly a trillion hard currencies in different monies to Eastnama. In economic reality, the monies pass from hands to hands and reach into hands of RL guys who become stronger and stronger, richer and richer thanks to the monies. Anti-RL organizations send monies out from the countries they lived for nothing in exchange. For sure, they harm the economies of these countries. If the currencies are circulated in these countries, the monies will help these countries prosperous and thriving. No budget deficits or economic depression happened."

Cordata and her inferiors probably brought all things they wanted to print to our print shop. Hard to understand, the things consisted of both pro-RL and anti-RL ones. But nothing touched their emperor and the clique.

One day, unexpectedly, Dadang confided his appraisals to me in a private conversation:

"I've worked for the RL clique for thirteen years. When I was fourteen, RL guys stuffed my head with idealistic hopes: freedom, democracy, equality, so I followed them. Badly, when RL clique gripped powers, they've done opposite things: cruelty, despotism, dictatorship, and odd policies causing peoples poor but making them wealthy as well as full of prerogatives and abuses. I realized their wrongs when I was in Eastnama, where I witnessed the prosperity and freedom of its people.

"Nevertheless, I cannot quit! To quit means to be killed. I know you fell in their trap because of gullibility. Nhutien, there appear sillies here again: a part of children and grandchildren of former officers and officials of defeated army and surrendered government of Eastnama don't heed and trust their parents and grandparents about ruses and propagandas of RL guys, they support and defend RL guys. Ah, RL clique have so many monies now, million times now than before the end of the war, so the children and grandchildren are lured by monies or promised high ranks. Ah, some former officers and officials are also lured by these things."

"I thank for your trust. Dadang, tell me your appraisals on patriotic volions of the peoples in Kanxono and Eastnama now. The peoples know despicable inherencies of the emperor and his clique. Can the peoples overthrow those deceiving and despotic guys?"

"I don't know the psychological circumstances of people in Eastnama. The great majority of people in Kanxono have subjugated negatives. For many decades, their patriotism has been misused by RL guys. Now, when the people hear any words similar to *patriotism*, they immediately think of deceiving schemes.

"To understand circumstances of the people in Kanxono, I'll describe two images.

"On material conditions, before and during the war, the people had only meager food to survive. Other products had been in severely shortage. For example, yearly, one citizen had two yards of cloth, one needle, ten yards of thread, and so on.

"Now, after the war, thanks to the different products taken from Eastnama, their lives became a little better. Thus they don't dare to struggle because of the fear to live in misery again as the periods before and during the war.

"On nonmaterial areas, all activities of the people were stringently enforced to be in dictatorial lines of RL clique like being in tight shackles. Now, the shackles are loose. They don't dare to struggle because of fear to be tightly chained again.

"By the way, I just had permission to marry. The woman that I firstly intend to marry is you. To me, you're the most beautiful and resourceful woman in the world."

"I'm sorry. You know I got rid of three men. Now, I'm very embittered with conjugal consummation. Don't waste your time. Marry a woman you love or you want. You're nearly forty years old."

"I presume Cordata gave me permission and expect me to marry her. But she's not the type of woman I want to marry. Furthermore, she's already thirty-six years old. She cannot have a child."

"Aha! You should marry her. If you marry another woman, she'll be jealous. Unsounded consequences will come to you and your spouse. As the matter of having a child, science can help her get pregnant. Furthermore, you can adopt children."

"You're right. If I marry, I should marry her. Being on this wrong way, it's impossible to jump onto the right way. By the way, be silent on what I've confided to you."

A month later, I received the wedding card from the couples Dadang Tynan and Cordata Vongdanh. In the wedding party, among the guests, I recognized some RL diplomats of the consulate from Kanxono to Unto Blumen. Near the end of the party, Cordata came to my table and thanked me specially. She did not say the reason, but I knew she thanked for my refusal to the proposal of Dadang's marriage.

I write these lines after five months of my attendance in the wedding of the couple Dadang Tynan and Cordata Vongdanh. In this period, no guys of Cluster 36 Spies including Dadang and Cordata have any contact with me. Probably, Cordata calculates that if I still work for them, Dadang can meet me. It harms their marriage. Thus, I hope they forget me, and I'll live in peace. I still have hope that my parents and sister will get visas of exit.

Will I marry? I really do not know how my future will be. Finally, I thank you for reading my story.

About the Author

Prudence Han Tranduc is an immigrant. He is a member of PEN International. He has two books on Literature and History in his native language. *Submitted to Work as a Spy* is his first book in English.

CPSIA information can be obtained at www.ICGtesting.com
Printed in the USA
LVOW13s0252180614

390555LV00001B/133/P

9 781628 385311